DAUGHTERS

AYANA ELLIS

Chapter 1

LATE NIGHTS/ EARLY MORNINGS

*N*aomi's signature long blonde and brown ombre faux locs covered her face as Damon steadily drilled her from behind for a third time this morning beginning at 5.am. She had to beg him to stop and promise him that if he let her go, the next time she saw him they could do whatever he wanted in the bedroom. He released her immediately knowing that his little freak would make good on her promise. He tapped her on the buttocks before jumping out of the bed and swiped his garments from off the floor.

Now Naomi was thirty minutes late to her standing mani/pedi appointment with her girls and she couldn't bring herself to care.

"Imma hold you to it," he said without looking at her. He slid a fresh white tank top over his abs. Naomi lay in bed watching him as he swiped up every article of clothing from various areas of her bedroom. She loved it when he pulled his hat all the way down over his eyes.

"Walk me to the door."

She did as she was asked, standing in the doorway naked as he ogled her body.

"Call me. You know the vibe," he said and slapped her ass playfully before leaving. As soon as he pulled off, Naomi showered and threw on some leggings and a denim button down shirt. She called a Lyft while sliding her feet into a pair of New Balance. Now she was eager to catch up on life with her friends. Shantel was probably already at the salon, prompt as usual, so Naomi decided to give Jameela a call to see if she was on her way once she got in her Lyft.

"I can't make it," Jameela said as her greeting.

"*Again*? Let me guess...something to do with Tyrone."

"Did I hear a woman with no man say something, oh..." she snapped back.

Naomi rolled her eyes.

"This is the third time you cancelled. Either your phone is on do not disturb, or you're not showing up for appointments, it's off-putting. You have a man, *great,* I love that for you, but come up for some air. You don't know what could be going on!"

"No news is good news! I know you beautiful dames are ok, so on that note, I promise to catch up soon. But seriously, I'm in the middle of something right now so I must run. I promise to get with you both next time. Toodles," she said and hung up before Naomi could protest.

Disappointed, Naomi dropped her phone in her small leather crossbody and settled into her seat. She could still feel Damon's sweet kisses on her neck. She smiled at the vision of his face while she rode him. He would always go to this pleasant place when she got on top, and she wished she knew what he was feeling or thinking. Normally he was serious, barely laughed or cracked jokes as if he didn't want to get too comfortable around her, even though they'd been sex buddies for a while. But when she was on top, his face softened, and a smile always crept across his lips.

Naomi snapped out of her daydream when she arrived at the salon. She could see Shantel being escorted to her pedicure chair through the window. Naomi had unfortunately missed her manicure and would have to come back another day. She rushed in and grabbed a seat next to Shantel who was noticeably agitated. She didn't tolerate lateness, especially without a phone call and thought it was disrespectful and dismissive of someone's time. She rolled her eyes at Naomi as she approached.

"So, you *and* Jameela are late. You sistas know you can do better than this," she said adjusting herself in her seat.

"She's not coming," Naomi said sliding her sneakers off.

Shantel just shook her head.

"I called her when I was on my way, and she basically told me I had no say so in her not showing up to anything because I don't have a man." Naomi said.

"You've got to be kidding me." Shantel zoned out for a while. "I hope he's not abusing her because the way she's acting over a man she hasn't even been with that long you would think this man has a gun to her head or a foot up her behind."

Naomi interrupted the rant Shantel for sure was about to go on. "Look, I cannot and will not spend my spa day talking about Jameela and her poor decisions so let's get on with the afternoon, please."

"You're late as well. What's your excuse?" Shantel folded her arms.

"The way your attitude and energy are set up right now I will not ruin a good story. Maybe later," Noami said with her eyes on the pedicurist.

"No sweetheart, you owe me some kind of explanation, so spill it, because you wouldn't be you if you didn't have some kind of story to tell. But before you tell me about your shenanigans, you know I must ask, how's your mind, soul, heart, body?" Shantel asked, adjusting herself in her chair.

"All is well in every department, praise Rakim Allah."

"I can't stand you sometimes." Shantel laughed.

"And, if you must know, I'm late because Damon spent the night."

After her ex-fiancé Cory's heartbreak and betrayal, none other than Damon found himself in the mix because of the disturbance Naomi caused when she found out about Cory's indiscretions, prompting the super to call Damon who happened to be her landlord and did not appreciate police presence on his property. But after what sounded like a domestic dispute, he was called and that's where he learned she was single.

When Naomi first met her landlord, she wasn't expecting this young, handsome, fly guy to introduce himself as such.

"Nice to meet you. I'm Damon," he said politely and extended his hand upon opening the unit door.

"Naomi. Nice to meet you."

Dressed in sweatpants and a white T-shirt with fresh white Nikes, Naomi could not keep her eyes off him as he walked ahead of her, leading the way to the different parts of the condo for her to check everything for anything that may need fixing.

"Everything all good?" he asked.

"Yes, all good, thank you. This is a beautiful place. Expensive but beautiful," she said, looking around.

"Everything is state of the art in here. You have built in speakers in your ceiling and in the shower. Your washer, dryer, refrigerator, and dishwasher are all Bosch and can be controlled through Wi-Fi. The jacuzzi in your bathroom works and you even have a half bathroom for guests, so people won't have to go into your bedroom. The neighborhood is one of the wealthiest neighborhoods in Brooklyn, steps away from Barclays, you have cameras up and down the halls and when someone rings your buzzer, it will ring to your phone, and you'll be able to see who you're letting in. I'll have the super set that up for you. These floors are brand new as well. This rent is actually cheap compared to what's really happening in this area."

"I looked at the rent increases from last year until now for this unit, and it's been raised $800. You don't plan on raising it again any time soon, do you?"

Damon smirked. The attraction between them both was subtle but undeniable.

"No, I don't plan on it. I fixed everything in here and made it brand new, that's why I raised the rent."

"Very good. Well thank you. I'll pick up my keys in two weeks."

"I'll leave them at the front desk," he said walking to the front door and opened it, allowing

her to walk out first.

"I've owned this unit for about ten years. It could have been fixed it up, but my last tenant was terrible, so I wasn't fixing shit until they left," he joked.

"I'm sorry to hear that. Well I'm glad you can recoup what you lost from a single black female." Naomi flirted.

"You look good on paper. You're doing just fine." He smiled. "Well, welcome to the building, let me know if you need anything. You have my number. Remember to pick up your keys at the front desk." he reminded as they reached the lobby.

"Thank you." Naomi said and watched him walk out in the crisp spring summer air.

Shantel snapped her fingers in Naomi's face bringing her back to reality. "Ma'am, spill it!"

"I was late because Damon was on me like the IRS!" Naomi bit her bottom lip.

Shantel only met Damon once when she came to pick Naomi up for brunch and immediately understood the attraction. He was hood but sophisticated, dressed in a navy-blue Sergio Tacchini sweat suit and a blue Yankee cap. The way he smiled at Naomi with those perfect white teeth and winked at her before jumping in his foreign ride was sexy. Shantel watched him as he walked to his car and pulled off. His swag was out of this world.

When Naomi got inside of Shantel's range rover Shantel looked over at her and said, "*Naomi, you in trouble girl!*"

"Don't I know it!" she replied through laughter.

"Good ole faithful, still hanging in there," Shantel muttered with a hint of judgement in her tone.

"I can't even be too mad. I'm not normally impressed by much of anything, but boy he is something. He just got that *je ne sais quoi*. He favors Method Man a bit, just a shorter version." Shantel said doing a little shimmy for emphasis.

"Body and all." Naomi agreed.

"He's been around for a long time."

"Yeah, but he was never right for me, and I was never right for him. We just fit where we're supposed to."

"You never thought maybe you and Damon are meant to be more? He's been your sex buddy and friend forever. I don't see why you feel the need to see other men when your needs are being fulfilled?"

"Because why would I put all my eggs in one basket? This is how women end up catching feelings they have no business catching. If you're not in an exclusive relationship, then you have two options, either date other men as well or spend time gingerly with the one you're dealing with. You can't be out here playing wifey games with a man that doesn't see a future with you."

"I hear that!" Shantel said while admiring the pedicurists' work. "I'm so glad you bounced back." She smiled warmly.

"Thanks to you."

"Nope, thanks to *you*. You are Naomi Lawson, always been a strong, beautiful, esteemed woman. That did not change because some man tried to play in your face. That was *his* bad, not yours. You had a moment of weakness, but you are far from being a weak woman." She winked.

"Well enough about a nonfactor. Cory was so many dicks ago. I really and truly wish that you ladies would stop bringing him up as if he's the bar! I've moved on, and I know you don't understand my lifestyle right now, but I'm happy to be in the space I'm in. But enough about me, how are you, what's going on in *your life*? How's your mind, body, soul and all that?"

Shantel went on to talk about her new tenants in the rental property she purchased, her new position as CEO at an African Bank and how good she and Yusef were doing. But it wasn't long before Shantel delved back into Naomi's personal life to Naomi's dismay. Naomi closed her eyes and took steady breaths as Shantel lectured her about the different energies of the men inside of her when having sex and how it could lead to anxiety, depression, and other mental and emotional disorders.

"I'm a grown woman and well aware of all of these things, but thank you Dr. Emmitt-James, seriously." she said gently touching Shantel's leg.

"Naomi, it's been some time since Cory, don't you think it's time to slow down? Don't you ever get lonely, tired?" Shantel softly asked.

"I've got gizmos and gadgets and vibrators plenty, a man in each borough, I can get dick from any!" Naomi sang.

"Why are you like this? I just really want real love for you and Jameela both."

"Me and the ill-nana are fine." Naomi said patting her private parts. "And despite what you're saying, what I'm experiencing right now is a form of love. I love me, I love sex, I love how I feel when I'm with a different man. I love the allure and excitement. I love the adrenaline rush when I'm about to get it on with someone I barely know. I love it all. I love where I'm at in life right now, and I'm sorry that it doesn't fit your expectations, but this is how I'm living right now, Shantel, and I don't want to feel judged or as if I have to hide it."

Shantel huffed. "My love, I just want to know why so many? Is dick going extinct or something? Is there a misunderstanding because I certainly do not understand this behavior at all. I'm appalled!" Shantel clutched her imaginary pearls.

"Stop slut shaming me. Can we move on from what I do in my bedroom?"

"I'm not shaming you, I just think that it has gotten excessive. In other conversations, you named at least five men you've slept with in a very short span of time, not including Damon."

"Five men, that's one for each borough, duh." Naomi giggled knowing she was getting under Shantel's skin. "How's Yusef doing, how are you guys?"

"That's a good man, Savannah, a good man!" Shantel smiled.

"I love that for you, you guys made it through."

"Yeah." Shantel briefly reminisced but changed the subject. "So what's up with our girl? She has this new man, and she is brand new hunty!" Shantel said changing the vibe, and Naomi was thankful to not be in the hot seat anymore.

"We may have to pay Jameela a visit to see what's really going on," Shantel said.

"What's his name again, starts with a T."

"*Terrible,* that's his name." Shantel rolled her eyes.

"Terry."

"Tyrone," she offered.

"He acts just like a Tyrone."

"What does a Tyrone act like?" Shantel asked laughing.

"*Trifling*." Naomi laughed. "But seriously, do you know Pops hasn't even met him?"

"Which is very odd as close as she and her father are. But she did say they've talked on FaceTime."

"Pops said she's a damn lie," Naomi confirmed to Shantel's surprise.

"What? Why would she lie about that?"

"I have no idea. Why won't she bring him around? Is he short or something?"

Shantel laughed. "Don't sleep on short men now, remember Phil?"

"How can I forget Phil! Where he lacked in height he packed in pipe. My goodness, and he was fine as hell."

"But too bad he couldn't keep a job." They both started giggling.

"Remember when he came to my house with that damn gadget, he was trying to get off the ground?" Naomi asked through tears of laughter.

"Please, do not start." Shantel started chuckling, covering her mouth. They both yelled out at the same time, "Pursuit of Happyness!" causing the women to go into a fit of laughter.

"Oh my God, I ran into him years later. Did I ever tell you?" Naomi asked wiping tears from her eyes.

"No way! What's he up to?"

"Not a damn thing! He was beating me in my head about some business he was starting. Phil was a whole bullshit artist!"

"My lord." Shantel said, calming down. "But back to our girl. I don't know what's going on, but I'm tired of pushing her to come out with us and to meet him."

"Do you know how many times I've made plans to be with her, and at the 11th hour she would cancel because *Tyrone* needed something from her? I mean I'm talking dressed, grabbing car keys, about to leave my house, and I get a call to say, hey girl, I am sooooo sorry, please forgive me, drinks on me next time? Her behavior is bizarre to say the least," Shantel said.

"That's not like Meela. She has never allowed a man to control her in any way. What does he do again?"

"She claims he's an ex-football player turned entrepreneur. Not sure what he does these days or what he's *"preneuring,"* and I know Meela is not open off his money because she's always had her own."

"Did you just say 'preneuring?" Naomi chuckled.

"I did."

Both women sat pondering on what hold this man could have on Meela for a moment, then Naomi's thoughts drifted back to thinking about Damon.

She wasn't in love with him or anything like that, but last night was different. They were more intimate, in tune and actually kissed while having sex, something they both had never done in the six or so years they've known one another. It had her mind blown all day. This was also the first time she allowed a man to sleep over since Cory. It felt nice waking up with someone in her bed if for no other reason other than it being a sign of her being free.

Chapter 2
SUMMER RAIN

*N*aomi's girl's day out with Shantel was a bit more under-whelming than she expected it to be, so she made up an excuse to skip brunch afterward. Shantel laid it on too heavy with her about her personal life and Naomi knew that the conversations would get worse over drinks. Once home, relaxed with Ferrari Red toenails, she peeled her clothes off and put on a robe and plopped down on her couch. The spa day had her thinking about when she could barely get out of bed after what happened between her and Cory several years ago. She scoffed a bit, thinking about what a broken bird she was and promised herself that she would never wallow in self-pity that long ever again because she had no intent on loving that hard again. It was extremely difficult for her to overcome the grief and sadness she endured at the hands of the only man that she had shared the deepest parts of herself with.

Naomi met Cory while living in Miami for six months for job training. He noticed her as she exited the popular nightclub Liv. He approached her as she slowly strutted through the lobby. She was instantly attracted to him because she could tell he was from some-where "up north" by his style. But it was when he opened his mouth and his baritone serenaded her ears that sealed the deal. She imagined how his voice would sound moaning and groaning in her ear.

"I saw you tonight, but I wasn't sure if you were alone or...." he said, looking around.

"I am. I just stepped out to have a little fun," Naomi offered.

"Cory. What's your name?" He extended his hand.

"Naomi."

"Nice to meet you, Naomi. I don't mean to be abrupt, but I do have to run but wanted to say hello to you first. Would you mind putting your number in my phone so I can call you?"

With nothing to lose, Naomi did as she was asked, and Cory called her within an hour, asking if she would like to have dinner with him, to which she obliged.

The next night, dressed in an off-white bodycon dress and heels, Naomi showed up at Prime 112 and waited for Damon, who arrived shortly after her, handsomely dressed in a yellow Polo shirt, jeans and yellow & white 97 Air Max's, the scent of his cologne led the way to the table. The server came over and Naomi asked for a glass of Dom Perignon to start, Cory ordered a bottle instead with appetizers for the table. When he took off his hat, Naomi was able to see how handsome he really was. He had jet-black waves, dark eyebrows, and the sexiest dark eyes. His forearms were covered in tattoos, his wrist adorned an expensive watch. They sat quietly, almost awkwardly until the server reappeared with a bottle on ice. He popped the champagne for them both and poured glasses.

"Cheers." Cory said, looking Naomi directly in her eyes while he sipped, holding his stare longer than she would have liked, as if he aimed to hypnotize her.

"What are we toasting to?" she asked, breaking his stare.

"Something new." He winked at Naomi and smiled.

"I can get with that." she said, happy he didn't throw out some cheesy line about love and the future. They ate their appetizers hungrily and didn't speak much other than asking one another how they liked their dishes and what they both did for a living where she learned he had two small children, was a restauranteur and had other business ventures as well.

"Two small children. What's up with their mother?" Naomi asked.

"She's around. We're not together. Our first child was planned, second one was a breakup baby to be honest. I love and take care of my children, that's it," he said cutting into his steak.

Naomi looked him over then decided she need not be invested because this was just a date, and she would be going home in two months. But in hindsight, she realized she should have asked him some crucial questions that may have saved her from the heartache she had yet to endure. Questions such as, if there was someone who would be upset he was out on a date or was there someone under the impression she was in a relationship with him or was there someone well within her rights to knock all this shit over if she walked into this restaurant right now.

"You look like your feeling alright." He stared Naomi down, noticing the toll that the champagne was having on her. She was smiling more and literally loosening up. Her shoulders were more relaxed, and she was no longer fidgeting with her flute.

"I hope you don't think that you can get me drunk and take advantage of me. I know how to hold my liquor."

"Not at all. I'd never take advantage of woman. I rather you be 100% coherent and in agreement with what you are about to do."

"IImph, I hear that."

He laughed. "You are something else."

"So, how come a beautiful woman like you doesn't have a man? You didn't meet anyone out here in Miami with all these ballers?" he asked mockingly.

"I'm not out here looking for ballers. I'm here for work, then I'm taking my ass home." She shrugged.

"But you're *here with me.*" He took a small sip of champagne.

"I've been out here alone. I deserve some male company. Besides, I could tell you were from where I was from. I knew you were my people."

He chuckled at that statement.

"I had tunnel vision since I've been out here, and I definitely didn't find myself to be sexually attracted to anyone since I've been here, until now."

Naomi let that last part slip and embarrassingly excused herself to the ladies' room to give herself *and her lady parts* a pep talk in the mirror. She ran into the bathroom and closed the door as if someone was chasing her.

"You just met him, down girl, down!" she said, patting myself in the vagina.

"But he's so damn fine!"

"What if he has a little dick?"

"Well, he doesn't know where you live so you can always just block his number."

"No way in hell a man that fine and rough has some wack ass sex."

"You would be surprised, ugh no, no sex, you haven't even known this man 24 hours!"

"So what! Grown people don't wait, go get you some. It's been too long!"

"What will he think of me?"

"Bitch when have you ever cared?"

"True."

"Put it on his ass and make him fall in love. You want love, right?"

"Yes, but not like this!"

"Grow up! Go out there and go with the flow, stop over thinking!"

She gathered herself and strutted back to her table noticing how Cory was fixated on the lower part of her body and not her breasts like everyone else typically was because of her natural triple D's. He kept his focus on her legs the entire time until she sat down.

"You have the sexiest, longest legs ever." He grinned like a Cheshire cat.

"Thank you." Naomi blushed. *I'd love to wrap these long legs around your neck like a scarf.*

She laughed at her own thoughts prompting him to ask her what was on her mind.

"You want to share?" He leaned in on the table.

"If I share, then I'd have to follow through, and I don't think that's a good idea," she flirted.

"I had a good time, Naomi. I'd like to do this again some time."

She instantly felt his energy charge her entire body. She was disappointed he didn't push to be with her tonight. Here she was filled with two bottles of Dom Perignon, horny as hell, ready to go and he wanted to be a gentleman.

"I'd like that as well." Naomi smiled softly, batting her eyes trying to send out the bat signal she wanted him just as much as she knew he wanted her. The waiter came by and placed the black book on the table. Cory slid his card into the booklet without giving the receipt a second look.

"So what are you doing for the rest of the evening," he asked.

"*You*", Naomi said and sipped her champagne seductively. She had to take matters into her own hands, and she knew that he would not turn her away, nor would he be able to walk away once she took his soul tonight.

A whirlwind romance ensued throughout her time in Miami and continued when she returned to New York. Cory professed his love for her within two months after they returned form the Grand Opening of a new restaurant he opened in Fort Lauderdale, but Naomi didn't return the sentiment. She'd never experienced having a man profess his love for her. She instantly began to overthink, wondering what Cory stood to gain by lying to her or playing games.

He responded to her silence by kissing her forehead while they stood in the doorway of her hotel room. He picked up his duffle bag and kissed her on the cheek.

"You good?" he asked her.

"Yes," Naomi said as she watched Cory dig into his pockets. He would always give her whatever he pulled out, and if it was less than $500, he would dig for more to give her.

"I don't know why you always ask me if I'm good and when I say yes you give me money anyway." She chuckled.

"You mine, I gotta make sure you're always good. I gotta go. I'll call you when I touch." Naomi watched Cory disappear onto the elevator and softly closed her door. She basked in the moment of being told she was loved and let it rock her into a deep nap.

But the trouble began when Naomi moved back to New York after completing her training. She started seeing him less, which was odd because when she was further away, she saw him more. Soon the arguing about "time spent" ensued, and they were at each other's throats. Naomi's suspicions began to increase when she came up with the solution for them to be able to see one another more once he blamed his time away on business.

She suggested she stay at his house for a week at a time since she worked from home most days, and he declined. Noami's natural reaction to that was to fall back from Cory who started to show lack of interest. Once Naomi made herself scarce his weekend only visits changed to four days a week, sometimes five. He even invited her to his home where she spent a weekend a few times.

Then to seal the deal once they made a year in, he proposed. A few months after the proposal he suggested she start to look for homes in New Jersey, which she gladly did with Jameela and Shantel by her side. But Cory was never happy with any of the homes she chose which began to frustrate Naomi, so he told her to focus on a wedding venue instead, which she did.

Cory treated Naomi, Jameela, and Shantel to an all-expense paid trip to check out two wedding venues in Costa Rica that Naomi found online, the dream was finally becoming a reality and Naomi was thrilled. With her girls by her side every step of the way, a blissful Naomi chose her wedding dress, a simple yet elegant spaghetti strap Vera Wang number with a fishtail silhouette and long train. She planned on wearing her natural hair with a big flower a la Billie Holiday. Under her faux locs hid a gorgeous full head of thick chocolate brown 4c hair she would get twisted out into a big coily mane for her special day. But within weeks of Naomi being excited about finding her dress and wiring a down payment for the venue, Cory slowly began drifting back into his suspicious ways. But Naomi was used to this dance and decided she wasn't going to stress herself out. Two years in at this point, she assumed she had Cory all figured out and when he was stressed, he would pull back and that there was no real need for her to be concerned. Even still, Naomi sought counsel in the only two men she trusted, Jameela's father, "Pops" and Shantel's husband, Yusef, who both told her to watch him closely but not to stress too bad.

Naomi was thankful when Shantel suggested a girl's trip to the Maldives for her 35th birthday. The night before she was leaving, Cory's energy was off, concerning Naomi a great deal. His typical rough, masculine persona showed signs of vulnerability.

She rubbed his waves as he lay face up on her lap with his eyes closed. He looked so handsome, almost angelic, and she could tell that something was bothering him by the slight wrinkle in his brow. Also, his migraines were coming on more frequently, which led her to believe he was stressed about something but wasn't willing to share with her. He looked up at her with those jet-black eyes that she would normally catch staring at her sometimes. Those same eyes that Naomi would look into, and find safety, promise, stability, a friend, looked back at her with uncertainty. His deep voice snapped her out of her thoughts.

"I want you to go have a good time baby and when you come home things will be better. I'll be right here."

"Do you have my flight information? Do you know what time I land? You know I hate waiting, so please be on time."

"When am I ever not on time when it comes to my baby? When am I ever not there?" He finally smiled. Naomi stroked his thick course waves as they locked eyes. Something in that moment told her there was trouble on the horizon when he didn't hold her stare.

"Baby, what is going on? Sit up and talk to me. Are you having second thoughts about getting married?" Naomi asked, trying to ease him off her lap.

He didn't sit up. In fact, he turned toward her and nuzzled his face in her crotch, inhaled then exhaled deeply. He kept his eyes closed and wrapped his arms tight around her hips and held on tightly. He mumbled into her private parts, and she could feel the warmth of his breath on her love, but she couldn't make out what he said.

On the way to the airport the next morning, the weather was unseasonably warm for the winter and the sun was bright. Naomi donned a pair of huge black designer shades, a yellow puffer coat and her signature waist length locs was tied up in a loose bun.

The drive to the airport was quiet with Naomi holding Corey's hand the entire way while he remained deep in thought until they pulled up to the terminal. Upon arrival, Naomi sat in the car briefly while

Cory retrieved her luggage out of the trunk. He gently helped her out of the vehicle and put her bags down. He cupped both sides of her face and kissed her tenderly, warmly, and slower than he had ever kissed her before, as if it would be the last time. His eyes shut tight like he was making a wish, his tongue danced around her mouth, he kissed her as if he was trying to take her last breath. Naomi wrapped her arms around his slim waist and inhaled his scent, her head on his chest as they lingered for some time holding one another until hearing an authoritative voice politely tell them that they couldn't stay there and to move along. Naomi opened her eyes slowly, trying to savor the moment.

"Be good. Stay away from Dexter St. Jock." He kissed her forehead.

Naomi laughed nervously. "You're going to pick me up from the airport, right?"

"Baby, yes, 6:15, I'll be parked out here somewhere waiting for you, alright? I sent you $1,500 too."

"I do not need all of that money!" Naomi dug in her pocket for her phone to check her account.

"What do I always tell you? Your mine, I gotta make sure you're better than good, besides that's pocket change."

"Whatever you say," Naomi said with a knot in her throat.

"I know whatever I say, come here, stop looking all worried and stressed. You're on your way to paradise," he said pulling her in one last time. "I love you. I'll see you next Sunday. Go before you miss your flight."

Why did it feel like goodbye? Naomi wanted to say to him, but the words wouldn't leave her mouth.

Naomi headed inside the airport and turned to look at Cory one last time. His smile was gone immediately, his face hardened. She could see him wipe his face, as if he was wiping away a tear then he pulled off. But her mind was at ease upon speaking to Cory daily up until day six. When she couldn't get through to him the entire day her nervous system felt like it was shutting down. She felt sick when she woke up on day seven and there weren't any missed calls or text messages. The flight home was long and stressful as she popped open small nips of tequila and took shots most of the time until falling into a drunk stupor.

"Girl, you sure you don't need a ride home?" Jameela asked as the three of them stood in front of the airport.

"No, I'm good. Cory said he's stuck in traffic, he'll be here in about fifteen minutes." She lied.

"Oh, well call us when he picks you up. Come on, girl," Jameela said to Shantel. Naomi watched her friends as they headed to the parking lot where they both parked their vehicles before hailing a taxi. Her tears were on standby, but she had no idea what she needed to cry for.

Everything was just up in the air. Upon entering her apartment she didn't smell any of the finest marijuana that would normally greet her in the hallway as Cory was a heavy weed smoker. The apartment was just how she left it except for the outfit he took her to the airport in strewn across a chair in her bedroom. She put her bags down and slowly looked around. She opened the closets swiftly and breathed a sigh of relief seeing that all his clothes were still there, his toiletries in the bathroom and his beloved peanut punch and Guinness in the fridge. His side of the bed was unmade, the comforters pulled down where he obviously lowered the sheets to climb out of bed, meaning he was here, because Naomi always spread her bed before leaving home.

Where are you, boy?

Still trying to understand why, and if he ghosted her, her cellphone began vibrating in her hand. Her nerves were all over the place, and she was disappointed when she saw that it was Jameela calling.

"Hey, girl, you made it home safe?" Naomi could hear they were still in traffic.

"Hello?" she asked as Naomi sniffed. "Naomi.... what's wrong?"

"He never came to get me from the airport. I knew something was wrong since yesterday when he didn't call me, and I couldn't get through to him."

"I knew something was wrong with you when you were so quiet yesterday and throwing back those drinks like that on the flight. I hope he's okay. Did you call his mother?"

"No."

"I would call her now Naomi. I'd let her know that he didn't show up!"

Naomi closed her curtains and then sunk deep into her plush mattress as Jameela started her rant about men were dogs and how she hates when they act stupid.

"Do you want me to come over? I can come over, I'm still in traffic." But Jameela didn't wait for Naomi to respond.

"I'm on my way," she said and hung up.

Naomi laid down until Jameela and of course Shantel showed up about two hours later trying to help her resolve the case of her missing man.

Chapter 3

JUST BE A MAN ABOUT IT

ory's mother said that she hadn't talked to him either so Naomi called the morgues, the hospitals, the precincts, and everything she could think of between New York and Philly and no one had heard of him. The next morning, while working from home, Naomi logged in to her rent portal to find that her rent had been paid for the next three months.

"Yeah, he's in the wind, and he feels bad about it, so he set you out for a few months. That's guilt money," Jameela said when Naomi told her about it on a Saturday evening inside of Naomi's stylish Brooklyn apartment. At this point, an entire week had gone by and Cory's mother stopped answering Naomi's calls the day after she came home from her trip. While trying to crack the case of the missing fiancé, Jameela poured a round of Sauvignon Blanc in pretty wine glasses and sat them on the small table in between the women as they sat in front of her fireplace.

"You think he's like a runaway groom or something?" Shantel asked.

"It's possible, and I wouldn't even be surprised. He was so back and forth with it, unenthusiastic about everything, just throwing money at me to handle business, but he wasn't involved. But what makes me angry is that I gave him an out a few times, but he kept telling me he wants to marry me and to stop tripping," Naomi said, aggravated.

"Does his mother sound worried? Like is she calling you to see if he has called you?" Shantel asked.

"No. She stopped taking my calls and when I suggested we file a missing person's report she told me not to, to sit tight." Naomi sipped.

"Because she knows exactly where her son is and what he's up to, you better believe that! These motherfuckas don't be no good, I swear! And his mama ain't shit either. You can't tell me a damn thing because *babyyyy*, my father, thee Preston White done showed me everything that I need to know! None of these men are faithful. They are all dogs, that's why I treat them how I treat them!" Jameela ranted.

"I'm so sorry you're going through this," Shantel said, rubbing Naomi's back while Jameela continued to rant.

"He's probably laid up with some bitch right now. I'm telling you, settling down is a joke, marriage is a joke, love is a damn joke. These men don't love nobody but themselves!" Jameela said.

"Jameela, relax, okay?" Shantel snapped.

Between Jameela being a man hater and the pitiful look in Shantel's eyes, Naomi just wanted tonight to be over so she could push through another day.

"My head hurts. I need to get some rest, you guys," she said setting her barely touched wine glass down and standing up.

"I know one thing, you better be done with him when he shows up. If he could pull a stunt like this now, imagine when you get married? He is fully capable of leaving you standing at the altar! I cannot stand these damn men. This is why I'll never settle down ever!" Jameela said.

Naomi rolled her eyes so hard it made her headache worse. Shantel looked at Naomi and shook her head while Jameela looked through her phone, still mumbling about how terrible men were.

"Get some rest, baby, we'll call you in the morning," Shantel said gently.

Naomi walked her girls to the door and closed it softly behind them. She could hear Jameela still talking on the way down the stairs saying how ridiculous this was.

Sunday morning, Naomi took a long stretch and reached for her cell phone. The sight of no missed calls from Cory irked her, so she jumped up and decided to clean. Her worry had turned to anger with the thought of him putting her through this unnecessary drama. She opened her windows letting in the crisp February air that swept the warm melancholy, heavy energy out of her apartment. She lit Palo Santo sticks and gave her place a thorough cleaning until it gave her the fresh free cleansed feeling she loved, reserved for Sunday mornings. She then closed her windows, adjusted the heat, and poured a glass of Rosé and plopped down on her couch to watch a little bit of television, when an unidentified number popped up on her cellphone. Before she could say hello, his baritone came across her entire body warming her to her toes.

"Baby," was all he said. It was all he ever had to say to get Naomi to melt faster than a snow cone in hell.

"Oh my God, Cory, where the fuck have you been?" She sat up, her heart beating fast.

"I can explain it all to you, but in person. I'll be there in a couple of hours, I'm about to leave the house now."

Naomi couldn't even speak.

What on God's earth could this man possibly tell me after pulling a stunt like this?

"Is this your new number or something?"

"Yeah, lock it in. I'm so sorry for having you worried. I'll be there soon, and I will explain everything."

"Why did you change your number?"

But he hung up before answering her question.

Naomi called the girls to let them know he resurfaced, and they of course bombarded her with questions that she had no answer to yet. Jameela was certain that Cory must have a family somewhere and reminded Naomi of how her father had a mistress for years. Naomi timed his drive and knew that his arrival time shouldn't be any more than 2.5 hours including traffic. Her nerves got the best of her, so she decided to complete her bottle of Moet Rose, eventually overcome by anxiety and a sweet buzz she decided to lay down on her fresh sheets. Cory had the key and could let himself in and wake her up when he arrived. Almost three hours into her nap, he called, probably to tell her he was looking for a parking space.

Naomi answered, "*Yes, hello.*" In her sweetest sleepy voice.

"Is this Naomi?" a woman's voice asked with the complete opposite tone. Naomi sat up slowly.

"Who's asking?"

"Is...this...Naomi?" The woman reiterated with more attitude this time around.

Naomi didn't answer, she put the phone on speaker and held the phone to her mouth.

"This is *Mrs.* Stephens; do you have a moment?" She emphasized the misses, and Naomi was too stunned to speak. But it didn't matter as Mrs. Stephen didn't give her permission to speak, she owned the conversation.

"The first thing I need to tell you is you need not wait up for Cory because he's not coming. The second thing I'd like to know is, how long have you been fucking my husband? You bitches have no shame, do you?"

"Pardon?" Naomi's eyes shot open.

"Don't act like you didn't know he was married. All of you bitches put on the same shocked act, and I'm just about tired of it."

Naomi's mind replayed everything going on over the course of time, specifically the day before she left for vacation. Everything Cory was doing led up to this moment right here, so a part of her wasn't shocked. As she paced her bedroom, waiting to hear what else the woman had to say, alerts came through her phone. She looked at the incoming text messages that Mrs. Stephens sent her.

"Like I said...*Husband.*" She rubbed it in knowing that Naomi had to have been looking at the pictures by now. Wedding pictures, honeymoon pictures, vacation pictures, pictures with the children all began popping up on her phone.

"We've been married for six years now!" she continued.

Naomi's fiancé's wife was on the other end berating her and calling her everything but a child of God, and all Naomi knew was to fight back because she wasn't like these other women that Naomi was surprised to hear he had, she was special. She wasn't some homewrecker this woman was making her out to be.

"I've been with this man for almost three years, and I had no idea he was married. We are in fact, engaged and planning a wedding," Naomi said feeling foolish as the words left her mouth.

His wife laughed hysterically. "Girl what? I know you lying," she shouted, and Naomi could tell that she was talking to someone else, more than likely Cory. It was confirmed when she heard a light scuffle then she got back on the phone.

"He bought you a ring? He proposed?" she asked, her voice cracking a bit, finally showing emotion which allowed Naomi to gain some confidence.

"Yes, he did."

Naomi then sent her a picture of her diamond encrusted left hand, her dress, and photos of her and Cory together. His wife let out a maniacal laugh.

"Where did you meet him?"

But Naomi was too busy staring at the woman's pictures wondering what they possibly had in common other than him. They looked nothing alike in style, body, height, nothing, so he clearly didn't have a type. The woman looked just as rough as Cory, tatted up, dark lips like she smoked more weed than him. She wasn't unattractive, but she appeared to be very unfeminine, rough... like him.

"Miami. I used to live out there," Naomi said.

The scuffle ensued again. Naomi could hear her screaming at him, "*So that is why your ass was always in Miami talking about some business, but you were out there fucking and tricking on some bitch?*

"Oh, I'm not just some bitch," Naomi attempted to defend herself, but his wife was having none of it.

"He's married, and if you're not his wife then you are indeed just some bitch! So no matter what you want to tell yourself sweetie, here's a fact for your ass, when that man dies, the only thing he's leaving you is alone! I am his wife! I will inherit the pain of his children, the businesses, the life insurance policies, everything! So like I said before, you are just *some bitch*, you and all the other bitches he sleeps with behind my back, so don't ever get it fucked up."

"I understand you're upset but I'm not about to be too many bitches. Did you not see that ring on my finger? You can tell yourself that I'm just some bitch but clearly, I am more than that to Cory!" Naomi cried out.

Naomi had to fight back and say something. She wasn't about be diminished to being just some bitch, even if that was the reality of it. She wasn't going to be humiliated and disrespected in that way. But the truth hurt so bad, so she did what any hurt person would do, she spewed out her own hurt and began sending pictures back. She sent vacation pictures, birthday parties, out with friends, out with his children who were too small and young to understand who Naomi was. She sent pictures of his family, his mother, his brothers, and uncles, pictures from the grand opening of his restaurants she sent them all. She even stooped as low as to send her a brief six-minute home video she had in her phone of her and Cory engaging in sexual acts. Naomi refused to be spoken down on as if she purposefully got into a relationship with her husband. She wanted to hurt Mrs. Stephens just as badly as she and her husband were hurting her. The long pause on the phone let Naomi know that she accomplished just that. But Mrs. Stephens' response didn't make Naomi feel good at all. She was not to blame, nor was Naomi and when his wife began to wail, it broke Naomi's heart. The sound was unlike anything she had ever heard in her life.

"What is it? I'm not pretty enough? I look like this because of you! Because of these babies I carried for you! Because of all the stress you put me through, and you go cheat on me? I've always been here for you, and you continue to do this to me! First it was the bitch in Virgina, then the bitch upstate but now this. You proposed to another woman?" she lashed out.

Naomi was torn between hanging up, feeling sorry for her, and wanting to jump on Amtrak and knock on his door. She wondered if that was the home that she had been to a time or two. Now it made sense as to why he was so against her staying with him so that they could spend more time together.

"Excuse me, but the home you share with Cory, is it in Fitler Square?" Naomi asked, reciting the exact address.

"You were in my home?"

She then went back to screaming.

"You had this bitch in our house, in our bed, around my kids!"

Then Naomi heard what sounded like glass shatter and Cory's voice finally appeared telling her to give him his phone. Naomi listened to her husband to be, and his wife argue. She listened to this woman cry and scream in agony at the heartache he had caused her. He pleaded with her, forgetting, not caring or not realizing that Naomi was still on the line.

She yelled, "Do you love her? Are you in love with her?"

Naomi then heard her man say, "She doesn't mean shit to me. I don't want to lose my family. Calm down before you lose the baby."

Lose the baby? She's pregnant?

Naomi continued listening as he consoled her. Cory assured his wife she was in no danger of losing him. Other than the sounds of a wounded woman, things got quiet. Naomi held on to the line for as long as she could then the lines disconnected.

Standing in the middle of her bedroom, Naomi held the phone in her hand. She couldn't even cry, she just paced her breathing to keep herself from throwing the violent tantrum that she felt brewing in her soul. About ten minutes later, Naomi began blowing Cory's phone up, texting him all kinds of hateful messages, leaving him threatening voicemails. She even called his wife's phone a few times, but it went to voicemail. About an hour later, Cory called but Naomi didn't answer. The phone kept ringing and Naomi ignored it as she headed into her living room and spun around not knowing where to place her energy. She slowly walked into the kitchen and grabbed a hammer out of the drawer and began ripping into the butter leather couches that Cory bought her and breaking all the pictures on the wall. She was screaming and crying so loud that her neighbors banged on the door asking if she was okay and if they needed to call 911.

"No, I'm okay!" she yelled out then calmed down some.

For hours, Naomi stayed up drinking, crying, fuming until night fell and her head spun, so she finally went to lay down. She dialed Cory's number repeatedly until she was tired and eventually fell asleep. In the middle of the night, she thought she heard keys jingling and light switches flickering. She felt a presence in her doorway.

It was him. She could smell him or was she dreaming. Warm tears began to fall down her face, slow but strong as he crawled in bed behind her fully dressed pulling her up under him and covering her. His touch sent her into a frenzy, and she began to bawl. Something in her died. It felt like a funeral, and she was inconsolable. She let Cory hold her; it was what she needed now.

Naomi woke up tucked under her down comforter with a bad headache. The day before was a blur, and she couldn't remember much. She reached for her phone on the nightstand and was furious at the sight of no missed calls from Cory. She stared out her window from her bed, deciding that she would spend the rest of her morning there. She didn't want to talk to anyone. She remembered her vivid dream of Cory rushing to her side to beg for her forgiveness but of course that wasn't a reality. His wife for sure was not letting him leave her pregnant side to go console his side bitch.

"Jesus, I need an Ibuprofen or something. My head," Naomi murmured, holding her head as she slowly crept out of the bed. She stopped short upon entering her living room.

"Where the fuck is my furniture? "Naomi looked around her apartment, head throbbing, vision blurred but shocked and nervous.

Was I robbed? Is someone still here?

She stepped back into her room, reaching for her cellphone; Shantel answered immediately.

"Where was Cory at all this time!"

Naomi shushed her.

"My head is pounding; hush listen to me. I think I've been robbed."

"Robbed, what?"

"My living room furniture is gone," Naomi whispered.

"Girl, what? Did Cory come over yesterday?"

"No."

"No? He did not even show up after having us all worried sick about him?"

"Shantel, please stop yelling, please, my head is pounding. Listen to me…. *Oh shit.*"

"Girl, what, what, what?"

"Someone just came in here, oh my God please, call Jameela, Pops, whoever, please." Naomi panicked.

"I'm calling the cops! But I'm on my way!" she hung up.

Naomi yelled out to the intruder, "Don't come in here or I'll shoot your fucking head off!"

But she didn't own a gun.

"It's me, baby, it's me!" the all too familiar voice said.

Cory appeared in the doorway. It did not make sense that seeing him made her heart melt but there was absolutely no way he could talk himself out of this. He approached her cautiously, his arms extended.

"I came over last night. You don't remember?" he asked softly.

"I thought I was dreaming," Naomi said somberly.

"I got rid of the furniture. Your super helped me bring the couches outside. I thought you heard us with all the noise we made trying to get those big couches out. He asked if you were okay. He said it sounded like you had a fight or something in here last night."

Naomi looked up at him in disgust.

"I sent you some money to get a new set…you know, extra pillows and whatever else you needed to replace," he said putting his hands in his pockets. He could not look Naomi in the eyes.

"Wow, I was a kept woman and didn't even realize it. You have been married all this time. It all makes sense now," Naomi said, her voice a whisper as the smallest of vibrations made her head hurt.

"I know you don't want to hear what I have to say, but Mimi please just let me explain."

"Where the fuck am I supposed to sit?" Naomi said to herself, ignoring Cory. She looked around her apartment and threw her hands up in the air in defeat.

"Naomi, listen to me. A long time ago I was someone totally different..." he said walking up to her, but Naomi backed away as if he was infested.

"Please, please, please do not touch me. I heard everything that I needed to hear, Cory. You love her, she's your family, I don't mean shit to you, and you know what else, your entire family aint shit for allowing you to parade me around knowing that you're married.!"

"It's not their fault. They love you, Naomi, they just didn't want to get involved."

"They got involved the minute they started smiling up in my damn face knowing that you were married!" Naomi snapped.

"Listen to me. I wanted to talk to you so bad, but I let too much time pass, and I knew it would look crazy. I didn't want to hurt her, so I told her what I needed to tell her to keep her calm."

"Oh, so fuck me? Hurt me then?" Naomi held her head. She walked off as he was talking to search for headache medicine in the bathroom cabinet.

"I didn't know you were listening, baby." He followed behind her.

Naomi turned around and mushed him with her finger. "*Exactly*! Which makes it even worse because you spoke from the heart and said how you really felt. And she's pregnant? You're having a baby?"

"It's not what you think," he said, having the nerve to seem aggravated.

Naomi hauled off and slapped him, twice. She could see the anger in his eyes, because the slaps hurt. He backed away from her, his face holding a scowl she had never seen on him before.

"I need you to get out of my house," she said walking past him into the kitchen for a glass of water to take her pills.

"What I never told you was a couple of years ago, before I met you, I was deep in the streets and was facing a lot of time and out of desperation I married my children's mother. But due to a technicality, I got off. I took the money that I had and opened a business and then things started going well, and I was able to totally leave life as I once knew it far behind me. I was way too busy running my business to file for a divorce from a marriage that wasn't even real. We weren't together at all, I swear. How could I have spent so much time with you over the years if I had a legit marriage?"

"Your wife said something real to me, and it made me put things into perspective. *God, forbid* you dropped dead right now. I'd be left with what? Some designer bags, memories, a few dollars you gave me. I wouldn't even be able to come to your funeral! Can you imagine me not finding out you were married until you were dead? Imagine me trying to obtain information about your funeral just for your mother of all people to say, hey I'm sorry you can't come to his funeral because he's married! Can you imagine me showing up and being confronted by a wife that I didn't even know you had?"

Naomi's chest tightened so she looked around for a place to sit. She hopped up on a small part of the kitchen counter holding her chest.

"You alright?" he asked, concerned, touching Naomi's knee. She pushed his hand off her.

"How could you ask me to marry you knowing it would be *impossible* to do so?" She grimaced.

Before he could answer there was a loud knock at the door, so she hopped off the counter to open it. Two officers, one Hispanic, the other black peeked inside, with Damon bringing up the rear.

"Fuck," Naomi said stepping aside letting them in.

"We got a call about a potential robbery?" the Hispanic one said.

"What's good, Mimi, everything cool?" Damon asked, ignoring Cory's presence. Since he was in no predicament to act like he held any weight, Cory begrudgingly stood on the side quietly fuming. Damon looked past Cory and around the apartment for a brief inspection. He even went as far as to walking around Damon into Naomi's bedroom. He looked inside then came back.

"What was going on in here?" Damon asked.

"Who are you?" Cory asked Damon.

"Her landlord. Who are you?" Damon already knew who Cory was but didn't care for the situation at hand. Naomi would often mention how cool her landlord was but now it all made sense. Naomi and the landlord use to be an item Cory surmised.

Damon looked into Naomi's eyes. The vibrant woman who's company he enjoyed looked downtrodden.

"It was a false alarm. I seriously thought I was being robbed. I heard footsteps, called my friend, she called you guys, yadda, yadda, yadda! Silly me forgot to let her know it was all good, it was just him." Naomi nodded her head toward Cory.

"Neighbors said they heard some fighting and screaming last night?" the black cop asked.

"Just me, I was here alone just going through some things. It's nothing officers, I promise."

"Fighting and screaming at yourself?" Damon folded his arms. Naomi took note of how fine Damon looked standing before her. Cory took note of how Naomi kept glancing at Damon.

The Hispanic one broke up the tension by asking if Naomi was in any kind of danger.

"No, not at all," Naomi said softly.

"Anything broken in here?" Damon asked.

"No, everything is fine, I promise."

"Ya'll can go," Cory spoke up. The officers looked at Naomi then around the apartment.

"You good?" Damon asked one last time.

"I assure you, I am fine. It was all a misunderstanding." She fake smiled.

One of the officers said something into his shoulder radio. Then the two of them wished her a good day and headed out with Damon slowly dragging behind them.

"Call me when you done," he said, closing the door.

"The fuck does he mean call him when you done?" Cory asked Naomi.

"Why don't you fucking go ask him what he meant?"

"So you gonna go fuck this nigga when I leave, probably was fucking him the whole time!"

"Typical. Look I think it's best you go, there isn't anything else I need to hear, and you can't make me understand shit!"

"I came here to talk to you man to woman."

"You're a coward. You could have told me your situation and allowed me to decide on my own. But it all makes sense, the way you've been acting, how you've been so stressed, so conflicted. That double life had you on Stressame Street, didn't it?" Naomi chuckled sarcastically.

"Yeah, it did," he admitted.

Naomi peered out of her window. She watched Damon talk to the officers for a bit then he got on the phone. He looked up at Naomi's window to find her staring back down at him. He winked his eye and mouthed, "You good?" to where she winked softly at him while Cory was busy on the other side of the room lying.

"You listening to me?" he asked walking toward her. She met him halfway, not wanting him to see that Damon was still outside.

"The day before I was supposed to pick you up, I stopped by to visit my kids. I left my phone on the counter because I didn't have nothing to hide. You must have been calling me, and she saw. She went through all our messages and pictures, and we got into this big ass fight. She was threatening to take my kids, take me for child support, just a whole bunch of shit. But even before that I had been going through a lot with her because she wanted us to be a family, and I knew that wasn't going to happen, but I was trying to keep her calm, so she didn't want to divorce me and take everything I worked hard for. I was trying to tame the beast, that's all baby. It was very stressful to have to hurt her and hide this from you. I planned on telling you everything once the divorce was final."

Naomi stepped a bit closer to Cory, looking up at him. "And let me guess, you gave her pity sex and that is how she ended up pregnant?"

"That is *exactly* what happened, on everything I love," he said, touching his chest for emphasis.

"You must think I'm a damn fool," Naomi said, picking up her vibrating phone.

Then there was another loud obnoxious knock at the door. Naomi swung her door open violently to find Shantel and Yusef, the new guy she was dating at the door. Shantel barged in. "Is everything okay?"

She hugged Naomi while Yusef and Cory exchanged firm hand-shakes.

"Yes, it was a false alarm. Cory came in last night while I was asleep. I didn't know he was here," Naomi said, exasperated.

"You had our friend worried sick. We all were worried, so where was he?" Shantel said, turning her attention toward Naomi. Cory put his head down.

"And where is your furniture?" Shantel said spinning around. "And why are the cops and Damon outside?"

"Wow, so she's really far along, this makes so much fucking sense, what is she about 6-7 months now!" Naomi spat as more pictures came through her phone. His wife began texting like a maniac, asking was Cory at her house to which Naomi replied yes.

"I'm sorry, who's pregnant?" Shantel said looking around.

"*His wife,*" Naomi spat out.

In unison, Shantel and Yusef both shouted out, "Wife?"

Naomi simply handed Shantel her phone. "Jameela was 100% right," Naomi said.

"Cory…. what is this?" Shantel said quietly. Cory wasn't saying anything that made sense to anyone.

"His wife is still texting me pictures. She asked were you here, and I let her know that you were so you may want to head home now before you get in trouble."

"Cory, how could you do something as duplicitous as this?" Shantel scowled.

Naomi looked at the man she would have to take time to learn to unlove almost immediately and she didn't recognize the person who stood before her. The man in front of her looked wicked, devilish, like a liar, a piece of shit. She was trying to see the man she fell in love with who would never hurt her, who vowed to protect her. The man who's chest she lay on telling him all her deepest hurts, secrets and dreams. He held them all inside of him now and for what.

Shantel held Naomi's face between her hands as if she was a child. "*Sweetie, do you want him here?*" she asked softly with tears in her eyes. Naomi, knowing that there would never be a future for her and

Cory, thinking of her own parents and the mess they created in her, shook her head.

"This is a nightmare, Shantel," she cried.

"She doesn't want you here. You need to leave," Shantel said to Cory.

But he didn't budge. He insisted on exercising his power, attempting to sweet talk Naomi into letting him stay so he could continue to convince her she should give him another chance. He approached her and rubbed her back as she faced a wall away from him. Shantel stood close by, making sure her girl didn't fold.

"I need to hear her say it. Naomi, do you want me to go?"

"She said leave," Shantel said raising her voice a bit.

Cory snatched up his car keys and slowly headed to the door as if he was waiting for Naomi to tell him to stay.

"Mimi…" he called out to her one last time.

Naomi's heart was screaming "don't go" because she needed more time to end this, but instead she just watched him walk out the door. Shantel slammed the door behind him and ran back over to her friend and held her.

"It's going to be okay." Shantel rubbed her back.

Naomi listened intently and could hear him slowly jogging down the stairs, further and further away from her and through her cracked windows she could hear the engine of his truck starting and him pulling off.

And just like that, it was over.

Chapter 4

HAVE YOU EVER TRIED SLEEPING WITH A BROKEN HEART?

The days following the betrayal were extremely difficult for Naomi, forcing her to take time off from work. Getting out of bed was hard and ignoring Cory's calls got even harder, so she changed her number. The girls would come over after work sometimes and sit with her even though she didn't have much to say. They played music and kept noise around her to keep her alive.

One or two times they even had to dress her and take her for a walk like a puppy so she could get fresh air, otherwise she'd live under her covers. After two weeks, Naomi began forcing herself to do better because she needed to get back to work, but it wasn't getting any easier to deal with. She cursed the day Cory was born, and begged God to push her to the acceptance part of the grief cycle. But it proved to be difficult as everything reminded her of him, every scent, every song, every show, every color, everything because he was her everything, her *only* thing. Laying alone in her king-sized bed reminded her of the betrayal, and it hurt like hell. One late night at around 2am the ache in her chest would not subside, so she called Shantel, who answered the phone half sleep.

"Shan, this shit hurt so bad girl," Naomi whimpered.

"I know, my love," she said in a sweet sleepy voice.

"I swear it feels like someone is hammering me in my heart. Sometimes I can't even breathe, and I get these sharp pains in my chest like I'm having now."

"When was the last time you had a decent meal? You can't keep drinking the pain away. Look, why don't you come stay with me for a few days so you can get the proper food and rest. I have plenty of room, and you know I cook. You need a change of scenery for a little while."

"That doesn't sound like a bad idea."

"You know, that man is not going through what he put you through. He's not home sick like you and as your sister, I need to tell you this and it's going to hurt but understand that his wife done forgave him, she's carrying his baby, they are a family, she deals with his infidelities, you weren't the first and you probably won't be the last woman he cheated on her with."

"But it was different. We were engaged."

"No my love, you were not engaged, he gave you a ring, that's it. He had absolutely no plans to marry you. I'm sorry, Naomi, I'm not going to let you sit in this any longer. You're about to start stinking in a minute and then nobody is going to want to come around you, so get up. This man has moved on with his life. If he wanted to see you, he would. He knows where you work and live, he has my number, Meela's number. If he so desperately wanted to get at you, he would have. You are better than being a side piece, jump off, mistress or any of those things. And I know you loved him, and dare I say it, he loved you too, but it's over Mimi. I'm not rushing your healing, I'm not saying get over it, but we got to turn the corner, my love."

Naomi thought about the night she found out Cory was married and once Yusef and Shantel left, Cory spun the block, and she allowed him to come back upstairs to talk to her, soothe her pain and make love to her. It was what she needed, even if it was a lie. She never told the girls because she knew they'd disapprove. But it was what she needed, it was the ending she desired. Cory made love to her as if he had something to prove. Naomi came with all her might that night and then she sent him home to his wife with no intention of ever talking to him again.

"I promise you, I don't want to feel like this. I be praying to God every night to please take the love that I have for this man away from me. I don't want to love him no more. I don't want to remember him anymore. You ever hurt so fucking bad you beg God to take the love out your heart for a nigga, like you would give anything to not love a motherfucka no more?" Naomi cried.

"Keep praying, baby, you know God will see you through this. Do your part and let him do his and in the meantime, keep in mind you have responsibilities and a full beautiful life ahead of you. So let's just bend the corner *just a little bit* so you can handle your business to keep a roof over your head. You can't lose your job; you can't lose your security or your sanity over this."

"Damon would never put me out," Naomi joked.

"Hey, you never know, didn't Cory just give you the shock of your damn life?"

Through her tears and grief Naomi agreed. "I'm going to pack a few things and head over tomorrow."

"Okay, you know where the spare is. But come Naomi or I'll come after work and drag you out of that house myself. You don't need to be there alone, let's get you across the finish line, sis."

Harlem was like a whole different vibe, and Naomi loved visiting. Harlem was filled with so much culture. Music always filled the streets, the air smelled like lemongrass and smoke, the old folks sat out on their stoops congregating with the neighborhood winos and dope fiends which probably used to be friends of theirs back in the day. Naomi arrived at Shantel's the next morning while she was at work and made herself at home in Shantel's beautiful brownstone that looked like something straight out of architect digest. Her home was adorned with exotic plants and beautiful art from all the places she traveled. Shantel was so sweet, she left Naomi a sandwich and a fruit salad with a note that read, "nourish yourself." Shantel was an excellent cook, she could even make a peanut butter and jelly sandwich taste gourmet. Naomi ate the delicious pastrami, muenster cheese, tomato, avocado sandwich then curled up on the couch watching Martin re-runs until she fell asleep. She was awakened by Shantel propping her feet up on her lap. She opened her eyes to find

Shantel's smiling face and Jameela on the phone fussing with some-one about something as usual.

"How was your day sunshine?"

"Better than it's been, but you know." Naomi rubbed her temples.

"Don't give it too much power today. Just relax, I'm going to cook, and we are going to just vibe today, is that alright?" Shantel smiled and happily headed toward the kitchen.

Naomi watched as Jameela and Shantel both did things in the kitch-en. She decided to see who was knocking at the door and opened it to find Yusef standing there.

"Hey, how are you holding up?" he asked, giving her a brief hug.

"I've had better days." She walked to the couch and sat down. Yusef walked into the kitchen to greet Shantel then made himself comfort-able on a chair across from Naomi.

"If a man wants to hide something, so don't beat yourself up too bad."

"You got that right." Naomi said leaning back on the couch with her eyes closed.

"You're a good woman, and by how highly Shantel always speaks of you, you're a good friend too. You're solid, and you don't deserve to be going through this. I hope you heal soon."

"Yeah, me too." was all she could offer Yusef.

"A whole wife and kids and the fact his family was riding out with him through the bull shit is nasty work." he said and stood up while taking a quaff of his bourbon.

"Get up, Naomi," he said one last time then extended his fist for her to bump into his then he walked into the kitchen.

"Baby, holla at me when dinner is ready," he said, kissing Shan-tel on the cheek before heading upstairs. Shantel gushed as she watched him slowly walk up the stairs. She did a lil shiver, shimmy move as she diced the tomatoes for salad.

Naomi smiled at how in love she was with her new man and remi-nisced on the days when she use to feel that way about someone but she had to get over it. Meela came back and sat next to Naomi with more bourbon.

Music blared through the ceiling. "Hold On" by the Internet played. Naomi closed her eyes and vibed, letting the tears run down softly, smoothly, unforced. But it didn't hurt this time. This time the cry felt like a cleanse, like taking her soul to the laundromat. It felt like the last cry, and she truly hoped it was because she was ready to move on and get to the other side. She was tired of feeling sorry for herself. As the women milled about doing one thing or another, she noticed how lighthearted their energy was. Their hearts were so free of heartbreak weighing them down, and she wanted that feeling again. She wanted to go back to a time when her heart wasn't so heavy, when love was innocent. But had there ever been such a time?

Shantel appeared with a plate of salad and handed it to Naomi. She loved how Shantel always served her food in courses like in a restaurant. Once she was done with her salad, Shantel placed a small plate of salmon bites in front of Naomi with homemade bang bang sauce and they were scrumptious as she hadn't had home cooked food in months. She ate the salmon in what seemed like slow motion. Once done, Shantel placed a small plate of chicken fried rice in front of her with all the fixings like a Chinese restaurant, scallions, egg, vegetables, light soy sauce. Hungrily Naomi ate, happy that her appetite was seemingly coming back, a clear sign of progression, and she was thankful. She belched and reclined into the couch, vibing some more to one of Yusef's many playlists. Shantel came over and sat next to her placing a cup of ginger tea in front of her. That ginger tea warmed her soul and pulled more tears out of her.

"I feel like the pain is leaving my body little by little," Naomi said in a low whisper, with no intention of anyone hearing her but her friends did.

"Good, my love, let it burn," Shantel said.

Naomi let out a deep groan as Jameela rubbed her shoulders.

"I got an idea," Shantel said getting up and quickly running downstairs. She returned with her foot sauna and a bunch of oils and salts. She laid a towel down and instructed Naomi to soak her feet in the warm sitzy water filled with Vitamin C Epsom salt and baby oil gel. While her feet soaked, Jameela oiled her scalp. The tears fell hot, warm, steady as Naomi took in the energy and love from her sisters. Shantel washed and massaged her feet then slid a pair of fluffy warm socks on to them.

"I needed this so badly," Naomi said.

No one said anything as Shantel handed Naomi a T-shirt to sleep in.

"You feel like you want to lay down?" Jameela asked softly.

Naomi simply nodded, so Shantel retrieved a pillow from her guest room that smelled like lavender.

"Turn the music down," Shantel instructed Jameela.

Then a blanket was put over her. She heard the words I *love you* and felt kisses on her forehead, activating tears. Soon after, there were whispers of goodbyes at the front door as Jameela headed home. Thankful that her tribe did not allow her to dwell on the pain today, she drifted into a most wonderful sleep and before she knew it, the morning had come, and today when she woke up, she decided everything she went through was beautiful. She had experienced love and lost it.

She compared finding out about Cory's marriage to what it must feel like to get hit by an 18-wheeler, landing you in ICU. Through the weeks, she found herself on bedrest and feeding tubes, while nurse Shantel and Jameela checked on her, giving her physical therapy to help her walk and talk again. Then there were times when she thought that she was ready to leave the hospital, but every time she stood up to walk it hurt. Now she was on the path to a full recovery, no longer needing crutches. Naomi knew that she had work to do. But abandonment issues were very real for her, and she realized it being one of the reasons why it was hard for her to assert herself when it came to men.

Her thoughts were sidetracked by the beautiful clothes in the department store windows as she strutted down Fifth Avenue. Retail therapy was much needed especially after her body transformed from using gym therapy to heal her broken heart. One weekend after Naomi proved to be in a decent head space, Jameela and Naomi came over to help her pull Cory's things out of the closet and sell them on eBay where she made a cool $8k off leather jackets, designer shoes, belts and a bracelet. Separately, she was able to sell his Rolex for 6k. She renovated her apartment, ridding herself of everything that Cory had ever touched or bought. She was pleased as she looked around knowing Cory hadn't touched anything in her apartment. It was all brand new and so was she. As she strolled down 5th Avenue, deep in thought while simultaneously looking for some place to spend her money, fate intervened.

"I'm so sorry, she's a friendly one!" The pale white woman with red hair said as her dog pawed at Naomi's legs.

"She really likes you!"

"I see! Look at her little tail go!"

Naomi played with the dog for a few more moments then made her way into the Fendi store where she was about to buy something that she didn't necessarily want or need then swiftly made an about face. She always hated walking into high end stores and leaving abruptly or empty handed. She felt as if the workers low key judged her for not buying something as if she couldn't afford it. But any way she knew where she wanted to spend her money, and it was not on a purse or shoes. It would be spent on love.

Chapter 5
BETTER DAYS

*S*am and Ginger, named after the main characters in her fa-vorite movie Casino starring Robert DeNiro and Sharon Stone, were the two most adorable, curly haired, yorkie poodle dogs she had ever seen in her life. Ginger of course was ginger colored and extra curly, and Sam was just as curly but chocolate brown with the biggest, prettiest eyes ever.

The moment Naomi saw them, her heart began beating rapidly. Like a little girl, she hopped up and down excitedly, pointing at them knowing they were going to bring her immense joy. Naomi was pre-pared to reorganize her 1 ½ bedroom apartment, turning the ½ bedroom into her pups room. She fully trained Sam and Ginger and put them on a schedule where she would be able to walk them. Sam and Ginger slept in her bed and followed her everywhere. She took them to the groomer consistently and purchased doggy clothes for them to wear. Naomi found her happy place for now. She began, "living her best life" dating and doing *who* and what she wanted. She felt free and happy to not be burdened and bogged down with the responsibility of love as she liked to put it.

"I'm impressed. I really thought you'd get tired of those dogs but here we are so many years later." Meela watched Sam and Ginger hop around on Naomi's lap.

"These are my babies and speaking of dogs, how is this new man of yours we have yet to vet and really spend time with?"

"How are you calling someone a dog and you don't even know them?"

"It was an easy segue girl relax a little bit. What's up with you being so defensive and secretive suddenly?"

"What is up with you being so pressed, my God."

"Nobody is pressed. Pops hasn't even met him so he called to ask me what I thought about the man and was befuddled by the fact I never even saw a picture of him, so what is up?" Naomia looked into the camera suspiciously while rubbing her fur babies.

Jameela rolled her eyes and shook her head out of frustration. "You all are making a big deal out of nothing. You act like I'm some child that needs permission to date. Furthermore, did you forget I started a business? I am swamped with all kinds of paperwork, I'm trying to open another location, I'm running around doing boss shit. Contrary to what you and Iyanla Vanzant over there are talking about, I'm spending most of my time handling my business not hiding some man, and any free time that I have, which is minimal is spent relaxing alone or with my man, is that a crime?"

"My man, my man, my man. You missed the last two mani, pedi appointments and for the record, you had this business before you met him, and you used to make time. Now things are just different so who else can we blame your reclusions on?"

"Now I'm a recluse. Stop reaching okay, I think you are noticing everything now because you don't have a man. But nothing has changed."

"Well, that would have hurt me in the past, but the fact I am over that nigga and so okay with being single, I am totally unbothered." Naomi shrugged.

"You know I'm the blunt friend, don't get all sensitive on me now."

"I promise you, I don't feel no kind of way, but you can try being the friend with couth sometimes for a change, blunt is just another term for classless in my book." Naomi rolled her eyes.

"Whatever, and then on top of everything else, I'm helping him with his business, so I am extra busy these days."

"Helping him how, shouldn't he be helping you?"

"Do I look like I need help?" Jameela asked offended.

"He's an ex-NFL player, he should have a few millions laying around, I assume."

"I had my business before I met him, what on God's earth could he or should he be helping me with? Because I'm a business major, earned several degrees in business management, I can assist him with the basics to start, it's nothing major."

"How's business going anyway?" Naomi asked shifting gears noticing she wasn't getting anywhere with Jameela.

"Running a 24-hour day care is more than what I expected, but it is so rewarding. The stories that I hear just inspire me to do so much more in the community for single parents. They're so appreciative of this business, and it makes me feel good. I hired the best of the best childcare providers. I have cameras everywhere and so many protocols in place and the location is chef's kiss. I'm hiring more staff. I need an Office Manager that knows bookkeeping. I need two more security guards and I'd like to have a chef on staff to make the kids nutritional meals. I need someone to handle the day to day so I can move on to other things. These Chanel bags aren't going to buy themselves baby."

"You have a whole NFL playing boyfriend, I think you will be okay in the Chanel department."

"Why do you keep bringing up my man's profession, like what is up with that?"

Because I don't believe him that's why, Naomi thought.

"I'm just saying that although you have your own and always have, now that you got this baller you can spend his money girl, lighten up!" Naomi said, trying to change the mood, but she noticed Jameela was extra defensive and deflective when it came to this man. Naomi's mind was made up, she didn't like him, he had a negative effect on her girl. Suddenly she had become secretive, easily offended, offensive, and mean.

"Well, don't watch my man's pockets, dear. And it is *ex* NFL; he's an entrepreneur now," she said snidely. "But anyway, as I was saying, I am simply happy to be doing my part is all! Imagine having to work an overnight shift without someone you can trust to watch your children. I'm just blessed to be able to provide some sort of relief, you know?"

"That's why you created Roun' The Clock Care beloved, you are a genius! I am so happy you didn't give up. We have to get out and celebrate everyone's accomplishments. Make some time, come on, Meela. I miss my sista, dammit!"

"Awe, I tell you what. How about this Saturday we link up for brunch? I think Tyrone has some affairs to tend to, so I should be free."

"Damn, so you can only make time for us when he doesn't have time for you?"

"I love my life, and I love being with my man, what can I say?"

Naomi rolled her eyes so hard she instantly caught a headache. She was just hoping Jameela took her head out her man's ass and re-surfaced soon. But she was so busy talking about "her blessings" she hadn't even noticed Naomi put the phone down to put the dogs on a leash in preparation for their walk. She could hear Jameela telling a story about how Tyrone almost crashed his G-Wagon and decided to park it up and pull out his *lambo*. She began listing a whole fleet of cars that Tyrone owned, happy to have access to them all and not having to put miles on her own Benz. Naomi interrupted Jameela's humble bragging to ask if she could bring Sam and Ginger to a girls' night out. Meela rolled her eyes.

"I don't care what you do with those mutts, just don't ever think to ask can you put any of those dogs in my man's Lamborghini when I'm driving it or any of the vehicles. I don't do dogs."

Naomi had enough at this point, "I'm taking my babies out for a walk then I'm hitting the gym, let's confirm our outing Friday night. I'd hate to get my hopes up and you cancel."

"Ok, well, I need to go anyway. I need to crunch numbers and get dinner ready."

Meela rudely hung up the phone on Naomi before she could say anything further.

It took the women about three weeks after that last phone call with Jameela to get her to pencil them in and on a rainy Friday night, like torrential downpours, Naomi jumped in a Lyft and headed to Bobby Vans on Park Avenue because she was a sucker for a good steak, and they had some of the best in the city in her opinion. Rain and all, she knew if she canceled due to the weather, it would be another six months before they all saw one another again. As Naomi approached the hostess to give the reservation name, she spotted Shantel at the bar sipping on an Aperol spritzer with a spray of tequila. They made eye contact, both breaking out into huge smiles. They hugged tight and warm, rocking side to side like sisters do when they haven't seen one another in a while.

"You look so good," she said cupping Naomi's face between her hands like she always did, like a mama bear would.

"Thank you, you look well yourself. How are things? How's the job?" Naomi sat on a stool.

"You first, how's your mind, body, soul and heart? How are you sleeping, eating, and getting on?"

That was Shantel. Though she was small in stature, she had the biggest heart, and her energy could fill up any room. If she needed to vent, she always asked your permission first. She always asked if you had the mental capacity to hear some complaining before she rambled on about anything though she barely ever complained. She valued time and her loved ones. She always asked about the other person before she told you about how she was doing.

"I am well. I really can't complain, you know. I do have some things I'm working through but other than that, life is good."

"Do you want to talk about it?" she asked.

"I think I may need to go see the lady."

"No bullshit," Shantel said excitedly.

"Yeah, I've been thinking about my parents, you know. This can't be normal for me to just go through life with these broken relationships. I want to have children one day, but I have to make sure I get my shit together first. It's been on my mind to level up some in my personal life. I love you ladies down, and you both give some of the best advice even if I don't want to hear it, but I think that it's time to go see the lady for real."

Shantel's face suddenly turned serious. "I am so proud of you, Naomi! Oh my God," she said, getting emotional.

"Girl, stop," Naomi said, making light of it.

But it was a big deal for her to admit that she had issues that Shantel deep in her heart believed that Naomi was suppressing through sex and alcohol.

"I'm not going to drag it, just know that I love you, and I support you and I know some exceptional psychotherapists," Shantel said.

"You know every damn body," Naomi joked.

"I'm part of the black elite, honey." Shantel winked. "Seriously, do you have someone in mind?"

"Why is finding a Black therapist so hard, especially finding someone in network! Now if I must pay out of pocket, cool but I still cannot seem to find anyone who has a CV that makes me comfortable. So if you have someone in mind you believe is a good fit for me, kindly send them my way so I can put their contact in my phone and take a few more years to use them."

"Naomi!" Shantel slapped her leg playfully.

"No, seriously sis, all recommendations welcome, it's time."

Shantel warmly nodded her approval and understanding and immediately forwarded Dr. Drummonds contact info to Naomi.

"So what's up with our girl? Are we sure she's going to show up tonight because you know I haven't talked to her in about a month."

"Seriously?" Naomi asked surprised.

"Yes. I got tired of calling her and getting sent to voicemail or our conversations getting cut off, plans being broken like come on sista you can do better than that. Ain't nobody that damn busy. I'm married and I always have time for my girls when necessary. She needs to come down off that high horse for a while and mingle with us peasants. I'm only here because *you* confirmed she was coming." Shantel scoffed a bit.

"I spoke with her while I was on my way, and she informed me that *her man* was getting dressed as well because he had some business to manage and so she would be here."

Shantel rolled her eyes. "Jameela has never been *that girl*, you know the, *my man, my man, my man,* type. Now suddenly, she's just...I don't know, it's not giving happy, it's giving *happy to have a man* you feel me?"

"The self-proclaimed *Product of Preston* as she likes to call herself is in love, that's all." Naomi said mockingly as she always hated when she branded herself as such, making light of the adultery her father committed throughout his marriage as if it had not affected her in a negative way.

The hostess escorted the women to their tables where they ordered drinks and appetizers while waiting for Jameela, who arrived 45 minutes late. Jameela was not tall but tall for a woman, standing about 5ft 9in flats. She always walked with her head up, shoulders back, long struts giving grand dame aura, but now it was to the max for some odd reason. Something about claiming a man had her confidence on a trillion. She strutted in wearing a black, wide brimmed, red bottom hat over her always sharp short haircut, skintight jeans and a black tank top, heels higher than her esteem and her staple, a large Chanel purse, this one was red. She caught the eyes of everyone she passed, and rightfully so. Jameela had "it" always have since she was young. Her parents always instilled morals and lessons in her, drilling it into her head that she embodied greatness. The women waved to her wildly excited and were met with a mediocre twinkle of the fingers as she neared them. Shantel scoffed and Naomi playfully kicked her under the table.

"You look good, girl, you look good!" Naomi said standing up and hugging her tightly. She missed her friend and had not seen her in months since she'd been in a relationship.

"And you smell delicious! What are you wearing?"

She hesitated to say then said, "I am not in danger of you buying it. It's called Jardin Nocturne."

"Why wouldn't she buy it? It smells nice, I would buy it!" Shantel agreed.

"It costs $2,000 a bottle, that's why," she said and tucked her purse next to her on the couch.

"You are so right. I damn sure am not paying for that! "Naomi said lightheartedly.

"So, what's going on with you ladies, what's new?" Jameela asked.

She looked at her watch long enough to show the women that it was a Breitling. No one bothered giving her the attention she was searching for.

"Are you with us for the night or do you have some place to go? I see you looking at the time already and you're an hour late, miss thing," Naomi said nudging her playfully. Jameela's body stiffened at her friend's touch as if it wasn't welcomed.

"Ah ah! No you did not stiffen up on me like you don't want to be touched, do you see this?" Naomi laughed. Jameela snootily picked up the menu to view.

"Well, I'm elated that the three of us are finally together! We have so much to catch up on, career, love lives, health, just every and anything! I say we pull an all-nighter," Shantel said, looking at both women from across the table. But Naomi was already getting turned off by Jameela's nonchalant attitude; she was acting as if she didn't want to be there.

"I'm too busy for such an indulgence, an all-nighter simply won't happen." Jameela hissed.

"Aren't we all, just relax, girl, damn and why are you talking like that?" Naomi said annoyed.

"Look, all because you don't have anyone to go home to doesn't meant the rest of us can be out gallivanting, isn't that right, Shantel?" she said, expecting an ally in her arrogance.

"I mean while I do respect my marriage, if I'm out with the girls then I'm out with the girls. Besides when I say all-nighter you know damn well my check engine light is going to come on around 10!" she laughed.

"Sure but do you really want to be out with the girls all night when you have a man at home?" Jameela pressed on.

"Why not?" Shantel shrugged, not understanding what point Jameela was trying to make.

"God damn, Jameela, act like you won before! You're really acting crazy over having a man, good for you! Gold star, cookies and confetti, shit already!" Naomi laughed.

Jameela responded by shaking her head as if she pitied Naomi, which upset her even more. The server came out with three flutes of champagne and set one down in front of each of the women. Shantel began a toast to shift the mood.

"So! Let me be the first to say I am proud of all of us. Life is beautiful for each of us, and I'm incredibly happy to see us all blossoming and living such a soft life, living in our divine feminine energy, and doing what we need to do to maintain our health, sanity, and happiness," Shantel said, extending her glass. The women followed suit.

"To the good life." She smiled as everyone clinked glasses and made eye contact while sipping.

"C-Suite baby yes, let me hold a dollar!" Naomi joked.

"Cheers, but there is a vast difference between being the CEO of a company and owning a company. While I do respect your position as CEO, you have the option to clock out at 5 or 6pm and be done for the day, whereas I'm running this business twenty-four seven. Having actual employees and doing payroll is a whole other monster."

"Why do you always have to do that Jameela, damn!" Naomi said but it fell on deaf ears.

"Speaking of, I need to figure some things out. I need to hire an experienced bookkeeper and office manager. The two that I hired are about to get the boot. How much do you make Naomi, I may have to hire you, girl!" she tapped Naomi's thigh.

Shantel intervened in Jameela's rant. "You need to hire some young girl fresh out of college, or maybe someone that needs a side gig."

"I'm willing to pay $70k" she shrugged.

"So you think that's how much I make? I mean there's nothing wrong with making $70k, but I'm just saying." Naomi asked.

"Considering that you don't have a degree, how much does admin assistants make these days? I really don't know, I've never been one." She shrugged.

"Oof," Naomi said and guzzled her champagne.

"Oh Jameela, why must you darken our doorstep with these little jabs? You should be happy about your success. How do you have time to be so hateful." Shantel said.

"Oh, I am very happy, trust me!"

"So then why are you being so nasty? We haven't seen you in a while and you show up with all this bravado."

Naomi, beginning to feel some kind of way chimed in, "Kudos to you too Shantel for winning in a space that was created by and for white men only and here your black ass goes disrupting the scene. Being the CEO of a company and institution built for white America to succeed is no easy feat," Naomi said making sure that Jameela did not try to downplay Shantel's accomplishments.

"And what about you? What's your success story?" Jameela turned to Naomi and sipped.

"I managed to survive another year." Naomi smiled genuinely.

"Oh hell yeah, I hear that hot shit, loud and clear my love," Shantel said and clinked glasses.

Jameela nodded her head and quietly sipped her champagne.

Everyone eyed the menu in search of an entrée, all of them in their own thoughts. The vibe was off, and it was all Jameela's fault. But the women planned to find the underlying cause of her attitude and arrogance tonight. She could not hide behind the phone by not answering or hanging up on a conversation this time. The waiter took everyone's orders, and it was not lost on the women that Jameela ordered a bottle of Del Dotto Napa for $1200. She closed the menu quickly and handed it back.

"$1200!" Naomi exclaimed.

"Don't worry about it." Jameela shrugged.

"Don't worry about it? Girl, we're trying to celebrate and have a simple girl's night out and you came through stuntin."

"When your man has millions and a black card, you can live a little, stop being so uptight." She shrugged.

"Well my man doesn't have a black card," Shantel said.

"But you could have one if you wanted to," Jameela said to Shantel.

"And as you like to point out, I don't have a man, so..." Naomi followed up.

Jameela sipped her drink and led the conversation by pointing to Shantel with her flute. Her wrists twirled around with her pinky up in the air as she spoke so matter of factly about everyone's finances.

"Girl, you're a CEO, I know you clear about $350k and your parents are rich, you got investments and brownstones, a PhD in Finance from Stanford. You don't have children, which is another factor in you having money because those little crumb snatchers are expensive. You should be pulling up to work in a Maserati or a Rolls, but I hear you trying to appear humble in your car choices. But anyway, your money, your business." She sipped.

"Are you sure it's my business and mine alone? I mean damn you should work for the IRS. And what do I look like parking a Maserati or a Rolls Royce in Harlem, or pulling up to a job in one?" Shantel rolled her eyes.

"Oh please you don't even have to work if you don't want to. Daddy's rich and mama's good looking." Jameela winked.

"What in the world?" Naomi said, looking around.

"All I am saying is live a little, damn! You can't take none of this shit with you. What's the problem with throwing away a measly $1200? You know Shantel, you can be very hypocritical sometimes."

Naomi leaned back in her chair and shook her head disapprovingly of Jameela's conversation choice.

"Okay, so tell me what you've been holding on to because clearly you have things to get off your chest."

"No, I'm just saying that you turn your nose up sometimes to material items, let people live if they want to wear expensive purses and things like that, because even though you may not walk around with double G's and LV's all over your clothes, you wear designer labels. You *only* wear white Louis Vuitton T-shirts." She gave Shantel a once over, "Three Van Cleef bracelets, I don't know what kind of earrings those are but I'm almost positive they're something high end."

"Well, damn," Naomi said, clutching imaginary pearls. "You did your homework on a bitch, didn't you?" She laughed.

"I don't have a problem spending $1200 if it's on something that I like or enjoy. I don't even drink like that, so I would never spend this amount of money on alcohol." Shantel stated.

"Girl, I guess." She rolled her eyes and sipped her drink.

"Well, now that we got that out of the way..." Naomi said.

"Naomi, what's is holding you back?"

"Pardon?"

"I just expected more from you after all these years. Shantel don't look at me all cockeyed. Your mother feels the same way."

"Wait, what does my mother have to do with anything?"

"Well that's your bad for putting your expectations of me on me. I'm doing fine."

Naomi turned to Shantel who had a nervous smile on her face.

"So you didn't ask me a few months back if you could live in my rent stabilized apartment so that you can save money?" Jameela said.

"Mmm, mmm, mmm, this is nasty work," Shantel chimed in.

"And, so what, I'm looking to buy property and figured I could save quicker if I was paying $1,200 in rent as opposed to the $4,000, I'm paying now, what's the big damn deal, *friend?* Oh and I'm aware your mother never really cared for me because she thought I was beneath you in some kind of way," Naomi turned her attention to Shantel.

"That's taking it a bit far, she never looked at you as beneath me. She just honors education and yes, she frowns upon anyone that doesn't take advantage of furthering their education but it's nothing personal. My mother isn't invested in my friendships like that so please don't think that."

Jameela was making it a point to attack everyone's finances because she hit the jackpot with her new man. She always resented Shantel for having the kind of mother she wished hers was, educated, rich, classy, bourgeois', all the things she aspired to be. And though her father was self-made and did right by his family, she sometimes wished he was part of the elite like Shantel's stepfather Kenny. But with Tyrone in her life and plans for getting married, she would one day have the life that Ms. Cheryl and Kenny lived.

"Wow." Was all Naomi could say sitting next to her friend who was acting more like a frienemy.

Shantel reached across the table to touch Jameela's hand.

"Sis, are you alright?" she asked her tenderly.

"Never better, why?"

"Because you're coming in here hot! I don't even know who I'm sitting across from right now! You seem to have some kind of chip on your shoulder. Is everything cool in *real life* because this delusion of grandeur you're living in has you acting out of order!"

"Delusions of grandeur because I feel as friends, we need to hold one another accountable when we see our friends not living up to their potential? I wouldn't be a real friend if I didn't point out where I see either of you falling short and I would expect you both to do the same for me."

"Can't nobody tell you when you're falling short without you getting defensive." Naomi snapped.

Jameela fanned her off as if she was speaking nonsense. "When have I ever fallen short in my education, job, career, lifestyle with or without a man, tell me when? All I'm saying is Shantel's mother is partially right, you can be doing better, why do we have to turn it into an argument?"

"Now you want to gaslight me like you didn't just sit here and insult the fuck out of me. What if this is my best and I'm happy about it, will you shut the fuck up then?" Naomi asked.

Jameela let out a deep sigh. "If mediocrity is where you choose to dwell, then suit yourself." She shook her head as if she were disappointed in Naomi, who looked at her up and down with the nastiest of looks, her lips snarled and her eyes turned into slits. This woman next to her was unfamiliar.

"You haven't been yourself for quite some time. We're your girls, what's up?" Shantel smiled softly trying to lighten the mood.

"What is this, a Destiny's Child video?" Jameela laughed.

No one else laughed. The women were pissed, turned off, upset and two seconds off Jameela's ass.

"Everything is great, you guys can't take real talk anymore. We always talk about pushing one another and uplifting each other, what's the problem?"

"The problem is you forgot what uplifting means clearly," Naomi said.

"So, is this what we're doing now, taking things seriously?" She looked around at her friends. She then fanned her hand at them in a never mind motion and that's when Naomi noticed the ring on her finger. She looked at Shantel first to see if she noticed. She had not, so Naomi motioned with my eyes. Shantel's eyes widened.

"Is there something you need to tell us?" Shantel sat up.

"*Need* to tell you? Nope," she said smugly.

Naomi inhaled deeply out of frustration and twirled one of her locs and shook her head.

"We're not about to do this with you. Are you engaged?" Shantel asked.

"Yes, I am. Look, I didn't plan on telling you ladies or discussing this tonight, but here we are!" She smiled the fakest smile.

"When the hell did this happen? Why didn't you share this with us?" Shantel drilled her but Naomi was at a loss for words. She just sat and listened, fuming from the insults that her best friend had hurled at her moments ago.

"He proposed about a month ago." She shrugged.

"You got to be kidding me, Jameela. You barely know this man, you haven't even introduced him to us or your family. Since when have you been so careless?"

"What's the problem? When you both decided to settle down, nobody batted an eye or judged. You met Cory out in Miami, and nobody vetted him, nobody said shit because you were happy. And Shantel you are the last person to judge how I am moving because let us not forget how Yusef used to get down. Now that it's my turn everyone has something to say?"

"Woah, woah woah now wait a minute!" Shantel said. "Why are you taking shots at me? Yusef and I have long gotten past his indiscretions, and we're in a healthy marriage!"

"All I am saying is he was not perfect then and he is not perfect now. Once a cheat always a cheat, trust me Product of Preston may tell a joke, but I will not ever tell a lie," Meela said.

"Are we being punked? What in the actual fuck is this?" Naomi spat.

"I never said Yusef was perfect." Shantel looked around, confused. "How do I act like my man is perfect? I'm genuinely happy. Is that a crime?"

"You want to be the only one happily married so you can sit on your pedestal like some martyr talking to us about what we need to be doing and how we need to do it as if you and Yusef arrived at this point unscathed, like ya'll are the blueprint. Whether you know it or not you do act like you and Yusef are the standard for what a marriage is supposed to look like. You may not realize it, but that's how you come off. And all I am saying is, that nigga was a wild boy before you all got married, so he without sin."

Shantel took a beat before she responded. "Maybe if you didn't watch us with a jealous mind and heart you wouldn't take it as us thinking we are perfect."

Naomi closed her eyes slowly. "This fittna be a long ass night." She guzzled her champagne. She waived down the server and quietly asked him for three doubles of Don Julio.

"Jealous of what? Girl, do not make me hurt your feelings because I can do just that," Jameela said.

"It sounds as if that was your intention for even coming out tonight! What has gotten into you? And for the record, let me just say this, I don't care what happened before I got married. Right now I am in a healthy, loving marriage, and I will never, ever downplay that to make anyone comfortable. So if my marriage triggers your damn demons or reminds you of what you deep down want for yourself that sounds like a you problem. But don't come at me with all this negativity. Embrace me, love me, talk to me, get in alignment with me not in fight mode. I'm your sister, and I would never look down on either of you for what you have or don't have nor will I ever throw your past or anything hurtful back in your faces, not never!" Marriage was sacred to Shantel, as it should be.

Naomi watched the women go back and forth until she simply had enough. It seemed as if Jameela had some things that she needed to get off her chest, and she came out guns blazing shooting at everybody.

"Did we do something to you Jameela, this is a serious question. I've never seen you act like this. Your energy is so negative. Is everything okay?" Naomi asked seriously concerned.

"Everything is fine, for the hundredth time."

"So then why are you attacking us? You've been shutting us out for a while now, and we're just trying to catch up, like we always do, but you're just insufferable at this point. What's going on?"

"Because I feel attacked. The two of you are always coming at me with all these questions about my man instead of being happy for me like I've been for you both any time you do anything."

"The irony of you asking someone to be happy for you while you're over here slighting your friend's happiness, girl bye. I can't stand it when you turn from villain to victim, you do this all the time Jameela! Why is it a crime that we want to meet the man that you love!" Noami rolled her eyes.

"Jameela, baby, you have been so mean. New love is supposed to make you nice, happy, soft," Shantel added.

"This is exactly why *we* did not want to tell anyone because *we* do not need the judgement. Everyone has something to say about *other* people's lives, rarely do they look in the mirror and judge themselves just as harshly." She said looking at Shantel. Not willing to match her energy, Shantel just shook her head and took the double shot that the server just placed on the table.

"So, you're okay with marrying a man that the people closest to you have never met? And you don't see why everyone has a problem with that?" Naomi said.

"I'm a grown woman, and my choices are my own. I don't need anyone's permission to get married. I've always told myself that when I meet the one, I'm going to keep him under wraps until I get married because I don't need anyone judging who I decide to be with. If I'm happy then I expect the people that love me to just be happy for me and leave it alone."

"But nobody said anything about you asking permission, we simply want to meet the damn man that our sister is marrying, why are you turning this into something other than that!" Shantel said.

"Jameela, this isn't even realistic, at least not for you. You've never been in a relationship before and now that you're in one, things are so extreme. I mean not once did I ever hear you express that you love this man or any kind of affectionate colloquialisms. I never heard you mention anything about him other than the material things that he has which is mind boggling because I never pegged you to be a girl impressed by such things because you have your own." Naomi said.

"You have this all thought out I see. So, what is this, like an intervention, like what are we doing at this dinner, are we celebrating or player hating." She snapped.

"Hating?" Shantel said.

"On what?" Naomi brought up the rear. "Look I don't know anything about no hateration, we came out here to have a good time, to catch up on one another. You're the one that came in with all this worldly energy, we're just matching it." Naomi rolled her neck.

Jameela scoffed at the *worldly energy.*

"Do you think Pops is going to give his blessings and walk you down the aisle when he hasn't even had the time to get to know this man? You're his only daughter, and you're robbing him of the opportunity to be a part of your journey. It's not like you're estranged from your father, he's like your best friend. Aren't you considering his feelings as well?" Naomi asked.

"You're always so overly concerned about my father. Look, when you get married, you deal with things the way you want to deal with things. I'm a grown ass woman."

"Wow." Was all Naomi could say. This man had her nose wide open.

"Okay, let's start over, scratch all the nonsense. Can we just erase the past 45 minutes and start over, fresh energy, because this isn't us. We don't do all of this." She looked form Naomi to Jameela who both shrugged.

"Okay,   so   our   girl   is   getting   married, and   this   is   wonderful   news,   right   Naomi?"

"Mmm hmm, wonderful, so, when's the wedding." Naomi forced.

Eager to talk about her upcoming nuptials, Jameela's attitude changed for the better and she rambled nonstop about her and her mystery man.

"We're still trying to figure some things out, but we do know that we want it to be a destination wedding, Anguilla possibly...next year. I don't want to be engaged longer than a year."

"So, what are the colors, what are we wearing?" Shantel inquired. But Naomi had checked out. She had nothing more to offer this version of Jameela.

"Well, his sister Robin asked to be my maid of honor. They're close, and she wasn't at his first wedding, she didn't like his wife, so I wanted to give her the opportunity to be a part of her brother's big day. I'm not sure if *her girlfriend* is going to be in the wedding. I think I would like her in seafoam and you guys in a pale yellow, I'm just envisioning us on the beach and how the colors will look against the ocean and the sky." Jameela daydreamed.

Naomi suddenly became alert again and involved herself in the conversation.

"I know you didn't just say some woman that you just met is going to be your maid of honor! We've been friends since the second grade are you crazy?"

"No, we met in the *third grade* and we didn't get close until you actually moved to Long Island in the fifth grade, and it's not a big deal, Naomi. Trust me, you are going to love Robin. Oh! I did give her you all's info so she can let you know the deets on the bridal shower, whenever that's going to happen. But I already know I want it at the Fontainebleau in Vegas they just built. It looks amazing!"

Naomi sat back in her chair defeated and heartbroken. Shantel was speechless. Jameela took up most of the airtime talking about her new business, her fiancée, his cars, her dreams, her new friends, and the high-rise apartment that she began renting in New Jersey.

More news for the women.

"What happened to the rent stabilized apartment and your house?" Shantel asked.

"I'm thinking about subleasing the apartment out to one of Ty's friends, I haven't decided yet."

"The same apartment I asked to stay in so I could save money because I wanted to buy a house?"

Shantel looked around bewildered.

"You would be miserable there, it's way too small. You can still save if you spend wisely and manage your money and they have all kinds of programs for first time home buyers. You will be just fine, you don't need my apartment." Jameela convinced herself. "So, about my new penthouse apartment, it is absolutely beautiful. It's right on the water, 3 bedrooms, 3.5 bathrooms, wrap around balcony, huge kitchen, I mean huge! It's on the 41st floor overlooking the Hudson River. I never ever close my blinds so at night, sometimes I just stand in the middle of that large living room and look out at the sky it feels like I'm standing in space. You guys must come visit when he's out of town so we can have a girl's night, maybe a sleepover. He's there a lot so right now, I don't feel comfortable having women over when he's home, not yet."

"Oh shit." Naomi laughed. "We are *women* now, women that she isn't comfortable having around her man. If you feel like that then why are we even friends?"

"Hold on, hold on!" Shantel said, putting her hands up.

"What, she comes galloping in her on her high horse looking down on us, because she has a man that has a few dollars? Is this what we've become? We don't know shit about her anymore, she doesn't want to include us in the things that matter to her any fucking more, so none of this shit matters, what comes out of my mouth doesn't fucking matter anymore!" Naomi was furious.

Shantel whipped her head around and glared at Jameela, "So, you wouldn't think that the best thing to do would be to invite your best friends over to show us your new place, your new ring and your new fiancé?" Shantel asked.

"It's not that deep, ladies, look can we just change the conversation please? Let's shift gears some, come on lets drink there's other things to talk about."

"Oh now you don't want to talk about yourself. Fuck outta here." Naomi snapped.

"So, in between homes, what does that even mean?" Shantel asked.

Naomi chuckled a little because this story was getting worse and worse, but Jameela did not see anything wrong with what was going on around her and she wouldn't listen to her friends.

"He was living in Dallas in *a mansion,* but I'm not moving to Dallas of course."

"Oh, so he use to play for the Dallas Cowboys," Naomi asked sarcastically. Jameela ignored Naomi and kept on with her story.

"Besides, he left the house to his ex-wife and the children, moved to New York and has yet to find a home that he wants to purchase so he has been living out of the Four Seasons downtown Manhattan until he finds something." She sipped her drink unapologetically.

Naomi mumbled, "*The plot thickens.*"

Jameela turned to Naomi. "Girl what is the issue? You think an athlete doesn't have children or an ex-wife somewhere, nothing to see here so stop looking for a flaw."

"Sweetheart, for a flaw we do not have to look far." Naomi sipped her drink.

Jameela was sounding like a young, dumb, star struck, dick whipped teenager and she was none of those things. She was a grown, intelligent, educated, well rounded, well-traveled, well-to-do, business owner, great friend, sister, daughter, boss. But the wrong man could send all of that crashing down if you let him and Shantel and Naomi were seeing all the red flags that she refused to acknowledge. It's like she had all the book smarts and no common sense or street smarts when it came to men. The product of Preston was a fraud.

"You don't know anything about this level of commitment, so it's useless having this conversation with you. Shantel might be better equipped to understand what I'm saying, as a married woman and all."

"Jameela Bridgette White, I am about four five seconds from wilin' on your ass, please cut the damn masquerade all right? You came here to play with us and punk us, you won, you got us girl, okay, please will the real Jameela please stand."

"So, Shantel, you understand when a man takes issue with a woman hanging around the single friend too much right?" Jameela said ignoring Naomi.

"The single friend?" Shantel asked confused.

"When I was with Cory *you* were the single friend that was sucking down different dicks and spitting the cum out like sunflower seeds, so don't come at me like I'm some single whore friend that you have. Is that what you're telling your new man about me?"

Naomi looked at Shantel with an expression of horror on her face, "Has she gone mad bruv?"

"I would never call you a whore but sweetheart, musical dicks is your game, let us not go there. Before Cory and after Cory you put hella miles on that pussy and I would never judge but you came at me first so he without sin? Tuh, girl." she said, turning toward Naomi aggressively.

"Girl..." Naomi said back just as aggressive.

She turned around and faced Shantel, *"Anyway, what were you saying Shantel?"*

But Naomi kept on her because she needed to be knocked down a few pegs.

"He sounds like a man that doesn't want to be seen because he probably has a whole damn family tucked away some damn where, *respectfully*," Naomi spat out.

"Now that is just too easy." Jameela chuckled smugly.

"What, say it. Stop speaking in codes and say what you have to say!" Naomi demanded.

She turned to her slowly, deliberately with a nasty grin on her face.

"Everybody is not Cory. So do not project your pain and jealousy on me because of what Cory did to you," she said and turned away.

"That's low," Shantel said.

"She's the one making accusations when she shouldn't be throwing stones!"

"No, it's all good, it is all good sweetie because today me... tomorrow you."

"What the hell does that even mean, whatever Mimi." She fanned her hand at Naomi in a go away motion. Shantel looked at both of her friends with sad eyes. All Naomi could think at this moment was that with the way Jameela was moving, it was inevitable that she would be eating humble pie soon because one thing was for sure and two things were for certain, she was blind to the red flags, in a relationship with a greaseball, and she could not see it.

"I don't like this," Shantel spoke softly. "We're sisters and this shit ain't right. Now Jameela, you do understand that some of the things that you're telling us don't add up. We just love you, and we ask you these questions out of love of course."

Jameela let out an exasperated sigh, "He has an ex-wife and children as does every other athlete or ex athlete. He left her the house. He's starting over, I'm giving him advice on how to start a business, and we are engaged to be married, what's the issue?"

"Are you sure that he use to play for the NFL? Why can't we even see a picture of him?" Naomi said, picking up the expensive bottle of wine and looking at it in disgust.

"Other than him telling you what he *used* to do, how can you confirm if any of this is true? What if there was no mansion in Dallas? Did he show you pictures? Why can't he be found on the internet anywhere?"

"Because he does not want to be found! In fact, he did show me pictures of his children and his home in Dallas! And why on God's earth are you searching for my man on the internet?"

"He doesn't even have a residence in New York for you to visit and confirm who he is and how he lives, you're being ridiculous, he has something to hide, I stand on that," Naomi said.

"Where was all of this detective work and intuition when Cory was out here married and living his best life behind your back, huh?"

"It's worth checking him out, Jameela. I mean you've never been so serious about any man in your life and now that you are, you are foregoing a lot of pertinent information that you need to know before you get married. Who are his parents, where was he raised, do you know any of these things?" Shantel inquired.

"Ok I get it, you're the only one that's supposed to be in a *genuinely happy* relationship."

"Do *not* go there. These are legit concerns, what if it was one of us? You'd be asking the same questions," Shantel said.

"Nobody questioned Cory with all the outlandish spending and shenanigans he had going on with Naomi, so why are you questioning me and mine?"

"You're renting high rise apartments, waiting for him to move in and take on the overhead when he hasn't even shown you his earning potential. If he wanted to marry you, and he has this NFL money as he's leading you to believe, why isn't he handling the bills? And you still didn't tell us what happened to your home, did you sell your Long Island house?" Naomi inquired.

"No, I'm renting it out like people do every damn day, what the entire fuck is the problem?"

"The problem is that this man is telling you he is in between homes, money tied up in a divorce, you don't know where he's living, he says he's living out of a hotel, but is he really? You can't find him on the internet, I mean come on Meela."

"I've stayed weekends with him in his hotel *suite* plenty of times," Jameela said.

"*And C,* Cory had *a home* that he took me to. I've been to his businesses, all three of them might I add. I met his employees, his family his children and most importantly he met you all, you guys saw him, he existed, he's Googleable, he was here, he was real, he was who he said he was."

"You sure about that?" Jameela asked.

"Cory has legit businesses; he was legit."

"Legit married," Jameela clapped back.

Naomi threw her hands up in defeat. "That's all you heard, that's all you received from everything that I just said to you. We are just trying to open your eyes Jameela and to be quite honest I cannot believe how green you are acting. If it were one of us, you would be reading us the riot act and calling us all kinds of stupid and letting us know all the lessons learned because you are a *product of Preston*! But you know what? Leave her be, Shantel, don't save her, she doesn't want to be saved."

"Don't you think that it is odd he doesn't want you to take pictures of him, show pictures of him, he doesn't feel the need to meet your closest friends and family, yet he wants to marry you and you haven't even met his children?" Shantel kept on.

"How can I meet his children if they're in Dallas?" Jameela answered annoyed.

"Have you at least talked to them on FaceTime, so they know who their stepmother is going to be?" Naomi asked.

"I don't have a problem with him not wanting to meet anyone because we don't need your permission, we are grown, and we choose to protect our relationship by not having it on social media or exposing it in any way until we're married. Why can't you just trust me?

You all will meet him when the time is right. Now can I please eat my dinner." Jameela said as the server began placing their orders in front of them.

Shantel sat back in her chair watching Jameela cut her steak aggressively. But Naomi wasn't done.

"How old are his children? Have you seen them in pictures or anything?"

She responded by aggressively pulling her phone out of her purse, "Seven and nine." she said slamming her phone down on the table. Shantel and Naomi observed the pictures then handed her the phone back.

"Chile these can be anybody's kids." Naomi rolled her eyes.

"So, he's just in a picture with random children? Stop reaching already!"

"This is his ex-wife I assume?" Shantel said looking at another picture.

"Yes, she's mixed."

"Typical," Naomi muttered. Jameela cut her eyes.

"Just be careful Meela, that's all," Shantel said, handing her back her phone.

Jameela began cutting her steak again.

"Well, I'm happy for you?" Shantel asked more than stated.

"I appreciate that Shantel," she said sarcastically.

"Where did you meet him again?"

Jameela inhaled deeply. "I met him at a conference for black women entrepreneurs."

"What was he doing at an event for women?" Naomi asked.

"He was accompanying his sister Robin, actually. But that's what attracted me to him, his business mind set. So, I have decided to help him with his business because right now his money is tied up with the divorce and all these other shenanigans."

"Helping him how?" Shantel asked and Naomi was glad she did because she was at a loss for words.

"I'm not sure, we haven't ironed out the details, right now I'm just helping him with the logistics. I'm not worried though he's a whole multi-millionaire. Once his account gets unfrozen, he can contribute in a way that would make you both happy."

"If he's divorced, then why is his account still frozen, how long has he been divorced?" Shantel's eyes were out of her head and on the table.

"Because he's still married." Naomi said.

"The divorce has been finalized; how else would we be able to get married? With that amount of money, things don't move along as quickly as it would if he was some average joe. There's prenups to iron out, all kinds of things."

"But this typically gets sorted out then you sign on the dotted line and be done," Naomi said.

"I've had enough, what's up with Yusef Shantel, let's talk about you guys for a second."

"Now you're asking about Yusef after you just threw him under the bus? Girl, are you okay? Ok I have one last question, just one because this entire situation is really yanking my tampon string...he doesn't have any football friends to ask for financial assistance instead of you?"

"First of all, he did not ask me for financial assistance."

"Ok, this shit is getting tired. Let's start over, please, just one more time. Tensions are high, let us all just take a deep breath and start over, please?" Shantel said putting her hands on the table for Naomi and Jameela to pile on. Naomi slid her hand under Shantel's so that she would not have to touch Jameela.

"Come on, ladies, let's talk about something else," Shantel suggested.

"I love you girl, don't even trip," Jameela said placing her free hand on top of Naomi's.

"Awe, this is what I love to see!" Shantel said clasping her hands together in prayer.

"Let's get a round of shots." Jameela suggested. Shantel signaled for the server to come over, but it took Naomi a second to thaw out.

Not wanting to spoil the mood for Shantel though she played along but she was hurt and pissed at Jameela.

"So, time to put you in the hot seat, how long is this *hoe phase* going to last?" Jameela asked Naomi.

"Lord, this girl just doesn't know what to say out of her damn mouth!" Naomi said. She looked over at her sister, her eyes watering with disappointment.

"Look, whatever you do, always do it classy, do it nice, meet nice men so when it's all said and done you don't have some bum beating down your door. You still want to keep a healthy track record as it pertains to the company you keep. You want to limit your regrets and not be embarrassed by who you shared your body with." Shantel warned.

"Amen to that! You're a grown woman and I do encourage you to live your life to the fullest before that special one comes along but I don't want you to have any regrets, no bums. Sometimes you can't control who you love and when you fall in love. So if you are surrounded by quality men then you can't lose!" Jameela warned.

"No bums!" Shantel reiterated.

"Now have I ever?" Naomi looked around offended. The girls started exaggerating as if they were thinking hard about who she dated.

"Don't do me, I ain't never!"

The women shared a good laugh for a while.

"I haven't hit up the globe as much as I want to! I'd like to see the world, meet men abroad. I have stamps on my passport, I'm well-traveled but now I want to be on some eat, pray, thug shit."

"You mean eat, pray, love," Shantel said.

"No, I mean eat, pray, thug...then love. I gotta thug it through my traumas before I can love anyone and let someone love me."

"Eat, pray, thug, I like that with your crazy ass," Jameela said.

"There's so much to do. I want to expand my mind, learn more, see more, do more and I want to meet a different caliber of men. I want to meet a man that teaches me things, someone that levels me up in ways that I can't even imagine. I want to meet them in museums and conventions. I just want to explore an entirely different echelon of men, you know?"

"Exactly! That is how I met mine! Go where the over achievers are baby, you can't lose!" Jameela raised her glass.

"Respectfully, I think not." Naomi laughed.

"Naomi!" Shantel scolded while laughing.

"It is all good, you will see. He is the real deal," Meela said, pouring a round.

"Here's to love, money, success, health and a lifetime of happiness." She smiled.

"Bomb ass sex with good disease-free men with lots of stamps on their passports and zeros all up and through their bank accounts!" Naomi added.

"And sisterhood. Should all else fail, we always have each other," Shantel chimed in.

"I like that," Naomi said.

"Me too," Jameela agreed.

Everyone took their shots, then spent a few more moments with one another when Naomi decided that it was time to end the night. She simply could not keep up the charade any longer.

"Jameela." Shantel pointed her finger in her face.

"I know, I know, you will meet him, I promise, please trust me on this and just be happy for me."

"I guess I don't have a choice," Shantel said.

She looked at Naomi.

"I have absolutely nothing nice to say so I won't say anything."

"What is it, Naomi?" Jameela asked.

"I am your best friend. Your parents damn near raised me, and I don't know who you're marrying, I'm not your maid of honor and you have been so mean to me. But if you don't see anything wrong with how you've been acting, the way you're treating Shantel and I, what you're doing and how you're moving then it is not my place to tell a grown woman how to live her life. I wish you all the best and I mean that. Be safe is all I can say."

She looked at Shantel to say something.

"Meela boo, she's right. But if you say you got this then we must trust that and pray for you."

"Trust me and pray for me? You know what..." Meela got aggravated and began digging in her large Chanel purse for her wallet. They watched her rifle through her purse until she came across what she was looking for. The waiter brought the check and Jameela slid her business Amex into the cardholder. She told Shantel and Naomi not to bother when they reached for their payment methods.

"I ordered the most expensive items; I'll cover it this time," she said with an attitude, handing the black book to the waiter while her friends sat quietly; you could cut the tension with a knife. Once the waiter came back, Jameela got up from the table hastily.

"Come on Meela don't leave like this, we were just starting to have a good time!" Shantel said.

"Yeah, and you ruined it. Look, I gotta run, let's catch up soon, toodles," she said and blew air kisses, no hugs no nothing. She just stomped off in her 5-inch Jimmy Choos as her friends watched her walk out the door.

"*The weather up there has gotten to her head*," Shantel mumbled.

"Hmph." Was all Naomi could add.

"Between homes? Mansion in Dallas? No pictures, didn't meet the closest people to her and she's about to get married? How could she be so naïve?" Shantel questioned.

"This is beyond ridiculous. I'm so exhausted let's get out of here," Naomi said, getting up from her chair. Shantel kept trying to crack the case as the women exited the restaurant and stood out on the busy sidewalk.

"Even more strange, she said Pops spoke with him on FaceTime a few times. Listen, Pops loves football, he would recognize the damn water boy so how come he doesn't recognize this man?" Shantel said.

"Because she's lying. Pops said he has never spoken to him. He also said that there's no record of Tyrone Richards, ex NFL player anywhere. Do you notice we can always hear him talking but she never wants us to see his face? So, there's definitely some man around but she got a stranger in her house."

"Oh, it is not lost on me that she is going out of her way to hide this man. And knowing her, she gave us a fake name on purpose because she knew we would google him."

"But it still doesn't explain why she's hiding him. Anything could happen, and we wouldn't even know where to start if he hurt her or something!"

"I do not know but mark my words this isn't going to end well at all!" Naomi warned.

"An ex-NFL player that we can't find on the internet. Then he doesn't want to be seen or talked about. I need some understanding, somebody call X-scape, Kandi, Tiny? Anybody but Toscha, she be stealing and shit," Shantel said giggling extra hard at her own jokes; the drinks had taken over. Naomi laughed along with her.

"She's grown as she reminded us quite a few times tonight, so we just have to pray for her and be there to support her, right?"

"I ain't supporting shit, fuck her and him," Naomi said half-serious.

"You need a ride home? After all of this I need to go home and purify myself in the waters of Lake Minnetonka," Shantel said, digging in her purse for her keys. The rain began again but for now it was just light drops.

"Oh, no ma'am, I just got this hair pressed, I gotta go baby, gimme kiss." She hugged Naomi. "Get on home, how far is your Lyft?"

"My Lyft will be here in two minutes. I'll call you. Can you drive good after all those shots?"

"Yup I feel like a million bucks! I'll be safe. I'll put Yusef on the speaker phone to keep me company. I'll text you when I reach home."

She twinkled her fingers and walked off quickly while opening her umbrella. Naomi watched her until she could see her turn into the parking lot. As she disappeared into the lot Naomi's Lyft appeared but before she could touch the car door, she heard a voice say, "*Excuse me, miss, do you have a moment?*"

Chapter 6

ONE NIGHT ONLY

The rain didn't get any heavier, so Naomi stood outside under her large black umbrella talking to Jeremy for twenty minutes. Jeremy was fine, jet-black complexion, perfect white teeth, and he smelled delicious; that was one of Naomi's weaknesses.

"I saw you inside with your girls having a good time. Nothing is sexier than seeing well dressed, beautiful women out enjoying the finer things without a man in sight." He smiled.

"All because a man wasn't seen doesn't mean one isn't on the scene." Naomi flirted back.

Damn that was smooth for a girl who hasn't been on the market for a while.

"Do you have a lucky man?" He stepped closer.

"No, I do not." Naomi smiled.

"Well, if it's okay with you I'd like to get to know you better. Perhaps you can put your number in my phone, and I'll call you?"

"That doesn't sound too scary," she said, taking his phone from him and inputting her work cell phone number.

"Baby steps, right?" he joked while looking at the number in his phone.

"Yes, one foot in front of the other."

"Okay *Bobbi*, well let me pay for your cab home since I made you lose the last one. I need to get back inside before my food gets cold."

Naomi allowed him to hail her a yellow cab as she was not letting him know where she lived by putting her address in his Uber app. He opened the car door for her when it arrived.

"Get home safe, beautiful," he said, closing her car door gently. Naomi winked at him as her cab slowly pulled off. Before the cab could turn the corner, Naomi already knew that she was going to add him to her roster.

After a few conversations over the phone, Jeremy invited Naomi over to his place. He lived in a 3-story walk up, *in the Bronx* nonetheless, and she regretted coming as soon as her Lyft turned the corner on the dark block with a bunch of dudes outside doing absolutely nothing. Naomi sat in the cab and asked Jeremy to come outside.

I am not getting out of this damn car.

"Thank you for waiting, he should be down any moment," Naomi said politely to the driver who seemed to be everything but patient. He was tapping his steering wheel and eyeing her through the rearview mirror. Jeremy appeared and nodded to some of the men outside, then flung her car door open.

"Come on, girl, nobody's going to bite," he said, gently pulling Naomi out of the car. He looked totally different from the night they met. He was still handsome, but he looked much younger than she was used to. Naomi liked her men mature, masculine, a little rough around the edges, but the way he was casually dressed brought out the youth in him. He didn't have on a button down, slacks and shoes but instead was dressed in basketball shorts, T-shirt and Fendi flip flops. Though he told her he was six years younger than her, she now had reason to believe he was lying about his age. She concluded it didn't matter – he was legal and looked fuckable in her opinion as long as he didn't say anything to turn her off and his living quarters were up to her standards as Naomi dubbed herself an "ambience whore." The smallest of details either turned her on or turned her off.

"Yawl hooligans got my lady scared!" He joked with the guys and gave them all dap which made Naomi feel a bit safer. At least he wasn't a mark. She could hear them complimenting her as she walked through them and to the building. Her jeans fit her nicely, showing off her slender curves, her plain white Gap t-shirt hugged her huge breasts, and her white toes were perfectly manicured, poking out of her Birkenstocks.

"Damn, she smells good too," someone said as she left the fragrance of Victor Rolf Flower bomb linger in the filthy Bronx wind. Naomi did not want to be in the Bronx, but here she was wondering if she had hit rock bottom. The men she dated or had experiences with typically owned homes and condos or at the very least had apartments in upscale or middle-class neighborhoods. Every step she took, she regretted it. But once upstairs, the inside of his apartment did not match the outside, it was beautiful and left her in awe at the décor.

"Wow, this place is absolutely stunning. Say you have a girlfriend without saying it!" she said looking around.

"I do not have a girlfriend, and if I did, I would not be bold enough to invite a woman over to my place."

"Do you have an interior decorator or something?"

"I do, luckily she's my sister." He smiled, relieving Naomi of her Chloe purse.

"Oh, is that what they are calling it now, *sister*? You know you have a woman, cut it out." Naomi laughed still looking around the nice sized apartment. All the details jumped out at her from the extra clean baseboards to the beautiful curtain rods. Noticing how in awe Naomi remained, he began to fill her in on the details of his apartment.

"Seriously, my sister is an interior decorator, graduated from New York Institute of Art & Design and the whole nine." He said placing a graduation photo of his sister, mother, and himself in her hand from off the mantle. He also handed her a coffee table book of his sister's work.

"She is amazing! I may need to hire her for some work when I purchase something, oh my goodness!" Naomi said flipping through the pages.

"You better catch her now before the price goes up. She was just hired by Niecy Nash to design one of her homes, as well as Fantasia. She is under contract until the jobs are done but once she posts that on her IG, it's over! Yesterday's price will not be today's price!"

"Shut the front door, let me get her IG."

"Of course," he said typing her handle in Naomi's phone.

"Have a seat, get comfortable. Are you thirsty? Hungry?"

"Not too hungry but what do you have to drink?" Naomi asked while looking through his sister's beautiful designs. He offered Rose' or Cognac. Naomi chose Cognac as she came to do damage and leave, nothing more nothing less. Rose' was for wining and dining and she wasn't there for that. He poured some Remy VSOP neat in a sifter and handed it to her. "Do you need a cube of ice?"

"No, I like it strong just like this." she said with a little sexual innuendo in there for a little razzle dazzle. He turned on his heels and headed to the kitchen without so much of a smirk, so she assumed he didn't pick up what she was putting down...*yet.*

"You look beautiful," he said upon his return from the kitchen, placing a bowl of cheese, crackers, and nuts between them as he sat down. For that she was thankful as she loved a nice dose of salt when sipping cognac.

"Thank you. So, what do you do for a living, *Bobbi*? Bobbi is your real name, right?" he smiled.

"Yes, I was named after my father whose name is Robert," Naomi lied so easily.

"Okay, I dig that. So, what do you do for a living?"

"I work at a bank." She lied some more. She wanted everything she told these men to be a lie until she was ready to settle down again. Right now she didn't want to be found, traced, sought out, nothing. Sort of like what Tyrone was probably doing to Jameela.

"Oh, that's nice. Do you like or love your job, is this a career or a pit stop."

"Why does it matter?" Naomi asked, irritated.

"Just making conversation love, seeing what interests you if anything at all. If you love your job, I love that for you I didn't mean to offend you."

"None taken, I was simply curious as to your line of questioning. No one has ever asked me that before."

"Understood, so..." he said waiting for an answer.

"I'm not really sure honestly. There's a lot of things I'm good at but I have so many tabs open in my head, I need to just narrow some things down so I can concentrate better."

"Ah, the curse of the talented." He smiled. Naomi thought how cute and safe he appeared to be.

"Well, I'm a computer software technician," he offered.

But Naomi didn't care. She was too busy trying to see if there was a bulge in his shorts but the way he was positioned was making it difficult to size him up.

"I work at Morgan Stanley, it's pretty cool but you know, very corporate. But it pays the bills for now. My dream is to be a DJ."

"A DJ?" Still, she didn't care but was intrigued by the drastic career change. "Um, how old are you again, Jeremy?"

"Twenty-nine. I've done some big events but not consistent enough to live comfortably. I do it on the side, I drive Uber as well. I'd like to buy a big house for my family within the next three years and one paycheck isn't cutting it, but I'm almost at my goal amount saved."

"You are a very ambitious man. That's sexy." Naomi winked.

"Thank you. And sorry I didn't warn you about the wolves outside of my building, they're harmless though. My uncle kind of runs these little cats over here if you know what I mean. I spent a lot of summers here, this is his old spot, he passed it on to me and moved up to Riverdale once his money started getting good, he just comes down here from time to time to check on things. Besides you look like you can handle yourself."

"The Bronx is definitely a different kind of beast. You would have to grow up here to really be unphased by what goes on up here."

He let out a chuckle. "I'm originally from Brooklyn."

"Oh really, what part?"

"Crown Heights. What about you?"

"I'm from all over. I've moved around a lot," Naomi said avoiding providing details of where she grew up.

"Well at least you have a beautiful place and the building itself isn't bad. But those boys outside will definitely keep the white people away and the rent decent."

"Cheers to that!" he said, and they clinked glasses. Naomi took a big gulp. She was ready for the cognac to start working its magic.

"So those women you were with, were they your sisters?"

"Not biologically but sure."

"Got you, you all were so beautiful, but it was your smile, and I am a sucker for a woman with faux locs." he said, making hand gestures to show the length of her locs that she had wrapped up in a top bun.

"Thank you."

"Yeah, I like that natural look, it's sexy. More Remy?"

He got up and Naomi was able to catch a glimpse of something in his sweat shorts, but still wasn't too sure. But she was happy to see he was athletic. Nothing turned her off more than a man who was not in shape.

"Can you excuse me a moment?" he asked then answered his call.

He spoke on the phone briefly then rushed back to Naomi.

"My man always wanna party."

He had a beautiful smile, big hands, and long feet. He was so polite, mild mannered, sexy.

"Do you like to party?" he asked her.

But she was too busy still sizing him up. He gave her a moment to snap out of her thoughts. He watched her as she zoned out then cleared his throat a bit to bring her back to reality.

"Something on your mind?" he asked seriously.

"No, not at all I just zone out from time to time. But you were saying?"

"Do you like to party?" he asked as he reached for a piece of cheese.

"It depends. I can't say I like to party, but I love music and a good lounge is cool occasionally, you know, mingle with other adults, fraternize a bit, vibe."

"Well I am unable to make this event as I have other obligations this weekend however my boy was telling me about some rooftop party that he wanted me to attend. He's normally good about these things so if you and your girls are interested in good drinks, vibes, music, and all that I can forward you the info."

"Please do, thank you. I think a night out with some music would do us all some good."

"No problem, beautiful. Can I show you around the rest of my apartment?"

He took his time giving her a tour. He had a few conversation pieces which she did enjoy hearing about as she was a conversation piece furniture kind of woman so she could appreciate a "weird" coffee table or something like that. Once they headed toward what she believed was his bedroom he gently touched her hand.

"What did you come here for?" he asked, stepping closer to her, his innocent boy demeanor slowly dissipating.

"To see you," Naomi said shyly.

"Yeah, but you could have seen me anywhere. I could have taken you out for dinner, coffee, ice cream, a walk in the park. But you decided to come to my home in those tight ass jeans and your breasts busting out of this t-shirt, so tell me again, what did you come here for," he said and planted the softest kiss on her neck.

"Is that alright?" he asked.

Naomi nodded yes. He kissed the other side of her neck.

"*What about that.*"

She nodded again.

He slowly lifted her T-shirt over her head to reveal her full triple D cups covered in a beautiful yellow lace bra.

Damn.

"You like what you see?" Naomi asked.

"I do. Forgive me, please but..."

Naomi already knew what he was going to say as she had to deal with it most of her life.

"Yes, they are real." she said.

"Take your bra off?" he asked with a hint of demand. Naomi reached behind her back and unclipped her bra professionally. Her full breasts stood firm, full, her nipples erect.

"Damn, these are the prettiest titties I've ever seen in my life, word."

He led Naomi to his bedroom, where he continued to massage her breasts, fascinated with them. Naomi could tell that he probably never seen breasts this big, this real in person. While he bit his lip and caressed her, she scanned his bedroom. It was clean, nice, and smelled good. Naomi got a whiff of his sheets when she plopped down on his bed, they smelled amazing. She began to relax a bit as she ran her hands across his high thread counts. He removed her slides slowly while looking into her eyes.

"I won't do anything you don't want me to do. Are you comfortable?"

She could appreciate him taking his time and making her feel safe. She nodded. He then gently grabbed her by the hand and pulled her to stand up so he could peel her jeans off her. Naomi stood before him in canary yellow lace boy shorts that matched her now missing bra. He took a step back and rubbed his chin.

"I don't even know where to start, you are so bad. Take your locks down.? he asked excitedly. Naomi did as she was asked, and Jeremy almost lost his mind. He began exaggeratively stomping around his room.

"Nah, you can't be real. Ain't no way you're real let me take a picture of you, please!"

"Um, no thank you," Naomi said perplexed and getting a bit turned off as his age was beginning to show. He clearly had never been with a real grown woman before.

"I just want to have it to look at when you're not around." He calmed down some.

"I don't do pictures, sweetheart."

"Okay, alright, fair enough. I don't even know where to start with you." He said holding her hand and spinning her around.

"Start anywhere." Naomi said slightly agitated.

He instantly grabbed one of her breasts and sucked on them. Her nipples were her hot spot and if he knew the right way to suck them, he could get her to come in minutes maybe even seconds. He kissed all around them, missing the sweet spot, he was rubbing his face all in between them; he was a kid in candy store.

"Damn, damn, damn." He said holding both jugs in his hands.

"They just sitting up all big and beautiful like two birthday balloons." He chuckled. Naomi did too inside, she'd never heard them described like that before.

"Turn around." He asked.

Naomi did as she was told and felt him parting her ass cheeks. Soon she felt the warmness of his tongue licking her up and down her crack then circling her hole.

Thank God for bidets, I was not expecting this.

Then, like a mechanic he slid under her and began sucking her clit. She allowed him to please her some more, then he came up for air and put his tongue down her throat. She did not like the way he kissed so she pulled away and stood up. He followed suit and gently pushed her on the bed then reached into his drawer for a condom. He stood in front of her and slowly slid the condom on his small dick. Naomi was mortified. She could no longer wither around sexily in the bed anticipating this mandingo to nail her to the cross when that thing couldn't even reach past his pubic hairs. She was now trying to figure out a plan to get out of this man's bed and pray that he didn't turn into a psychopath and try to hurt her if she said no. Her purse was too far so she wouldn't be able to get to her mase or taser.

Think girl think, think, think!

Naomi let out a big groan and held her stomach. He continued to stroke his dick, unphased by the "pain" she was in until she sat up and keeled over, "wait." She put her hands out for him to stop.

"Are you okay?" he asked with his penis still in his hand, trying his best to be patient and keep his thing erect but Naomi had her own set of rules, she wasn't catching a body for anything under six inches and if it was six it had to have a "girth certificate". This was a preemie, underdeveloped penis and she wasn't willing to lay down and allow this man to enter her body. She continued the charade and even keeled over at the edge of the bed.

"Can you please get a glass of warm water and an Ibuprofen or something?"

Dickappointed, but still a gentleman he obliged. He sucked his teeth and walked off. That is when Naomi texted both Jameela and Shantel with the S.O.S. They knew what that meant. It took about ten minutes for one of them to see her text. Naomi took her time sipping the water as Jeremy sat on a chair opposite her impatiently. She apologized profusely and asked him to please give her a moment. She wanted to tame whatever beast was in him and didn't want to risk possibly getting sexually assaulted for turning a man down. All kinds of crazy thoughts ran through her head then her phone rung finally. She knew it would be Shantel to call because Jameela was on her bullshit.

Shantel played her roll and yelled, *"You need to come home now!"*

"What is going on?" Naomi said into the phone.

Shantel just began yelling as Yusef looked at her from the kitchen like she was crazy not knowing the protocol. Naomi responded, *"Oh my God, okay let me gather my things and I'll be on my way!"* She said jumping right into character. Shantel continued screaming and all Jeremy could hear was a woman's voice in distress, but he was unable to make out the words. He sat at the edge of his chair concerned.

"Please just relax, I will get there as soon as possible, okay?" Naomi said.

Naomi tossed her phone in her purse and went back to holding her stomach, wincing in pain as she looked around for her jeans.

"Is everything okay?" Jeremy stood up. Naomi could tell he was buying it now. She was able to conjure up a little bit of wet eyes.

"I don't know, I hope so. Where's my bra, please, and my shirt." She said looking around frantically.

"Do you need me to drive you?" Jeremy said, handing her all her garments.

"You're so sweet but no I need to go, please."

Naomi got dressed quicker than she ever did in her life while simultaneously calling a Lyft.

"I am so sorry for this, please accept my apologies." Naomi began laying it on thick.

"You gotta do what you gotta do. I just hope everything is okay, will you call me when you get home?" he said, walking her to the door.

"Yes." Naomi said tip toeing and kissing him on the cheek.

"I'll walk you downstairs, let me just throw on some sweats."

"No, I'm fine!" she said, rushing out the door and running down the stairs quickly, sniffling as if she was crying, breathing hard as if she was stressed because she knew he had the door open still watching her as she ran down the stairs. Naomi ran passed the hoodlums in front of her buildings straight into her Lyft. Once the Lyft pulled off, she exhaled and called Shantel.

"Breaker, breaker, subject is safe, in a Lyft heading home. Thank you for saving me from a little dick terrorist, over and out."

Shantel burst out laughing. "Who is this person?"

"I met him right after we left Bobby Van's that night. Fine chocolate brother, good job, ambitious, a little young but well spoken, beautiful place, dick look like a burnt piece of bacon."

"Bye Naomi." Shantel hung up and would not take her calls. Naomi laughed all the way home, even the Lyft driver tried to stifle his laughter.

Sam and Ginger met Naomi at the door as did the stillness and loneliness of her apartment. She kicked her slides off and headed to her room while her phone vibrated. It was Jeremy asking if she was okay. She hit the block button and peeled her clothes off. The stillness of the night along with the bright light illuminating from the street cast a sexiness through her bedroom window, mixed with the cognac in her system, she began to think about the last man she shared her body with *that meant something.* She tried to remember his touch without remembering his heartbreak but that was impossible. She lay across her bed caressing her body, imagining it was Cory. But no matter how much she touched herself, nothing could bring her to the sweet orgasm he once did. Frustrated, she sat up and turned her television on. Living Single reruns were playing, and it was her favorite episode with Jenifer Lewis as messy TV show host Delia. Her phone vibrated again; it was Shantel asking did she get home safe. Naomi texted her back a heart emoji. She did the same. Naomi spent a few moments scrolling through social media while simultaneously watching Living Single and decided that she was rolling to that all black party this weekend that Jeremy told her about. She needed some fresh energy and was ready to replace the men on her roster, everyone but "ole faithful."

Chapter 7

NEVER KEEPIN' SECRETS

*E*verybody loved Yusef. He was educated, charming, and the way he commanded attention when he walked into the room was a sight to behold. The way Yusef would fill up a sweat suit when he wasn't in tailored suits for work was a sight to see. Shantel fell in love with Yusef at first sight when visiting Oak Bluffs in August for the annual African American Book Festival. She watched him from across the way, the way he handled the men he was speaking to, the way they all looked up at him hanging on to his every word, even the ones that were his height. She looked at his body up and down from his follicles down to his wing tip shoes. The way his biceps took up space in his short-sleeved button-down shirt had her imagining him picking her up and carrying her away. But she was so short, there was no way he would be able to look over and see her but instead see one of the much taller women within his view. There were tons of beautiful, brown, educated, go getters in this space. Surely Yusef would have his pick of the litter as all the women were vying for his attention in one way or another.

He shook hands with the men in attendance and began to make his rounds through the crowd. She watched as the women watched him and how the men nodded as he approached. He then walked over to the outside bar for a drink. He ordered 1942 Don Julio, neat with a lime. He stood close to the bar and sipped his drink, looking around with a smile in his eyes like a proud parent watching his children get along.

That is when Shantel made her way over to the bar, donning a light-yellow knee length A-line cut dress that gracefully hugged her petite but curvy body. Her thick natural long dirty blonde hair was in a half up half down style giving her a youthful appearance and show casing her slim neckline that was adorned with an elegant emerald teardrop necklace with small dangling earrings to match. But it was her French manicured nails and toes that got his attention and how sexy her legs looked in 4-inch heels with the ankle strap that compliment her tone calves. She had no idea that her future husband was a sucker for the French manicure and a woman that had a full pinky toenail. He watched her through his peripheral and listened to her order Aperol Spritz. Her voice was warm, sweet but heavy like hot syrup and she smelled delicious, like sunshine and citrus.

He turned his full body around to look at her and concluded that there was no doubt that she tasted like butter cream. Shantel felt him staring at her, but to her disappointment, he didn't speak, and she was a lady and had no intention of introducing herself first or looking his way, so she headed back outside to join her colleagues as he watched her body move so graciously in her tall heels. He could tell she took care of herself. Her body was toned like she put in a few days a week at the gym. Being an avid gym goer himself, he could appreciate a woman that was disciplined in that area. He watched her from across the way such as she did to him moments ago. She was graceful, soft, sweet. She was attentive while listening to the women in her circle speak. The fabric of her dress was high quality, he could tell by the way it fell on her body which also revealed that she didn't have any shapewear underneath her clothes as he was not a fan of Spanx, girdles, waist trainers, none of that.

As the event came to an end and everyone disbursed, he noticed she was alone and wondered what brought her out this way. She tucked her pretty clutch under her arm and looked at her dainty watch. She was so precious to him. He followed her, catching up to her just as she was about to disappear around a corner and into one of the vehicles lined up.

"Excuse me." He said gently touching the back of her small, toned arm. Delighted, holding back a huge smile, Shantel turned around and looked up at the man she knew she was going to marry. It was

love at first sight for her. She slowly took her shades off and Yusef could have fainted at the beauty of her eyes, not because they were a beautiful chestnut brown, but the shape was sexy, kind and inviting to him. She shielded her eyes from the bright sun with her hand and looked up at him all 6feet 5 inches of him as she was only 5 feet.

"My name is Yusef James." He placed her petite hand in his large one.

"Shantel Emmitt." She smiled softly.

"It is an honor to meet you, Shantel, are you an author?"

"No, I'm here supporting a colleague's sister, she's an author. What about you, are you a writer?"

"No, well sort of. I'm in education."

Educated and fine, God I see what you've done for others!

Shantel was always the settle down type because of how she was raised by her mother Cheryl who married her stepfather Kenny when Shantel was 11 years old. Her father, a heroin addict, passed away when she was ten. But over the years, growing up in Harlem, Shantel would see her father on the street and Cheryl would all but threaten Shantel to stay away from him.

"Stay away from that corner and those damn addicts, they will do anything for drugs including kidnapping little girls!" Cheryl warned.

But one day one of those drug addicts that always seemed to be outside and in Shantel and Cheryl's line of vision approached them as they were heading home from Shantel's after school program.

"Uptown Cheryl!" The man kept calling out and Cheryl kept walking as if he wasn't talking to her. She pulled a 9-year-old Shantel along and warned her not to look back.

"Crazy ass addicts." Cheryl mumbled.

"But Mommy, he knows your name!" Shantel said, defying her mother and looking back. The man was upon them so out of slight fear, because of how quickly he was approaching, Shantel stopped and jerked her mother's arm to alarm her.

"Come on Cheryl, I'm not gonna hurt nobody you know me." the stranger said. He then looked down at Shantel who smiled at him, he smiled back.

"I'm your father." He said simply.

"Are you mad?" Cheryl barked.

Cheryl pulled her daughter along and walked briskly until they got inside of their gate, but the man was on them. He stepped inside the small gate and closed it so now they were all standing in a small circle. He reached into his pocket and pulled out a picture showing it to Shantel. It was a photo of him holding Shantel when she was around two years old as Cheryl looked on. Shantel looked up from the picture to the man who was still good looking just weathered and his clothes were old.

Bilal was on his way to becoming an architect but hanging out with them white boys at work, getting turned on to coke then something stronger thwarted all his plans to be a successful family man as his white colleagues got help, kicked the habit and went on to be successful. Cheryl couldn't take much more of him stealing out her purse, not coming home and catching him doing dope so after giving him one too many chances, she kicked him to the curb and plans for them getting married and living happily ever after were null. With nowhere to go, he hung around Harlem jumping from house to house, inevitably ending up homeless where he would watch his daughter grow into a beautiful young woman from the sidelines. In his heart he wanted to get clean to be in her life, but he was no match for the heroin. Bilal would have dreams of getting clean and walking his daughter down the aisle, but the heroin habit was too hard to kick.

"I need that picture back baby, it's all I have of you." Bilal reached for it while Shantel held on to it tightly.

"What's your name?" Shantel asked, handing him his picture.

"Bilal Campbell." He smiled.

"We made a deal that you would not talk to this girl unless you were off drugs, what the

fuck are you doing?" Cheryl said.

"Why did you call my mom Uptown Cheryl?" Shantel said, looking between her parents.

"Your mother has always strived for the best out of life. That's why I fell in love with her."

"But then you chose that white bitch over your family." She said tussling with the small gate to open it to let him out.

"So you're my dad?" Shantel's eyes lit up.

"Yes, I am." Bilal said.

"Shantel, sweetie, go upstairs, now!" Cheryl demanded. Shantel looked from her mother to

Bilal then slowly stomped up the stairs. Once she was inside the vestibule, watching from afar, Cheryl turned her back so that Shantel wouldn't see the look of rage on her face.

"I can't believe you pulled a fucking stunt like this. My daughter will never, ever be around you, so don't hold your fucking breath."

"You know I'm not a bad person I would never harm her, she's my daughter and she deserve to know who her father is. You telling me this little girl never asked who her father was?" Bilal said.

I told her you were dead." She snapped. "She doesn't deserve to know her father is a fucking drug addict. I don't need her growing up thinking she can date a man like you and it be acceptable. Now do me a favor, don't ever let me catch you by my house and you better be sure that I will be watching to make sure that Shantel isn't anywhere near you! Now get the fuck out of my gate." She said and opened it for him.

Bilal slowly exited the gate with his hands in his pocket. He looked up at the door and could see Shantel's pretty little face glued to the window, he winked at her softly and she waved. Cheryl looked up at her daughter then quickly went back to Bilal.

"I swear to God, Bilal, you better stay away from my fucking child."

"She's my child too." he said and walked off before Cheryl could say anything else. Cheryl hurried up the stairs and looked down at her daughter.

"Mommy you said my father was dead."

"Baby that man is dead."

"A few weeks went by, and things were quiet, with Cheryl constantly asking Shantel did she see "that man" to where Shantel would tell her no. She was sad that her mother had scared him off until one day he appeared out of the shadows as she headed home from school.

"Hey Angel." He whispered from the threshold of an abandoned store.

"Hi!" Shantel waved looking around.

"Is your mother with you?" he crouched down in the doorway. Shantel shook her head no.

"Come give me a hug." He whispered.

Shantel looked around to make sure that nobody would see her then she ran into her father's arms where they embraced for a while. Bilal took in the fresh scent of his daughters' hair.

"I haven't seen you." Shantel said.

"But I have seen you!" he tapped her nose.

"Well where do you hang out at, I can stop by after school!" she said innocently.

"No baby, I tell you what. Make sure you walk home the same way every single day from school and just know that your father is watching you and every once in a while, I'm going to step out and say hi, how's that."

Shantel didn't understand but she just nodded her head.

"Stay away from drugs or anybody that does drugs you understand me?" he said, his tone getting extra serious.

"Yes, Dad." She said.

"You don't have to call me dad, your mom won't like that. In fact, you need to head

home. I don't want you to get in trouble."

"But you are my dad." Shantel said so innocently.

"Is your last name still Campbell?" He asked.

"Yes. Shantel Angel Campbell." She said proudly.

Bilal just smiled and wiped his tears before they fell. He dug in his pocket and handed her a dollar.

"Get yourself some candy after school tomorrow, now go before you get in trouble and don't tell your mother!"

"Okay!" Shantel said, scurrying off.

Every night, Shantel would fall to sleep thinking about her father, excited to know that he would pop out and surprise her. She couldn't get the kindness in her father's eyes out of her head, nor could she understand why her mother was so mean to him and forbid her to see him. Shantel quietly kept in touch with her father sometimes spending her allowance money to buy him McDonalds and they would sit together, in that little alley way that he always jumped out of and eat their fast food while sitting side by side on a crate. It was the best of times for Shantel. Shantel would even hide leftovers and bring him a home cooked meal wherever she could find him. She would beg her mother to let her clean the kitchen so that she could stash food for her father.

Then one day, Shantel went on a hunt to find her father to bring him a piece of birthday cake the day after celebrating her tenth birthday. It was always so easy for her to sneak and see her father because Cheryl would let her run down the block to her best friend Daphne's house where Shantel would wave from the top of the dilapidated brownstone steps from the end of the block. Once Cheryl saw she was safe, she'd go inside. Shantel would wait a few moments then high tail it a few blocks away to spend at least twenty or so minutes with her father. Shantel saw her father the week of her birthday, but it was cold, so she wasn't coming outside much. To her delight when he saw her, he asked her, "who's having a birthday this week?"

"You remember my birthday?" Shantel's eyes lit up.

"How can I forget Angel. Til this day it is the most important day of my life, the day you were

born. I was right there when you came into the world."

"I'm going to bring you some cake!" she said excitedly.

"You know where to find me baby." He said as she kissed his cheek and ran off.

The evening of her birthday Cheryl watched her walk up the block to Daphne's with her cake wrapped in aluminum foil for her best friend. Cheryl waved at the top of the steps and Shantel went inside the vestibule. Cheryl started calling randomly so Shantel started going upstairs first before running off to see her father and she was right to do so tonight as she heard Daphne's mom confirm that Shantel was actually in the house. Moments later Daphne's mother was in her bedroom with a drink watching TV, leaving the girls to themselves. Daphne quietly opened the front door and begged Shantel to be back in fifteen minutes.

"I'm just giving him the cake then I'll be right back!" Shantel whispered then she quickly ran down the steps, the big fuzzy ball on the top of her ski hat flopping, her mittens keeping her little hands warm.

She went to Bilal's usual spot but didn't see him, so she dipped into a doorway and waited, holding her birthday cake knowing that her father would come. But when he didn't show up, she walked around some but was unsuccessful at finding him in his usual hang out spots, nor could she find any of his associates, so she gave up, somberly dumping her cake in the garbage on the street on the way back home.

She was so upset that she ran down the block to her own house forgetting she was to be at Daphnes, but she wanted nothing more than to be in her own bed. When she got home, Cheryl was on the couch nursing a glass of wine, she stood up upon hearing her daughter come in the house.

"What are you doing back in here?"

Shantel was crying and visibly upset.

"I don't feel like being outside, I want to be in my bed." Shantel lied.

"Did something happen? Are you and Daphne arguing or something?" she said approaching

her daughter. "No mommy no!" Shantel snapped.

Cheryl, not taking Shantel's word for it stomped into the kitchen and got on the phone immediately, calling Daphne's mother who had no idea that Shantel had left the house. She could hear Daphne's mother yelling at her, and Shantel felt bad that she didn't let Daphne know the play when Daphne was looking out for her. Their friendship never recovered after that. Shantel lost her best friend that night as Daphne got in big trouble for sneaking Shantel out of the house. Daphne's mother and Cheryl exchanged a few words about the girls needing to do better, then Cheryl politely said goodnight and hung up.

"You cannot do that again, it is dangerous out there. I don't care if it's on the same block you should have let someone know that you were leaving! Somebody could have snatched your ass up between Daphne's and here, do you understand me little girl?"

"Can I go in my room now?" Shantel asked with an attitude.

"What is your problem?" Cheryl insisted.

"Mom, I don't want to talk about it, I just have a stomachache can I go lay down now?"

Cheryl sipped her wine and nodded her head as Shantel stomped off to her room. About a half hour later, Kenny came over as planned.

"How was your day, you're here later than usual," she said helping him out of his coat.

"It was a long day as I suspected it would be." He kissed her lips. "It's cold out there tonight baby, where's Shantel."

"In her room, upset about something or another, she said her stomach hurts, but I think it's something else Kenny. She went over to Daphne's and was there all of thirty minutes before she came back upset and didn't even tell anyone where she was."

"Hmph, she will be alright. What did you cook, it smells good."

Cheryl didn't like Kenny's nonchalant response to Shantel's outburst. "Did you hear what I said? Shantel is upset about something."

"I heard you baby but she's ten years old. It can be a boy, hormones, anything. It's nothing for you to be so worried about, like I said she will be alright now what's for dinner." He sat down at the dining room table.

"My day was fine, my courses were challenging and I am glad that I am soon to graduate with my Masters." Cheryl said sarcastically.

"I'm so sorry baby, how was your day." Kenny said but Cheryl ignored him.

"I made some beef stew over white rice." She said blandly.

"Okay, not too much on my plate." Kenny said pulling his shirt out of his pants. Cheryl leaned against the kitchen counter dangling her left hand.

"I do not plate or serve for no man that is not my husband. Please feel free to come over here and make your own plate. I ate already." Cheryl said sitting down at the dining room table across from Kenny who shot her daggers.

"You know I was thinking about the conversations we have been having about us getting married, me adopting Shantel and your concerns about her relationship or lack thereof with her father. You know I want you to leave Harlem."

"Yes, we discussed this over and over but all it's ever been, is a discussion. You know that I am not leaving my place until you make an honest woman out of me. I cannot just uproot my daughter to shack up with a boyfriend no matter what you promise me."

"I understand that, and I respect that about you more than you know. I love you Cheryl and I want to marry you and I love Shantel. I'm tired of going from my place to yours, spending a few nights here then going home. I want us to be up under one roof, but you are just too concerned about taking Shantel away from *her roots*. Where does that leave me, where does that leave us?"

"You haven't done anything to show me how serious you are so what do you expect me to do? I have to continue doing what I need to do as a woman and a mother because you can walk out of here tomorrow and where will that leave me and Shantel? I do pretty good for myself and I have every intention of doing better and better."

"Yeah, but you could be doing much better if we were married. You wouldn't have to work you could just focus on your studies. We could live in a better neighborhood in a big ass house and send Shantel to the best schools. Baby things are about to change for me, and I want you by my side. I secured investors. I'm resigning from Deloitte on Monday."

"Baby that is wonderful news I am so happy for you!" Cheryl said jumping out of her seat and hugging Kenny.

"I don't need you still at Deloitte when I leave. I don't even want you working to be honest, not right now at least. I just need you to focus on your studies and raise Shantel and when you go back to work you should be going into business for yourself, baby I can handle all of that for you...as my wife."

"Kenny I am happy for you, but that is your money, your success. I must make my own money. I am *not your wife,* so I have no security with you as my man, just your promises and we all know promises ain't nothing but comfort to a fool."

"I can't do nothing with you as long as Shantel is running behind her junkie father."

"Kenny that has nothing to do with you, we discussed this!"

"It has everything to do with me! And you were none too happy to find out that Shantel was sneaking off seeing her father, when I told you that I was driving by and saw her ass sitting on a fucking crate on Lexington Avenue surrounded by a bunch of dope heads! You have to let that shit go."

"I have let it go! I can't help that my child loves her father. She doesn't see drugs she just sees the man she loves, I tried to keep her away but when can I do when I am at school after work and she's a latch key kid coming home. She is bound to run into Bilal."

"You haven't tried hard enough. It's almost as if you want her to keep going around her father so you can know what is going on with him."

"What are you implying Kenneth." Cheryl said walking up to him.

"All I'm saying is you need to focus on your future, not your past. Shantel will be alright she is young she will forget about him."

"You sound insane. I'm still not understanding how you're starting a lucrative business and wanting to marry me has anything to do with Shantel's father."

"He hasn't been her father since he put that shit in his veins. I've been the one taking care of her."

"It's the price you pay for fucking her fine ass mama. And if you decide to stop taking care of my child tomorrow my child won't starve. You forgot who you're dealing with?"

"Oh I didn't forget at all. I am *well aware* who I'm with. And that is why I want you with me and baby I'm going far, very far, places not many African American men get to go. And what I don't need is the shadow of some junkie motherfucka hanging over my success because the woman that I married has a past that she can't let go of. You gotta put an end to this shit with him and Shantel or you will not be my wife."

"You know that I want to be with you, so I'm not following what more you need from me!"

"Just tell me that you are okay with her never talking to her father again. That's all I need to hear."

Not sure of what Kenny meant, Cheryl hesitated as she looked into his eyes.

"Kenny, we were born and raised in Harlem. Her father and I were superstars of this neighborhood and so everyone knows us. We get a lot of love and support here, this is our home. I'm not willing to leave here just for any old thing Kenny so you have to come out and be straight with me. What is it that you want from me? Do you want to marry me and provide for me and my daughter? Or do you want to continue to spew out these empty promises and threats making me feel as if I have to do something strange to keep you. I feel like you are playing games with me to be honest."

"I want her father out of the picture." He said bluntly.

"He's not in the picture, what are you talking about?"

"As long you're in Harlem, he's in the picture."

"So what do you have in mind Kenneth. What would you have me do."

"Nothing, but I just want to have a man to man with him." He said eyeing the pot on the stove.

"What are you up to Kenny, why are you coming in here all hot and bothered over Bilal. You're supposed to be happy about your new business venture, you haven't told me not one detail about it. I want to know what's going on?" Cheryl sat down next to him and began rubbing his leg.

"I saw Shantel's father and I asked him to stay the fuck away from my family. So it might be some time before Shantel sees her father again."

Cheryl looked Kenny up and down. "What did you do?"

"Something you should have done a long time ago. We're getting the fuck out of Harlem." He said, grabbing his plate and heading to the stove for some beef stew.

As the days went by, Shantel took the long route home, walking around Harlem trying to come across her father and his friends. She would brave the cold and stand on her stoop for hours, hoping that he would walk by, but the weeks turned to months until Winter gave way to Spring, and she was surrounded by boxes as they were moving to Long Island. Cheryl would join her on the steps as Shantel sadly watched people walk by.

"Hey, my pretty girl, how you doing today?"

"I'm okay." Shantel said somberly as Cheryl toyed with her long ponytail. She wrapped arms around her daughter, kissing the top of her head.

"Something has been troubling you, you wanna talk about it?"

"You wouldn't care." Shantel mumbled.

"I'm so sorry, I know you wanted to build a relationship with him but drugs are bad and well there's no future in it. You either end up dead, in jail or a zombie, you see what it looks like over there on the east side, that's why I don't like you going over there, and this is why I didn't want you to build a relationship with him because I knew that eventually he would break your heart. I'm so sorry baby." She put her arms around her daughter.

"We could have helped him mama, now he's gone." Shantel cried as her mother consoled her.

"You can't help someone that doesn't want to help themselves baby."

"He wanted the help, he told me so." Shantel sniffled into her mother's arm pit.

"People on drugs say anything Shantel. He was suffering baby, he is now in a better place. I know you don't understand that right now but one day you will. But look, we are moving far from here into a house of our own and you will have a backyard, a front yard, and a way bigger room than what you have now. Oh and I have some news that might cheer you up a little bit."

"Not right now mama."

"Okay baby. Well come on and do a walk through and make sure that you have everything packed." Cheryl said, leaving her daughter on the stairs heartbroken.

Later that week, once they were semi settled into their new home Cheryl and Kenny sat Shantel down and explained to her that they were married, and that Kenny would adopt her and change her name from Campbell to Emmitt. Shantel cried so hard and begged her mother not to change her name, but she had no dog in this fight. Kenny wanted to erase any remnants of Bilal. Shantel went to a private Junior High School and when it was time for her to go to high school she begged to go to a public school for a little bit of normalcy. She didn't want to be in a uniform and hang around the stuffy, privileged kids. She desperately wanted to connect with her people.

Her parents agreed and she went to public school where she would meet her best friend Naomi before going away to Spellman. By then Kenny's business had taken off far beyond his expectations and they were living large. While in college, her parents bought a 3.2-million-dollar home in Sands Point, NY. No matter how lavish the home was, Shantel didn't want to move in with her parents after graduating with her Masters as she yearned for the culture of Harlem. Her parents fought hard for her to not move back to Harlem, but she was an adult and there was nothing that they could do about it. Harlem was her heart, it was where she was born and it was where her daddy died. She would never leave Harlem no matter how bad Cheryl turned up her nose to the place that made her. And though Kenny was a great provider and a great father to her, knowing that she had a father out on the streets never sat well with her. She wanted him in her life, she didn't care if he was a junkie. But Cheryl would have none of it so when he passed away, he took a piece of Shantel with him.

The one thing Cheryl knew was she wasn't going to be a statistic or a single mother and that even though her fairytale of having a happy family with Shantel's father wasn't going to happen, she knew some way somehow that the life she dreamt of since a little girl was going to come to fruition if she had anything to do with it. She pursued higher her education, worked two jobs, and made sure that Shantel always had the best of everything. She rented out a duplex apartment in a brownstone in Harlem for her and her daughter to live in and manifested owning one, one day by hook or crook.

She went to school at night to earn her bachelor's in information technology while working as an Executive Assistant in the daytime at Deloitte where she met Kenneth "Kenny" Emmitt who already held a position there as an Executive. Fifteen years her senior, Cheryl made sure to put herself on Kenny's radar. She was a red bone with dirty blonde hair a beautiful smile and a small waist. She didn't need much else to hook a man back then. She needed a lifestyle for her daughter and so she asked Kenny to mentor her knowing that the inevitable was bound to happen with Cheryl's good looks and intelligence and Kenneth's ambition and charm. Quietly the two began dating, as it would be frowned upon to date one of his colleagues' assistants so after quietly marrying Kenny, Cheryl quit her job and focused on her education while Kenny went on to become the President and CEO of a technology company building a net worth of $7 million and counting over the years.

Not having an education was not an option in Shantel's home and once she graduated with her Phd in finance her parents gifted her a fully renovated brownstone in Harlem since the neighborhoods were becoming gentrified, along with stocks. Her mother's expectations of her made it very hard for her to date. There wasn't anyone that her mother thought was good enough for her, Kenny even worse. Her mother always drilled into her head, get an education, make your own money, get married and travel the world. Watch the company you keep, don't hang with a bunch of low vibrational women, always thrive, and strive to be your best self and you will attract a great partner.

Well, here she was, thriving in her career, owned a beautiful brownstone in Harlem, no children, made upper six figures and counting, great credit, money in the bank had wonderful friends that were far from low vibrational *even though Cheryl judged Naomi for not having her degree in anything,* and simply needed someone to share her gracious energy with. The way Yusef looked at her she could see herself peacefully and comfortably sleeping on top of him like an expensive mattress. He had it going on, and Cheryl would love him.

"Where are you from, Shantel?"

"Harlem, and yourself?"

"Queens, St. Albans."

"Well, Mr. St. Albans it has been an extremely taxing day as you know. I need to head back to my room and get some rest. I have an early flight in the morning and some work to catch up on." Shantel said, backing away from him a bit hoping that he followed suit. Jackpot when he explained that he was leaving early as well. She could only hope that he was on the same flight as her.

"I have an 8am Delta flight, what about you?" he asked.

"8:25am United." She responded.

"Ah close but no cigar, well where are you staying tonight perhaps, I can give you a ride if you're comfortable with that." He persisted to Shantel's delight.

"I'm staying at Harbor View." She gladly provided information.

"Well, what do you know, I'm staying there as well."

Shantel smiled warmly and bashfully.

"I'll let my colleagues know that I have a ride, allow me a moment?" Shantel said and headed over to the group of women who were grinning, eager to know what was happening between her and the handsome stranger that everyone was eye balling.

"Okay, alright. I'll be right here waiting for you." He smiled.

He watched Shantel saunter off, the hem of her skirt swayed quickly from side to side as she tip toed to her associates to inform them that she had a ride home. He smiled at the women as they giggled like little schoolgirls once she told them who she was leaving with. He thought it was adorable how she maintained a straight face upon her return to him when she was just cutting up not knowing he could see her.

"I just want to say that you look so beautiful by the way, like a ray of sunshine in that yellow dress."

"Thank you." She said as he opened the car door for her. They drove silently until reaching their destination. Yusef made sure he got out of the car first and opened her door for her again.

"So is this your representative or is this what you do?" Shantel flirted.

"For a classy lady like yourself, this is the treatment you will get from me, always. May I have your number so I can call you in the morning, perhaps go to the airport together?"

"Sure," Shantel said and took his phone out of his hand, inputting her phone number trying to contain her excitement.

Shantel tossed and turned all night, visions of her and Yusef getting married kept her awake. The fact that he texted her at 6 a.m. to make sure that she was up, knocking on her door gently after she gave him the okay, carrying her bags to the airport and seeing her off before heading to his gate sealed the deal for Shantel. Once they arrived back in New York, within days he took her out to dinner at Capital Grille where they talked for hours, her telling him that her lambchops were way better, finding out that they had so much in common career wise, family, future. The look in his eyes each time they agreed on something confirmed to Shantel that what she was feeling was real. It was love, early on, his eyes did not lie. She shared her glee with Naomi and Jameela, Jameela being the pessimistic man eater that she was, after seeing his picture advised Shantel to get a hold of herself, to just give him some pussy and have fun but Naomi the hopeless romantic was all for the fairytale especially once Shantel showed her a picture.

"God took his time when he made this man, God damn Shantel! Lock that down immediately!" Naomi squealed and that she did.

Within three months of dating, Yusef professed his love to her verbally even though she had known he loved her from day one as she did him. He asked her for a commitment, and she accepted. He knew that he couldn't keep Shantel just hanging around under any other circumstances. She wasn't a "situationship" type or a casual woman, she meant business and she didn't even have to say it. Shantel did not give herself to Yusef until he confirmed that they were in a relationship which made him adore her on levels that she couldn't begin to comprehend. He was motivated and impressed by her and her parents' drive. The one thing Yusef yearned was a mother that was proud of him for all his accomplishments, such as Shantel's mother was proud of her, not a mother that was proud of him for how many women he brought home. But their whirlwind love affair didn't come without hiccups.

About a year into their relationship, Yusef was asleep, and Shantel couldn't help but to look at his phone that vibrated ferociously in the middle of the night so many nights in a row. Yusef always slept through it, but Shantel knew that someone was desperately trying to get in touch with him and always after midnight. She peeked over at the phone and realized that it didn't have a name attached to it which made her suspicious. With one swipe she took his phone and headed downstairs and hoped that the person would call back. After waiting five or so minutes while getting a glass of water, she was about to head upstairs when the phone vibrated again, this time with a text message that read. *Are you sleeping or are you at her house?*

There was no doubt that it was a woman demanding his time. Shantel scrolled through his phone finding a thread of messages from eggplant emojis to ass and breast pictures all from a chocolate woman. There were some pictures of the chocolate woman and another woman kissing sensually. Shantel decided to call back and the woman answered on half a ring.

"*Are you at her house or are you home?*"

But Shantel didn't answer right away.

"*Hello, Yusef?*" the woman asked.

"Yusef is at *her house,* sleeping right now sweetheart, who are you and what do you want?"

The woman hung up. Shantel sat with the phone for a while, but it didn't ring. She called the number back several times, but the woman didn't answer so Shantel texted.

"*You're brave enough to knowingly deal with a man in a relationship, but you can't talk to me.*"

Shantel watched the three dots appear then disappear several times indicating that the woman was typing something then deciding not to. She was heated, she called again and this time the woman answered.

"He's never going to leave me alone; I hope you know that." The woman confidently said.

"Is that right, then why isn't he with you? Why are you home, alone, begging for a man to contact you when he is laid up with his woman?"

"You don't have a prize sweetie, Yusef is for the streets."

"Well, if that's the case then why are you being bothered with him? That says more about you than anything, sweetie."

"He provides a service I need, and I provide one for him as well, something you can't comprehend and that you clearly *don't* provide." The woman said starkly. "You might be number one, but you are not the *only* one. I've been around for many years, *way before you* and more than likely I'll be here *after* you. So do me a favor and tell Yusef to call me. No need for a name, he knows who I am." She said and hung up.

Before heading upstairs, Shantel flustered, took deep breaths and tried to calm her nerves. Not one to ever get out of character, she began scrolling through the phone looking at the raunchy pictures. She regulated her breathing while trying to calculate when Yusef had the time to commit such heinous acts of the heart. She began to pace. *My God.* She said to herself then headed back upstairs and placed his phone back next to him after deleting her text message to his side piece. She watched him sleep so peacefully in her bed. Shantel dosed off finally and was awakened a few hours later to the sun creeping through her bedroom blinds and Yusef smothering her with kisses.

"Good morning, beautiful." His huge brown presence towered over her.

"Morning." she said in a faint voice.

"I woke up extremely hungry this morning. What about you? You want some breakfast? I'll cook," he said hopping out of the bed. He dropped to the floor and did pushups. Normally Shantel would love watching Yusef in her expensive kitchen cooking up a delicious meal in nothing but his boxer briefs. Breakfast somehow always ended with him propping her up on the island and giving her long strokes. But not this morning. The thought of him touching her repulsed her.

"Sure, that sounds nice. What do you have in mind." she said dryly.

Yusef did three reps of twenty like nothing then stood up and let out a grunt. He loved working out and would do pull ups or pushups anywhere. His naked body perfectly sculptured, his manhood semi hard and still bigger than most men that was fully erect, stood before Shantel while she lay in bed, disgusted but in love with this Adonis of a man.

How could I possibly think he was all for me? Jameela was right.

"French toast, fruits, egg whites, crispy bacon, some good Café Bustelo, *then some of you.* You know you are my favorite meal of the day. My breakfast of champions." He winked.

He leaned on the bed and kissed her forehead. Shantel put on her robe and followed Yusef downstairs where he made her a cup of coffee while he cooked breakfast. She watched him from her huge oversized comfy couch.

"Do you love me, Yusef?" She sipped her coffee. He looked up at her perplexed.

"If you don't know, then you will never know, girl." He laughed.

"What would you do if I was untrue?" she asked with a more serious tone.

"What do you mean?" He asked walking over to her while scrambling eggs in a bowl.

"What would you do? How would you feel if you found out that I had another lover?"

"First of all, that would never happen." He scoffed.

"How do you figure that?"

She was now seeing his arrogance.

"Well aside from everything I have to offer as a man and a partner, I mean, I'm supportive, I take you out, I buy you things, I listen to you, I make love to you, I compliment you, I put you first, second, last. I can go on and on about what a bomb ass partner I am not to mention all the things I do for myself which reflects you such as you reflect me. They say you date at the level of your esteem, right?"

"So much for humility," she said sarcastically.

"You asked me a question but to stay on topic, *smart ass*, nobody and I mean *nobody* never has and never will have the opportunity to make you cream and scream like me. Why would you ever waste your time with another when you have a man that does everything to you and for you sexually. You think another man will make your body react the way that I can? Doubt it." He said and laughed.

He kissed her forehead and headed back into the kitchen. Yusef didn't understand the severity of the moment and was taking everything for a joke. He had no idea at that very moment Shantel despised him. What was so special to her was being given away to someone else and here he was, making a mockery of her feelings.

"Well, what about me, what is it that I do for you sexually?" she followed up.

"Oh, that's easy, so many things my petite pudding." He smiled while preparing a fruit salad as if he was having a flashback of a fond moment.

"Expound." Shantel demanded.

Yusef leaned against the counter holding the bowl of fruit in his hand. "Where's all of these questions coming from?"

"I just want to know. I think it's important to check in with your partner occasionally, to make sure they are satisfied, right? One just can't assume that everything is everything."

"Right, okay then. Well to your question, your body's reaction to me is like no other. What it does for my confidence sexually as well as how secure it makes me feel in this relationship is something I never had, and I wouldn't forsake for anything in this world."

"I find that hard to believe." Shantel said.

"Pardon?" Yusef asked.

"Nothing. Go on."

"Anybody can have sex Shantel, but you're not a man, so I don't expect you to understand what I

mean."

"Paint me a picture, Yusef, I'd truly like to understand the minds of men, especially *my man*."

"Alright then, put it like this, women feel used, sexualized and objectified a lot, right?"

"Right."

"Well, men feel that way sometimes as well. We may not express it and to be quite honest, some of us allow it because we have no self-control or we feel as if nobody will take us seriously because as men, we are supposed to like the idea of women throwing themselves on us, but when we mature and become adults it can manifest into something else, something negative toward women. When you hear a grown woman telling a young boy, you are going to be a heartbreaker when you get older, that's objectifying him or when you turn 18 call me, that little boy is being sexualized. But everyone looks the other way, grown women calling boys their little boyfriends, I can't stand even when a mother calls her son her King. Your son is not your King! You can't look at your son and see your equal, your King, a man, the man that you wish you had in your life be it that boy's father or some other man. Women don't realize that they are objectifying their sons when they do that, and it allows other women to objectify him as well. You put that young man in a position to grow up too fast because now as a boy, as a son, he is going to want to be there for his mother, he's going to want to love her and make her happy and instead of doing that by getting good grades and just being a decent young man, he finds himself doing that by wiping her tears, fixing things around the house, going out to get a job at an early age so he could help his mother, vetting and sizing up any man she brings around to throw his little weight around as the man of the house or the worse part having to bare the weight of all of her bad decisions as it pertains to her personal life."

"I agree with you. It's no different than men doing it to young girls either even as young as five years old telling a little girl that *she's going to be trouble* when she gets older is totally unacceptable and that is a man that I would not let near any child of mine or any child that I am responsible for. Because for you to look so far into the future and envision what an innocent child is going to look like is creepy and pedophilic."

"Any man that says some shit like that to a little girl isn't looking into the future, he's looking at her now!" Yusef said and turned his back to finish prepping breakfast.

"Yeah, you're right. But how does this tie into what I'm asking you as it pertains to us?"

"Because when a man meets a woman that makes him feel loved and not objectified, you can't deny it or compare that feeling to anything else. That is a feeling that you provide for me. I never felt this way before. Every woman I've been with made me feel as if it was all about the sex, the optics of being with someone that looks like was most important to them. Most women want a man that's tall, dark, handsome, successful, got a big dick, some money. I have all those things and got the nerve to be educated with a beard that connects, come on man." He chuckled at that last part.

"As conceited and self-absorbed as this sounds, you have a point."

"Baby, a lot of women can't handle this kind of pressure, and I promise you I am just being honest, stay with me on this, just listen." He said recognizing that Shantel was turning her nose up.

"I've come across some of the most beautiful, educated, smart sisters in the world. I've dated up and I've dated down. You're neither, Shantel. You are in a class all by yourself because when you look at me, what I see is a woman that isn't easily impressed. You love me for me, and I have never had that feeling before, do you understand what I am trying to say to you?"

"I do." She said sipping her coffee.

"I told you I was in a long-term relationship before, right? I was with this woman for six years, but something just wasn't clicking. Now sure, we had a ball together, we traveled and shopped, ate at expensive restaurants but it became so overwhelming. I started to feel like all those things we did were just a way to cover up the fact that we didn't really love one another the way two people should love one another. I never felt as if I could sit around and do absolutely nothing with her and be okay. There was always a spot filler or something that we needed to be doing to enjoy one another. As highly as I thought of myself and as hard as I worked, I felt as if she would leave me if the next man made a little bit more, was a bit taller, was a bit more accomplished. I didn't feel safe. Ironically enough, we didn't work out and she is married to a well-known basketball player, so my gut was right. But you are so grounded, so pure, so real, I love you Shantel like I've never loved another woman before in my life. I can sit with you and do absolutely nothing and feel as if I am doing everything."

"But is love enough." Was all Shantel could ask him as she tried to steer the conversation back toward sex so that she could bring up the infidelity. There was no way that she could let this slide.

"The kind of love you and I share, yes, I believe it's enough as long as we continue to grow, respect one another, and remain committed. The key is to not be stagnant, to always try to impress one another. I'll never let my body go. I'll never not chase and accomplish my goals, I'll always present myself to be my very best for you and I ask for the same in return which I know I will get because that is just the kind of woman you are. So yes, it absolutely is enough."

"I know that sex is very important to you, Yusef. You are a highly sexual man. I've never been with someone like you that really enjoys sex as much as you do. Do you think what we have is enough for you to be faithful to me forever? I may not want to have sex all the time. I may not be okay with doing some of the things that you want to do in bed. So how important are these things to you?" She baited him.

"I want to have sex with you all the time because I am in love with you. And let me just preface what I'm about to say by saying this, yes, I love pussy, I love it so much. I love women, I love your bodies, the noises you make, the faces, your breasts, ass, everything about women, I love. But we are talking about *you* because each woman is different. So, if we're going to talk about sex between you and I, let's talk about it then. It's the way you feel inside, the way you taste. The way you lay there breathing heavy after I'm done having my way with you, the faces you make. The way your pussy feels as if it was molded and made just for me. It just feels like home. *I know* that's mine; *I know* it's safe, *I know* it's precious. That alone drives me crazy. The way your soft hands caress my face when we make love, the way you love me, the way you make love to me even when we are supposed to be fucking. The way you take your time when giving me head, like you love it so much. The way you look at me, the way you sometimes cry when we have sex. It's so many things girl! You are always such a lady even when you're not supposed to be. You just can't help being who you are, and I love that."

It was at that moment that Shantel realized what that other woman was doing for Yusef. This woman was probably pussy popping on a handstand and taking cum shots to the face while Shantel played it safe.

"I get it now."

"Get what, babe?" Yusef said walking over to Shantel to take her mug for a coffee refill.

"I get why you have been cheating on me," she said, barely audible.

Yusef stopped in his tracks and stared at Shantel. She stared back intensely.

"What did you just say?" he asked.

"You are cheating on me, and now I know why. I am not wild enough for you in bed. Your side piece is into threesomes and does all those nasty things to you, probably calls you daddy while I'm over here being a lady, even when I'm not supposed to be, right? That is what you just said right? Because that's what you like right? Nasty, freaky porn shit."

"Baby, what side piece, stop it. Is this why you wanted to have this conversation because you think that I'm fucking around?" He walked back into the kitchen.

"So, who is the darkskin woman in your phone, the one kissing the other woman."

"You were in my phone?"

"Is that all you can say?" Shantel stood up and placed her mug on the table. "She wouldn't stop calling you. All night she was blowing your phone up, she wanted to know if you were here with me or ignoring her, so I let her know that you were here with me, and she let me know that you two have *something special* and she was not going anywhere. Now please do not insult me, Yusef. Before you start lying to me, *do not.*"

"Shantel, baby, it's nothing. She is an old friend; we used to hook up early when you and I started dating, but that was before we got into a committed relationship. Yes, she is someone I use to call when I wanted sex, but that is it. That been over, whatever pictures you saw in my phone are old."

"You do know I explored your phone last night while you were sleeping so peacefully in my bed. She literally just sent those pictures to you a few days ago. Now do me a favor on this lovely Saturday morning Yusef, turn my stove off, march your big ass upstairs, get dressed and go home."

Yusef turned off the stove but didn't go upstairs. He headed over to Shantel. "I cannot stop someone from sending me dirty pictures Shantel. All because she sent those pictures does not mean that I've been sleeping with her."

"The text message reads, and I quote, *can't stop thinking about last week, that was one for the books. I got a new girl for you next time. You're going to love her, Daddy.*"

Yusef stood there rubbing his forehead out of frustration. "Shantel, listen to me. I promise you I am not cheating on you." He continued to blatantly lie.

"Yusef, listen to *me.* I am not the one for lies and games. I am not going to put up with infidelity, so I'm going to ask you nicely to please leave my home, now!"

"Baby," he pleaded.

But Shantel ignored him, marching up the stairs ahead of him and tossing his clothes outside of her bedroom once she got upstairs.

"Do not step foot in this bedroom. Take your things and go!" she yelled finally.

Yusef gathered up his clothes and got dressed outside of her door then headed downstairs. She could hear him grabbing his truck keys. He closed the door softly behind him and headed home.

Shantel's emotions were all over the place the days to follow. After ignoring Naomi's calls, she called her back once she could stomach telling her that Yusef cheated. Naomi was empathetic. Jameela not so much to no one's surprise. Shantel continued lying to her mother whenever she would ask how Yusef was doing. She didn't want Cheryl to judge Yusef, mainly because she wasn't sure how things would turn out. Over the months, Shantel kept her head down, consumed with work while Yusef continued to call, sending flowers and asking for forgiveness.

"I'm not sure what to do." she confided in her friends.

"I say go with your heart. No one can tell you what to do, this is your life and if you want to take him back, I won't judge." Naomi offered.

"I will. He cheats once he'll do it again and again. Once you take him back you'll become his fool." Jameela said.

"I hate to admit it, but Jameela is right. I can't take him back. He'll lose all respect for me."

"She may be right but this is your life. And if she's your friend, she'll support you no matter what you decide."

"I'm not supporting low self-esteem, I'm sorry."

"It's not about self-esteem, it's about forgiveness and understanding. Shantel, do what you feel is best." Naomi said dismissive of Jameela's pessimism.

"What's best is leaving his cheating ass alone!" Jameela warned.

"I hear you both. I'm going to pray on it. He wants to come over, talk things out."

"Meet his ass in a public place with some big panties on and do not shave!" Jameela said.

"Baby I'm a size four I don't own nothing big." Shantel laughed.

"No seriously, I can't believe this woman is right again. Meet him in a public place and let him say what he has to say. You don't want him sweet talking your panties off."

About two months later, Shantel finally forgave him all the while he was still sleeping with Brandi. But he was also so in love with Shantel and knew that he needed to ween off his sexual exploits sooner than later because his sexual needs were deeper than the freak show he was a part of, it was something in his mind that he couldn't turn off and sometimes he would feel guilt. Shantel and Yusef got right back in the full swing of things with Brandi in the shadows. All was well until Shantel used Yusef's laptop.

Chapter 8

STRANGER IN MY HOUSE

ost of the time, friends will not forgive your man for hurting you even long after you have, but for whatever reason, Yusef was the exception, at least to Naomi. Everyone gave Yusef the one off that most men get, cheat once, beg for forgiveness once you realize your woman isn't taking you back so easily, get put on probation by the friends, then everyone sweeps it under the rug. Enough time had gone by for everyone to believe that Yusef was a changed man. Shantel loved entertaining in her home and Friday nights were for her divine cooking, music and sometimes Yusef would invite some of his partners over. Tonight, she had her big, beautiful bay windows open and the breeze that swept through her place kept everyone in a beautiful mood. She had her cards laid out for spades if anyone chose to indulge, Uno, board games, Cards Against Humanity, charcuterie boards and champagne on the table accompanied by laughter in the air. Yusef was accompanied by his cousin Dwayne.

"Put some music on!" Naomi suggested as she tore into Shantel's delicious lambchops. Her and Dwayne greedily devoured the lollipop lambchops long after everyone else had their share. Yusef shook his head in play disgust at them both.

"Cousin, you need to marry this woman already so we can keep the chops in the family!" Dwayne joked.

"Don't worry, it's coming." He said wrapping his arms around Shantel's waist. Jameela sucked her teeth.

"What Meela, what now?" Yusef said.

"Naan ring in sight talking about marriage, please." She rolled her eyes while twirling her drink.

"There is no rush, right baby." Yusef kissed Shantel on the neck.

"Not over here." Shantel confirmed. Jameela laughed unnecessarily loud and exaggerated. "Now Shantel, say that again, with your chest, in front of Uptown Cheryl."

"Baby, did you bring your laptop? I'm going to connect it to my Alexa." Shantel said removing Yusef's arms from around her waist and heading upstairs.

"Yeah, it's on the chaise." He said while shaking his head at Jameela. Shantel could hear Yusef and Jameela having friendly banter about relationships and marriage as she made her way up the stairs with Naomi on here heels, having to use the bathroom and loving the one in Shantel's room.

"How much did you spend on renovating that bathroom, girl that look like something Diddy would have in his home!" Naomi said wiping her hands and grabbing a seat next to Shantel on the bench at the foot of the bed.

"You know his password?"

"Yeah, from seeing him log in a million times," she said, hesitating as she hovered over a few folders on his desktop. Noticing her dilemma, Naomi began shaking her head disapprovingly.

"Don't go through that man's things, hit the Spotify app and let's go. Come on." She said standing up encouraging Shantel to follow her downstairs, but Shantel decided to click on the Drop Box anyway and it opened with a single sign on, prompting her to use the code that was sent to Yusef's Gmail. Shantel immediately scrolled through, seeing mainly business folders until she stumbled across the one titled, "Dark Place." Naomi had an uneasy feeling as they sat waiting for the video to load. She covered her mouth in shock when a dark-skinned woman with a huge backside appeared in the frame, crawling across the floor in a leather mask and an outfit made from chains. Then another woman appeared, crawling toward the darkskin woman and on their knees in similar outfits they began to tongue kiss.

"Oh my," Naomi said clutching imaginary pearls. A man's voice could be heard, instructing one of the women to pleasure the other one orally. After having been gone from everyone for too long, Jameela came bursting through the door.

"What are you both doing up here?" she asked suspiciously.

Naomi shrugged slowly as Jameela grabbed a seat next to the women.

"Yawl up here watching porn?" Jameela said looking at the laptop.

"Shhhh" Naomi said.

Shantel was still quiet. She clicked on another video. Immediately Yusef appeared in the frame and the two women from the other video were devouring his entire body. One was riding him, the other one was riding his face. Shantel clicked through several of the videos, each getting raunchier and raunchier, the same two women, sometimes joined by other women. Bondage, Dominatrix, role playing was all a common theme. Shantel kept clicking through each video, the dark-skinned woman was in each one, accompanied by other women most of the time until the last one that Shantel decided to click. It was just Yusef and the woman.

"Shantel, baby, maybe you shouldn't watch any more of these videos. I think you've seen enough," Naomi said softly.

But Shantel would not turn the videos off, it was like she could not look away. She sat in between Jameela and Naomi who were both having a challenging time trying to find something else to look at, but the way this woman was moaning Yusef's name was enchanting to say the least. The way he was managing her was enough to make any woman go mad. Shantel did not blink as she watched her man stroke this woman into oblivion up against a wall until the woman literally began to cry and beg him to stop in pure sexual bliss.

"Shantel, baby please turn this off I think you've seen enough," Jameela said, trying to push the laptop closed but Shantel shrugged away from her and stood up, still watching. Her face held no emotion as she studied her man making love to another woman.

"Go back downstairs, tell Yusef that Shantel is up here fixing my locs and hurry back but don't make it obvious."

Jameela did what she was told then came back upstairs confident that Yusef and Dwayne were cool. They were leaned up against the kitchen counter while Dwyane was leading the conversation about work.

"The time stamp on the latest video was from two days ago." Shantel said to no one as she continued to watch. She put the laptop on her dresser and stood back, folding her arms, just watching like it was the news. Naomi and Jameela looked at one another, unable to understand why she was continuing to torture herself in that way. Yusef had the chocolate woman nailed to the cross but when Yusef began to tongue kiss the woman feverishly, that is when Shantel showed emotion by punching the laptop off of the dresser. She let out a snarl and covered her face.

"Shantel, listen to me, we are going to go downstairs, and we are going to tell Dwayne that it is best that we all leave so that you and Yusef could have some privacy to handle this." Naomi said. Shantle ignored her and picked the laptop up from off the floor.

"So this is her, she's still around." Shantel choked on her words.

Her friends sat by feeling helpless as there was nothing they could do or say. Yusef was caught out there in the worse way. Shantel was trying to speak but the words were not coming out. After a few moments, laptop in hand, she made her way to the stairs as Naomi and Jameela followed behind her cautiously. Shantel did not have a mean, angry bone in her body. She never raised her voice and barely cursed. She was the one that kept everyone calm and believed that mediation and meditation were the answer to everything. She was calm, patient, and poised, always. But with all that being said, there was absolutely no way that Shantel was going to be able to practice any kind of couth after watching her man getting down and dirty with so many women.

"I say we go knock on that hoe door, she like whips and chains let's go whip her ass with a chain then." Jameela suggested.

"Shantel, baby, what's the plan. What are you about to do? What do you need us to do?" Naomi asked softly.

But Shantel just kept walking down the long corridor, laptop in hand until she reached the top of the stairs. She paused for a while then launched the laptop right at Yusef's head, hitting her target. Dwayne jumped up and Yusef held his head in agony. Before he could look up and cuss, he realized that his laptop was on the floor. You could see the lightbulb go off on his head. He knew exactly what was about to go down.

Dwayne was not sure what was going on, but he knew that it couldn't be good the way Shantel came flying down the stairs and began hurling slaps, kicks, and punches at Yusef. Jameela and Naomi stood on the side allowing her to go off until she was out of breath, her hair wild and all over the place. Though Dwayne did not know what was in that laptop, he knew his cousin, so he had an idea of what it was all about.

"I think I'm going to head on out, bro," Dwayne said looking around for his hat.

Shantel whipped her head around like the exorcist.

"Nah *bro*, stay right here because you know damn well what this is about. You come in here, you eat my food, you smile in my face, you are always teasing him about marrying me when you know damn well that this man is incapable of committing to anyone!"

Shantel reached for one of her statues that she brought back from abroad, but Jameela grabbed her wrist.

"No Shantel, no…uh uh… Not this one… *get another one!*"

"Jameela!" Naomi said standing between Shantel and Yusef.

"Move Naomi, move!" Shantel yelled.

"No Shantel. Please, Jameela take the statue from her!"

Jameela struggled a bit to pull the statute from Shantel's hand, but she was eventually successful.

"You dirty, nasty, filthy… I don't even know who you are!" Shantel yelled.

No one said anything for a while as Shantel hurled all kinds of insults at Yusef. She called him everything but a child of God. All Dwayne could do was shove his hands into his pockets.

"Did you ever think about what it would do to me if you gave me a disease? You are on camera, repeatedly, having unprotected sex with different women, oral sex, anal sex, all kinds of sex and then you come home to me." She choked on that last part. "*Why* am I not enough?"

It broke her friends' heart to hear Shantel say that about herself. She was more than enough, it was Yusef who lacked, not her.

"No baby don't do that. We are not going to let you take the blame for his behavior you hear me. Don't you dare do that to yourself." Jameela said. But it fell on deaf ears.

"Why am I not enough, Yusef? This is why you always want me to *wear this, do that, suck this, make this sound, make this face*, so that I can be like those fucking sluts that you are on video having sex with. Why am I not enough!"

"Baby, you are everything to me. I can explain." Yusef said.

"Explain what?" Jameela began laughing hysterically. "Do you hear this? I told you not to take his ass back the last time!"

"Now is not the time to make it about you Jameela, damn." Naomi said.

"But am I right though, did I not tell her once a cheat always a cheat?"

"Right because you are the product of preston, girl just chill out it's not about you! As a matter of fact, I think we should all leave." Naomi suggested.

"The way you were kissing her." Shantel said quietly, her voice cracking. She held her chest as if she were having a heart attack. Jameela and Naomi ushered her to a nearby chair where she sat and heaved up and down trying to catch her breath.

"Get her some water." Jameela instructed everyone.

Yusef just stood there not knowing what to do or say. The mood was somber over the next few minutes or so while everyone stood around waiting for Shantel to make the next move. Yusef didn't budge from the spot he was standing in. His face held so much embarrassment, remorse, and hurt. Naomi walked up to Yusef and asked him was it worth it. Yusef, realizing in that moment it certainly was not worth it, shook his head no but he had taken it too far. Shantel took a sip of water then abruptly got up, swept her hair out of her face, and walked up the stairs.

"Do not follow me!" she warned with a sinister tone to whoever had any intention of doing so.

Everyone watched her disappear at the top of the stairs, waiting for what would come next. Yusef took a step in her direction and right when he got to the bottom of the stairs an avalanche of shoe boxes came flying down the stairs.

"I wouldn't go up there if I were you." Jameela said as Shantel began screaming, "Get out! You nasty ass son of a bitch, get out!"

But Yusef didn't listen, he marched up the stairs two at a time and soon you could hear screaming, crying, yelling then it got quiet. After a few moments Jameela and Naomi ran up the stairs to make sure everything was okay. They found Yusef on top of Shantel on the bed with her arms pinned over her head. She was crying and grunting for him to let her go.

"What do you need from us." Jameela asked gently while entering the room.

"Just leave, I got this." Yusef demanded.

"I know you are not trying to tell us to fucking leave *Jason Luv*, get your ass out of here." Jameela said.

"Listen, I get it. I know you all want to be here for her but please can you both leave let me handle this as best as I can."

"Handle what? What are you going to do, try to convince her that it wasn't you on that tape, like R. Kelly tried to do? Boy, don't even waste your time we all saw everything!" Naomi said.

"Shantel, baby, what do you need us to do." Jameela asked while Naomi bickered back and forth with Yusef, but Shantel had no words. She just lay there with her eyes closed, tears falling in her ears.

"We are going to go downstairs and clean up that mess, okay? Then we are going to come check on you again and you let us know what you need or want us to do." Naomi said grabbing Jameela's hand and pulling her along before she popped off on Yusef.

"Everything good up there?" Dwayne asked as the women came down the stairs, but nobody answered him. After being ignored he decided it was best that he left. He stood up and stretched then grabbed his hat off the arm of the couch.

"For whatever it's worth I never condoned it. Honest to God. I hope your girl is going to be okay." He said and headed out the door.

Naomi stopped wiping the kitchen counter once Dwayne was out the door. "Can you believe this shit?"

"I sure as hell can. Remember when you were all, *oooh God took his time with him, forgive him, follow your heart*, I said a nigga like that will not ever be faithful not ever and you know Shantel is the settle down wife type. She's too soft for him, I knew he'd run all over her. Like I said, she should have just had a good time with him instead of trying to spend a lifetime with him. When he cheated the last time there was no way she should have taken him back!"

"Look, everybody deserves a second chance, and she gave him one, that's that." Naomi said as she swept the kitchen floors.

"I can sniff these dog ass men out a mile away you forgot who my daddy is? That's why I treat these men how I treat them. It's the reason him and Yusef get along so well. Product of Preston is never wrong when it comes to these men," she boasted.

"You really need to let whatever your father did go, that product of Preston shit isn't even cute at this point. You can't blame your daddy on your poor decisions or insecurities."

"Oh but you can? And where did that even come from?" Jameela shot back and picked up the few drinking glasses that were on the island and began loading them in the dishwasher.

"When have you ever heard me refer to my father when I make bad decisions or when a man is acting an ass? I don't ever even talk about that man at all." Naomi followed behind Jameela.

"You don't complain with your mouth about your father, it's your actions and how you move, you are a product of the lack of your father's love whether you see it or not."

"Oh so you think you can psychoanalyze me. I take full responsibility for all my actions. I don't boast about being the product of Kareem or wear the pain of my father's abandonment on my sleeve. I handle mines."

"You think you do." Was all Jameela said, hitting start on the dishwasher.

"What is it that I am doing that has you thinking I got some damn daddy issues? Clearly, you've been sitting back watching and judging so what's on your mind?"

Jameela walked past Naomi and began wiping down the counters with peppermint oils like she'd seen Shantel do.

"What's up Meela? What do you know about me that I don't know because last time I checked it wasn't a crime as a single woman to play the field!"

"Naomi, nobody is judging you, it's just that I know you, and I think that you are hurting deep in here." She said tapping Naomi's chest. "There's a thin line between playing the field and playing yourself." she said, turning her back, continuing to wipe the counters down.

"Playing myself how? What are you even talking about?" Naomi asked.

"Listen, if you like it I love it."

"I'm enjoying my life, what's the problem? When I was in a relationship and you were single I never made you feel no kind of way about how you decided to live your life, as long as you weren't being mistreated and in full control over your actions who was I to judge you just because that's not where I was in my life?"

Jameela didn't respond, she just continued straightening up. Pissed at Jameela for her unwarranted opinions, Naomi continued straightening up by lighting coconut incense and spraying the furniture down with lemon grass like Shantel would do.

"I'm going to check on her and see if she needs anything then I'm out." Naomi said curtly, walking ahead of Jameela who was unapologetic about her judgement of her friend.

She felt that Naomi needed to slow down, there were too many men in her cypher and one of these days she was going to get hurt, is what Jameela told her mother time and time again whenever Naomi would excitedly tell another story about another random man she met while running, walking the dogs, on her way to work, in the supermarket or wherever. Her mother would just tell her to support her friend and be there for her and to be mindful of her words because she knew that her daughter sometimes had no filter and shot straight from the hip and it could hurt.

Chapter 9

FRIENDS, HOW MANY OF US HAVE THEM?

The next morning, Naomi and Jameela met at Chocolat in Harlem where they got breakfast and coffee before heading over to Shantel's with Naomi still salty at Jameela for what she felt was disrespect yesterday. But Jameela showed up, dressed in a one-piece denim military suit, a cropped flight jacket, 5-inch Jeffery Campbell block heel lace up ankle boots and a signature Chanel waist bag. She had gotten over yesterday and was unbothered by Naomi's silent treatment. Both the women scanned the block noticing that Yusef's truck wasn't anywhere in sight which was a good sign but neither of them said anything to each other. Jameela pressed on the bell a few times but there wasn't an answer.

"There's no telling what time she went to sleep, poor baby probably can't get out of bed." Jameela said to herself. Naomi didn't say anything, she just headed down the stairs, retrieving the spare key from an old rusty mailbox. They entered the lower level then made their way up stairs through the beautiful plants, artwork, conversation pieces and statues from different countries. Once on the top level, they headed up the set of stairs off the kitchen that lead to Shantel's lair. A huge master bedroom and bathroom with a jacuzzi, double sink and shower, more plants, art, huge closets. Her place was truly like a museum. The women peeked inside and could hear Shantel in the bathroom taking a shower.

"Knock on the door and let her know that we are here so we don't scare her." Jameela suggested. Naomi knocked on the bathroom door and heard the water being turned off. The women backed away from the door anticipating Shantel's appearance but all they heard was the sink running and her humming while she brushed her teeth and did whatever she needed to do in the bathroom. Jameela and Naomi waited patiently until Shantel finally opened the door with gold eye patches under her eyes and a face mask, her hair up in a messy bun with a towel wrapped around her. She smiled softly at her friends.

"I could see you girls on the camera. I have one in my bathroom in case someone comes while I'm in the shower. So, what are you girls doing here so early in the morning?" She kissed them both on the cheek then headed to the edge of her bed where she sat, lotioning her body and humming as if everything was copasetic.

"We brought you coffee and breakfast." Jameela said cautiously.

"Okay, I'll be right down, you guys can go downstairs, put everything on keep warm please, you know I hate microwaves and cold food." She said almost shooing them away. She then continued tending to her body as if the women were not there. They headed downstairs and waited for Shantel who appeared about 30 minutes later with her mask off, dressed in a cute grey yoga pants set. She looked refreshed but her eyes told a story.

"What did you beautiful queens bring?" she rubbed her hands together.

"Food from Chocolat." Naomi said.

"Oooh, yes!" she said and began putting place mats on her dining room tables.

"Are we doing brunch, mimosas, bellinis?" she gushed.

"Sure." Naomi said.

"Bellini is my preference." Jameela said.

"Coming right up!" Shantel said heading to her bar and pulling out ingredients to make morning time drinks for her friends.

The women made small talk while eating their brunch, Shantel noticing some light tension between Naomi and Jameela. Happy to take the spotlight off her for now, knowing that's why they were there so early she questioned their energy.

"Everything is cool." Jameela said, cutting into her French toast. Shantel looked over at Naomi who gave her a look, a look that Shantel was familiar with.

"You bitches can give each other bat signals all you want as if I'm not aware. If you have anything that you need to say just say it." Jameela snapped.

"You are always right Jameela so what is the point in any of us saying anything." Naomi said.

Jameela dropped her fork.

"Tell me what I said that has your ass itching so badly." She folded her arms.

"Calm down just a little bit Meela, damn." Shantel said.

"It's not about what you said, my skin is thick. It's just that you have been coming off really rude, crass, insensitive lately and it's not cool."

"What are you being judged for, what did I miss?" Shantel sipped her bellini.

"Last night when we were cleaning up your place, I just checked her on how she's moving out here in these streets." Jameela said.

"First of all, ain't nobody checking me. I am a grown ass woman, so check that." Naomi shot back.

Jameela flipped her off. "My concern is that she has some unresolved daddy issues that has her out there fucking for her father's attention."

"Jameela!" Shantel said.

"You see, it's that kind of talk right there." Naomi fumed. "How far down in the gutter did you dig for that insult? Not far at all, because you live in the fucking gutter with your opinions."

"You understand exactly what I am trying to say Naomi. I really think that you are hurting maybe about Cory still, I don't know but you have really turned the heat up and it just has me a little concerned."

"So lead with that then Jameela and not with all of this back hand-ed concern, damn!" Naomi banged the table with her fist extra hard then turned to Shantel.

"We just love you sweetie, that is all." Shantel touched her leg soft-ly.

"Ugh, so what happened after we left because I don't have time for this shit." Naomi said pushing her plate aside, having lost her appetite.

No one spoke, it was just the sounds of Jameela cutting into her brunch and Shantel sipping her bellini. Naomi picked up her phone and began scrolling through Instagram until someone decided to speak.

"He just kept telling me that it's complicated and it's not what I think. He totally exhausted me to be honest. At some point I fell asleep to the sounds of him begging and trying to explain to me that what I saw wasn't what I saw. He left maybe an hour or so after you guys. After he left, I popped two Ibuprofen and went to sleep for a bit but couldn't really get into a good sleep so at 5 o'clock I was on my Peloton, did some weights, made a smoothie, meditated, washed, and deep conditioned my hair and then you lovely gals showed up."

"What made you want to watch those videos so intensely, that's what I want to know." Naomi had to ask. Shantel was watching those videos like they were re-runs of Martin.

"This woman has been around long before me, and I guess I called myself studying their dynamic which was an epic fail, because it will be some time before I can get the visuals out of my mind. It sounds silly I know but I was trying to find any similarities in how he deals with me versus her."

"Well did you come to a conclusion?" Jameela asked.

"Yes, I did." She sat with her thoughts for a beat before responding.

"He really enjoys having sex with *that* woman. I mean he loves having sex with me but with her it's like he's having the time of his life, he's free. With me it's for love, with her it's for enjoyment and pleasure if that makes sense and I don't know how I feel about that to be honest. Yusef needs more than I have to give sexually. I refuse to try and keep up with his sexual deviance which I am honestly concerned about. I mean you all saw the footage. I am not willing to crawl around and drink his cum out of a bowl. That is just *beyond savage*, have some self-respect. Why would a man that respects a woman ever allow her to stoop so low, for sexual satisfaction? That is ridiculous. It really makes me look at him differently and not in a nice way."

"You wouldn't be able to bend not even a little bit, even if he was your husband?" Jameela asked.

"Why would any man that respects his woman demean her in that way, *especially* my husband. There is a thin line between reality and fantasy. That is not sex, that's abuse. We can have amazing sex without the disrespect."

"Come on now, what's sex without a little slap and cuss." Jameela said.

Though Naomi wasn't speaking to her at the moment she had to laugh but now wasn't the time for jokes, yet she let out a light chuckle that caused Shantel to side eye her.

"I'm sorry Shantel." Naomi shook her head and fought for her life to stifle her laughter.

"Listen, I'm not making excuses for anyone, but I can't fathom having boring sex. I need a little disrespect." Jameela continued.

"But to the detriment of what, your self-respect? Come on Meela, you are telling me that you would do some of the things that those women were doing?"

Jameela shrugged, "I cannot say yay or nay but to each his own. Outside of golden showers and a feces fiesta, I would be down for anything if me and the person I was sleeping with had that kind of chemistry."

"Feces fiesta, I know that's not what I think it is. People actually do that?" Shantel said gagging.

"Yeah, I hear a lot of those IG models fly out to Dubai and be having these rich sheiks shittin on them and shit for some shingles." Naomi said.

The women burst out laughing for a few seconds.

"Lord have mercy, I guess I am never getting married or keeping a man because this new sex that they have out now is just beyond my comprehension!"

"There is definitely some new sex out now, it's a lot to take in, no pun intended." Naomi said.

"So give it to me girls. Product of Preston, what's your take on all of this, give it to me. Come on Naomi don't hold back, let me hear all of it!" Shantel pushed.

"I don't know what's the right or wrong thing to say to be honest." Naomi said.

"Just speak the truth. There's no right or wrong."

"Well, I mean I don't have an issue with what was happening on the videos because to me, sex is freedom right? I don't kink shame. If you are willing to lay down with someone and let them enter you, then why not push it to the limit if that's what the situation calls for and if you're compatible in that way. My only issue is that he cheated *on you* and hurt you if I'm being real, not with what was happening on the video." Naomi said.

"Okay, fair. You are entitled. Jameela, what about you, what's your take on this."

"I told you that nigga wasn't no good from day one. He cheated before and you took him back so I'm not surprised that it happened again, and it will continue to happen. It's just who he is, it's in his DNA. And to Mimi's point, I just hate that it happened to you."

"Okay so I get it. I'm a prude so I got cheated on, got it." She folded her arms and shook her head.

"Yusef is wrong for cheating on you but he's not wrong for having kinks and fantasies. And you do sometimes kink shame and now I understand why." Naomi said.

"Why is it that I kink shame, enlighten me." She sat up.

"Because your man is into things that you frown upon. Come on Shantel you mean to tell me there is not *anything* sexually unconventional that turns you on?"

Shantel thought for a second. "I don't like porn but to please my man when I do watch porn it's lesbian porn."

"Okay so what's the issue?" Jameela said.

"I prefer girl on girl because it's more sensual and softer. I do not like watching all that gang bang, double penetration, all of that is just too much. I'm sorry, it's barbaric to me and nothing about that turns me on."

"You're most certainly entitled to your preference Shantel but as I'm sitting here thinking about what I saw, all jokes aside, how do you expect to…. Never mind."

"No, say it Jameela, please, don't hold back." Shantel said confrontationally.

Jameela looked down and Naomi knew where she was going with this, because she was thinking the same thing.

"What? Why are the two of you looking at one another in code. Say what you have to say Jameela!"

"Well, I was going to say, how do you expect a man with that kind of sexual appetite to be faithful to you sexually if you are not willing to try anything that he likes to keep your love life healthy. I don't know what he has suggested and what you have turned down sexually, but I just feel like, maybe Yusef isn't satisfied and so he is able to compartmentalize his sexual deviance in that way, meaning he probably doesn't even see it as cheating as much as he sees it as getting his needs met."

No one said anything for a while after that. It was a hard conversation to have but they were exposed to her man's infidelity in ways that made everyone uncomfortable, so a conversation like this was inevitable.

"I think I speak for both of us when I say that we are in no way condoning him cheating and breaking your heart Shantel so please don't take it as you are to blame. I think what we are both feeling and saying though is that if Yusef doesn't get those desires and fantasies under control, he will never be faithful to anyone. So this isn't even about you as much as it's about Yusef and what he's into." Naomi said.

"All I'm saying is that you and she are totally different in every single way and Yusef struggles with that, it's the whole 80/20 rule thing." Jameela said.

"That bitch ain't zero percent of me." Shantel seethed.

"Agreed." Naomi chimed in "but let me ask you this, do you think maybe he has an issue like a sex addiction or something?"

"Now what would make you come up with that?" Jameela asked with a hint of sarcasm that Naomi let slide.

"It has certainly crossed my mind because who needs that much stimulation? But still there is no excuse for what he has done at the level he's done it. I am so turned off and just done with Yusef at this point. He can't be trusted. I have all these doctor's appointments scheduled to check myself for STD's. This man has lost his mind *and my respect.*"

"Did you tell Cheryl?" Naomi asked.

"Are you mad? I didn't even tell her about the first time he cheated. She has no idea that we broke up."

"You did take him back pretty quickly so she would be none the wiser." Jameela said.

"What is that supposed to mean?"

"Nothing Shantel, nothing. Right now, you are sensitive and ready to pounce. I am not here to hurt you friend."

"Right, you're just blunt." Shantel said.

Naomi turned her attention toward Shantel. "Per the usual, and what she doesn't understand is that one of these days she won't be able to apologize for it or hide behind being *the blunt friend.*" Naomi rolled her eyes.

"Here we go! Can we stick to the script?" Jameela said peeling off her high heeled boots.

"But let someone say anything to you about whatever the hell you got going on, you have a million reasons why it's not the same as what others are doing like your sin is somehow better or different than everyone else's."

"Well shit how long have you been holding that in?" Jameela laughed.

"I don't want to deal with you two and your drama, please park it for now." Shantel said.

Jameela maintained soft tones and reverted her energy back over to Shantel.

"I apologize if you feel as if I'm attacking you. I'm just trying to provide some clarity from my perspective. You didn't let him suffer long enough the last time he cheated so he didn't feel in danger of losing you is all that I'm saying. You let a man shenan once, he will shenan again."

"Girl." Naomi said stifling a laugh.

"I'm serious. He was back in your bed within 2 months or something like that. It just reminds me so much of when my dad use to cheat and I would never hear any smoke from Monica. They just moved on like nothing ever happened. It makes me sick to my stomach how she never made him pay for all the heartache and pain he caused her when we were growing up."

Shantel sat on that for a while and agreed with what Jameela was saying, but in her mind.

"Yusef didn't break any vows though." Naomi said.

"That makes it any better?" Jameela snapped.

"Well, there's no reconciliation here because I'm not willing to go that far to please any man. I am not licking his ass, I'm not calling him daddy *like ever*, I'm not doing the things that these women have done and I'm definitely not *ever* having a threesome. I really can't get with the women calling a man daddy, what is up with that?"

"Never say never." Jameela said.

"I agree." Naomi agreed.

Shantel looked at her friends up and down for a while.

"So let me guess, you both are out here calling men daddy, sharing your bed with multiple people at a time and just out there straight buck wilding in the place to be? I'm saying never! To hell with that never say never crap. I stand on my boundaries and my principles and when I say that I will never share my body with two men at once, or another woman or any of that freakiness I stand on that. I am into monogamy just me and my man and it needs to be enough for him and if it's not then he can go find someone else if it means that much to him."

"Or if the urge is that strong, he will step out like Yusef did." Jameela said.

"Jesus Meela you really don't have to say everything that you are thinking!" Naomi shook her head.

"No, it's fine. I need to hear it all! So you two are out there having threesomes and licking bootyholes and what not?" Shantel snarled.

"I have never had a threesome, but it's a fantasy of mine to be with two men, but that's just me. It may never happen. Everyone's sexual appetite is different. I personally want to try everything under the sun before I get married, *whenever that is*. I want to explore different races and experiences. I want to experience voyeurism, bondage, sex clubs, I want to explore it all because when I do get married, I'm not sharing my marital bed with no one." Naomi shrugged.

"Wait, you want to watch people have sex?" Jameela asked.

"I want to be watched. I think it's sexy." Naomi said.

Jameela nodded her head, "interesting, that never appealed to me but whatever floats your boat." She picked up her drink.

"Well call Yusef and the two of you can fuck one another into oblivion because it sounds like the two of you are on a freaky ass island by yourselves." Shantel spat.

"Oh wow." Jameela said.

"I know you're upset so I'm gonna let that one go over my head, out the front door, down the block and in the sewer with Jameela's opinions." Naomi said, her eyes wide open in disbelief. Shantel didn't apologize verbally but she put her head down and began shaking her head. She took deep breaths then joined the conversation again.

"Now how did I catch a stray?" Jameela asked looking around.

"He's free to go be with whomever he pleases and that's that."

"But see this is where you're wrong at Yusef aside, this is just generally speaking, what you do sexually is never about pleasing a man, it is about satisfying yourself. When I satisfy a man orally, I am not doing it for him, I am doing it for me. Everything that I do in bed with a man is for me. I never feel forced to do anything."

"Well see, this is where *you're wrong* at Jameela, I can't just give oral sex to any man in the name of being sexually liberating. So you're telling me that every man you have slept with gets oral sex from you because it's a part of sex to you? I'm dumbfounded totally. It took me seven months to go down on Yusef."

"Seven months!" Both Naomi and Jameela yelled out.

"Yes! You have to mean something to me in order for me to go down on you. We have to be in a committed relationship before I could even sleep with you let alone go down on you and even then, there is no guarantee that I am going to do that! So that is where we differ, sex is just sex to you, sex is more meaningful to me. This is my sacred body, this is mine." She said running her hands across her body for emphasis.

"I can't just give that away and let anybody have their way with me, I'm sorry. I can count on one hand with fingers left over how many men have been able to put their dick in my mouth. All that freak shit is overrated. Folks need to stay off the internet and stop watching porn and truly get in tune with real life. In real life you have grown women that are busy chasing careers, in school, working, raising children and when they come home at night, they do not have the energy to be the freak of the weak for their man. It's not reality, I don't care what you two have to say."

"I agree to an extent, but you have to make time to please your man." Naomi said.

"Agreed, you think big Mama back in the day wasn't lifting that big polyester nightgown up at night and letting Earl back shot her into oblivion? She didn't push out 15 kids from missionary. Earl was turning Big Ma the fuck out and he was paying all the bills because Big Ma was swallowing dick on the regular!" Jameela laughed.

"Hell even India Arie probably let a nigga rub Shea butter on that booty hole and take her to pound town." Naomi said.

"You two are so damn ridiculous, it's not even funny." Shantel tried not to laugh. "But Big Mama always had to deal with that pain in her chest every time she looked into the eyes of a child that shared similar facial features of her husband. Big Mama didn't have it easy."

"Oof, that's real." Jameela agreed.

"Be it Yusef or some other man, you have to loosen up Shantel. Have your standards but break the rules a little bit for your man, have some fun! There is nothing wrong with being a little open." Naomi suggested.

"Being open is subjective. My open, your open and some other women's definition of open is different. Me being open in my relationship sexually does not mean that I am going to allow any man to disrespect me all for the sake of love and keeping him satisfied. And why are you both making me feel as if it is my fault that he cheated on me? He put my health at risk!"

"We are just trying to open your mind up a bit Shantel." Jameela insisted.

"I do not need my mind opened Jameela, I am heartbroken! I just saw the man that I love having a fuck fest with multiple women on multiple occasions and all you two can tell me is suck it up butter cup your man is a freak, and you need to get with the program! This woman told me that he would never ever leave her alone because she provides a service for him that I cannot. He was clearly telling this woman that I couldn't satisfy him. Do you have any idea how hurtful that is? I have pride, I have feelings you know!" her voice cracking.

"I had no idea she said that to you Shantel I'm so sorry." Jameela said.

"Yes, and so when I took him back, we talked and I asked him what he needs from me, what does he want that I didn't give him that made him step out on me and he said he didn't step out because I didn't satisfy him, but he did suggest some things that would make our sex life better. But he clearly left out a lot of stuff that he was into because he knew I'd feel some kind of way about his kinky side. I did take his sexual appetite into consideration, so I opened myself to porn. I even swallowed a few times and I hated it but he loved it so much." She frowned.

"Atta girl!" Jameela said.

Naomi laughed and Shantel tried her best to ignore the two women's ignorance.

"I started talking dirty during sex. It was awkward at first, but he made me comfortable. He would talk me through my orgasms which I found to be very sexy. So yes, it may be amateur to him, but it is a big deal to me, I tried. But the way he enjoys himself with that one particular woman really bothers me a lot. He was in his element when he was kissing her, so passionately." She bit her lip hard and put her head down.

"We don't have to talk about this anymore Shantel." Naomi spoke softly.

"The way that he was looking into her eyes, making love to her mouth, he has never, ever done that with me. What they have is something that I won't even try to compete with."

"What they have is filthy nasty sex and that shit will fade after a while. Just like us, men want love too so don't ever get it confused!" Naomi said.

"They want love, and they want you to be their porn star wrapped in one and I just don't have it in me. I'm sorry."

"May I dare ask what has made you this way like, so squeamish when it comes to thinking outside of the box when it comes to sex?" Naomi asked.

"Nothing has made me this way, this is who I am. You all are the damn freaks, not me! All you ladies are offering me is sex tips to keep my cheating ass man. It says a lot about the two of you and how you handle relationships." Shantel said and got up from the table.

She walked into the kitchen and grabbed a bottle of water. She didn't come back to the table with the girls but instead stood up guzzling her water and staring out in a daze.

"We just don't know what else to go on after what we saw because outside of that you both seemed so solid and happy." Naomi replied.

Shantel nodded her understanding. "Yeah, I guess you are right. And I am sorry Naomi, about that comment I made, I know you would never."

"It's okay." Naomi said touching her hand as she came and sat back down.

"Call me crazy but I would not have been too upset if it was a different woman. But it is the same woman that was there before me and like she said, she will be there after me, she can have him."

"But it's not love Shantel, that is lust and fantasies. That ain't about nothing!" Naomi said.

"By Monday I have a job to go to, tenants to interview for the apartment upstairs in my other brownstone, other properties to look at, meetings to conduct, power points to compile, life goes on."

"This is a lot." Jameela said.

"And to think, I wanted to marry this man." She scoffed and finally showed some emotion. Her eyes watered a bit. "I know my mother is going to be so disappointed." She shook her head.

"So, you don't ever see yourself getting back with him" Naomi cautiously asked.

Shantel whipped her head around and looked at her like she was crazy.

"Would you get back with your man if you were me? Would you get back with Cory?"

"Well no he's married so that doesn't count."

"Yeah, but Naomi, please.... you will cut a man off if he sneezes two times in a row. You run through these men more than Mary J. Blige has boots."

"Now that's a lot of damn boots." Shantel said.

"First of all kiss my ass because I'm not in a relationship so I can sleep with whomever I want. I can cut em off and sew them back together again!" Naomi said getting angry that her sex life was always brought into question.

"Just throw a number out. What do you think your body count is?" Jameela inquired.

"Don't answer her Mimi, Jameela stop." Shantel warned.

"A girl is just curious, no shade." Jameela mumbled while fixing herself another bellini.

Naomi walked into the living room to get away from Jameela's energy for a while as she and Shantel continued with light conversation.

"I know that a lot of times women don't forgive their man because we are too afraid of what our friends and family may think so, please don't do that for us. It is your life, and you must make decisions that are best for you." Jameela said as Naomi came walking back to the table.

"Yeah, and you will be the first one calling her a stupid bitch for taking him back, man Jameela you are a trip!" Naomi laughed. "It is worth finding out if he has suppressed sexual traumas, I'm just saying. Maybe that's why he kept saying to you that it's not like that. Maybe there is something inside of him that he needs to let out."

"Is he behaving in a way similar to someone you might know or something?" Jameela sipped her mimosa. Naomi closed her eyes tightly out of frustration. She breathed in deeply before responding to Jameela.

"I understand that no man has ever claimed you or loved you since you came out of Preston's nut sack and it might be difficult to absorb, but your business and degrees got you covered, right?" Naomi said and rolled her eyes. She turned her attention back to Shantel.

"That was a good one, you came up with that all by yourself? Not bad for someone with no education."

Naomi whipped her head around and started to verbally attack Jameela, but Shantel stopped them.

"This is not cool you guys. This thing that the two of you have going on has to stop, the nastiness, the cattiness the mean girl shit, this is not cool at all."

"Look, forget all of this, okay? Forget Yusef and his wayward dick and that mask wearing clap having Jezebel he been laid up with, okay? All of that aside, someone is hurting, someone is heartbroken. I know what it's like to have dreams of settling down with a man and then the rug gets pulled up from under your ass because he's not who he said he was. It hurts like hell and friend I am so sorry that you're experiencing this Shantel, I truly am. You are the most beautiful inside and out, deserving of real love woman that I know, and I pray that your heart heals from this. Whatever you need from me I'm here for you just like you've been there for me." Naomi got up and warmly hugged her friend.

"This...this was all I needed from my girls." Shantel said squeezing Naomi.

"Not clap having Jezebel." Jameela echoed.

Naomi continued holding on to Shantel, asking her how her soul, heart and mind was. Shantel gently pushed away from Naomi to answer.

"Too soon to say you know. It hasn't even been 24 hours. It's a lot to unpack."

"You should have never taken his ass back the first time." Jameela said.

"I keep telling you Jameela, today them and tomorrow you." Naomi said.

"And I keep telling you Naomi that I don't know what that cryptic shit means, so I don't care. The bottom line is, he got dirty dick and Shantel deserves better. Ain't no way around it!"

Realizing that Jameela wasn't going to show compassion and had some kind of gripe with Naomi, Shantel decided to wrap up the conversation about her personal life.

"I don't want to spend the entire day talking about this please if you ladies don't mind. It happened, it's gone now, we must move forward, and I'll figure it out along the way. I will heal, I will be okay, this will all be behind me soon. But for now, you all are here, breakfast was delicious, the bellinis are flowing. Your company is all I need even if I do not say a word, your presence is enough. I am happy that the both of you are here with me right now, because I do need it."

She reached across the table and touched both their hands.

"I admire your strength." Jameela said.

"Please don't. There's nothing admirable about fighting to keep your head above water while someone is trying to drown you."

With that, Shantel stood up and headed toward the living room with her flute in her hand.

"Wanna watch our favorite movie?"

"Of course." Naomi and Jameela both perked up.

She cleaned off her dining room table, lit her favorite coconut incense and instructed Jameela and Naomi to head to her big comfy couch where they watched Set It Off and cried when Latifah's character died for what had to be the 100th time. They always said that Shantel would be Stoney, Jameela would be Cleo, and Naomi would be Frankie. *None of us would ever be Tisean. In the words of Jameela, that bitch is just too damn scary for me.*

CHAPTER 10
JUST LIKE DADDY

The Whites had one of the biggest homes with the best exterior on the block. It was a predominately white neighborhood, so Pops stood out like a sore thumb being the only black father and husband. Jameela's mother Monica was such a beautiful, sweet woman. She looked like Judge Lynn Toler, short haircut, and all. She took temp jobs here and there, but her main job was to take care of her children, Jameela and Jamel and her husband Preston aka Pops. She would cook these magnificent Sunday dinners and invite Naomi over when she was visiting during any school break which is how Jameela and Naomi became friends in elementary school.

Pops did extremely well for himself, owning three body shops that afforded him the opportunity to put his kids through college with no financial aid and allowing Ms. Monica the opportunity to be a stay-at-home wife, which she took pride in. Ms. Monica was always dressed like she had somewhere to be but she in fact was just making sure that when her husband came home, she was always presentable, hair done, a nice outfit on, some jewelry, smelling good and something was always on the stove or in the oven. But sadly enough, it wasn't enough to keep Pops faithful.

Naomi was spending the weekend at Jameela's house while her aunt Zola was away. The two pre-teens played in the yard, jumping rope, playing cards, and talking about the boys in school when they decided to go inside because of a car that kept circling the block slowly. They couldn't see inside the car, but it was enough for them to go in the house out of fear of ending up on the back of a milk carton like so many other children who had reportedly gotten snatched right from their doorstep according to the news. They decided to go in Jameela's over the top girly decorated room, light pink pillows, teddy bears, comforters, and bean bags that smelled like cotton candy. The girls had a friendly competition about who's room could be prettier. They both had canopy beds, pretty collectibles all around their rooms, posters of their favorite rapper or singer, vanity sets and everything a young teenage girl could want. For a while Naomi was winning but according to Jamel, the unofficial referee, she lost her first place slot when Jameela's parents somehow found a pink TV, trumping Naomi's pink stereo. While up in the room watching videos, they heard a car pull up in the driveway. It was that same black Cadillac that they saw circling the block. A woman exited the car and looked the house up and down while making her way to the front door. Jameela and Naomi went running down the stairs as Ms. Monica went to open the door.

"Hello?" Jameela's mother asked opening the door with just a screen door separating her and the guest.

The woman, darkskin, wavy hair up in a bun, lots of baby hair, red lipstick, a cute denim outfit on and an arm full of gold bangles stood on the other side of the partially cracked door. She looked younger than Ms. Monica but she was not too young. She was very pretty but she seemed terribly upset.

"Does Preston live here?" the woman asked trying to contain her attitude.

"Who wants to know."

Ms. Monica's stance changed a bit. Her voice got a bit deeper, and she stood up a bit straighter.

"Are *you* his wife?" the woman looked Ms. Monica up and down from head to toe in what seemed like slow motion.

Ms. Monica stood there dressed in an emerald, green, turquoise and yellow sun dress, her short chocolate brown pixie haircut always on point. She was a put together elegant woman, the way she spoke and carried herself, gracefully no matter what. But by the energy coming through the front door it seemed as if today would be the day that Ms. Monica would be anything but ladylike. There was no doubt that this woman was sizing Ms. Monica up but she was no match for the *Mrs.*

"I'm the woman of the house, yes, what do you want with my husband?"

Ms. Monica now opened the door a bit wider and stepped a little bit closer to the woman with nothing but a screen door between them. Jameela and Naomi waited anxiously on the staircase unaware of what was about to go down. Jameela left Naomi on the steps and ran down to the man cave where her father was.

"Daddy, some woman is at the door asking for you." An out of breath 12-year-old Jameela said. Pops did not bat an eye. He stood up slowly, tall, strong, and headed upstairs behind Jameela. When they emerged from the basement, Ms. Monica was still at the front door with Naomi a few feet behind her, listening as the woman told her that she was having an affair with Pops for two years. Naomi whispered the message to Jameela when she came upstairs as Pops walked to the front door, gently standing in front of Ms. Monica now blocking the woman's view of his wife.

"May I help you?" he asked, annoyed.

The woman's eyes welled up with tears at the sight of Pops who was dressed in his infamous house wear, Adidas track pants, house slippers and a muscle T-shirt that always had a picture of either a black activist or famous black boxer on the front. This shirt had a picture of Sugar Ray Leonard on it.

"I told you that I would do this. You can't keep playing with my heart! She knows everything now!" the woman said whispering through clenched teeth.

Pops opened the screen door to let her in to everyone's surprise.

"Okay, you're here now so come on in."

Ms. Monica folded her arms while Jameela looked at her mother to protest or do something, *anything*. But this woman stepped inside of her parents' home and that was the moment that Jameela's remarkably close relationship with her mother changed and her outlook on love was tainted.

"Everybody, this is Shelly." Pops said. Shelly stood there awkwardly holding her car keys.

"So... what can I do for you?" Pops said walking deeper into the house.

"I am tired of you playing games with me and hiding me." Shelly whimpered. Pops pointed at Jameela and Naomi.

"These are my daughters."

Though Naomi knew that Jameela's entire family loved her like she was one of them, Pops had no idea how in that moment he healed a small part of her that Naomi thought could never be healed. No one had ever called her their daughter and she was overwhelmed by a sense of belonging in that moment and held on to his words for a long time, so much so that unbeknownst to her, it caused a bit of friction between herself and Jameela. Jameela always felt as if Pops took more of liking to Naomi than to her. Pops walked out of the foyer and into a small room that led to the living room.

"This is my son." He said and pointed to a picture of Jamel who was away for the weekend at a friend's house. The woman followed behind Pops into the living room with no idea what he was up to. But he spoke sternly to the woman who was looking up at him with schoolgirl crush eyes.

"This is where *my family* and I gather after a nice meal that my wife makes for us. My wife is an excellent cook." He said doing a "chef's kiss" gesture for emphasis.

"Upstairs are my children's bedrooms and bathrooms that I renovated with my bare hands. Downstairs is my man cave where I go to relax after working hard all week to provide for *my wife and children*. Sometimes they're all in here making noise, talking, laughing, gossiping, playing video games, running up and down stairs, pots banging at the same time. I sit in the big chair aggravated as hell with all the noise but thanking God for it because all that noise simply means that I have family, I have love around me, and I don't know what I'd do without it." He staired Shelly down.

Pops then walked near the kitchen; he summonsed the woman to look. Begrudgingly she headed toward him.

"What is all this? I didn't come here for a tour of your house! You said you were leaving her! You said that you were divorcing her and that you weren't going to wait until the kids were out the house, that you were ready to leave now to be with me because you loved me, and I told you that I would come here and tell your wife about us if you didn't stop playing with me!"

Pops ignored her and began talking about his kitchen.

"Look at that Hibachi style stove. I spent so much money to have this kitchen remodeled as a 10-year anniversary gift for my wife. Have you ever seen a stove like that in somebody's house?"

He then turned to Jameela and asked her how old she was.

"Twelve." Jameela said with uncertainty in her voice.

"I've been married for fourteen years. So the point of me showing you all of this is so that you can get a clear picture of what I stand to lose, what is at stake here. I need you to read my lips Shelly, there is no way on God's fucking earth that you could have actually believed that I would leave all of this that we built together for you or for anyone." He grimaced.

Shelly took a deep sharp breath in and held it as Pops, who had to be about 6ft 3, close to 300 pounds, mainly muscle towered over everyone while talking down to Shelly. He pointed his finger very close to her face.

"You think I'm going to leave my home to live in a tiny ass apartment with you and your two kids? You want to come in here and tell my wife I've been having an affair and then what, she put me out, ask for a divorce and you take her place?"

"Preston that's enough." Ms. Monica stepped in, but Preston firmly moved her way from him with one sturdy swipe. He was beyond mad at this point and was coming for blood.

"You thought I'd leave my family and give you the life that I give my wife and kids?" he laughed making a mockery out of Shelly.

"Preston, enough, you proved your point. Miss.... whatever your name is, you can go now, you did what you came to do." Ms. Monica said, walking toward the door to let Shelly out, but Shelly stood firm staring up at Preston with daggers in her eyes.

"Let me put you up on game, a man will never give another woman what he gives his wife. So you take that back to the chicken coup and tell them that your plan failed."

Shelly was in shambles standing in the middle of the foyer. She was fidgeting with her car keys, appearing to not know what to do with herself. She was in a state of shock, her face held so much pain and angst. She struggled to get her words out as Pops looked at her like she was old gum on the bottom of his work boots.

"Why are you talking to me like this? You weren't disrespecting me last week when you were in my bed," she said in a broken voice.

"You come to my house with this mess, and you think I'm going to have mercy on you? This is my fucking family!"

Pops punched the wall, and everyone jumped out of fear. No one ever saw him angry like this. He's been heard raising his voice, being mad, stressed, and downright ornery from time to time sure but violent, never.

"You crossed the line coming here. There's the door!"

"Fuck you Preston, fuck you! Don't ever call me again! Lose my number, forget you ever met me! And you're a damn fool of a woman." She yelled at Monica as she headed to the front door.

"Bye bitch!" Jameela spat out since her mother clearly could not find any words.

Shelly turned around briefly as if she was going to address Jameela but quickly came to her senses. Ms. Monica watched the debacle as Shelly hurled insults at Pops bringing some of the neighbors out. She stood in the yard screaming *"This motherfucka is a lying, two timing adulterer! He cheats on his wife, he's a liar! I hate you Preston I fucking hate you! Two years he's been seeing me behind his wife's back, two whole years! Her life is not as perfect as she pretends it to be, she's a damn fool and her life is a façade, she's a fraud They damn sure aint the fucking Huxtables!"* She screamed like a maniac as everyone watched her angrily pull out of the driveway and screech down the street still screaming obscenities. This incident would be the talk of the neighborhood for years to come embarrassing Jameela in a way that affected her greatly as she had to endure the whispers and snide remarks from the neighborhood kids and sometimes even their parents. Naomi closed the door, and everyone remained standing in the foyer.

"I'm sorry baby." Was all Pops said to his wife who shook her head and walked off. He then turned to Jameela and Naomi, but Jameela had quickly run up the stairs not giving him a chance to say anything to her. Pops made a gesture with his head suggesting that Naomi run along after her friend. Once Naomi closed Jameela's bedroom door behind her, World War III broke out. Her parents were arguing loudly.

"Let's go to your house." She suggested while grabbing her house keys off the dresser.

Naomi and Jameela headed out the door while her parents argued in the kitchen not realizing that she left. Once inside Naomi's aunts house, she offered Jameela a cup of juice and asked was she okay.

"I don't know why my mother just lets him do this to her. He's always preaching about how a man is supposed to treat a woman but look how he treats my mother, and she never does anything about it." She said.

"I could never, ever be a woman like my mother and I'll never settle down, like ever. And I'm going to make sure that I always have my own stuff so that I don't have to deal with any man's stuff. She lets him get away with anything because she doesn't have a job." She shook her head.

And as Jameela got older and entered the dating world, she would go on to eat and spit out every single man she met until she came across "*Tyrone*" who came along and put that "Product of Preston" mess to rest.

HAPPILY EVER AFTER

*I*t was a warm muggy August day, and the skies were threatening rain as Naomi peered outside of the window of the bridal suite while Shantel's mother fussed at her dress and makeup, making sure that her daughter's day did not have one discrepancy. Cheryl had a mean classist demeanor, the total opposite of Shantel. She had no idea the hell that Yusef had put her only child through. She thought that he was the crème de la crème. Yusef charmed Cheryl and because of his education and career, Cheryl thought he could do no wrong. Kenny, however, was not impressed, and you could tell by how he spoke to Yusef that he did not care for him too much. His words to Yusef were always short, to the point, unwelcoming and giving very much, I'm just talking to you because you are marrying my daughter.

A few months after the "freaky folder" debacle, Yusef contacted Naomi, pleading with her to assist him in getting Shantel back. Once he shared a bit of his story with her, she brought a wildly skeptic Jameela into the plan. Naomi had assumed right about Yusef possibly having some kind of trauma, so she coerced Shantel into giving him the time of day to at least explain himself without giving her an inkling of what Yusef shared with her. She knew that her friend missed her man, she just buried herself in work so that she wouldn't have to think about him and would present herself as healed and over it. Shantel deserved some clarity and closure if nothing else so she agreed to let Yusef stop by so that he could say what he need-ed to say. But she couldn't imagine him saying anything to her that would change her mind and wanting to rekindle anything with him, missing him or not.

Yusef arrived at Shantel's home around seven in the evening on a Saturday night, dressed in a black Polo sweatsuit and black Yeezy's. He needed a shave and looked like he had not been sleeping well. Shantel let him in and instructed him to have a seat in the living room where she sat on the other sofa, away from him so that she could get a clearer view of him while he talked. She was not sure what this conversation would do for her as her heart started to heal over the months, and she was ready to close this chapter of her life even though she did yearn for him from time to time. Shantel had learned early on how to compartmentalize once she lost her father, being forced into adoption and changing her last name. She just nev-er saw the sense in dwelling over anything that you had no control over.

"How have you been." Yusef stated, looking over at Shantel who he missed so much. She was *home* to him, she looked so warm and approachable as she curled up on the couch with a tall glass of water with lemon, donning a pretty Mumu that she got from one of her trips abroad, her hair in two long cornrows, her skin glowing. She didn't look like she missed him at all, and it was easy for her to feel that way until she saw him. She tried her best to keep her emotions under control.

"I'm okay, what about you, how's your soul, your heart, your mind, how have you been getting on." she asked.

"I have so much that I want to share with you, and I just want to say that I miss you and I am in no way looking for an excuse or a sob story. But I have some things that I need to tell you. I owe you that, I owe it to myself. I realized not just when I cheated on you but long before all of this, that I had some issues that I needed to sort out. I guess there's no better time than the present so, I just want to share a part of my life with you that I should have shared when we first made a commitment to be together."

"Would you like some water or anything before you start." Shantel asked.

"Nah, I'm good. I won't be before you long."

"Okay, well whenever you're ready." Shantel said and sipped her water.

Yusef moved around uncomfortably before he began to speak. He was rubbing his hands together and shaking his head.

"Take your time." Shantel offered noticing how the normally confident Yusef who spoke in front of people for a living was nervous. He breathed in then looked directly into Shantel's eyes.

"So when I was about 8 years old, I had a babysitter, she was the daughter of my mother's best friend. She was 16 years old, and she use to walk me home from school and keep an eye on me when our mothers would go out and run the streets, during which time she use to have me watch porn." He paused. Shantel adjusted herself in her seat.

"My moms would have these card games, fish fries and shit, house full of people everywhere drinking, loud, playing music and me and her would be in my room playing video games, well that's what they thought. But she would have me watching porn and then she began to touch me inappropriately. I never said anything to my mother because Gail was always unhinged. She was one of those card party throwing, cussing ass, E&J drinking mothers that kept bottles of liquor out on the table. You never met my mother and not because of what I told you. I lied, she doesn't live far way on the West Coast. She's right here in Queens." He said.

She could see the wetness in Yusef's eyes, his hands trembled slightly. She didn't ask him again but instead got up and poured some bourbon that he had left in her bar months ago. She handed him the sifter and he sipped thirstily.

"Thank you."

"Yeah, sure, so go on." Shantel encouraged him.

"Every Friday and Saturday there was a concert hall amount of people in the house. My mother was always on some man's lap." He shook his head.

"What about your dad, were you telling the truth about him being dead?"

"Dead to me. I never cared to see him. I met him one time when I was five or something like that. He came and brought me some little green army men toys on Christmas. I heard him and my mom's having sex that night then I never saw him again. He lives in Delaware, married to some white woman, doing pretty well for himself according to Dwayne and my uncles. But um, yeah so when I was ten or somewhere around there, she started performing oral on me."

Shantel put her glass of water down and covered her mouth with both hands.

"I was always *big* for my age as my mother would say. So the older women that Gail would hang around would always make passes at me, letting me know that as soon as I turned 18, they were coming to get me and my mother would never check them, she would be in on the joke, laughing, telling the women how *he was built just like his father* and that I was going to be giving these young girls hell. I was 11 years old when I lost my virginity to the babysitter... *and* her friend."

He wiped tears away from his face aggressively as if Shantel couldn't see that he was breaking down. She wanted to hold him, but she wanted him to get his story out without any interruptions.

"Imagine having a threesome at 11 years old." He shook his head and covered his face for a while. Shantel nervously twirled the ends of her braids not sure if the story could get any more devastating. Yusef began telling his story again, but he was still slightly covering his face.

"So they had some gathering at my house when the girl was leaving for college. I stayed in the room, and I could hear my mother calling me to come out and say bye to her, but I wouldn't. They thought that I was sad because she was leaving but I didn't want to see her. She came in the room to say bye to me and when she hugged me, she pressed me against her breast and put her tongue in my mouth when they weren't looking. Once she was gone, I told my mother everything the next day."

He guzzled the rest of the bourbon placing the glass on the table and Shantel decided it best not to give him anymore.

"The next day Gail was in the kitchen, cleaning up and what not so I decided that this would be a good time to tell her what was going on."

"I know she had to be besides herself!"

"Actually, no. She was proud that her son wasn't gay and that I had sex. She lectured me about STD's and gave me condoms."

Shantel placed her glass on the table and sat at the edge of the sofa mortified at what she was hearing.

"She said it would be best if we kept it between us. She was always trying to push some daughter of a friend on me. It was hell."

Shantel continued listening to the horror stories that Yusef had to endure as a child and her heart hurt for him. "So, you never valued sex." She said.

"Not until I met you." He responded but didn't look at her.

Shantel got up and sat next to Yusef, "I am so sorry."

He paused his story for a while, gathering himself so that he could continue. He began to speak again as Shantel rubbed his back.

Yusef continued to emotionally share the sexual abuse that he encountered but worse off how it was ignored by his own mother. He also shared with her that when he was in Junior High, a group of girls attacked him at first in a playful manner because he was always handsome and tall, so the girls always had crushes on him, always wanting to play fight with him. This time a group of young girls began pulling him into a corner in the gym where they touched all over him, one girl getting on her knees and giving him head while the other girls served as lookouts. A few of the girls took turns putting their mouth on him and groping him then ran out of the gym leaving Yusef exposed for incoming students to see. He was absolutely humiliated.

"This is not an excuse, I swear Shantel, but I never thought of myself as anything more than a sexual object to women, until I met you. It was something that I suppressed but I knew that it was something that I needed to address. I would have never addressed it had I not met you and even if we don't work out and you don't take me back, at least I know now that I have a problem and I am going to get the help that I need so that I don't hurt another woman." He said.

Shantel pulled Yusef to her lap where he stretched out across her couch. She could feel his tears on her lap.

"Let it out big baby, let it all out." She said rocking him.

Her heart was breaking for him as she thought back to how passionately he spoke about the objectification of young boys the first time he cheated on her, and it all made sense.

"I never meant to hurt you. I know I need help, I know I do." He went on to plead and Shantel sympathized with him. She didn't take him back immediately, but she was there for him, helped him find the right therapist and encouraged him to make his mental health a priority and he did.

Once Shantel shared everything with Naomi and Jameela, her decision to take him back if he completed therapy was supported by Naomi, Jameela just promised to *ride with it.* Yusef went to therapy while also practicing abstinence while maintaining a friendship and support from Shantel. Coming up on a year of therapy, his therapist suggested that he bring Shantel in if this was in fact the woman that he wanted to marry, so that she can be provided with a clear, professional understanding of what Yusef had experienced, how it affected him emotionally and mentally, how he viewed himself and women and the progress that he made.

During this time, Shantel and Yusef's bond was solidified, they became intertwined in one another, mentally, spiritually, and emotionally. About a year and a half into therapy, Shantel and Yusef resumed their relationship, and he would begin to spend nights, where they would pray before going to bed every night, but they didn't resume a sexual relationship until one morning, as soon as she woke up and opened her eyes, he was holding a ring. Shantel didn't say yes but instead climbed on top of Yusef where they made love well into the afternoon.

Shantel and Yusef got married in an exquisite ceremony in the Hamptons on her parent's beach front property with Naomi as her maid of honor and Jameela and her cousin Nicki as her bridesmaids. It was a beautiful, elegant evening, dancing the night away under a tent with what seemed like thousands of white lilies and orchids everywhere. Champagne was plenty and the food was divine. Shantel looked like an angel in her wedding dress, a sleek classy number from black owned Pantora Bridal, against her mother's wishes who preferred her daughter in Vivian Westwood. All and all Shantel looked like royalty as she walked down the aisle alone to the tunes of Jill Scott, "He Loves Me". Her mother was livid when Shantel protested walking down the aisle with Kenny however, she agreed to dance with her stepfather to Be Ever Wonderful by Earth Wind and Fire. Everyone looked on in awe as the newlyweds shared their first dance as husband and wife to Luther Vandross, So Amazing. Yusef's mother sat in the front row emotionless with her date and did not fraternize much with anyone.

After therapy, Yusef was encouraged to reach out to his mother who he was estranged from for many years other than the occasional conversations for birthdays, holidays, and a few in between calls. She still resided at that home in South Side Jamaica Queens where he had no desire to visit but he would send his mother money to help her with the bills from time to time even though she received a good pension after retiring from the city as a 911 operator. Gail didn't know her son to be in a serious relationship let alone getting married and into such an upper-class family. She stood out among everyone with a not so exquisite dress, drawing judgement of course from Cheryl who was draped from head to toe in Saint Laurent. Yusef's mother did not seem to put much effort into her look, her hair in a bun that could have been brushed up a bit neater, a blue lace frock was ill fitting, and she wore a pair of shoes that were in decent shape but not wedding appropriate, more suited for the office, her nails... undone. Her date, a man that looked like he may have been good looking back in the day accompanied her in an ill fitted beige suit, a scruffy beard, and the eyes of an alcoholic.

When it came time for mother and son to dance, Yusef assisted his mother out of her seat and danced with her to A Song for Mama by Boys II Men. Gail appeared stiff as her son pulled her into him closely, at one-point tears fell from his eyes, causing her to wipe his tears. That gentle sign of showing emotion toward him broke Yusef down. Yusef hugged his mother long after the song had ended. The two stood in the middle of the dance floor, holding one another.

"I love you son." Gail said holding her son's face in between her hands that were in desperate need of a manicure. Yusef walked her to her seat before making his way to his wife. His mother sat in her seat unable to compose herself for some time after the dance, so she excused herself and disappeared for most of the evening.

"Look at you, looking all lost in love. I'm so happy for our girl but couldn't be me. I ain't never getting married especially to a serial cheater? Shantel crazier than a soup sandwich." Jameela said as she noticed the loving gaze in Naomi's eyes.

"Just once in your life, try to not be a pessimist. We're at a wedding, find the joy," Naomi said irritable.

"You can call me a pessimist all you want, but I'm just a realist. Now that they're married, Shantel has all this money, brownstones worth millions and shit. I hope she made him sign a prenup." Jameela said watching her newly married friend slow dance with her husband. Naomi let Jameela's words linger, wondering if Shantel did in fact make Yusef sign a prenup, but she wasn't about to have this conversation with Jameela. She would ask Naomi herself.

"I'm sure her parents made sure of that. But they won't need one, they're going to make it; I truly believe that." Naomi offered.

But Jameela just scoffed as the two of them sat side by side like the devil and angel on Shantel's shoulder.

Chapter 12

NASTY BOYS

The drive home from Bobby Vans was quiet yet aggressive and quick as Jameela sped through the streets, in her fiancée's Lamborghini, enraged at her friends who were judging her relationship. She was so pissed that they raised valid points and held a mirror up to her face, a face that she was not ready to see because she wanted what she wanted, and she was not trying to hear about any red flags. She was grown and would manage whatever came her way.

He can't be worse than what Yusef or Cory has done, she surmised.

Tyrone was everything that she had envisioned that the man she would decide to settle down with would encompass. He was financially stable, he met her height requirements, he was sexually satisfying and a goal getter, he was strikingly handsome, exceeding her expectations in that department. She wanted someone as business oriented as herself and he checked all the boxes. And though in her gut she felt that something was off, she just needed some time to see things through, when Naomi and Shantel brought up obvious signs of something not being right, she didn't appreciate it. Jameela pulled into the underground parking lot of her swanky high-rise building, jumped out of her man's Lamborghini, and headed upstairs to her deluxe apartment in the sky. She was living "the life" and there wasn't much you could tell her. She could hear Tyrone on the phone out on the balcony, but he hung up the phone as she approached. She opened the glass door, "who was that?"

"One of my partners." He said leaning to kiss her.

"So why did you hang up when I came in, you could've kept talking." she said suspiciously.

"We were already on the phone for a while, it's no big deal. So how was it seeing your girls, you're home early? I wasn't expecting you back before midnight." He asked, looking at his watch.

"Interesting." She said dropping her large purse on the island in her kitchen.

"What happened? I thought you ladies would be so happy to see one another you said it had been a while since you last hung out, come tell me all about it baby." He pulled her into him and hugged her from the back as they leaned against the island in the kitchen.

"They just had a lot of questions about us, well about you."

"Oh yeah, such as." He sniffed her hair.

"They want to know how come they haven't met you, how come my father hasn't met you and they're right."

"Because the time isn't right, you know that, and you know why. Did you tell them

everything?"

"My friends ain't trying to hear that you're married and going through a divorce. I told

them that you were already divorced."

"Baby all that matters is that you trust me when I tell you that I don't feel comfortable meeting your loved ones while I'm still technically married. It just feels wrong, you know. I proposed to you because the divorce is happening, and I want to marry you." he said, turning her around to face him. "You trust me, right?"

"I do, I just hate that you have this baggage. It just feels wrong."

"Not for long baby, look, I got you something speaking of baggage." He said, heading to the bedroom. Jameela stood in the middle of her huge living room, surrounded by floor to ceiling windows, the Hudson River in the background feeling like she had arrived. Tyrone reappeared with a large black shopping bag poorly hidden behind him. Jameela knew exactly what it was.

"You got me a Chanel purse?" she squealed excitedly.

"Yeah, now I know what you're thinking, you have plenty, but you don't have this one." He said revealing a Chanel Diamond Forever bag that cost about $250k.

"Oh my God, Tyrone, no you didn't, no you did not!" she said as she began jumping up and down. "Where on God's earth did you get the money to buy this bag, this bag costs six figures!"

"You forgot I'm not broke? Just being frugal until everything is situated."

"You call this frugal? Baby, this is too much, oh my goodness. I have been looking at this bag for so long knowing that I could never drop that amount of money on a purse. It's a collector's item, you know I will never, ever wear this bag! This is for like the rich Hollywood folks!"

"I just wanted to buy you something for once that you can't buy for yourself."

"Oh Tyrone baby thank you so much!" She tip toed and kissed him on his lips.

"Anything for my wife to be, now is this the kind of gift a man gives a woman that he doesn't intend on marrying? Forget about your friends, they'll see soon enough that what you have is the real deal."

"I love you so much baby." She said, admiring her bag.

"I love you too and I know how this looks and I care about your family and friends' perception of me I truly do. But I was married a long time, and I'm about to get married again. I just have to do things my way, I'm jumping out of one family into another it's a lot for me."

"I understand Ty, I really do, but I have a question." Jameela said holding her bag up to the sky and twirling it around.

"What's up."

"How can you afford to spend all of this money on a purse, but you can't help me pay this rent?"

"Who said that I couldn't? I simply said that it wouldn't be wise for me to be paying on a place that I'm not living in. Until I move in, this all you baby we discussed this before you got the place and you agreed, you said you could handle it until the top of next year when I move in."

"But it just doesn't make sense to me. I mean I love this bag, my God I'm in shock but the rent on this place is steep, and you sleep here a lot, so ...."

"So then I can sleep here less, problem solved." He said leaning up from the counter and walking across the room.

"Oh, there it is, so you buy this expensive ass bag to shut me up and run game on me, huh?"

"I need a moment to myself to just breathe. I left a home with a wife and kids and now I'm about to get married and I'm still married! Can I have a moment to process all of this, please! I'm jumping from taking care of one household right into another, let me live for a second!" He snapped.

Jameela didn't really know what to say at this point. She watched Tyrone pace back and forth and then he walked past her and plopped down on the couch.

"Come sit down, you're so uptight! That dinner was supposed to be fun and relaxing, but you came home more stressed than you were when you left." He said patting the seat next to him. Jameela walked over to Tyrone and sat next to him, he put his arms around her and pulled her into him.

"We really do need to solidify some things, Ty. The girls did have a point. My family and I are close, my friends are my sisters. I don't have too many people in my life like that. It's necessary that they meet the man that I am going to marry."

"And they will." He said squeezing her shoulders.

"I sometimes feel like you have no urgency or understanding of anything that I'm feeling. I just want you to try to compromise some because I have. You don't want me to post pictures, show pictures which is odd and definitely feels like you have something to hide."

"I just told you that I understand. The issue now is *you* don't understand *me* and it's pissing me off."

"I don't want you to get upset, I'm just trying to make you see my perspective, that's all."

"I don't want my soon to be ex-wife to see anything about me on social media because she will try to take me to the cleaners and then what kind of life would you and I have? I got a few dollars in the bank but do remember I did not play in the NFL for long so I'm not sitting on twenty million or anything like that. I gotta play it smart. If she finds out I'm in a relationship or engaged before the ink has even dried on our papers she'll take me for child support, alimony, and everything else. Right now she's playing fair, we get along and all is well. You gotta trust me baby, this is for the greater good."

"I understand which is why I haven't done the picture thing and honestly, I'm not pressed. I'm a very private person anyway."

"And you don't want to risk your friends having my pictures and randomly showing them or anything like that. You never know who knows who. Once everything is finalized you can post away baby I couldn't care less, just not right now. I don't want my ex-wife to feel as if I'm rubbing things in her face and plus, I have children. I have to ease them into this."

"I understand that part baby, I do." She said and kissed his cheek. "But my parents are the most important people in my life, why can't you understand how important it is to meet them, you were married, and you know the importance of meeting family."

"For one, I'm *still* married and morally I just don't feel right meeting someone else's family while I am still in one."

"Well you know what Tyrone, you seem to have a million and one excuses. You should have thought about all of this before you started dating. We've been dating for almost a year and you haven't met anyone? I'm sorry but meeting my folks within the next few weeks has to happen, its nonnegotiable. I've had enough of playing by your rules, give me something!" She said and stood up.

"You see, you're already letting these bitches get up in your head. You go out one night with these lousy bitches and you come back with all this strong black woman energy. No high valued man wants to, nor does he have to deal with this! One bitch doesn't have a man because he had a whole wife and secret life and she's out there fucking everything that moves, and the other bitch can't keep her man faithful because she won't perform in bed. But these are the women you're listening to?"

"Don't call my friends bitches, you outta order. And don't you ever bring up anything I told you in confidence and throw it in my face. You have the facts all wrong! And you know what, remind me not to tell you anything else because you're twisting my words."

"No, I'm not, I'm repeating *exactly* what you said out of your mouth. So, try watching what you say about *your so-called friends* if you don't want it thrown back in your face. Now I love you, please can we just enjoy the rest of the evening?" he said snatching up the remote. Jameela walked away from Tyrone and decided to take a shower then get in the bed leaving Tyrone out in the living room until he realized that Jameela had retired for the night.

"Baby, come out here and spend some time with me, stop being a baby!" he shouted from the living room.

"Go fuck yourself," Jameela said tossing the covers over her head and forcing herself to get a good night's rest.

Tyrone knew that Jameela couldn't stay mad at him for long. He let her cool off overnight then in the morning he dicked her down so good, she went back to sleep and didn't want to get out of the bed until 3pm. He awakened her with brunch, his famous sausage and egg casserole, a mimosa and a kiss on the lips.

She rolled her eyes and inserted a fork full of eggs into her mouth.

"I gave what you said some thought and I am willing to meet your folks."

"When." Jameela asked, not looking up at him.

"Whatever works best for our schedules. I'll meet them but no pictures or anything like that." He warned.

"That's fine, I'll set something up. Let me call my parents and everyone else to see what their schedules are like, it might be a few weeks before I can get everyone together at the same time." She said knowing that she had to mend her relationship with the girls after acting a fool last night, plus get her father's mind right to meet Tyrone. Because of how Jameela was moving, nobody was really interested in meeting him genuinely anymore, now it was simply about putting eyes on the man that got Jameela acting brand new.

"Sounds good just let me know. So what do you have planned for the rest of the day." he asked, sitting on the edge of the bed.

"Nothing much, but I was thinking we can go out to dinner later. It's been a few weeks since we've been out on a date."

"Not tonight baby, the fellas invited me out. It's been a while, you know that."

"Well when can you and I go out to dinner?"

"I'll plan something for later on in the week, maybe dinner at Bartello's." He kissed her lips succulently.

"I like that." Jameela purred.

"I see you stuffing those eggs in your mouth. I got something else you can stuff in your mouth." He flirted.

"I rather the eggs, gawn somewhere." she said playfully.

Jameela spent the rest of the evening under Tyrone until it was time for him to go out. Once he was gone, she showered and returned to her bed, wanting to call her friends but she knew that they weren't going to answer. She tried anyway and Naomi sent her to voicemail.

"I deserved that." She thought then called Shantel who sounded as if she was sleeping.

"Old lady! Why are you asleep so early?"

"It's almost midnight." Shantel said dryly.

"But still, where's Yusef?"

"Sleep, why do you have so much energy."

"No reason, I was just calling to make sure that there wasn't any bad blood after dinner yesterday. I know that there was a lot of tension and that I left with an attitude. I was just overwhelmed with all of this talk about my relationship and what not."

"That was more than tension beloved. And honestly, I can't talk about that right now so, I'm glad you made it home safely. We'll catch up soon." Shantel said and hung up.

Jameela stared at the phone momentarily then tossed it to the side.

Tyrone exited the beautiful high rise building and walked out into the beautiful summer air and his whole demeanor changed like Keyser Soze, the moment he reached the parking lot. He hopped in his vehicle, pulling up next to his partners Archie and Shawn who were double parked up the block. They exchanged pleasantries then headed into midtown for the black party.

Once they fellas secured a table on the rooftop, Tyrone began catching them up to speed with his latest antics, filling them in on Jameela, her not knowing his real name and his plans to cut her off soon. But when he revealed that he proposed to Jameela with his wife's first engagement ring, that's when his friends got more engaged in the conversation.

"Man, this is the most fucked up shit I've heard in a long time." Jimmy said.

"You gave a woman a ring and you expect that shit back?" Archie snapped.

"The damage is done. I have to tell her that I need to take the ring to get cleaned or upgraded or something then break out."

"That's foul Gerrod." Archie said.

"I'm a foul motherfucker, what do you expect?"

"This is low, even for you." Shawn said to Gerrod who almost choked on his drink.

"You don't get to play Mr. Morale now bro. You out here doing the same dIrt!"

"Absolutely the fuck not. I get the occasional trim if I come across an exceptionally sexy female that's throwing herself on me and if I'm in the mood. I can't tell you the last time I cheated on my wife." Shawn said as he twirled his glass.

"Last month, remember the Spanish chick when we were out at the cigar bar in Brooklyn." Jimmy said.

"And you hit that chubby chick in the bathroom at Burger and Lobster a few weeks back." Gerrod chimed in.

"The motherfucking point being is that I'm not gaming nobody for money, proposing, catching feelings or sticking around long enough for a bitch to even pull her panties back up over her ass."

"Your sin isn't any greater than mine playboy so you can try to convince yourself all you want."

"Man go head, you're in that hell by your damn self. You gave another woman your wife's engagement ring; we are not the same, I don't care what you say!"

"Look, old girl will be just fine. This'll be just another story for her and her girls to get drunk and get over while listening to Mary J. Blige."

"Wow." Archie said. "I'm still stuck at how she thinks you're an ex-NFL player. You're driving *your wife's* cars."

"Shit man, you're really committed to being a greaseball." Archie said.

"The way karma is going to spin the block on your ass, I don't want to be around when it happens!" Jimmy said and sipped his drink.

"How are you getting that ring back that's what I want to know." Shawn asked.

"Yeah, what's the end game, this woman thinks you're going to marry her."

"She wants to meet my children."

"You ain't got no damn kids, what are you talking about?" Shawn threw his hands up.

Gerrod pulled out his phone and showed the guys a picture of his sister-in-law and her two kids on vacation and pictures of them in Dallas.

"Please tell me that you didn't tell this woman that these kids are yours. And you're trying to convince me I'm as bad as you? Negro please." Shawn shook his head.

"Also, my mansion in Dallas."

All the men started laughing but they didn't think it was funny. Shawn left the men mid conversation and headed across the rooftop toward the beautiful stranger that just appeared.

"Tiffany is a good woman. Then you wonder why she's always on your ass." Jimmy said.

"She knows who she married. Did you forget she was my side at one point?" Gerrod tossed his drink back, ready to catch up to Shawn and the woman.

"That was a long time ago man, give it up." Jimmy said, defending Tiffany.

"I give up. You just insist on swimming in a pool of garbage choices." Archie said walking away. Jimmy was also turned off, so he made his way over to where Shawn and the woman were standing. Feeling a bit bad for what he was doing especially since the fellas weren't amused by his behavior, Gerrod went into the hallway to call Jameela to check her temperature to see if she was serious about her light ultimatum, but she didn't answer, so he called his wife who was questioning what time he planned on coming home tonight.

"Hey baby." He said sweetly.

"Make sure you come home at a decent hour tonight. I don't want to hear any excuses, Gerrod. And if the sun catches you, I *will* call and report my car stolen!" she said and hung up.

"Love you too." Gerrod said.

Chapter 13

YOU, ME AND HE

*N*aomi almost didn't make it out tonight, thinking about the things her friends had been saying to her about the way she carried herself regarding men. She argued that she was single and safe and couldn't understand why they were so concerned about her sexual appetite. She tried to settle down years ago and it didn't work. She concluded that maybe settling down just wasn't for her. But the guilt she felt after those comments and conversations left her feeling heavy, in bed all day channel surfing.

"I'm not a homebody, I don't want to be in the house. Why am I staying inside when I can be outside doing what I want to do, aren't they doing what they choose to do?" she said out loud to herself while flicking through the channels. She glanced over at the clock which read 10:11pm. She then checked the weather. It was still sweltering 82 degrees outside.

"I missed a good hot summer day lying in bed to please these bitches who are home laid up with their men." She said snatching the covers off her. Naomi took a long hot soapy shower then sprayed her body in Replica Beach Walk.

"I'm doing me." She said standing naked in the door of her closet. Sam and Ginger danced around her ankles while she picked out outfits as if they knew she was going out.

"What should mommy wear?" she asked them, pulling out a black jumpsuit, a black flirty short set and a black body con dress.

How are you feeling girl, you feeling sexy? Chill? Coy? What are you giving tonight. She said tossing the outfits on the bed.

"Ah, pregame time." She headed into the kitchen with the dogs on her heels. She tossed them some snacks then opened her kitchen cabinet revealing a selection of alcoholic beverages.

"Hmm, that brown makes you get down, that tequila makes you feel fun, festive, nope no wine that shit is a drag, Sunday shit. Ugh why do I even have Vodka in here, this will make you fuck, marry, kill, stab." She laughed at herself then grabbed the La Gritona tequila from the shelf. She poured a healthy serving, squeezed a fresh lime in it and added a drop of Agave. She guzzled most of it down before even getting back to her bedroom.

"Let the liquor guide you to your outfit child." She said staring out of the window. Moments later she put her glass down and swiped up her outfit.

"Oh so you are feeling naughty tonight I see." She said and licked her lips in the mirror.

Naomi decided on a black bodycon spaghetti strap dress and stilettos for the all-black affair. She scanned the rooftop and was pleased with the variety of well-dressed men and classy women that showed up.

"You are one beautiful woman, the finest woman in here that's for sure."

Naomi turned to find an attractive stranger in her personal space. His breath smelled of cognac and fresh mint. His cologne mixed with light sweat was sexy to her. She glanced over his entire body and was pleased with his thick physique and how well-groomed he was. His chocolate brown skin looked healthy. She concluded that this was a man that took great pride in his appearance and health as she admired the whites of his eyes and his manicured nails.

She smiled, "Thank you."

He smiled bashfully, recognizing that she was taking him in. Her erect nipples made him stutter a bit.

"What's your name?" he asked, trying his best not to look at her body. But he couldn't resist, nor did she want him to.

"Bobbi." She lied.

"I'm Just." He extended his hand and placed her dainty manicured hand into his and kissed it. His lips were very soft.

"What's Just short for."

"Justin. Can I order another drink? You look to be running low."

"Sure."

Naomi smiled and turned her body ever so slightly so that he could take her in. He eyed every inch of her body and bit his lip unintentionally. She could see him through her peripheral looking at her lustfully.

"I'll have another glass of champagne please, a splash of St. Germaine." Naomi asked the bartender then averted her attention back to Justin.

"So, what brings you hear, are you alone?" he asked her.

"I'm not sure if I should answer that. You might try to kidnap me or something." she flirted.

"If I kidnap you, I promise I won't hurt you." he said leaning in a bit closer to her.

"What if I want you to." Naomi said to his surprise. He kept his cool and responded, "I'll do whatever you want me to do."

Just then, his friends came over and formed a semi-circle around them.

"Who's this?" the short chubby one asked excitedly while giving Justin a slap on the back.

"This is Bobbi."

The men all raised their glasses and exchange pleasantries.

Gerrod's eyes lingered over the length of Naomi's body and the sexual chemistry was immediate. After a few minutes of small talk, Naomi decided to excuse herself to the restroom. She could feel the presence of someone following behind her. She was certain of who it was. When Naomi reached the bathroom, Gerrod was close on her.

A smirk crept across her lips. The session was quick, hard, wet and nasty. Gerrod held Naomi up by her buttocks as her legs wrapped around his torso. They breathed heavily and as her breaths got slower, he kissed her neck and in between her sweaty breasts. Once he put her down, she handed him a few wipes then turned her back to clean herself up as he flushed a condom down the toilet. The door closed as she stood at the sink freshening herself up. She took enough time to make sure she didn't look flushed then put the phone to her ear as she headed back to the roof. She knew that once she reappeared all eyes would be on her, not sure if Gerrod would say anything to his friends, so she continued with a fake conversation until she got closer to the group of men that were all eyeing her like a piece of meat.

"I thought you ran off and left me, you good? You were gone a minute." Shawn said pulling her close to him by her waist as she tried her best not to wince in pain.

"Sorry about that, I took a phone call and was trying to convince my girls to come meet me tonight, you know, maybe get with your friends?" she lied.

"They as fine as you?" Archie asked.

"Well, that's not for me to say, but yes my friends are very attractive." she answered, wondering where Gerrod went after leaving her pussy with a black eye.

"Where's G? He's been gone for a minute." Jimmy asked to Naomi's delight.

"He's outside either talking to that chick that he's running game on or his wife."

"He's a wild boy. He took things too far with this new chick for sure." Archie said.

"What's that line women love, the same way you get him is how you lose him." Shawn said matter of factly.

Jimmy shook his head, "I'm never getting married. I can't deal with someone telling me how to come and go. And furthermore, I want to marry a woman that I have no desire to cheat on. I need to be sure that I'm ready." He sipped his drink.

"I don't think marriage is that complicated." Naomi interjected. The men all turned their attention toward the beautiful stranger who's scent lingered amongst them in the small circle they stood in.

"Are you married, *respectfully.*" Jimmy asked intrigued.

"I was engaged once but the problem is people get married for the wrong reasons or they think that they can change someone after the fact. You have to marry you're a-alike."

"How would you describe your a-alike?" asked Archie.

"Someone that's spontaneous, free but structured at the same time if that makes sense. Someone grounded, has a purpose, someone that knows who they are, most importantly that knows who I am and doesn't try to change me. Someone not afraid to take risks in any area of their life. A man's man, masculine, strong, someone certain, safe, someone sure of themselves and sure of me."

"So, you wouldn't mind having a husband that goes out a lot, gets a lot of attention from women?" Shawn asked.

"I go out a lot and I get a lot of attention from women so no." Naomi laughed.

"I hear that! I can see that." Jimmy said, raising his glass.

"That sort of thing doesn't bother me. We're married, not blind. Men are going to look at other women. Women are going to look at other men. But there's a thin line between finding someone attractive and being attracted to someone."

"So real quick before he gets back, my partner is married to a woman that thought marriage would change him. That nigga ain't never gonna be faithful to no woman."

"As usual, when he's out she holds him hostage on the phone." Archie added.

"What's keeping him on the phone going to do? He could be fucking someone in the bathroom right now while talking to his wife. "Naomi said.

"And he has definitely pulled that stunt a time or two!" the men laughed giving each other high fives.

Don't I know it Naomi thought.

"So back to you beautiful, you want to get out of here, maybe go someplace a bit more intimate? I know a spot not too far from here, dim lights, live music, ambience where I can get to know you a little better." Shawn asked, reaching for her hand.

"That sounds lovely, I'd like that."

Upon exiting the building, Gerrod was immediately to their left still on the phone. Naomi pretended not to see him as she grabbed Shawn's hand.

"You all are leaving already?" he asked.

Shawn turned around upon hearing Gerrod's voice.

"Yeah, we're heading to Lee's for a night cap."

"Okay, I was heading that way too as a matter of fact, meeting up with a joint." Gerrod lied.

Naomi's mind was on Gerrod the entire 20-minute drive. Shawn (Justin) was sweet and attractive but Gerrod was sexy. He had that *je ne sais quoi* about him that she loved in a man.

Naomi had another drink once they arrived at Lee's, that she nursed as Shawn put his moves on her, kissing her neck and rubbing her leg while she kept her eyes on Gerrod who was at the bar "waiting for his friend" that never showed up. Naomi began getting bored.

"Let's get out of here. I have a suite at the Mandarin, Columbus Circle." She said standing up.

Shawn's eyes widened *with* excitement. He downed his cognac and placed the glass and some money on the table. Naomi made her way toward Gerrod with Shawn in tow, who was trying his best not to react to her large breasts softly jiggling as she headed toward him. Once Naomi got close enough, she informed Gerrod that they were leaving.

"I want you to come too." she said seductively.

Shawn and Gerrod looked at each other like it was their lucky day.

"You okay with that?" Naomi asked softly.

"Yeah, I'm cool with that, G you good?" Shawn asked.

"Oh, he's *really* good." Naomi answered.

Naomi headed up to the room while Shawn and Gerrod parked their vehicles. She texted Shantel to let her know where she would be tonight then slid out of her dress, placing it on a chair by the front door. When Shawn and Gerrod arrived she instructed them to take their clothes off. Tonight she was going to fulfill her fantasy of a threesome with two men.

Gerrod was all but drooling as stripped while Shawn concentrated on taking his clothes off. While he fumbled with his belt and shoes, Naomi walked slowly up to Gerrod and got on her knees, placing his penis into her mouth.

Shawn finally undressed and Naomi took a glimpse at his manhood. He wasn't well endowed like Gerrod but it had girth. Naomi reached for him with her free hand pulling him to her face and took turns pleasing them both.

After a while, Gerrod picked her up tossing her on the bed where they had sex like no one else was in the room. When it was Shawn's turned, he propped her up on her knees and inserted himself inside of her anally, slow, and steady as she groaned in agony until he was all the way in.

"You nasty bitch. I knew it as soon as I saw you." He growled in her ear.

"Fuck me like the nasty bitch I am then." Naomi growled back.

Naomi screamed at the feeling of his thickness entering her without lube. But he knew his way around the back door, so it wasn't long before Naomi got wet and caught his rhythm. For the next 45 minutes, the men took turns devouring and feasting on her body like vultures with no intentions of slowing down. Naomi's body creamed from the pleasures of double penetration and the sounds of the threesome sounded like a beautiful sexual symphony that sent Naomi's body into orbit as they all climaxed together making for a perfect ending to such a salacious night.

As the men thirstily guzzled water while lying in bed, no doubt waiting for a another round, Naomi made the announcement that she was leaving as she slid her dress over her head.

Shawn sat up as Naomi snatched up her purse and heels.

"This was fun." She said then headed out the door quickly knowing by the time they made it downstairs to the lobby, she would be safe in a yellow taxi on her way home.

Sam and Ginger greeted her at the door excitedly jumping up and down as if they wanted to hear the details of her night. Naomi knew that a night like this should be kept a secret because she was sure to be judged. She showered then poured herself a drink to take the edge off so she could lay in bed and replay the night's events.

"Well babies, let me tell you what mommy got into tonight!" She said to Sam and Ginger who were now in her bed, their little tongues out and tails wagging as if they were ready for a story.

Chapter 14

SOMETHIN', SOMETHIN'
JUST AIN'T RIGHT

*G*errod pulled into the garage and tossed his burner phone into his car before heading up the stairs. Jameela would just have to be angry because Tiffany was home fresh off a business trip, and he needed to give her his undivided attention. It was a quarter to four in the morning and he was playing it close knowing that Tiffany would make good on her promise of reporting the car stolen. He had run out of excuses and was conjuring one up in his head as he tossed his house keys on the entry table and kicked his shoes off.

"That's you?" He could hear Tiffany asking from upstairs.

"She doesn't sound too upset." Gerrod thought as he headed toward the winding stairwell.

He knew she was used to his shenanigans, but he had to admit how outlandish he'd been since meeting Jameela. But with Tiffany going out of town on business trips more frequently and for longer periods of time, it made it easier for Gerrod to get away with infidelity.

Tiffany appeared at the top of the steps looking like a goddess, standing 5ft 11, slim-thick, dirty blonde tresses with blonde highlights that hung to the middle of her back, complimenting her chestnut brown eyes. She slowly walked down the stairs, almost gliding in a long emerald, green silk robe. Gerrod could smell her as she approached, she clearly just finished taking a shower having lathered herself in La Prairie skin products. For a 46-year-old woman, Tiffany looked to be in her early thirties in the face. But the Caucasian side of her family showed in her neck and around her eyes sometimes.

"So, enlighten me husband. Where are you coming from this time of the night and *this time*, tell me something clever, make me a believer." She taunted bypassing him to lay across her chaise.

"I was at a rooftop party then we went to a strip club and got totally inebriated. I had to sober up before I drove home that's the only reason why I'm home so late, honest to God. I didn't want to risk getting into a car accident."

Tiffany didn't believe one word out of his mouth, but she was too tired to play detective. The truth would find her eventually. He covered his tracks too good most of the time, except for that one time, a few years ago.

Tiffany looked at him suspiciously.

"So what have you been up to?" She lay across her chaise chair elegantly waiting for her husband to fill her head up with lies.

"Now, before you start lying, you need to know that I check the cameras and I see that you're gone for three, four days at a time! So instead of working on a business plan that we discussed, I don't know 5, 10 years ago, you're out here chasing pussy while I bust my ass. Is that what we are doing these days beloved? You plan on working that dead end job at Black Rock until you die?"

"How soon do we forget that you worked at that same company, with the same title as me and got fired and it was my dead-end job at BlackRock that took care of the bills so that you can build your brand and your business and become the multimillionaire that you are. That was *your dream* not mine, and I supported you!"

"But the plan was for you to start a business of your own, that was years ago, you haven't done much of anything. A few months back you rocked me to sleep showing me some bullshit plan and I fell for it, so what's up, what's going on."

"I love my job and it pays well. Not everyone is cut out for entrepreneurship." Gerrod said, growing frustrated as he was not in the mood for this topic for the hundredth time.

"250k is a well-paying job to you in this economy? Do you see where you live? You would not be able to live like this on your salary alone!" She said looking around her monstrous sized home for emphasis.

"Really Tiffany, wow." Gerrod shook his head.

"You've outgrown that salary, that's all I'm saying. What happened to all your dreams? It's like you got content letting me chase the bag while you just lag and drive the cars and live in your big ass fancy house and do whatever you want. You wouldn't be able to pay this mortgage without me you do know that right? You wouldn't be able to live like this without me. Yet here you are just enjoying yourself without even trying to pretend that you're trying to get on my level. Do you know how much the mortgage is on this house? No, you don't because we don't have one anymore, thanks to me. You can barely manage your own car note let alone mine, oops *my cars* are paid in full but not yours, you have a note!"

"I told you out the gate that we didn't need all this house so don't start that shit." Gerrod said, grabbing a seat on his recliner. He rubbed his head out of frustration knowing that Tiffany was about to be on a rampage for another hour or so and all he wanted to do was get in bed replay the events of the night.

"Baby you just got home. Why are you trying to beef with me this time of the morning instead of making love to your man?" he asked softly.

"You think that I bust my ass to live in a condo. I'll buy a condo just to put clothes and purses in it! I bought *all this house* because I worked damn hard for it! So, if I decided that I wanted a house worth 2.5 that is my damn business!"

"If it's your damn business then why are you complaining to me about how much it costs then."

Tiffany sucked her teeth long and hard. "You used to want the finer things Gerrod, now you just *pretend* to want them." She shook her head disapprovingly. "We could have so much more if you would just get in line."

"Get in line, who do you think I am, one of your employees? Get in line, you better watch it, all because you make the money does not make you the man of the house."

"And what makes you the man of the house? What separates you and I, other than you having a penis, what makes you the man?" she challenged.

"I'm not doing this shit with you tonight!" Gerrod stood up.

"Your lack of ambition is a turn off." Tiffany said and with that she walked into the kitchen and began boiling water for tea.

Gerrod followed behind her.

"It's not always about money Tiffany, how much more money and success do you need huh? I get that you don't ever want to go back to that place that you grew up in, but you're a long way from the projects in Baltimore. You have to shake that mentality and stop being afraid of being poor. That will never happen again because you are too smart, ambitious, successful and so far removed from that life."

"It's so unfortunate that you aren't understanding what I am saying. It's not the money, it's the principal Gerrod. You and I both were at Black Rock, 15 years ago I met you at that job and I had dreams of owning a construction business, now I have two about to have three. We shared a love of being business owners, getting rich, building a life and a brand, that's the reason you left Miranda for me, at least that's what you told me. You said that she wasn't ambitious and that my drive turned you on. Was that a lie?"

"No, you know it's not a lie." Gerrod said trying to sweet talk Tiffany. He attempted to wrap his arms around her waist, but she pulled away, placing her hand on his chest to stop him.

"We got engaged, bought that little condominium in Jersey City, and thought we were doing something. Then I got fired because I knew I was destined for more and was always distracted at work. I knew that my life wasn't about sitting behind a desk, wearing stuffy suits, and crunching numbers for other motherfuckas and you said don't worry about it, focus on your dream, go back to school I got this, and I thank you for being the man of the house and allowing me to pursue my dreams without blinking. I will always respect you for that because you stood up like a man is supposed to. But we've outgrown those times. If all else fails for whatever reason, my husband can't even hold me down. So don't talk to me about being the man of the house. It's not about money it's about stability and security."

"We're in a place in our marriage where none of that shit even matters Tiff. Why can't we just enjoy our success?"

Tiffany shot him a look like what you could imagine someone would look like when choking. Gerrod clarified what he meant before Tiffany could speak.

"You just said that by me holding you down, you were able to succeed, so why isn't this my success as much as it is yours. Why can't you just accept me for who I am and what I bring to the table."

"You aren't the reason for my success, I am! It's like the minute I started making it, your ambitions just faded to black and that was not the plan. The plan was, once I got on you would jump on with me, we would trade places, I would take care of the bills while you work on your thing. I told you out the gate that I would not take care of you because it would make me lose respect for you. You were supposed to get busy building while I held it down, not wait for me to give you a handout. I got it on my own and I needed to see my husband do the same and yes, I would have extended help along the way, but it's the principle. I fell in love with an ambitious man that had goals. So, it's not about the money, it's the lack of any personal goals and growth, it's the laziness that's really turning me off."

"I get my ass up every day and go to work!" He raised his voice.

Tiffany yelled louder, "Did you not hear anything that I just said? Stop chasing pussy and start chasing your dreams because baby if you think for one second that you're going to divorce me and take everything I worked for so you can share it with some bitch then you have another thing coming I'm telling you right now!"

"Oh, there it is. So, we're introducing the energy of divorce in this house now? Who the fuck knows what you're out there doing on these *so-called* business trips, you can be out there fucking somebody."

Tiffany stepped up close to Gerrod and looked up at him, "Look around you motherfucka, there isn't anything *so called* about my damn business! *So called* doesn't get you all of this. I worked my ass off and you're out there riding around in the fruits of *my labor,* not coming home at night, lying to me about your where abouts so where the hell are you all those nights when you're not coming home?"

"When you're not here, you know *when you're out being a boss*, I stay close to the job at the Four Seasons, we had this discussion already, it's redundant at this point." He said walking off.

"Spell it, motherfucka." She snapped.

"Tiffany, I want to take a shower and get in bed." He shrugged and unbuttoned his shirt and headed up the stairs.

"Gerrod, I promise you, if you're cheating on me, I won't take you back this time, I mean it." She said following behind him.

"I'm not cheating on you Tiffany. I don't know how many times I gotta tell you this. You travel a lot what am I supposed to do? I'm a grown ass man. I don't have to sit on my hands while my wife is away to make her feel secure, get over yourself already it's tired."

She walked past him in the bedroom with a cup of ginger tea, her robe swaying behind her.

"Listen, marriage is not a means to keep me locked up in the house, I told you that from day one. I love going out, partying, hanging with my partners specifically when you are not around but when you are home, *I am home*, phones off and it's all about us, you know that and when I do go out with my partners and you're in town, don't I always invite you?"

"Yes, because you know I am going to say no. You know that I have no desire to sit around your friends that know you're cheating whilst looking like a fool. Oh, and do not get me started on their wives, those *mediocre bitches* that are constantly asking me where I got my clothes from and how much this or that cost, as if them *or their man* could afford it. I hate for my time to be wasted. I do not delight in hanging out on rooftop bars, I rather be on a yacht in St. Baarts for crying out loud and I make enough money to do that, but my husband is stuck on rooftop bars and hookah lounges like a fucking video vixen."

"Watch it, Tiffany."

"No, *you* watch it. You know even before I became successful in my business, I still was not that girl. I was never into clubs and things like that, I was about my paper, always. I just don't understand how I haven't rubbed off on you yet!"

"My bourgeois ass wife." he said, grabbing her by the waist and pulling her in aggressively.

"You are so sexy when you're mad. You make so much money you don't need me to do anything. All you need is a man that's going to love on you, cater to you and have a nice big hard dick for you whenever you come home."

Tiffany shook her head and pulled away from him.

"Well while you stress yourself over nothing, I'm going to take a nice long shower to wash the smell of strippers off of me, then I am going to lay across my California King in hopes of my beautiful, gorgeous, successful, self-made, rich wife coming to lay on my chest so that I can play in her hair until I fall asleep." He said entering the shower.

Tiffany sat on the edge of the bed, watching her husband watch her, watch him take a shower. She couldn't deny how sexy he was. He took pride in his body, skin, and health. He was a very handsome, sexy man, but he was unfaithful. But sometimes she made excuses for him, blamed it on karma because she started dealing with him when he was engaged to marry her coworker. She let a lot of things slide because of their past but at this point, she paid her debts and could no longer use that as an excuse to let him cheat.

"You see something you like?" he asked her through the glass doors.

Tiffany tilted her head to the side, "I've seen better."

"You wish." Gerrod laughed and turned his back to her so he could rinse the soap off his body.

Gerrod knew that Tiffany anticipated the hardness of his love against her back once they got in bed but instead, he kissed her hair, said I love you, good night. He didn't have an ounce of energy or desire to sleep with his wife after what he just experienced.

"Baby." She spoke.

Wearily he answered. "Yeah babe." Hoping that she didn't want to have sex.

"I forgot to tell you, I can't find my ring, have you seen it?"

Gerrod's eyes shot wide open in the dark. "What ring?"

"My engagement ring. I was rearranging my jewelry chest, and I didn't see it. I'll look again tomorrow but I know for sure it's not in that drawer where I left it. I may need you to pull the drawers out and look in the back. It's possible that it may have fell out as I have a habit of over stuffing my drawers sometimes."

"Okay baby, I'll do that this week." He kissed her hair.

She began toying with her huge 6 figure engagement ring that she received years down the line.

"You spent your hard-earned money on that ring before all of this...it means the world to me." she said genuinely.

"My hard-earned dead end job Black Rock money?"

"Whatever Gerrod. You know exactly the point that I'm making."

Gerrod stayed up an extra 45 minutes staring at the walls wondering how he was going to get that ring off Jameela's hand.

Jameela continuously called Tyrone's phone, but it kept going to voicemail. Frustrated, she tossed her phone on the nightstand and went to bed. He ended up calling her two days later on Monday morning when he was on his way to work.

"Good morning sweetheart." He said sarcastically awaiting the verbal rainstorm that was sure to come.

"Don't sweetheart me, where the hell have you been?"

"I got absolutely fucked up Saturday night and it took me all weekend to recover. I am so sorry, but I'll be by there later around 6pm."

"What's all that noise in the back where are you now." She asked while powering up her laptop to start her day.

"Oh, I'm on the train."

"The train? What the hell are you doing on the train?"

"I have a few meetings and it's easier to get around on public transportation as opposed to dealing with traffic."

"Mmm hmm. What kind of meetings do *you* have?"

"I'm just handling business like you're handling yours."

Jameela closed her eyes and breathed in deeply. "Look, I have a long day ahead of me so I guess I'll see you later, so you say."

"Indeed you will." He said knowing that he needed to see Jameela in order to attempt getting the ring back.

Chapter 15

I APOLOGIZE

Jameela knew she had been unreasonable and unnecessarily shady to her friends, and she needed to extend an olive branch, especially now because she needed counsel. She text Shantel and Naomi in a group chat, *"Hey can we get together this weekend?"*

Only Shantel responded later in the night with, *"Hey love, sure."*

Rightfully so, Naomi did not respond. Jameela knew that she earned the right to be left on read. But it wasn't that Naomi was ignoring her, she was caught up with the personal trainer she met at Juices for Life. Naomi responded to the group chat two days later by simply sending a "thumbs up" emoji.

In hopes of rehashing a nostalgic feeling among her friends, Jameela suggested that they meet in Harlem at Blvd Bistro for good music and a boozy brunch. She kept in touch with Shantel throughout the weeks leading up to their pow wow, but Naomi was in the wind, however Shantel had assured her that Naomi would make it, she was just tied up literally and figuratively. Jameela parked her man's wife's Lamborghini in a parking lot up the street while he laid up in her high rise apartment awaiting her return from her girls' day out. Tiffany was in Colorado for only three days and now he knew that she was checking camera footage, so he was never leaving the cars with Jameela again, nor was he going to continue spending multiple nights out. Shantel showed up first, dressed in a bright white button-down shirt, distressed jeans, Angela Scott loafers and an oversized leather clutch, her hair up in a signature messy bun with light tresses intentionally left out to frame her face. She looked well rested and happy as usual. She walked up to Jameela who was at the bar nervously nursing a mimosa.

"Hey beautiful woman, how have you been?" Shantel warmly greeted Jameela.

Jameela embraced her friend, a total difference from the last time they saw one another. But Shantel wasn't going to lean into her until Naomi arrived.

"You look nice as always." Shantel complimented Jameela who was dressed in a teal-colored fitted jogger set, Louboutin heels and a large red Chanel duffle bag, her short hair in its natural state, tapered and curly like it was freshly washed, signature big sunglasses and a red lip.

"Thank you." She said.

"What's in the duffle bag girl, you running away?"

"No, another bag that Tyrone got for me." She said. Shantel noticed the somber undertone of Jameela's energy.

"Naomi should be here soon, she was close when I spoke with her. So what's up, how's your soul, your heart, your health, your mind, how are you getting on?" Shantel asked softly.

"I'm okay, business is growing, money flowing...."

Shantel interrupted her. "That's a blessing, more abundance to you sis but I asked about this." Shantel said lightly touching Jameela's chest where her heart would be. Jameela inhaled and let out a sigh.

"I'm in way over my head."

Before she could speak on it, Naomi showed up, her face stoic showing signs of already being on the defense. She didn't have her signature faux locs but instead wore her natural hair which was still in a beautiful brown and blonde shade, styled in a large, gorgeous healthy twist out. She said hello to Jameela as if they were strangers, then embraced Shantel long and invitingly. Jameela felt the drastic difference in greetings.

"Your skin looks amazing what have you been using?" Shantel said to Naomi.

"I stumbled across Kelis' skin care line on Instagram and decided to give it a shot, but you know I have my Le Roche Posay on standby." She cracked.

"Your face is flawless do you have on any make up at all?" Shantel observed.

"I do have on a tinted moisturizer by Laura Mercier but other than that no. And as you can see, her hair products are equally amazing."

"Obviously! Your curls are so juicy, okay go girl you look like a breath of fresh air!" Shantel continued.

"I've been working out and just staying away from negative energy." She said, shifting the energy in that moment.

The hostess came over to seat them and placed a pitcher of margaritas on the table. They made small talk about work, life, the dogs, needing a vacation and then there was a pregnant pause where they hadn't any more small talk in them. It was time for Jameela to speak up. Naomi looked at her watch impatiently as Jameela had done months ago, prompting Meela to get the ball rolling.

"First of all, I'd like to say that I love you both dearly and if I offended you the last time that we were together, I'm truly sorry." She said looking into their eyes, but no one said anything. Jameela looked at them both dissatisfied with their reaction to her apology. She leaned back in her chair and folded her arms. She then realized where she went wrong with her apology and reiterated.

"*I know* that I've offended you both the last time we were all together and I apologize for my behavior." She spoke. Both women took a satisfying sip of their beverage but remained silent. The floor was Jameela's to spill her guts and let her sisters know why she felt the need to be so indignant toward them.

"I don't know where to even start." She spoke.

Upon realizing that they were not about to make this easy for her, she conjured up the courage to speak.

"Well let me just admit that you ladies were right. Tyrone has something going on, I'm just not sure what it is. At one time he was all in, now he seems to be back peddling a little bit. I was already feeling a bit uneasy about how he was moving and after leaving you ladies it just confirmed that I wasn't tripping. I did some deep diving, trying to understand why I was allowing him to shortchange me when it came to pretty much doing the basics. I have everything I need and honestly, I don't know what it is I need a man for. But I know that a woman is supposed to need a man for something, right?"

Naomi and Shantel shrugged and made faces, unsure of how to respond to Jameela in the moment. "A part of me feels as if I just snatched up a man to know what it feels like to be in a relationship at this big age. I don't know, there's just so much confusion in my brain right now. Then I went down this rabbit hole, and I started doing a little bit of soul searching. I realized that I may have some forgiving to do."

"Forgive who." Shantel asked.

"My parents." she said softly.

This was a surprise to Naomi who never experienced Jameela being vulnerable regarding her parents. She always presented as if nothing bothered her and that being successful was the answer to everything. She always let it be known that under no circumstance would she ever get married. But now it was all too obvious that the tough girl act was just that, an act. Jameela wanted love.

"Growing up most children that don't have a two-parent home always tend to romanticize those of us that do have it." She said looking at Naomi.

"But what about those of us that have a two-parent home and it's unhealthy? I've never expressed to anyone how my parents' marriage did more harm to me than good. Yes, I love my father, I adore him and yes, he has always supported me, been there for me. He's a good guy. But my dad never gave me the quality time that I needed as a little girl. The optics are great, you know having this big, tall strong hard-working father in the house, but he was always working and when he wasn't working, he was out cheating or doing something when he could have been spending that time with his family. And I love my mother she's the most sweet, compassionate, beautiful woman in the world to me. She always spoke life into me, never hit me, or called me out my name. I mean she is just a big bag of sugar. She has always encouraged me to be my best self, but how could I take that advice from a woman that let a man run all over her, a woman that didn't do all the things that she loved to do because of a man?"

"Such as." Shantel asked sweetly while reaching across the table to touch an emotional Jameela's hand.

"She didn't finish her education, she didn't chase her dream to become a Chef and open a restaurant, food truck, nothing. She just let my father do whatever he wanted to do. I vowed to never have someone run all over me how my father runs all over my mother. So I became obsessed with being independent and financially success-ful and made it my business to be the opposite of her and become the woman that she didn't have the balls to become herself." She said choking just a little bit.

Naomi began to soften up as she heard Jameela speak about her family because she was there for it all, but Jameela never articulated how she felt in this way.

"I'm just so disappointed in her, you know?" she said softly.

"Everyone sees sweet Ms. Monica but all I see is a weak woman. And I love my mother, I feel terrible even speaking about her in this way but it's my truth. I resent my parents so much sometimes, espe-cially when everyone fawns all over them like they're the greatest."

"But why are you putting the blame on your mom when it was your dad doing the wrong thing." Shantel asked.

"Because my mother could trust my father to be exactly who he was while she hid in a shell. *She* shrunk because of my father; he didn't shrink her. *She* chose to play small. She had her thing going on before she met him, she's the one that allowed him the opportunity to become successful."

"Damn." Was all Naomi could say.

The table held silence for a while with everyone processing what Jameela was putting out.

"But there's power in the tongue sis and you have branded your-self, proudly might I add, a product of Preston. What do you think that has done for your love life?" Shantel inquired.

"Yeah, I thought about that. I mean it's partly true, I rather be the hunter than the prey. But that started to get old real fast. The last few men I was with before Tyrone it just felt wrong like I was miss-ing something. All this success, aspirations and goals are all good but then what? Who am I going on romantic vacations with? Who's taking me out to dinner, who am I cooking Sunday dinner for like Ms.

Monica does for Preston? Let me tell you, I watched you fall in love with a beautifully flawed man." She said to Shantel, catching her off guard.

"You talking to me?" Shantel said confused because Jameela was just dragging her husband for filth, and she still was having a hard time sitting across from her as a result.

"Yes, I'm talking to you Shantel Emmitt-James. When Yusef fucked up, I was like *aha!* I knew it, and I gave you hell. I was not kind to you. I didn't consider your feelings. I was too busy trying to prove a point to myself so that I could make excuses for my decisions and thoughts. It wasn't even about you. I judged you for taking him back and marrying him and for that I'm sorry."

"I appreciate this more than you know, Meela, and just know I never held a grudge or malice behind your behavior at the time. It did hurt me tremendously, but a person can't hurt you unless you care about them, right? And I do care about you deeply. But I did recognize how pungent you were being, and it did concern me, but thank you for your apology. Perhaps you can apply that to your parents' situation and be more forgiving about what they went through? They were just trying to find their way?" Shantel said softly.

But Naomi wasn't so forgiving. Jameela really turned up on her and said some low vibrational things and she needed to know where all this came from and how long she'd been feeling that way. Each of them picked up their drinks and began sipping, taking a moment to ingest Jameela being soft and pink, because they knew this would probably be the only time they would see this side of her.

"Naomi, you have been my best friend since the third grade, in fact my only friend until we were in high school, and Shantel came in the mix."

"Fifth grade." Naomi could not help but remind her of how nasty she was in Bobby Van's.

"I deserve that. But you've been in my life forever. I can't even remember a time when you weren't there. There was my little brother and then you, like Pops and Monica, just adopted you one day and that was that. I also want to apologize to you for the hurtful things I said to you. You didn't deserve any of that." She said this time a tear escaped from behind her oversized Celine shades. Shantel reached across the table and gently removed the glasses from her friend's face.

"We need to look into your eyes, and you need to look into ours friend. You need to understand how ridiculously insufferable you have been over the past year." Shantel said.

Jameela put her head down, but Shantel reached across the table and lifted her head up with her chin. She looked both women in their eyes and noticed that Naomi was still emotionless.

"I'm in my mid-thirties and never had a real relationship even if it failed. I have no idea what being in a real relationship looks like. I don't know what intimate love is. And so, I met Tyrone and I convinced myself that he had something special when all it really was to me was timing. And I'm going to hold myself accountable in this moment and say that even if there was infidelity, lies and scandal, I have always envied how you both were never afraid to give love one more try. I have always been lowkey jealous at your approach to love Naomi. No matter what you go through, you still eat, pray, thug as you like to say. Love has found you both at one time or another, it never found me."

Shantel handed Jameela a linen napkin from out of her purse to dab her eyes. Naomi shifted in her seat, seeing her friend so emotional was hard, it was something that she wasn't use to but it was something she had to go through to grow, so as bad as she wanted to get up and hug Jameela, she had to fight the urge and let her friend regurgitate all of the negativity that seemed to be plaguing her over the past few months.

"I went hard trying to make it seem as if I had something that neither of you had."

"Which is what?" Naomi asked.

"A man with no bad track record. Someone that I could show off and say look, he doesn't have any bad history or baggage like you guys experienced. Here is this perfect man, let me show these girls how it's done."

"And have you found this to be accurate?" Shantel asked.

Jameela's silence said it all, but the women already knew this.

Naomi took the opportunity to speak.

"I'll tell you what hurt me the most. We have never been the type of women to hate on any other women, especially one another. We never competed with one another, we've always supported and pushed each other to go big, go far, be successful in whatever our endeavors were. So, when you assumed that I was jealous of you that broke my heart Jameela because I've always been the type of friend to celebrate everyone's wins even when I wasn't winning in life myself and you know that. You attacked my education, my finances, my home, my character, and it fucking hurt to my core Meela. I don't know if I could ever look at you the same again." Naomi said and began to tear up.

Jameela nodded her head aggressively in agreement as Naomi continued to push through her tears and hurt.

"You know I'm a transparent person. I don't like to lie about how I feel or what I have going on. I never had to because I had women around me that I can trust and you changed that Meela, you said some really hurtful things. You were mean, disrespectful, arrogant and you looked down on your friends and that's not cool. I questioned whether I was losing my friend, my sister. Your behavior was beyond bizarre, and I had so many questions like, is this who she really is and is this what she thinks of me? Outside of you and Shantel, who do I really have that I can trust?"

"I fucked up Naomi, I know I did." Jameela said in a low tone.

"My abandonment issues run deep so if I love you and I call you a friend, then that's what you are to me, I don't take that shit lightly. I don't have anyone except you two, no co-workers, nothing and I have been consistent." Naomi spat growing a bit angrier as she thought about the things that Jameela said to her. Shantel reached over and began rubbing Naomi's back to calm her down.

"I'm begging for your forgiveness Mimi. I'm sorry for hurting you. You know you can trust me, you know I'll hop a fence for you, I'll do anything for you. I wasn't being myself because I had some shit in me to fix, I know this now. Please forgive me Naomi. You're my sister and I love you." Jameela extended her hand across the table. "Over the past few weeks I've never felt more alone after that fall out we had. But it gave me time to think about life and what it is I wanted. I've been snappy with my parents too. It's not one of my proudest moments."

Naomi loved Jameela and since this was the first offense in their entire friendship, she decided to forgive her but, in her heart, and mind, things weren't the same. She needed time to heal.

"I get that you are the blunt friend but practice some tact, some couth. Blunt doesn't mean right. This level of clownin' can't ever occur again, I'm not forgiving you next time, you've been warned."

"Noted." Jameela said.

"'You totally went against girl code, like I don't know who you've been over the past year."

"I don't know who I've been either, allowing this man to run game on me. Everything you all were saying had me so upset because I knew that you were right. Something is up with this nigga." She said and chuckled to herself.

"So tell us something we don't know." Naomi said.

"I need my sisters to go off on me. If I can dish it, then I must be able to take it so lay it on me."

Naomi folded her arms exaggeratively and looked at Shantel who was shaking her head no but laughing.

"She asked and she shall receive right?" Naomi said rolling up her sleeves.

"Take it easy on me, I'm feeling like a gentle little lamb right now." Jameela said.

"So what's up, talk to us."

"Well for starters, women's intuition is a real thing, we know this. I keep catching him in little lies, for example last week he told me that he would be in Albany all day handling some paperwork, but who do I run into in the city. He looked like he saw a ghost when he saw me."

"What did he say?"

"He told me that he was meeting with some investors for his business."

"But I thought you were helping him start a business." Naomi said.

"I was until he started to move a little differently."

"What about him moving into your deluxe apartment in the sky?" Shantel asked with a hint of sarcasm.

"That's not happening... until he meets folks." She said toying with her ring.

"And the wedding?" Shantel said.

"And these two non-descript bitches you tried to replace us with?" Naomi added in.

"I must say, that was a bit over the top." Shantel said.

"Again, he was all up in my ear but there will be no wedding without the two of you in it and until he meets my parents. He talked a good one but it's as if the mask is slowly falling off." she admitted.

"Another example, a few weeks back, he went out with these friends but didn't come back to my place. I didn't hear from him for two days! He calls me bright and early on a Monday morning claiming that he was hungover all weekend."

"The writing is on the wall baby." Naomi said.

"So, what's your next move?" Shantel asked.

"Right now, I'm just watching. He's always busy, I'll speak to him either early in the morning or in the evening, never late at night anymore and get this, he's no longer living at the hotel. Allegedly he's couch hopping when he could just stay with me. He claims he's staying between two sets of married friends but that the wives are close to his ex-wife, so he doesn't want me to come over because he doesn't want the ex-wife to know that he's dating and try to fuck him over in the divorce."

"Please do not tell me you're still buying that divorce story." Naomi rolled her eyes.

"I have to be honest with you both."

"I already know what you're about to say." Naomi sipped her drink.

"What, he's still married?" Shantel asked naively.

"He's going through a divorce now. He says that he didn't want to meet anyone until it was final because it doesn't feel right."

"That sounds ridiculous. So he can be in a full relationship with someone but meeting her folks is where he draws the line? Let me let you in on a little secret, men do not leave their wives. Your father didn't leave your mother, my father didn't leave his wife, Yusef isn't leaving Shantel, Cory isn't leaving whatever the fuck that bitch name is that he's married to. These men will sell you a bridge honey, they are not leaving, so please understand that." Naomi said.

"Did you ever google him, do a background check on him, get your hands on his ID and look his ass up? Is his name really Tyrone?" Shantel asked.

"Yeah, I may have to do just that." Jameela said, twirling her glass.

"How haven't you done that already is surprising!" Naomi said.

"No he really manipulated me into believing that he needed to be so down low and secretive with everything so that he wouldn't get fucked over in his divorce."

"How did you fall for that is what I'm having a hard time compre-hending. I mean at this big age, you meet a man, you vet him in some kind of way, by either going to his place, meeting friends and what-ever have you." Shantel said.

"I wish I had an answer, I truly do. I just know that his sister and her friend addressed him as Tyrone, so why would I think that his name isn't Tyrone?" Jameela said staring out of the window.

"So, what else this no-good negro been up to." Naomi leaned in.

"Other than clearly being up to no good, it's anybody's guess what this man has up his sleeves."

"Do you think that he use to play in the NFL?"

"Now why would someone tell that big of a lie? I kind of believe him, I do." Jameela said. Shantel and Naomi both rolled their necks and bucked their eyes open at her in disbelief.

"Girl..." Naomi laughed. "Pops has never seen this man and you know Pops knows every and anything about football, shouldn't that tell you something?"

"Yes, it should but right now I'm just watching him you know?"

"What more do you need to see? You need to cut your losses I'm sorry." Naomi said.

"Hold on now, let's get to the bottom of this. Do you love him Jameela or is he just filling a void in your life because you want love?" Shantel asked.

"A little bit of both." she admitted.

"You deserve a man that you're sure of and that is sure of you, do not settle. Would you want to see either of us setting?"

She shook her head no and began playing with her ring.

"A man asked you to marry him doesn't mean much of anything. Didn't Cory ask me to marry him with his already married ass?" Naomi rolled her eyes.

"Yeah, and now I know what you meant when you would always say *today me, tomorrow you.* That was some prophetic shit, where you learn that from?"

The women shared a good laugh after that.

"I want love, I want a husband, I want a life with someone. I just don't wanna be a fool." she admitted.

"I'm proud of you, Jameela, I know that took a lot of courage to admit." Shantel said.

"I'm just so afraid that I'll never get it, so I act as if I don't want it. A bitch is getting old, these degrees and businesses cannot dick me down out night!"

The women started laughing and clinking glasses. "Listen, you ain't never lie." Shantel said.

"Speaking of degrees, you know I don't be tripping over no paperwork. I'm sorry about what I said in Bobby Vans, you know, calling you mediocre." Jameela said to Naomi.

"And to you too Shantel. Your mother didn't say all of that, I was just being a mean girl. I don't know what came over me!"

"I just don't understand what was in you to make you do and say all of that!" Shantel said rubbing Naomi's back. Naomi then excused herself to the restroom as the women watched her walk away. Shantel leaned in on the table.

"Meela boo, it's just really hard to understand or come back from that debacle at Bobby Van's, I mean you were on some real mean girl bullshit!"

But Jameela had no words, she just embarrassingly twirled her drink waiting for Naomi to come back. Shantel leaned back in her seat and was about to check on Naomi when she reappeared and sat down quietly.

"You good Mimi?" Shantel pouted.

Naomi nodded and signaled for the server so she could order more drinks.

"I'm sorry, Naomi," Jameela said again.

"Mmm hmm, so let's finish talking about this old dirty bastard you're dealing with." Naomi said wanting desperately to change the subject.

"Not too much on Tyrone now, he may end up being my husband."

Naomi rolled her eyes. "Girl please, he's still somebody else's husband. God don't bless no mess."

"You're right about that! I don't understand how some women can be so delusional to think that they can take a man away from his wife. Like what in the Shirley Murdock be wrong with these hoes?" Shantel said causing Naomi to burst out in raucous laughter.

"Shantel, you have been extra funny these days have I told you that?"

"I'm serious though!"

"No seriously, that's why once I found out about Cory, as much as it hurt me to my core, I knew that was a fight that I would not win. Because wifey ate me up when she said, *when he dies the only thing, he's leaving you is alone. Like*, biiiitch, what?" Naomi laughed.

"Not a crumb was left." Shantel laughed as well.

"Ate you right on up, like Ms. Pac Man, wacka, wacka, wacka, god damn!" Jameela said.

"Oh, I'm so glad I can laugh about it now. But I have a secret, well not a secret but I didn't tell you guys he came back upstairs after you and Yusef left, and we had some of that I know I'll never see you again type sex."

"I'm not surprised at all, you truly loved that man." Shantel said.

"I did. Hell I still do. But I'll tell you now, make up sex is overrated. I don't regret it, but it did nothing for me."

"So what's been going on with you anyway?" Jameela asked.

"Same ole same. I've been having some wild adventures but I'm not sure if I want to share, no shade but you two have a way of making a gal feel judged. I know, you just want me to be safe but alright already." She rolled her eyes.

"Give that kitty kat a break is all I'm saying." Shantel said.

"She doesn't need a break, she needs the breaks beat off her ass every chance she gets!" Naomi chuckled.

"What's up with ole faithful, he still around?" Jameela inquired about Damon.

"My lover boy, of course he is. When he's in town, he calls, I go running, we both get to cummin, creamin and screamin, same shit."

"Don't you ever want more sis?" Shantel asked softly.

"Here we go! Can we just have fun with it and not be so serious? You have a married woman's mind, so I don't expect you to understand. I'm not bothering anyone, so I don't understand why you both are so bothered by me and what I choose to do."

"You know what, you're right. You're a grown woman and as your friends we just want the best for you and if this is the level you're at right now in life, then so be it. So, what's the latest story." Jameela pried.

"I agree, I second that. No more preaching and judging." Shantel raised her glass as they all toasted. Naomi took a beat before sharing her some of her stories. She warmed them up about the fitness guy she met at a Juice Bar to start.

"Some of these men I've been coming across don't count. If your dick doesn't touch your belly button when it's erect, you just don't count to me."

Laughter filled the table for a while as the women began cracking jokes and talking over one another while the server brought out their food orders.

"Girl it was like he worked out too much his dick shrunk or something I don't know it was disgusting. Then girl, the night we left Bobby Vans, Shantel knows this story, I met this fine chocolate brother, I got to his place, and he had burnt bacon dick."

Shantel covered her mouth, and her shoulders were jerking up and down as she stifled a laugh. Jameela's mouth was agape.

"What is bacon dick?"

"I said *burnt* bacon. What does a burnt piece of bacon look like, girl bye! I faked a stomachache, sent out the S.O.S Shantel called back and got me clean up out of there. I blocked him as soon as I got home. But before I left, he was telling me about some party that he thought I'd be interested in going to, so I went alone, and you both are not going to believe what happened *that* night."

"I am afraid." Shantel said.

"I met this guy I can't remember his name honestly and I'm vibing with him right, he's there with a bunch of guys. He was a catch, embodied everything that a man is supposed to be on the outside right but then his friend showed up and baby, this man was a big ole fine goddess of a nigga and we catch a vibe, the sexual tension between us was so thick. So, I go to the bathroom on another floor and the friend follows me. Tell me why I fucked the friend in the bathroom."

"Girl shut the front door, what?" Shantel's eyes bugged open.

"Oh my goodness, Naomi!" Jameela said.

"Oh, it gets even better."

"Wait, first how was it?" Jameela asked.

Naomi did the chef's kiss to show how good it was.

"Wow, okay so then what happened?" she leaned onto the table.

Naomi lowered her voice as she began telling her story about the threesome. Shantel was clutching her fake pearls as Naomi told the story of how the two men took turns devouring every inch of her body from the inside out.

"What got into you that night?" Shantel asked.

"Besides those two beautiful men, what else did I need, it was phenomenal." She bit her lip.

"Would you do it again?" Shantel asked as Naomi stared off into space.

"If it never happens again, I'll be okay, fantasy fulfilled. But when I tell you they were like synchronized swimmers or something they were so in tune, it was magical." She said zoning out and reminiscing.

"Wow, it was like that?" Shantel asked.

"It was nothing short of amazing, honestly. All those hands, tongues, and mouths on me at once I didn't know whether to shit or go blind. But the best part was the control that I was in. It felt good to be running the show, leaving when I felt like it. But I think that I've become insatiable in a sense but it's unrealistic to chase that high."

"Wow." Shantel said really taken aback by the story she just heard. The table was quiet for a while, everyone digesting the details of what Naomi just shared.

"So now what, what else is there for you to do sexually, women?" Shantel asked.

Naomi chuckled softly, "We're in two different places in our lives Shantel, just leave me be. I'll be okay."

The women didn't say anything. They began digging into their dishes quietly.

"I'm feeling judged again." Naomi sang.

"Nobody's judging you baby, I just really think that you should take some time to yourself, lay off the dicks for a while." Shantel advised.

"I don't want to be the poster child for healing. It's shit or get off the pot, life goes on." She said with a mouth full of eggs.

"Maybe you're not as over that hurt as you think?" Jameela asked cautiously.

"Meela, girl, come on now don't do me, you've had your run."

"And I just sat here and admitted that it was fueled by my parent's marriage. You have way more trauma then I do Mimi, you know it."

Shantel nodded her head in agreement as she slowly cut her French toast. Naomi looked at them both.

"You know what I think? I think trauma has become a trend now. Everything is not fueled by trauma you do know that right? It's perfectly normal for people to make decisions and live their lives based off the present and how they're feeling not based off some shit that happened decades ago that nobody remembers nor gives a fuck about. I'm not going to just sit on my hands like a good girl and wait for my husband to come along because daddy left me and mama didn't give a shit."

"This is less about you finding a man and more about you finding yourself." Shantel said.

"Oh, so I'm lost now."

"Don't be so defensive, we're just telling you how it looks." Jameela said.

"How it looks to who? You guys talk to me as if ya'll shit don't stink." Naomi put her fork down.

"Oh we are not about to do that again." Shantel said easing up in her seat thinking about when Jameela went on that tangent in Bobby Vans.

"That's not where I'm going with that. Look, I'm good, it is not as bad as you think."

"You know who you sound like?" Shantel asked.

"Who." Noami rolled her eyes frustrated.

"Yusef, back then." She said cutting her French toast as she could feel Naomi's eyes piercing through the side of her face.

"I want to share something with you ladies that I've never been able to articulate, however, the remnants of what I'm about to tell you has been lying dormant in my soul" Naomi said as the server removed their plates from in front of them.

"When I was about seven years old, I remember sitting in the back of my classroom feeling down as I watched my classmate Shaniqua's parents sit on either side of her to sing happy birthday. The immense sadness that came over my young body was inexplicable at the time. I hated Shaniqua because she had a father, and I didn't. I remember looking up at him as he approached me to hand me a chocolate cup cake and I couldn't stop staring at this man. It was the closest that I've ever been to a dad. I had never been around anyone that had one. It was just me, my mom, and my aunt until she bought a house on Long Island, so she didn't come to visit us as often as she once did. Shaniqua's parents kept kissing her and her father picked her up and she playfully told him to put her down in front of her friends. Everyone giggled and surrounded her dad. I wanted him to pick me up, but I just stared from the back of the classroom."

"I can relate." Shantel said.

"On the walk home from school, for some reason I suddenly started seeing fathers everywhere holding the hands of their children. When I got home, I asked my mother how come my dad never comes to visit and all she said was why am I asking now?"

"Has she ever had conversations with you about your father prior to this?" Jameela asked.

"No, not really. It was just understood that he was alive and just wasn't dealing with us. But I remember telling her the story about Shaniqua and all she said to me was, *so now you want a dad too?*"

"Damn." Shantel said under her breath.

"A few weeks later, on a Saturday morning, my mother was in an exceptionally good mood, and I didn't know why. She was blasting Stephanie Mills, *I feel good all over* and seemed, to have a little joy in her heart. Normally she was always consumed with her schoolwork, so I loved seeing her show emotions. I remember being so in love with my mom when I was little. She looked like Gladys Knight to me."

"So what was she so happy about?"

"My father was coming but I didn't know at that moment of course."

"*Ohhh.*" Shantel and Jameela said in unison.

"So he comes over and introduced himself as Kareem then he just stared at me for a while, then told my mother that he couldn't do this. They started arguing but I didn't know who he was. I was so confused."

"So he never introduced himself as your father and your mother never gave you the heads up that he was coming, how old were you?" Shantel inquired.

"About seven or eight, something like that. Anyway, my mother blurts out, *it's time that you start acknowledging your daughter.* When I tell you I got so excited and I really started to look at him and realized how much I looked like him, so now I'm getting giddy! I wanted to say the word Daddy like I heard Shaniqua say so in the middle of them arguing I called out, Daddy? Well, he walked up to me, cupped my chin, looked me dead in the eyes and said, don't ever call me daddy again. Then he walked out the door."

The girls gasped in horror at the cruelness of her story. No one said anything for a while as Naomi began sharing the emotional details of her childhood.

"All of this is how I ended up spending so much time on Long Island, specifically when my father's wife left a nasty voicemail on my mother's answering machine calling me a bastard and my mother a tramp."

"Jameela, she never shared this with you growing up?" Shantel looked on in shock.

"No ma'am." She answered with her head down.

"Then one day I was coming home from school and this car was following me. Out jumps a woman and a young boy about 13 years old. She tells me that her name is Diane and told me to tell my tramp bitch of a mother to stay away from her husband or something like that. Then, the little boy kicks me, and they get in the car and drive off. I was done. I went home and I told my mother and she just stared at me. She didn't hug me, explain anything to me, she just stared then told me to wash up for dinner. A few months later she decided to move down south to set up shop for us but she never came back for me. I'm telling you both this story because I want you to understand that I have experienced a level of betrayal, abandonment and hurt like no other and yet I still manage to smile, be joyful, blessed, happy. So when you see me out, living my life, doing what makes me happy, please don't disrupt it with your expectations of me, please, stop worrying about me."

"I'm at a loss for words. We grew up together and I knew that your mother left you and that's how you ended up with Zola, but you never shared details. I only experienced you showing emotion once you got to Junior High, and you would be so upset with your mother when she called. This is a lot I am so sorry friend." Jameela said reaching across the table placing her hand on top of Naomi's. Shantel followed suit. The women sat quietly for until the server appeared asking were they ready for the check.

Chapter 16

GUESS WHO'S BIZZACK

Benjamin was the oldest man that Naomi had ever had an encounter with, but he was handsome and in shape. Men in shape was her preference. She met him on the C train on her way to work. His Brooks Brother's suit fit him well. Naomi appreciated a man that enjoyed reading so she watched him as he stood up, holding on to a pole, deep into, "The Four Agreements." He caught her looking at him twice and each time she would turn her head away, embarrassed. The next time she looked at him he was already staring. He had on a pair of Cartier frames, that he adjusted and smiled. He then made his way over.

"You ride this train every day?" he asked now standing over her while holding on to the pole.

"Give or take a few minutes."

"Benjamin." He said and gave her his fist. "Germs, the pole." He explained.

"Bobbi."

"Nice to meet you Bobbi, I'm about to get off next stop, can I get your number?"

Naomi quickly put her number in his phone.

"I'll call you tonight!" he promised as he jogged off the train. He had such a nice smile and he wore his salt and pepper beard well, but all Naomi could think about was if he had a nice dick to go with it. She quickly forgot about the stranger and went back to listening to her podcast. Once off the train she made her daily stop at Dunkin Donuts for her French vanilla coffee, three creams, three sugars with a shot of espresso when her cell phone rang. It was a 910-area code.

"Yes hello." She sang as she hot stepped down John Street.

"Hello, Naomi, this is your mother."

Naomi stopped in her tracks.

"Naomi, baby how are you sweetheart. I just want to talk, is this a good time?"

At ten years old, tired of hearing her mother's lies about coming to get her and starting school in the South, Naomi decided that she would not talk to her mother until she came to get her. No matter how hard her aunt Zola tried to get her to understand that her mother was just working hard to secure a future for them both, Naomi didn't want to hear it. Her mother would always send gifts on the holidays and birthdays, but never did she once show up. By the time Naomi was in the 8th grade, she had become a "woman" when she lost her virginity and her outlook on life began to change. She was no longer that innocent girl waiting on mommy and daydreaming about daddy. She had her mind made up; she was on her own.

"How did you get my number?"

"Well hello to you to Naomi. Is this a bad time?"

"I'm on my way to work, so I guess you can say it's not a good time."

Naomi suppressed any memories or thoughts of this woman so far deep down into her mind. Her aunt, whom Naomi always remained close and in contact with once she moved out of her house right after high school must have given her the number. But the sound of her mother's voice just reopened a very deep wound.

"I need to talk to you, when's a good time to call you back?"

"What do you need to talk to me about?"

"Naomi, please. Can I please call you later today?"

Naomi thought back to the last time she had a conversation with her mother when she was in her twenties. She loved her mother and wanted to forgive her for leaving her. But after expressing the mental and emotional load she had to carry when her mother and father abandoned her, she was met with lack of accountability on her mother's part, her feelings downplayed and her being called dramatic. They got into a huge argument with Cherisse calling Naomi a liar, trying to convince Naomi that she sent for a few times, but she didn't want to come. She flipped everything on Naomi leaving her heartbroken and she vowed to never talk to her mother again. She begged her aunt not to ever give Cherisse her number, but she was guessing now that the statute of limitations had run out. She hesitated for a while then told Cherisse that she would give her a call later once she got home and settled.

Shantel genuinely enjoyed dog sitting for Naomi when she would go away on her "hoeasis" as she liked to call it, this time, she was in St. Thomas for a few days with "Benjamin the older gentleman" much to Shantel's disapproval as she thought Naomi was moving too fast and not being careful. She had only known him a month and was already going on trips with him. Though Naomi swore she "wasn't going through anything just living her best life" Shantel knew better, especially after that heart breaking story she told in Blvd Bistro. But when the time was right, she was really planning to have a sit down with her good girl friend who seemed to be racking up sex partners like frequent flyer miles and this time she didn't care if Naomi got offended.

It had been a long time since Shantel took in Harlem's beauty, strolling through her neighborhood and enjoying the culture. With Sam and Ginger along for the ride, Shantel stopped at a few stands, purchasing incense and Sage, gaudy African jewelry and even dipped inside of a health store for a green smoothie. It was a gorgeous fall day, and a sea of sweater coats and denim jackets swarmed the streets, the music was blasting, and the strong smell of dope or marijuana was in the air. An African braider seemingly came out of the crevices of the concrete begging her to come get her hair braided to which Shantel politely declined and was met with a scowl. She walked along the streets of Harlem, past the Red Rooster where she was flooded with memories of her childhood. Shantel stopped briefly in the middle of the sidewalk to adjust the straps on the dog leashes and to secure her messy bun that had fallen out because of the strong and steady but warm winds when she felt the large presence of her husband behind her as he wrapped his arms around her waist and picked her up slightly to kiss her neck.

"What are you doing out here? I thought you would be at Dwayne's all day helping him move."

"He has more manpower than he thought, so they don't need me."

"But you're the biggest and strongest of course they need you." Shantel flirted with her arms around Yusef's waist looking up at him.

"Don't hurt your neck girl." He joked and grabbed the leashes from her as Sam and Ginger jumped all around him to get his attention.

"Hey girls." He began to do a light jog as the dogs tagged along. Shantel watched in admiration as the women passing by on the street all eyed Yusef, leaning into one another to whisper to their friends, no doubt discussing what a beauty he was. She was so thankful that in her soul and spirit, she knew that her husband was all for her and no longer in the streets, so she didn't mind the stares, one woman even blurted out to her, "*Yaaaaaz sis, you did that!*" to which Shantel winked and said thank you. That was black women for you, the ones that didn't hate at least. Shantel trailed behind, texting Naomi on WhatsApp, asking her was she safe and enjoying herself and in true Naomi fashion she had a funny story to tell.

"Can I call you, he's at the gym, he just left so I got time." Naomi text. Shantel replied sure and soon Naomi's beautiful, tanned face appeared by the poolside with a mimosa close to her lips.

"So, how's the trip, what's going on out there?"

"Oh, the place is beautiful, we're staying on Sapphire Beach in luxury villa it is absolutely amazing, we have a private chef, the water is pristine, the food is chef's kiss." She said making the kiss gesture.

"Sounds so divine, I'm glad that you're safe, *crazy* but safe."

"I'm just living my life girl, where are my babies?"

"Your babies are with Uncle Sef, they ran ahead of me. So what's going on, what's up with Bernie."

"Benjamin." Naomi laughed.

"I can't keep up, you got a Bernie in your roster I'm sure." she teased.

"Girl so, his dick gets pretty hard still, I guess we can contribute that to him working out and he doesn't drink but he smokes a little joint here and there when he's trying to get in the mood so you know, we were out here smoking feeling all sexy and what not and I'm rubbing on that thick delicious thing, it looks like a caramel snickers bar with all the veins, his dick is beautiful girl! I mean he knows how to eat *and* beat!"

"So, what's the problem?"

"I can't really say it's a problem, but he got some OG Bobby Johnson dick on him." Naomi said laughing with tears coming down her cheeks.

"Naomi *please* alright?" Shantel laughed as well. "What does that even mean?"

"I feel like he's trying to do like a sexual seance on me, something isn't right. But girl get this, I was doing a reverse cowgirl on him this morning and baby I thought I was about to sink into quicksand, his old ass knees were so damn soggy both my hands sunk into his damn knees!"

"Naomi!!!!"

"I can't make this stuff up Shan. So anyway, to save myself from drowning in his knees I grabbed his ankles. The sex is good he has a nice body for a man his age, but I can't lie, old balls is old balls and I'm a visual woman I'm not ready to see old balls, have you seen me naked?"

"I have not had the pleasure of seeing you naked sweetie, my bad." Shantel said full of sarcasm.

"Well you don't know what you're missing. My body is a wonderland baby, and I cannot have no Access-A-Ride pulling up to this here pussy. I'm still quite young, I got Lex coupes beamers and Benz pussy still, so baby it's going to be a no for me after this trip."

"Naomi, you have got to be stopped, I'm serious." Shantel chuckled.

"Come on, how are you going to take me to pound town on a hover round!'"

"Naomi!" Shantel began cackling. "You are so ridiculous, I swear!"

"Look, he's fine and in shape and I have a confession."

"Do I really need to know this." Shantel was shaking her head with her eyes on Yusef and the dogs running up and down the block.

"You don't *need* to know but I got to tell somebody. The dick was so good I cried."

"Wait, what?" Shantel slowed her walking. Naomi was nodding her head yes, "I don't know if it was the alcohol, the weed, but it was something about how good he felt on top of me and in me, he was just delicious and next thing you know he's fucking me so good I got the ugly cry going."

"You cried? Like … a tear rolled down your eyes?"

"No, I cried like somebody died, maybe it was my pussy, maybe the pimp in me died, I don't know but something died, and I cried!"

"Can you be serious for one moment. I think I know why you were crying."

"Here we go, let me guess, I miss Cory, I got daddy issues, what." Naomi rolled her eyes.

"You said it. You're with that older man, he probably gives you some security that you never had even though, hear me out, even though you just met him, energy doesn't lie. And if he was giving you that OG Bobby Johnson then you know that's what has you all in your feelings. That grown man, secure, I got you, kind of loving. Sweetheart you ain't never had that shit before and you need it."

"That sounds wonderful Shantel but uh no, I think I was just drunk, so anyway, as I was saying with your ole philosophical, I think very deeply KRS-1 ass, it was just emotional sex, that's it. I hope he doesn't think he's the bomb or no shit like that."

"Denial is a river in Egypt girl, when are you going to see *the lady* because I can't with you."

"Soon Dr. Shantel Emmitt-James. I don't need you to try and psychoanalyze me while I'm out here with this sexy ass AARP peen, okay?"

"But you have a problem with him because his knees are soggy or because he made you feel

extra, good."

"I have a problem with him because he got somebody."

"Naomi! Come on now you know we talked about this, we don't willingly get into situations

with involved men! How involved is he, relationship, or marriage."

"I rather not say." Naomi sipped her drink.

"Mimi." Shantel said disappointingly.

"Once I come home, I'm blocking him and moving on. And don't give me that look girl please, you're married so you don't have any conversation for me right now, we are not the same, why are you over there talking to your single friend anyway?"

"What is that supposed to mean?"

"Just let me live my life on *my* terms and when I'm ready to get married or settle down, I'll let you know so that you can chime in and help me find a husband, deal?"

Shantel rolled her eyes, "So go on, finish your story." she said trying to keep the peace.

"*As I was saying*, I'll do a brother in his low 30's, I'll even do 40s, but upper fifties, knocking on 60s is giving Isley's. I don't know girl, it's so confusing because older men are so experienced, passionate, they know how to treat a woman's body so damn good but it's just something that I'm not ready for right now. But here he comes with his soggy ass knees I think he lost the cartilage or something I don't know but smooches boo I'll be home in two days! And I forgot to tell you that I spoke to Cherisse."

"*Whaaaat.*" Shantel laughed at the soggy knees comment but was taken aback by hearing that Cherisse called.

"Yes, long story but I'll tell you all about it when I get home. Kiss my babies for me." she said quickly and hung up. Shantel continued laughing at her friend as she turned the corner and headed toward her brownstone. As she got closer, she could see Yusef inside of the gate talking to a man. They seemed to be in a very engaging conversation. The gentlemen had his back turned and Yusef towered over him facing Shantel. As she neared them, the gentleman turned around to face her as Shantel asked, "hey baby, is this our new neighbor?"

EMOTIONS TAKING ME OVER

ameela was on a mission to catch Tyrone in a lie. She knew that he was up to something because his behavior changed drastically. He wasn't spending nights or taking her out as frequently. He claimed to be working on his business venture and flying back and forth between New York and Dallas to see the children and though Jameela couldn't argue with that, her suspicions were confirmed when he was supposedly in Dallas but when he face-timed her while going for a run in the neighborhood she was able to see a street sign as he stopped to catch his breath. She googled the sign and found that it was a street in New Jersey.

As she drove around the affluent neighborhood with beautiful trees lining the streets and million-dollar homes tucked away down circular driveways, she stumbled upon the street that Tyrone was last seen on a few days prior and it led her down a road. Looking left to right for any signs of Tyrone by way of his cars, her mouth was left agape at the beautiful multimillion dollar homes. She drove slowly admiring the homes when she saw her man's Lamborghini behind a large gate that protected an enormous home, a home fit for an (ex) athlete.

"I got you motherfucka." she said and pulled out her phone to take pictures. Tyrone had driven his G-wagon to her home, and she insisted time and time again that he bring the Lamborghini because she loved driving it and he told her that it was in the shop, but there it was sitting pretty amongst a small fleet of foreign cars. Cars, she had never seen him drive nor did he mention owning. Jameela sat back and stared at the house. There was no way to pass the gate unless she had access or was with someone that lived there. The lights were all off and you could tell that nobody was home. She took a few more pictures then called Naomi as she made her way back to her apartment.

"I knew he was up to something, this motherfucka has a whole mansion that he's living in, can you believe it!" she said to Naomi who was out walking Sam and Ginger.

"I'm such a damn fool!" she said banging the steering wheel.

Naomi could only empathize with her friend with whom she tried to warn, based on the red flags that this man was up to no good but alas here they were, and this wasn't the time for I told you so because Jameela was furious driving home. Naomi had to warn her to slow down and be careful, reminding her of that woman in L.A. that killed 6 people as she drove in a rage after an argument with her boyfriend. She slowed down and drove with her hand on her head most of the way until she pulled into the underground parking lot of her building.

"Is he upstairs?" Naomi asked.

"Yeah, he's up there. You know he's the one that convinced me to get this expensive ass apartment because he said once he moved in that he would take over the rent."

"Are you having trouble paying the overhead?"

"It's a lot of money every month! I'm paying $8,500 by myself."

"Shit girl!"

"I'm so damn upset I don't know what to do." Jameela said as she pressed PH on the elevator.

. "Are you going to say anything to him about this?"

"Nope, I'm going to build my case and get his back against the wall until he can't take it anymore and is forced to tell me about this house and cars that he has. I'm not going to make this easy for him at all and he's going to start paying this fucking rent!"

"Damn well keep me posted and keep your cool girl!"

"Hmph, I'll try. Well let me go inside and deal with this lying ass negro, this calls for a Friday night at Shan's, call her up and give her the tea and let me know if she's free."

"I don't know what is up with Shan. I didn't even see her when I picked up Sam and Ginger, she left them at doggy day care."

"She's a busy woman. Well let's all try to link soon."

"Will do, love you."

"Love you too." Jameela said, disappearing behind the door.

Naomi was about to call Shantel but that 910 area code popped up from before. Naomi never bothered to save Cherisse's number.

"Whassup." Naomi said dryly.

"Hello to you too Naomi."

The sound of her mother's voice bothered her immensely, but she wasn't about to give her birthing person any negative energy. There was so much she wanted to say to her mother, but she silenced her years ago by turning against her and downplaying her hurt when she attempted to open up to her. It hurt Naomi's heart to think about how much she used to adore, look up to and be in love with her mother as a little girl.

"Do you have some time to talk, I don't want to rush the conversation." Cherisse said cautiously.

"What's up." Was all Naomi could ever manage to say. She could hear her mother take a deep breath on the other end out of frustration and she did not care.

"Well, for starters, I'm coming to New York next month." She paused, waiting for Naomi to care enough to ask her why.

"There's something that we need to settle." She went on and Naomi still said nothing.

"Naomi are you there?"

"*Mmm hmm.*" Was all she said.

"Look Naomi, I'm coming next month because Kareem wants to see you and talk to you." She blurted out.

"I'm listening." Was all Naomi said.

"He asked that I give you his number so that you can call him, but I thought it be best that I take a trip so that the three of us can sit down together and clear the air. He reached out to me some time ago on social media and we cleared up a lot of mess between us."

"I'm happy for you both. Was his wife privy to this reconciliation." Naomi said sarcastically.

"As a matter of fact, she was."

"Well great for all of you, you guys going to double date or what?"

"Naomi, I just want to be there to not only support you when you see him face to face but to talk about you and me. It's long overdue."

"I'm a full-grown adult now, why would I need to sit with either of you when you could have cleared the air all throughout my teens when I asked questions, throughout my twenties when I asked questions. There's nothing you can say to me now, especially in front of Kareem to appear as if you truly care. I tried to clear the air with you, but you had amnesia and called me ungrateful, you forgot? Does he know that you abandoned me too? Is he aware of the kind of woman that you are?" Naomi snapped.

"I did not abandon you. Your aunt Zola took great care of you, you went to a good school and built a nice life for yourself. Why would I take that from you when you seemed so happy? Whatever decisions you made as a young adult is on you."

"And still, no accountability." Naomi said feeling herself get pissed. But this time she wasn't going to hang up the phone and fester in her hurt. She was ready to unleash.

"Naomi, I know that I've made some terrible decisions in my life. But we're both grown, and I want to fix this."

"We are both grown but I am still 7 years old. That's the person you left. You don't know me

past that! That's what you're not understanding miss psychotherapist! You weren't there for my Junior High or Highschool graduation, what excuse do you have for that?"

"I couldn't get off of work for your Junior High graduation and that graduation is not that important Naomi."

"Oh my God, do you hear yourself?"

"And when you were graduating high school, I was graduating with my Ph.D, I couldn't miss my own ceremony!"

"You were disgusted that I didn't go to college, and I know you disowned me for not living up to your standards. I lost my virginity in the 8th grade, did you know that? And I didn't have you to talk to, I didn't even know why I was in that predicament, all I knew was that whatever was inside of me was leading me to make some terrible damn decisions. My first date, my first heartbreak, my first job, anything having to do with being a woman, I had to go to my friend's mother. As much as auntie does for me and has done for me, I thank God for her, but I had to hide everything from her because I didn't want her to tell you, because you didn't deserve to know anything about me because you weren't around!" Naomi yelled.

"You act like I left you destitute on a stoop with a crackhead in the projects. How the hell do you think you ate, and were able to dress and have the latest clothes and go places? You think your cheap ass aunt was funding all of that? No sweetheart, I was sending her money and making sure you had the best of everything!"

"Is that what you took from everything that I just said! For a person with so many degrees you are so damn ignorant and have no common sense. The best of everything would have been a mother that loved me and a father that acted like he gave an ounce of a fuck, but you managed to fuck both of those up for me."

"Naomi, watch it okay? I'm still your mother."

"You are my birth giver. Ms. Monica is a mother, Cheryl is a mother, Auntie Zola is a mother but not you, you left me, got married and became a *mother fucker* and a mother to a fucking stranger!"

"Naomi, you have one more time to say something disrespectful out of your mouth to me and I promise you..."

"You ain't never promise me shit in life so don't start now. Let me explain something right quick. I don't care if you slept with a married man or that you hid me from him, that's between ya'll. That's something that's going to haunt you both! Him cheating on his wife and you being a side bitch, you both have to answer to the most-high when it's all said and done. What I care about is that you put your love for a man before being a mother and when that man didn't want you, you left me, you said fuck me because I was a part of him which lets me know that you got pregnant to keep him and when you couldn't keep him you decided not to keep me either. Then you met a woman, married her, and helped her raise her son?" Naomi's voice cracked.

"Naomi, you're my only child and I love you with everything in me. I would never hurt you on purpose." Cherisse said softly.

"What if I didn't have auntie, where would I be? Then you got the nerve to become a psychotherapist and calling me like we're best friends, getting mad when I go months and years not talking to you. You left me! Why should I care about you! You need psychotherapy your damn self!"

"Naomi Latrice Lawson, you think you understand and know everything. You don't know much and that's why I want to come and talk to you with Kareem present."

Naomi laughed, "I did good without your guidance, your love, your assistance, your help, your conversation, your presence. I had abortions without you. Not just one, but three, my first one in the 9th grade. I got my heart broken and healed it without you. I bust my ass to be a good woman, to be the kind of woman that you will never be, without you! And I didn't go to college because I was too busy trying to heal and survive and make sure that I never needed any one for any fucking thing because my own parents abandoned me, who could I count on? I would never ever do this to my child. You're a coward and I don't respect you at all, you know that? You leave me then go start a whole new life, taking in someone else's child? Does your wife know what a piece of shit you are?"

"Naomi!" she shouted in her proper tone.

Naomi didn't feel good saying what she said but she couldn't take it back, it was too late. It was how she felt in her heart, but her aunt didn't raise her to be disrespectful to her mother, she knew better but couldn't bring herself to apologize.

"I'll text you Kareem's number, do what you want with it." Cherisse said and hung up.

Naomi knew that her mother's feelings were hurt, and she didn't delight in disrespecting any woman, even if it was the woman that gave her life and abandoned her without as much as a goodbye, sit down, an explanation, and broken promises of *I'll send for you*. Moments later Kareem's contact came through to her phone. Naomi gave the dogs a bath, then herself, put on some lounge wear, poured herself a glass of champagne and curled up in her King-sized pillow top mattress bed, pillows surrounding her for safety as she was sure to be crying into one if not all of them before the night was over. She stared at the number for a while then decided before reaching out, to look him up on the internet and see what he was about. If he was a bum, alcoholic, looked like he was on drugs or showed any signs of stress or strife, getting acquainted with Kareem Lawson would be absolutely null and void. However, if he looked as if he was living a positive life then she would consider the possibility of texting him, *one day*. Kareem Lawson, 62 years old, Brooklyn New York, married to Diane Lawson. Naomi clicked on his wife's page first before looking into his. That was the mean woman that accosted her when she was just a little girl walking home from school. Naomi scrolled down her page, her lips were still black, and she put on weight, edges still nonexistent, her hair pulled up in a tight ponytail.

This heiffa ain't learn.

She scrolled and scrolled and there was her brother, the one that kicked her, with his cap and gown on, having graduated from Morehouse College. More pictures of Kareem, Diane, her brother whose name was KJ- Kareem Jr., friends, and family.

Naomi thought back to how many times over the years she called his house to speak to him and his wife would be so mean and would tell her that her father didn't love or want her and to leave them alone. Finally, their number changed. Naomi was way out on Long Island with no way or reason to visit Brooklyn once her mother left so plans of going by his house never came to fruition. But when she got old enough to take public transportation on her own, one day she headed to Brooklyn after school and went by his house. She of course didn't knock on the door but instead just sat in the park across the street for hours not knowing what to expect. Then finally, Kareem came out of the house with his son, the two of them laughing about something. She followed them from the opposite side of the street down four or five blocks and both went into a barbershop. The boy sat down first to get his haircut while Kareem flipped through a magazine. Naomi wanted to speak to him so badly but what could she possibly say to the man that looked her dead in her eyes and told her not to ever call him daddy and allowed his wife to call her a bastard. Naomi was 16 years old now, clearly, she looked different from when he saw her as a 7-year-old child, but he would always recognize her. She was his twin, his only daughter. Naomi watched him for so long that he must have felt it because he turned to look out the large barbershop window and they locked eyes. She was so nervous, expecting him to come outside and curse her out for being a stalker, but instead he smiled softly and nodded his head then went back to his magazine. It was then she realized that he didn't even recognize her. Naomi ran to the train station and headed home and cried her eyes out to Pops and Ms. Monica while Jameela was at work.

Naomi's chest tightened as she scrolled through social media, watching the life that her father had lived without her. He didn't have many pictures other than the ones Diane tagged him in. Based on his bio, he was an Ophthalmologist, his wife was a dentist, and upon clicking on KJ's page she found that he was married and was an English Professor. She began to take deep breaths, thinking of the life she would have lived if both of her parents poured into her like they poured into themselves and KJ. Her mother left, moved down south, continued her studies and became an African American History Professor and a Psychotherapist. She never thought to take her only child with her and make sure that she became the best woman that she could be. Yet she remarried and made sure her stepson got an education, as he graduated from Shaw University. Naomi began to grow angry, though her life decisions were her own, the seed must be planted by your parents for you to go on and become what you are destined to be, those seeds hatch when opportunity meets hustle. She was only given a seed of survival and how to navigate through heartache and "*make it*" so that she didn't need anyone because truth be told who would she be able to call for anything?

She so desperately wanted to reach out, but she wasn't ready. She could still feel the pain of when KJ kicked and jumped at her, scaring her half to death. She could still remember what a monster Diane looked like towering over her and the names she called her mother that back then, she loved and adored so much. She still remembers Kareem telling her not to ever call him daddy. It all hurt like hell, and for her mother to run away from the pain and leave her there to pick up the pieces as a little girl was just inhumane. The irony of it all was her studying to become a psychotherapist. If she didn't know how to be a mother, why didn't she at least look at Naomi as a patient and help her through this once she got a bit older.

Naomi wasn't ready to regurgitate her emotions and relive what she had been through. Her feelings had been suppressed for far too long. She tossed her phone across the couch and leaned back, allowing the warm feeling of alcohol to take over her body and before she knew it, she didn't remember a thing, just how she liked it.

Liquid courage made her call her favorite guy on the roster, Damon hoping that he was in town. Naomi was feeling emotionally needy after what she had come across on Facebook. She needed to be held and adored, even if it was fake, and Damon was the only one she felt comfortable calling. Damon and that Bruce Lee body with a dick longer than church service on Easter Sunday answered quickly and sounded like he was busy. He told her to take an Uber to Queens and that he'd meet her there, he was handling something. He left the door unlocked for her and upon entering his house, she saw the white crotchless body stocking lying across the arm of the couch.

"Oh, he wants Kitty to come out tonight?" Naomi said as she slid into the sleezy outfit and came into the kitchen to fix herself a drink when Damon came walking in.

"You look nice." He grinned and tapped her on the ass before heading into his bedroom to drop off the duffle bag he was carrying. Loving that he seemed to be in a good mood, Naomi relaxed a bit and poured Damon a shot of tequila.

Damon would play the game, he would get into character and make love to her sometimes like he loved her. Maybe from time to time he needed to live a lie as well. But in the back of her mind, she would sometimes question *how a man could pretend this good, he had to love me in some kind of way,* but then she would snap back into reality when he would sometimes treat her like a piece of ass, like the one time he said he was coming to get her. She had no intentions on fucking him in his car. She came outside dressed in a cute flirty dress, her signature locs wrapped up in a bun, her body smelling like Kilan, Don't Be Shy. She thought it would be one of those fake love nights where he would take her to his place, order take out, make love, she would spend the night and they would talk shit over breakfast then he'd drop her home and let her know rent was on him for the next two months. But he clearly had no intentions or time for that when she got into his vehicle and he pulled off, finding a parking spot a few blocks down on a dark street.

"I've been thinking about that mouth the entire ride up here." He said, the hardness of his manhood in agreeance. Naomi did as she was asked as he reclined the seat in his Ferrari back, allowing Naomi to get on her knees and pleasure him. He pulled her up on top of him after a while so she could ride. Once they were done, he asked her what her plans were for the rest of the night. She lied and said she was going to wash up and meet friends in the city, so he dropped her off in front of her house and sped off. Naomi in turn went upstairs, undressed and cried herself to sleep.

But tonight was going to be the fake love night that she needed. She handed Damon a shot and they both took it together.

"So, Damon, why haven't you settled down. I've known you for how many years now?"

"A really long time, more than ten years. I have settled down. I have two kids now."

Two kids were a shock to Naomi. She knew about one when they met.

"Where the hell have I been?" Naomi asked, trying to appear unphased but for some reason she was very bothered that Damon didn't share this information with her.

"My son is twelve you know about him, and my daughter is four." He said pouring another round of shots and handing one to her. They both took shots again.

"Wow, so do they live up here or...."

"My daughter lives up here. My son lives down south with me."

"Like custody?" Naomi asked.

"No, like me him and his mother live together."

"Oh okay." Naomi answered trying to appear unaffected. Though she knew that she and Damon were just sex buddies, it had been made very clear that she was even less than that to him now not knowing personal information like him having another kid. Sensing her emotions, Damon walked up to her and nudged her with his elbow.

"I know you're not over there catching feelings when you were in a whole relationship about to get married and all that. You forgot? I got feelings too!" he said leaning against the kitchen counter with her.

"You're right." Naomi said grabbing more tequila but this time adding seltzer water and fresh lime to it to make an actual cocktail.

"My daughter is a break baby. But everybody gets along. I don't have time for baby mama drama."

"Not surprised. You don't have the temperament for bullshit and games."

"At all." He reiterated and slid out of his fresh pair of retros. He pulled his shirt over his head and revealed his beautiful body. All Naomi could do was stare. Damon smiled.

"You really do stay your ass in the gym." Naomi said sipping her drink and watching him as he walked around his living room looking for the remote. What turned her on about Damon was that he was never pressed when she was in his presence. These were the "fake love" moments she enjoyed with him. They would spend quality time, watch movies, eat in, talk about air and when the opportunity presented itself, they would get down.

"Let's watch some TV." He said patting the seat next to him. He put on a hood movie that came on Tubi and they both watched and laughed tearing apart how terrible the acting and action scenes were. Then abruptly Damon jumped up, "come on kitty." He said leading the way into the bedroom where Naomi began to dance for him and do all kinds of sexual freaky things as he sat back on his bed with his dick in his hands, watching, his diamond bracelet glistening, his long diamond chain danced along with Naomi. Damon had the sexiest smile, he smirked at the sight of Naomi's cheeks shaking as she did her little stripper dance. No other man had ever asked for this level of entertainment so she enjoyed when Damon would. He reached into the nightstand and grabbed a stack of bills and began tossing them at her which made her giggle. Naomi did her best stripper moves as he egged her on. He was winking at her and rubbing his privates until he demanded her to crawl across the bed and ride him.

The mood was always sexy, exciting, and unpredictable with Damon and tonight was just the kind of evening that she needed after what she saw on Kareem's Facebook page. She needed to let all her emotions out and for whatever reason, Damon was the only man that she would have unprotected sex with. But finding out that he had a steady woman at home rubbed her the wrong way. She put the thoughts of him having a woman at home and any other cock blocking thoughts out of her mind as she rode on top of Damon while he rested his hands on her hips, his eyes closed, biting his bottom lip, enjoying every moment of Naomi. She was his favorite throughout all these years, but she didn't know it because Damon was always too cool to show it.

The night ended in missionary, Damon on top of her, slow grinding, kissing her on her neck, stroking her and whispering nastiness in her ear that would always get her to cum. He was a great sex talker and knew exactly what to say and when to say it. He would talk her through her orgasms, and it would drive her crazy. They both came together, and Damon rolled off her immediately and lay on his back, breathing heavy. Naomi looked over at his beautiful body and inched over closer to him. After such a beautiful night, she felt the need to cuddle up closer to him and began rubbing his chest, kissing the side of his face and running her fingers through his soft hair when he slapped her hands off of him.

"What the fuck is wrong with you?" he said sitting up.

Confused Naomi sat up as well.

"What happened, what did I do?"

"Don't touch me like that." he said, staring at her with the meanest face she had ever seen on him.

"I was just rubbing on you, what's the problem?"

"Ayo, you heard what I said." He said abruptly getting out of bed.

She could hear him in the kitchen. It sounded like he was getting water, so Naomi went into the bathroom to clean herself up. He made her feel so low at that moment, but she wasn't going to cry in this man's house. Yet her eyes were getting cloudy with the chance of showers. *I want to go home.* She thought to herself and so she entered the bedroom and began gathering her clothes. Damon watched her as she looked around the dark room trying to find her things. She didn't want to turn the lights on because she didn't want him to see her cry.

"Nay, come here sweetie." he said. He hadn't called her "Nay" or "sweetie" the last few times they were around one another. He would always call her sweetie and give her tight strong hugs when he saw her, he'd call her Nay when they were relaxing, comfortable in a good place. Naomi did as she was told, crawling into the bed. She needed to feel loved.

"I didn't mean to snap like that. Man, you are the freakiest most emotional woman that I know. You're so sensitive, I gotta remember that." He said tapping her leg. But what she didn't know was that she had a way of making Damon feel too good and vulnerable and it was a feeling that he liked but didn't know how to deal with it. Naomi had so much love inside of her that she wanted to give to someone, and Damon, although she was very clear that they did not love each other but had love for one another, he was the only man of them all that she felt the most comfortable with because she knew him before love and he was still around after love. So she gave him a little bit of what she had, and it was too much for him at times because he always had someone unbeknownst to Naomi and didn't want to get caught up emotionally. So as long as Naomi continued to be the "cool chick" they could get along but the moment that she showed any signs of having feelings, he would be gone.

"Don't leave, it's 4 in the morning. Get some rest. It'll be alright." He said pulling the covers over them both. Naomi didn't have anything to say. She felt terrible so she turned her back to him and closed her eyes, crying quietly into the morning. The next morning when she woke up Damon was gone so she called him, and he asked her not to leave because he was out grabbing breakfast for them both and that he'd be back in about 45 minutes.

"I just left not too long ago. I'm almost at the spot, I'm picking it up and bringing it back, okay?"

"Alright." Naomi said and hung up, but she had no intention of waiting for him. She put her clothes on and snatched up the bills that he gathered for her and placed on the nightstand. Naomi called her Uber and counted while she waited, to the tune of $1,200. She put the money in her small Telfar purse and jumped in her Uber, with plans to never talk to Damon again.

Chapter 18

WHERE HAVE YOU
BEEN ALL MY LIFE

"*H*ey baby." Yusef responded and pulled Shantel up under his wing.

Shantel's smile quickly faded, shock and terror set in as she stared at the man that Yusef was talking to. She was at a loss for words as Yusef rubbed her back.

"Dad?" Escaped her throat.

The three of them stood still in a circle until Yusef suggested they all go upstairs to talk. Shantel obliged by walking up the steps quickly, the men trailing behind. She was standing in the middle of her living room, pacing with her hands on her head when they walked in behind her. Her father walked up to her and gently touched her hand. He pulled her in cautiously until they were touching.

"This is not real; this is not happening, daddy?" her body lightly shaking.

"There is so much to tell you sweetheart." He said choked up.

Shantel pulled away from her father and stared up at him acknowledging that he looked good and clearly was off drugs. He was dressed well in a navy-blue polo sweater and a pair of black yeezy's.

His hairline and teeth were intact, and his nails were manicured. He sat down nervously dangling his Cadillac car keys between his legs.

"The last time I saw you, it was right before my birthday and...." She said tearing up. Her father reached out and touched her leg.

"I came looking for you, I had birthday cake, Arizona juice, water. I even had a camera for us to take our own pictures. I walked around the streets, and you weren't anywhere to be found, neither were any of your buddies." She sniffled.

The day that Shantel could no longer find her father, it broke her heart. She kept looking up at him, in disbelief because he was supposed to be dead.

"The last time I saw you Angel," he said addressing her by her middle name, "I was so happy that we were building that bond and I looked forward to seeing you every single day, it was the highlight of my day and the catalyst for me to get clean. I just had to be a part of your life, but you didn't deserve a father like me."

"But I loved you anyway. None of that stuff mattered and I would have helped you." Shantel sniffled.

"I know baby but that wasn't your burden to bear you were a child. And your mother didn't think it would be good for you to know me or be around me. I wasn't a good example of a man for you, I gotta side with her on that. She was just trying to protect you. Well, she somehow found out that you were sneaking to see me and so her husband came to see me, and he asked me to please leave you alone. He paid me to go away."

"You've got to be kidding me right now!"

"He approached me, Benny, Carl and Sticks and gave us some money to disappear and not come back. As drug addicts, we took the money, but it didn't last long. He knew it wouldn't, so he'd come around often, slide me some money to stay away. He came around on your birthday and gave me the most money he had every given me. Benny and Sticks overdosed in front of me at the same time. I was too high to grieve. Carl and I would see you from time to time, and your mother's husband would come to find me and give me more money to keep me away from you. When I look back on it, he for sure was trying to get me to kill myself. Carl ended up in prison for life, he killed a woman while trying to take her pocketbook. She wouldn't let go so he punched her so hard she hit her head on the ground and never woke up."

"I am just... I'm at a loss for words right now. This is like the twilight zone. That woman watched me suffer over losing you every single day! She told me that you were dead, twice!"

"It's not her fault Angel. After Carl went to prison, these anti-drug advocacy people came around trying to get folks off the streets and into a shelter. One of them recognized me. She was someone I used to get high with, turned her life around. She convinced me to go into rehab and I ended up in rehab in Brooklyn and man it was rough, it was so bad, I found myself back uptown and Brenda found her way uptown to come get me repeatedly. This time she had a connection to put me in a rehab in Connecticut and deep in my heart I wanted to get clean for you." He said reaching in his pocket and pulling out the picture of him, Cheryl and Shantel when she was 2 years old.

"You still have this picture." She said gently removing it from his hands.

"I don't go anywhere without it. I pray to it, talk to it, it's all that I had. So, I went to Connecticut, and I had no choice but to get clean because I didn't know anybody up there, it was like a prison, I couldn't leave. I was there for about six months can you believe that? Then they gave me a job cleaning the facility. I hadn't worked in so long; you know so I'm cleaning and feeling like a man again little by little. I saved my checks, and I enrolled in school online, and I worked hard." He said tearing up.

"A friend of Brenda's let me stay in his basement where I went to school online and got my Masters. I already had my bachelor's when I was with your mother. I worked so hard and by the time I graduated I had a job, money saved, I was so occupied with getting my life together I didn't even realize that five years went by, and I was clean! Then I met my wife while taking my physical exam. She was a nurse assistant. We got married, bought a nice big house in Rye, New York and had a son named Angelo, named after you. Other than some red wine, I've been sober with no desire at all to do drugs, it's been over 20 years now can you believe that?"

Shantel listened to her father's success story enraged that she could have been with him along the way and that her mother lied to her. Noticing the anger appearing on her face, Bilal continuously tried to comfort her with his words.

"She was only trying to protect you angel don't be mad at her, it was me that chose drugs, it was me that left you, it's all my fault. Just try to understand baby." Bilal said.

"How? Do you know the level of evil you have to be to do something like this? And Kenny, all that money he was giving you, why not just pay to put you in rehab? If they loved me so much, they would have done that for me!"

"Angel, God don't make mistakes, you know that right?"

"Yes, I know."

"I have a career. I helped build those big, beautiful buildings in Brooklyn down by the Barclay. I am drug free, happy and blessed to be alive. I have become everything that I was destined to become a long time ago. God is merciful in that way baby. I ain't easy to kill. God had bigger plans for my life!"

"I hear that hot shit." Yusef said from the sidelines.

"I just can't believe you're alive. How did you know where to find me?" Shantel said wrapping her arms around her father.

"Google." He laughed. "Your mother did what she had to do, Uptown Cheryl was never nothing to play with, she just wants the best out of life. Try to find it in your heart to forgive her."

But Shantel was just shaking her head no. She was beyond hurt and couldn't fathom forgiveness at the moment.

"So baby, tell me a bit about your life. I can tell you're living large!" he joked trying to lighten up the mood. "What do you do for a living, and do I have any grand babies?" he nudged her playfully.

Shantel wasn't ready to talk about herself yet. Her father had risen from the dead and she had a million and one questions and feelings running through her mind.

"You know what's crazy? It doesn't even feel awkward. I feel as if you've been right here all my life because you've always been right here." She said softly tapping her chest where her heart is.

"I've loved you all my life and when I saw you for the first time when me and mommy were walking down Frederick Douglas and you told me you were my father, I knew we were attached in some kind of way. You have the kindest eyes and gentle spirit."

"Like you angel. That's why I named you angel, you looked so angelic when you were born. I said look at this little angel, but your mother wanted to name you Shantel from day one, she said that it was a sophisticated name and angel sounded like a stripper name." they laughed. "So, I settled for angel being your middle name. I've always called you angel."

"Well, your angel is the CEO of an African Bank in midtown."

"Is that right?" He leaned back exaggeratively.

"Yes, and Yusef is professor at NYU, and a psychologist for young adults."

"You don't say, that big ole man don't play sports?" He teased.

"I love boxing but other than that surprisingly I am not a big sports fan."

"Is that right?" Bilal said to Yusef.

"Yeah, your daughter hates boxing though."

"It's barbaric!" Shantel said.

Bilal smiled at her and touched her hair.

"This all yours?" He teased.

"Yes, it is, all 40 inches!"

"Damn that's a lot of hair, it's so beautiful, like your mom." He said.

"Please, let us not bring her up for the rest of the evening."

"That's fair, okay, well what else about my Angel?"

"I love to cook and if you're not in a rush, I'd love to feed you. I left over lollipop lambchops, my specialty."

"Oh, sweetheart I'd love that, and I know you get your cooking from me because your dad throws down!"

"Oh really, box mac and cheese don't count!"

"Pardon me? I can cook veal, pork chops, a mean steak, chicken parm, steamed fish, my eggplant parmesan is to die for, you name it, I can cook! "Do you have any red wine?" He smiled as he watched his daughter move around in the kitchen. She then asked Yusef to pour her father a glass.

Shantel was smiling like a little girl on Christmas glancing over from the kitchen to see her father and husband getting acquainted discussing boxing, politics, women, and her little brother. The men ate hungrily, complimenting her food with each bite, but soon it was time for Bilal to head home.

"I am never ever going anywhere again." Her father reassured her by kissing the top of her head.

"I'm so glad you're back." Shantel said hugging her father tight.

"Yusef, good meeting you." He shook his son-in-law's hand.

Yusef and Shantel stood at the top of the steps waving bye to her father as he pulled off in his black Cadillac truck.

"Pops doing it big that truck is mean!" Yusef said admiring the ve-hicle as it disappeared up the street. He put his arms around his wife's shoulder pulling her in closely.

"Come on, I'll clean up the kitchen. Take a shower and let's relax."

Yusef watched her jog up the stairs.

It's about to go down, he said out loud as he loaded the dishwasher.

Chapter 19

CALL TYRONE

The air felt fresh and crisp on this night, so Ms. Monica kept the backyard door cracked as she cooked up a feast for her daughter and her guests. The house would be full tonight with friends of Jameela's, which had Ms. Monica in her element preparing dinner. She had her "Saturday Cleanup" play list on with tunes from Chaka Khan, Chic, Womack and Womack, and so many others playing. Monica pranced around her large state of the art kitchen singing, "Whatchya gonna do for me when the chips are down!" in her best Chaka Khan impression. Preston loved seeing his wife in her bag, cooking and blasting music, however, he was none too pleased about the reason for her good mood.

"I don't know why you all happy to meet this motherfucka, he ain't about shit."

"Damn Preston, all that?" Ms. Monica said, still dancing, she danced her way over to her husband and handed him some bourbon.

"Drink up, you are so grumpy. It's not just about him. I haven't had my children under one roof in a while. The weather is nice, the mood is right, and it's going to be a good night...when the chips are doooooooooooown!" she sang. Preston shook his head and sipped his drink.

"Where did we go wrong with that girl. I thought I taught her how to move since she was a little girl, she still ends up making the wrong choice in men."

"Why is it the wrong choice P? because he didn't come running to meet the *mighty Preston* as soon as he met her. Keep in mind he's a grown man as well. Jameela isn't some little girl that needs to bring her little boyfriend home to meet daddy. They are grown Preston, respect that."

"Yeah, you got a point, but you don't ask a woman to marry you without coming to her father first if her father is in her life. We wait all our lives for this shit and its disrespectful to men, to fathers, to me!"

"Oh big Papa, don't look so deep into it baby I promise you it's alright, gimme kiss." She tip toed to reach her husband's lips, he bent down to meet hers.

"I love you." She winked while stirring her pot and doing a little shimmy dance. Preston smiled at his wife thinking to himself how attractive she was.

"Love you too baby." He responded, leaning against the wall watching his wife move around the kitchen.

Tonight was a big night. *Tyrone* was coming to meet the parents. But his plan was to do this only to keep Jameela quiet for a while so that he could somehow retrieve his wife's belongings that he foolishly gave away to this woman. As he got dressed, Tiffany seemingly unbothered sauntered around the large home in her usual silk robe with a mug of tea, pretending to not watch her husband get extra handsome tonight. Dressed in jeans, a grey cashmere long sleeve shirt and Ferragamo shoes, Gerrod spritzed himself with Santal 33 and slid his Hermes watch on to his wrist. He kissed Tiffany on the top of her head as he whisked by her.

"Where to tonight?" she asked dryly.

"Celebrating an engagement. I told you that already." He said checking himself out in a full-length mirror.

"Who's this person getting engaged again?"

"Black Rock employee, you know that place *you despise* so much?"

"Yes, the company that pays you a salary to make you forget your dreams, that place *you love* so much."

"Not tonight my beautiful wife, be nice, okay?"

"Mmm hmm, what time can I expect you back here?" she asked, setting her mug down on a sterling silver coaster.

"Not too long actually, I want to be there for the proposal, take a few pictures, then I am coming home. It's not a big party, it's a small gathering at his parents' house so it's not like a big turn up or anything."

Tiffany nodded her understanding.

Gerrod kissed Tiffany's lips succulently, paying extra attention to the bottom lip.

"When I come home tonight, I hope my wife is nice and oiled up, smelling like one of her expensive body creams, her hair swept to the side, dressed in nothing but a pair of 5-inch heels, draped in diamonds." He said between kisses.

"Depends on what time my husband comes home." She flirted.

"It doesn't matter what time I come as long as I come home to you. I'll call you when I'm on my way so you can get that body ready for daddy, I want to make love to you until the morning sun warms our bodies. I want to fall asleep in it like I use to."

"Go enjoy your night so you can get back to me." She kissed his lips and playfully pushed him away.

Gerrod could feel his manhood getting erect. Just thinking about how good Tiffany looked naked was enough to get him started, he didn't need any help getting hard for her. He admitted to the boys that he took things way too far with Jameela and that once he retrieved Tiffanys things he was done with Jameela and cheating for good. He would let her keep the Breitling watch because Tiffany was convinced that she "lost it" while on vacation.

"I'll be back soon baby, love you." Gerrod kissed his wife one last time, slapped her on the buttocks and headed out the door. Once the large black gates closed behind him, Tiffany peeled out of her robe, tossed on a black skintight work out apparel and dad cap, jumped into her sleek black Benz coupe and rode out like Knight Rider trailing her husband.

Chapter 20

CAUGHT OUT THERE

Ms. Monica was elated to finally meet her soon to be son in law, but Pops wasn't thrilled at all as he watched his wife fuss over the table settings, making sure that everything was immaculate for this big shot that was marrying her beloved daughter who she thought would never settle down.

"I'm not sure why you're pulling out all the stops for a motherfucka who took all this time to come meet the parents of the woman *he claims* he loves and wants to marry. I ain't impressed. I'll be in the basement, come get me when this joker arrives." He said, grabbing his bourbon off the kitchen counter and heading downstairs as Jameela and Naomi came walking through the door. He stopped to greet them both, "hey daddy!" Jameela said hugging her father. He kissed the top of her head.

"Hey baby. Hey Naomi!" he said excitedly. He put his drink down and gave her a bear hug.

"Hey Pops! How are you?"

"I'm good now that I'm seeing you, how are you, love? How's everything?" he asked her as Jameela embraced her mother warmly and kissed her on the top of her head because she was so short.

"Hi baby, you look really nice. I love that jacket." Ms. Monica complimented Jameela.

"Thanks ma, it smells good in here!" Jameela said, heading into the kitchen while Naomi hugged Ms. Monica.

"It has been too long, Preston you see this one!"

"I see her." Pops stood by looking Naomi over.

Pops smiled like a proud dad whose child just came home from the war. Naomi could never get enough of the love that the Whites gave her over the years.

"I told you that you don't have to wait for Meela to come by for you to come by your family!"

"I know, I've been so busy, but I need to do better. But how are you? It smells wonderful in here! I haven't eaten since lunch, I saved my belly for this!" Naomi said excitedly walking into the living room to accompany Jameela who was on the phone questioning Tyrone about his ETA.

"Everything cool baby?" Ms. Monica asked.

"Yeah, he'll be here in 45 minutes or so, where's Jamel?"

"Mel is on his way with Tammi, and FYI, your daddy is some kind of mood." She mumbled.

"About what? He seemed fine just now."

"Well, you know your father feels some kind of way but don't worry about all of that, my baby is going to be a wife!" Ms. Monica said giddily but Jameela knew that this was far from the truth, at least for now.

Forty-five minutes went by quickly and Jameela's brother and his fiancée showed up first. No one was surprised that Jamel was marrying a white woman. He had always given off that type of vibe growing up, but Tammi was cool and so was her family. Jamel could not have picked a better person to marry, they were so much alike, quirky, into anime, loved pets and being childish together even as adults. He found his person and Jameela could not be happier as she embraced her soon to be sister-in-law and hugged her brother tight.

"It's been too long, big sis, how you doing? How are things?" he said, draping his arm around her shoulder and leading her into the living room. Jamel towered over his sister like his father did everyone in the house.

"I'm good, baby bro."

"So you're about to get married for real or what?" He joked, picking up her hand to look at the ring. "That's a serious ring, don't let Tammi see it she's going to start complaining," he joked.

"My baby." Ms. Monica came out of the kitchen with her arms extended to embrace her baby boy who picked her up slightly and let her legs dangle.

"My favorite girl, hi mama."

"Hi baby." Ms. Monica said, smiling, staring up at her son. She quickly turned to Tammi and gave her love as well, "how are you sweetheart, ready for the big day?"

"I am! I'm going to look at dresses next month, I'll call you with all the details, my mom sends her love."

"Send her my love right on back and I'm looking forward to it. God is so good, both of my children, educated, hardworking, doing well and getting married! My God and when yawl give me some grandbabies, I'm going to be besides myself!" she squealed then headed back into her kitchen.

"She trippin'." Jamel said, causing everyone in the circle to laugh. "Sis! Oh shit what's up?" Jamel said hugging Naomi extra tight.

"Melly!" The two embraced long and hard like long lost siblings.

"How have you been girl?"

"I'm great. Hi I'm Naomi," Naomi said to Tammi.

"Heard everything about you, nice to meet you." Tammi hugged her.

"Where's Pops?" Jamel asked.

Jameela motioned to the basement with her lips.

"Bet," Jamel said, disappearing downstairs to see his father.

The women all headed into the kitchen, grabbing seats and opening bottles of wine.

"No wine for me, got anything stronger?" Naomi asked.

"No, like seriously we need some tequila up in here." Jameela agreed.

"There's a little bit of everything you need in the bar." Ms. Monica said.

Tammi headed over and came back into the kitchen with Grand Marnier, Tequila and triple sec.

"My girl! Ms. Monica do you have lime juice?" Naomi asked.

"I have fresh limes in the refrigerator." She motioned with her head as her hands were full with cooking.

"Ooh let me do the honors of making these grand margaritas please!" Jameela volunteered.

"Make me one as well." Ms. Monica chimed in.

"Say no more!" Jameela said and began shaking up margaritas.

"I just want lime juice and Agave in mine," Naomi said.

After drink number three, two hours later, there was a knock at the door. Jameela's attitude was out of this world that Tyrone had the nerve to show up so late, adding more fuel to the fire for her father.

"That must be him, I'll go get your father and your brother, you ladies go in the living room." Ms. Monica instructed.

"My stomach hurts, I think I need to use the bathroom *way upstairs* if you know what I mean." Naomi joked as she ran upstairs. Jamel came upstairs first with Pops walking slowly and cool behind him, unbothered and uninterested in meeting Tyrone but he would support his daughter. Tyrone walked in casually with an arrogance that turned Jameela's stomach and she for sure knew that her father picked up on it.

"Daddy, this is Tyrone, Tyrone, this is my father, Preston." Jameela nervously introduced them.

Pops shook Tyrone's hand hard, strong, and aggressively as the two men stared one another down. Tyrone cracked a smile first remembering that he was here for one reason only.

"I've heard so much about you, Jameela adores you."

"Is that right." Pops scoffed and sipped his bourbon, "This is my wife, Monica."

Tyrone took in how beautiful Jameela's mother was. She was soft and elegant.

"It's my pleasure to finally meet you, Monica."

Tyrone shook her delicate hand softly, and she was smitten. Ms. Monica just smiled and escorted him into the living room to get comfortable while still holding his hand. Pops rolled his eyes and looked at Jameela.

"Daddy, please, he hasn't been here five minutes!" she whispered.

"Five minutes is all I need to know that I don't like this mother-fucka, but it's your life," he whispered back. They all sat in the living room with Pops being quiet and intimidating. Ms. Monica was doing her best to fill in the gaps.

"We have a full bar son, may I offer you a drink? Whatever you want, I'm sure we have," Monica said softly.

"I'll take a bourbon as well." He said looking at Pops.

"This is a man's man drink." Pops smirked.

"Exactly, one of my faves, neat please." He said to Ms. Monica.

"Pappy Vanwinkle." Pops said.

"Pardon?"

"What kind of bourbon you like."

"I'll take Makers Mark if that's what you have, I'm not picky."

"Makers Mark." Pops scoffed. "Rich man like you never tasted Pappy" he said as Ms. Monica appeared with a snifter of high-end bourbon with a large cube of ice. She then took Pops sifter from him for a refill.

"One bottle cost thousands of dollars, on the lower end you can pay around $400. Give it a quaff." Pops winked.

Tyrone did just that and had to admit that this was the best, most high-quality drink he had ever tasted in his life. Tiffany wasn't a drinker, and he didn't have the luxury of spending thousands of dollars on one bottle of liquor. He wasn't sure what Pops purse looked like but by the looks of the home, the quality of his wife's jewelry and the way his children presented, the man did more than alright for himself.

"Let me show you my man cave downstairs, come on." he said as Ms. Monica appeared with his drink.

"Thank you, baby." Pops said kissing her on the cheek. She blushed and watched the men disappear down the stairs. Jameela instantly went up to her mother.

"Ma, Daddy is being ...."

"Daddy?" she interrupted.

"Sis, I don't know what you expected given the circumstances he's being quite nice!" Jamel chuckled.

"It'll be fine." Ms. Monica reassured her.

"In the man cave? Alone with daddy?" Jameela panicked, following behind her mother in the kitchen.

"If he's the man for you, then he'll come upstairs, unoffended, un-bothered, and understanding of your father's stance. You know your father is a straight shooter and no nonsense when it comes to his family. Let him do what he needs to do to make sure that you're in good hands. After all you're going to marry this man so he's going to be around for a while. It's going to be okay." She said as Naomi came jogging down the stairs rubbing her stomach.

"Girl, I had no idea I had all that in me! Phew! So where is he?" Naomi said looking around.

"In the man cave with Pops." Jamel teased.

Naomi's eyes bucked open, "What?"

Jameela shrugged and threw her hands up in surrender then went to answer the door.

"You play pool?" Pops said picking up a stick handing it to Tyrone.

"I do actually." Tyrone said. Both men stood on opposite sides of the table.

"So, what do you do for a living?" Pops said as he sharpened his stick.

"I'm a retired NFL player and now I'm currently starting an agency for young men that want to get in the league. My goal is to teach them the fundamentals of the business first before they even get to high school with big dreams of getting drafted, there are things about the business that they need to know."

Pops scoffed again, "Listen, my daughter may be a fool but I'm not, so cut the shit. What do you do, and who the fuck are you, because

I scoured the earth trying to find a Tyrone Richards and I couldn't find that motherfucka nowhere!"

"Respectfully sir, there's no record of me on the internet because I don't do the internet. You won't find a picture or records of me anywhere. I live a very private life. Your daughter can attest to that."

"Private life while dating my daughter? You must be crazy. You want to marry my daughter but waited all this time to meet her loved ones? Has she met your children?"

"No, not yet. It's kind of difficult with them being in Dallas."

"What about your ex-wife, does she know you are planning to get married?"

"No sir, not as of yet."

Pops began knocking balls all around the pool table.

"I'll be straight to the point, I don't like you. I don't trust you, but it's Jameela's call. Just know that she has a father that doesn't play about her, at all."

Tyrone swallowed his drink hard and assured Pops that Jameela was in good hands.

"You hungry?" Pops smiled and began heading to the door.

"I can eat." Tyrone said but he had lost his appetite the minute he met Jameela's father.

Once upstairs, the first person Tyrone saw was Shantel who was also very beautiful. Naomi and Jameela were in the backyard trying to figure out how the night would go while Shantel held court with Ms. Monica discussing marriage and recipes.

"Oh, Shantel this here is Jameela's fiancé, Tyrone." Ms. Monica introduced.

"Finally!" Shantel said warmly and extended her arms for a hug. Tyrone embraced her and let her go. He took note of how wonderful she smelled and tried to decipher which friend this was as Jameela talked about them often.

"Where's Jameela?" he asked.

"Out back with Naomi, let me go grab her so we can all sit down and eat."

Ms. Monica hurried off. Pops walked past Tyrone and embraced Shantel. "Where's my main man at?" he asked, having a genuine love for Yusef.

"He's home, not feeling too well, but he sends his love! He asked me to call him when I got here." She said pulling out her phone so Pops and Yusef could chat on FaceTime quickly. As Yusef and Pops exchanged pleasantries, Shantel made her way to the backyard to catch up with her girls.

"I didn't think you would make it, where have you been?" Jameela said embracing Shantel.

"You have been M.I.A., everything okay?" Naomi asked hugging her friend.

"If I told you what was going on you wouldn't believe it. I literally needed time to wrap my head around the fact that my father is alive."

"What?" Both women exclaimed.

"Alive and well. I've been in therapy, trying to wrap my head around everything. I

haven't even confronted my mother yet, but let's put a pin in this. Tonight is about *miss thing* and ole boy in the living room!"

"I am gagging at your father being alive, I cannot wait to hear all about it!" Jameela said as she made her way back into the house with Shantel right behind her.

"Oh my God Shantel, this is crazy!" Naomi said.

The women lightly continued the conversation as they entered the living room.

Chapter 21

GUESS WHO'S COMING TO DINNER

Tiffany parked across the street and a few doors down from where the tracker led her and saw her Lamborghini parked outside of a large corner house with a manicured lawn and Black Lives Matter flag planted in the grass. She stood directly across the street and tried to see as much as she could through the vertical blinds that moved ever so slightly. She knew this had to be the house because other than this home, the lights were off in front of every single house. She could make out a ceiling fan, a few women, a man that wasn't Gerrod and some white chick. But she knew that her husband had to be in there, but she wasn't going to ring the bell unless she was sure. She waited a few moments then there he was. Was he really at a friend's engagement or was he visiting whomever he would spend days with when she was out of town. But her questions were answered once he draped his arms around the shoulder of a woman who was looking up at him as he spoke, it was as if he was giving some kind of toast or speech.

"Oh hell no." Tiffany said and went marching across the street.

Naomi had to rub her eyes a few times as she entered the living room.

"Hold up." She said to herself and stopped short.

"What happened?" Jameela asked.

Naomi couldn't form the words as Tyrone turned toward the women. He draped his arms around Jameela's shoulder and began apologizing to everyone for taking so long to meet them when there was a knock at the door.

"Who could that be?" Ms. Monica asked as Pops headed to the front door to find a woman, dressed in all black standing before him.

Tyrone looked as if he saw a ghost when he saw Naomi. He recognized those breasts anywhere. Seeing how stuck he was on Naomi's lady parts protruding out of her black V-neck sweater, Jameela inquired, "You good bro?"

"I'm good." He stuttered. Jameela rolled her eyes.

"This is my *best friend*, Naomi." Jameela introduced.

Naomi didn't say hello to Tyrone but instead turned to Jameela.

"I have to tell you something and it cannot wait!"

Tyrone stood rubbing his head nervously, but before Naomi could say anything, they were interrupted by Pops announcement upon entering the living room.

"We have a guest." He smirked looking at Tyrone.

Pops moved out of the way to reveal Tiffany who had taken off her dad cap and let her long hair flow. She tousled it a bit and unzipped her windbreaker jacket.

"Who's this?" Ms. Monica asked.

"I don't know, she said she knows *Tyrone*." Pops sipped.

"Hello Gerrod." She said to Tyrone who stood dumbfounded.

Jameela folded her arms and looked from Tyrone to the woman who was strikingly gorgeous even though she was dressed like a night crawler. Jameela walked up to the woman and extended her hand.

"I'm Jameela, this is my parents' home, who are you?"

That's when Tiffany saw the ring. She held Jameela's hand for a spell and looked at it.

"Tiffany Michaels."

Tyrone walked up to the two women, "Tiffany let's go." He gripped her arm and tried to rush out.

"Ah ah." Tiffany said, pulling away from him violently.

"This woman has on my engagement ring? I've been tearing the house apart looking for it and you gave my ring to some other woman?"

"Wait, say what now?" Shantel said stepping out from the shadows. Naomi covered her mouth. Ms. Monica stepped into the circle of women.

"Sweetheart, what's going on here?" she softly asked Tiffany.

"I'm Gerrod's *wife* of fifteen years. And *she* is wearing my engagement ring!"

"So, your name isn't Tyrone Richards." Jameela asked causing Tiffany to chuckle.

"Really? Using my dead father's name?" Tiffany shook her head in disgust.

"Oh my father in heaven." Tammi said in the background.

Jameela stood tall, confident with no intention of letting anyone in that room see her sweat...like she had seen her mother do so many times. Her girls came and stood by her side. Tiffany looked around at all of them, sizing them up.

"It's not even like that sister, we're on your side." Shantel assured her. Tiffany relaxed just a bit.

"So, tell me all about this? This is who you were spending days on days with while I was out of town working! Driving my cars and just living it up, have you ever been in my home?" She asked Jameela with wild eyes that only a scorned woman could have.

"No."

"Let me just reassure you right now that everything is mine and I do mean everything. Every car, every damn thing, mine!"

Tiffany then googled herself and passed her phone to Jameela. Jameela did a quick glimpse and understood that this woman was the baller and was filthy rich, Gerrod was not.

"What do you know about this man, what has he told you?"

"Well..." Jameela started.

"I'm out." Gerrod attempted but Pops smoothly stood in his way.

"You have an obligation son. You're not leaving here and you're not touching me to get out of here." Pops sipped his bourbon unbothered knowing although Gerrod was tall, he could still body slam him if he had to. He was half of Pops weight and not as strong.

"He said he has two children in Dallas and that he was an ex-NFL player. He showed me a woman and two children, the woman clearly is not you."

Tiffany let out a maniacal laugh.

"My sister Sasha along with my niece and nephew, live in Dallas and she's married to an NFL player."

"*Wooooooow.*" Jamel said.

"I know this isn't the right time, or maybe it is, this is so hard for me to say, and I'm embarrassed because your family is here so let me just say this, remember that time me you and Shantel had brunch and I told you about *that thing*, that situation I was in?"

"You mean the DP thing?" Shantel said, quickly covering her mouth.

"Double Penetration?" Jamel said.

Everyone turned and looked at him. Naomi's face was red with embarrassment.

Jameela looked at Naomi trying to gauge what she was trying to say then a lightbulb went off in her head.

"Wait, it was him?" Jameela said.

Naomi nodded her head slowly. "I'm so sorry how could I have known?"

All Jameela could do was cover her mouth. Her mother stepped closer to her and rubbed her back to calm her down.

"This has Tyler Perry written all over it." Shantel said causing everyone to look at her.

"That's my first engagement ring, he proposed years ago when we both worked at Black Rock where he has worked for the past 17 years." Tiffany offered.

Jameela slid the ring off her finger and handed it to Tiffany who begrudgingly accepted it back, but she knew she had no intention of keeping it. She was done.

"Look, we need to take this outside and go home, I can explain everything to you." Gerrod attempted.

"Has my husband ever taken you on a vacation?" Tiffany asked ignoring Gerrod.

"Look, respectfully I understand that you have a lot of questions about your husband and right now I don't feel like answering any more questions. Both of you get the fuck out of my parents' house." Jameela said, heading to the door to let them out.

"You know what, I respect that, you're absolutely right." Tiffany agreed as she wrapped her hair up and put her cap back on.

As she canvased the room looking into everyone's eyes, her eyes set sight on a large red Chanel bag. She closed her eyes tightly and began saying somewhat of a chant or something. Her fists were balled up and her shoulders were tight and upwards towards her ears. Everyone stared at her, Pops sipped his bourbon enjoying the show but feeling for his daughter. He was glad that Jameela would have to end this relationship.

"Gerrod." She spoke in low tones with her eyes still closed. "Tell me that is not my purse that I've been tearing the house up looking for, please tell me that's not my purse!"

The house turned and looked toward the large expensive purse on the couch.

"Jameela, did my husband give you that purse?" she asked with her eyes still closed.

"Yes, he also gifted me a very expensive Chanel purse that I now know belongs to you."

Tiffany's eyes shot open.

"You gave her my six-figure collector's item fucking Chanel?" she screamed at the top of her lungs.

"Say what now for a purse?" Pops said looking around bewildered.

"Give that woman her purse back." Ms. Monica whispered to Jameela.

"Shit, if she doesn't ask for it, I wouldn't." Naomi said.

"Mimi!" Shantel pushed her. "She doesn't need any of the crosses that binds her to this man, give everything back, you don't need shit from him." Shantel grunted.

"Did you hear how much that purse cost, that's six figures she can sell that shit and pocket the money! She deserves that for her pain and suffering." Naomi said.

"But his wife does not, that's her hard-earned money." Shantel shot back.

Jameela was too busy watching Gerrod and his wife argue in her parent's foyer until Pop's finally intervened.

"Enough!" he said standing in between them.

"Now little Sista, I'm going to tell you the same thing that I would tell my daughter so you both listen to me. I don't know you, but you've found out some real deal Holyfield today. You would be a fool to stay with this man after the levels he has stooped to. And Jameela the same goes for you, you know were raised better than this!"

To everyone's shock Jameela responded, "Was I daddy? This scene doesn't look familiar to you. I guess mommy's a fool then!"

"Jameela!" Ms. Monica said.

Pops stood frozen briefly, then without a word he reached back and opened the door for Tiffany and Gerrod.

"Don't ever come this way again, you both be blessed." He slammed the door and headed right to Jameela.

"Are you out of your fucking mind disrespecting your mother like that?"

"Were you out of *your mind* when you disrespected her? You're no different than that motherfucka that just walked out the door!"

"You're going to compare me to a low life who lied about his profession, lied about having kids, lied about having a wife, gave you his wife's possessions, cheated on her with you, your friend and God knows who else? I damn near built this house with my bare hands! Put you and your brother through college and your mother too if she wanted to go, no financial aid, no student loans, all me! I worked three jobs, started businesses, made something of myself to set an example for everyone in my family for generations to come. I've been married to your mother your entire life, no outside kids, never denied being married or having children, sure a few indiscretions here and there because I'm a man and I make mistakes, but I'm loyal to my family, good to my kids and my wife and I have never *not* come home, never missed nobody's birthday, recitals, games, graduation, nothing! And you're gonna sit up in my face and tell me that I aint shit? You try being married for almost forty years and not making a fucking mistake, while keeping your family intact. Man, you got me fucked up Jameela you're a grown ass woman, *you chose* to ignore the red flags, *you chose* to stay where you weren't respected and protected, don't put that shit on me because I ain't never made no woman in my life, in my family or in my presence feel disrespected and unprotected. How dare you!"

Jameela began slowly clapping while walking up to her father.

"That was a great speech, *Preston*. But let me remind you of Shelly that you let in this house, Miranda that was pregnant and lost that child, so you got away clean, yeah, I know all about that. The red head in the next town over, oh the married woman that lived a few houses down...*yes her.*" She said seeing the shock in her father and mother's eyes that she knew.

"So, when you would go hide in the basement to avoid hearing your wife's heart break, to avoid her crying eyes, to avoid her frowns it was me that sat with her for hours and kept her company while she fake smiled thinking that I didn't know what was going on. Big Preston's name is spread all around this fucking town, why do you think your son moved out so young and got with a white woman? He doesn't want to be anything like you or have a family like ours!

"Hold up now Jameela that's enough." Jamel intervened.

"Jamel don't even start because we had the talks about you loving Pops but not respecting how he does mommy so spare me. Everybody walks around here ignoring how dysfunctional this house is, on their fake ass high horse and I'm the fucking plague because I was real enough to not fall for the bullshit? Daddy you're a hypocrite! You should have shaken that man's hand and told him job well done for being such a great piece of shit because he certainly dethroned you." Jameela said stomping into the living room and grabbing her purse amongst the sounds of shocked voices and murmurs.

"Jameela, you don't get to disrespect us like this just because you're upset or embarrassed or whatever it is that you're feeling.

You need to relax and sit down so we can talk about all of this!" Ms. Monica said.

"Ma, respectfully you are the last person I'd take advice from."

Pops stepped in front of Ms. Monica and stared down at Jameela.

"Apologize to my wife right now." He said through clenched teeth.

Pops was so pissed he punched the wall right next to Jameela's head and everyone jumped. Jameela's eyes were closed and when she opened them they were filled with water. She didn't say a word, she just wiped her face and ran out of the house. Shantel and Naomi each picked up their purses, said hushed good nights as they ran out the door behind Jameela who they found stomping up the street unaware of which direction to go.

"Jameela, slow down, stop!" Naomi said, grabbing her friend and spinning her around. "What the hell is wrong with you disrespecting your parents like that?" Naomi snapped.

"Look, I get that you are mad, but you need to be taking that anger out on that joker you were in love with." Shantel said. Then they all stopped arguing long enough to listen to the faint yelling in the far distance.

"You need to go address *that* shit." Naomi said as they began following the voices that they found on the next block.

Tiffany and Gerrod were outside screaming at one another causing some neighbors to turn their lights on, most of them flickering their lights as a warning to lower their voices. Upon reaching the arguing couple, Jameela asked Naomi to open her large leather purse to where she dumped out all the contents.

"This belongs to you." Jameela said, handing Tiffany her purse.

"Where the fuck is my six figure Chanel purse, I need that shit back now!" Tiffany said snatching her purse from Jameela.

"I have it, I can mail it to you." Jameela offered with an attitude.

"Did you not just hear how much that purse costs? You will not be putting my purse in the mail. We will come pick it up!"

"That's not a problem sweetheart and you can definitely calm down because I'm not pressed."

"I don't have time for this Gerrod, you have me out here this time of night dealing with this down-market bullshit? Let's go now!"

"...the hell does down market mean?" Shantel asked Naomi.

"Look, I don't have an issue with you so there's no need for you to try and disrespect me. The only thing down market is this son of a bitch that *you* married. So relax, this community dick nigga is all yours, your problem, your husband, thank God not mine."

"Baby girl... you know what." She hit the alarm on her coupe. "I don't have time to be down here dealing with whatever kind of people you are. I have way too much to lose. I don't know you and I don't care, Gerrod, let's go now and I'm not going to say it again!"

Before Gerrod could walk off, Jameela stepped in his way, "Really?"

"You act like you didn't realize that I've been trying to cut you off for months. You just wouldn't take a hint. Me not wanting to meet your parents, me not staying over anymore, me barely having sex with you, but you were too damn desperate to let me go. You knew I was married, I told you that. I had no intentions on being with you." He turned to his wife, "baby the only reason I came out tonight was to be nice to her to get your ring and your purses back. I fucked up bad, I know I did. But that's the only reason that I'm over here."

"Sis you're okay with how your husband is carrying on and dogging my friend right now?" Naomi said to Tiffany.

"I know you're not talking about a woman being dogged when you let me and my friend dog you at the same time, you ain't got shit to say to me freak bitch."

He literally took Naomi's breath away with disrespect. She gasped for air and her reaction only gave him the fuel to act more of a fool.

"You had a threesome with my husband?" Tiffany asked, shocked.

"This is unbelievable, unbelievable!" Shantel said.

"What happened that night has nothing to do with me and everything to do with what a piece of shit husband you are." Naomi shot back.

"Wait, which one of you was the one that found out the man you were in love with was married too?" Gerrod laughed.

By Naomi's response he knew it was her.

"Why am I not surprised. You spent how many years with that man before you *supposedly* found out he was married? Jameela told me how unstable you were. It makes sense now since I had you sucking my dick in a public bathroom and then you let me and my partner run a train on you, despicable." Gerrod chuckled.

"Gerrod!" Tiffany said shocked at how her husband was disrespecting these women, but he was just warming up.

"Oh, so you must be little miss I think my life and marriage is perfect. What did you call her Jameela?" He said snapping his finger trying to jog his memory. "Stepford wife? Perfect Patty? You compared her to Janet Jackson's character in that Tyler Perry movie." He laughed. "Yes, you're the desperate to be married one, so you married the sex addict that cheats on you because you don't suck dick. You better keep Naomi away from his ass, she's a dick sucking machine. She had two dicks in her mouth at once. I ain't never seen no shit like that before in my life, man!"

"Gerrod that's enough!" Tiffany said, beginning to feel embarrassed by her husband's behavior. But she couldn't walk away. Shantel was fuming on the side at Jameela.

Tiffany walked away, stomping toward her sleek black Benz coupe as Gerrod hit the alarm on her Lamborghini across the street. The two expensive cars made a lot of noise as they pulled off, leaving Shantel, Jameela and Naomi to eat their dust.

Hurt, embarrassed and exhausted, Shantel and Naomi hugged one another.

"My car is up the block." Shantel said softly to no one in particular.

"I'm going to catch a Lyft." Naomi said and started walking.

"All the way to Brooklyn? No, it's been a long night, I'll drop you home."

"You sure?"

"Positive, come on. It's going to cost a fortune to get to Brooklyn from here in a cab. How'd you get here anyway?" Shantel said, her voice barely audible. The two women began walking off, leaving Jameela standing there.

"So, fuck me? With the night that I just had, it's fuck me?" she yelled.

Shantel and Naomi stopped in their tracks and turned to Jameela.

"Jameela, baby it can't always be about you. I'm sorry this happened to you, but we warned you and you were feeling yourself too much to come down from that high you were on to listen to the only two people in this world that would never, *ever* tell you no wrong. You don't get to play victim my love." Shantel said.

Jameela walked toward the women.

"When have I ever not been there for you bitches no matter my attitude? When have I not been there! And you two are going to stand on my block, walk away from me right now, because I had a little pillow talk like you never pillow talked with your man about the things that we all did before?"

"I have never, ever in my life spoken ill of neither of you to anyone, nor have I ever shared your personal business with no man that I was with, I put that on everything that I love." Naomi said, her eyes welling up with tears. "I've endured so much abandonment and hurt in my life, I never thought that it would come from you, not ever and especially not involving a man. You are so fucked up for talking about us like that." Naomi's voice cracked with every word.

"You act as if I told a lie." Jameela had the nerve to respond.

"Just because you pour syrup on shit don't make it pancakes. You had no right to lay up in bed with this trifling negro and tell your friends business." Naomi said.

"The fact that you're trying to justify this makes me question you as a woman. This probably isn't the first time you've done this but the first time you've been outed for being a shady friend." Shantel said.

"Oh, so now I'm a shady friend?"

"You laid up in bed with this man and told him our deepest darkest hurts, the things that hurt us the most. You tell me what kind of woman or friend would do that?" Naomi yelled.

"You were really dogging us to this man for what? So that you can look like the friend that has it all together? So that you can look like you're above your friends so you can be more appealing to him?"

"What are you even saying Shantel?"

"I said what I said. Your insecurities get louder and louder the older we get. You need to get it together. And for the record, any man that entertains his woman's gossip is a bitch! Real men are turned off by that kind of thing. Yusef would never."

"There isn't anything insecure about me, what reason do I have to ever be insecure? Have you seen me lately? Have you seen what I've built for myself, *by myself!*" she yelled.

"Maybe that's the problem, maybe because nobody has ever come into your life to help you build anything, you wear it as a badge of honor." Shantel said.

"Unlike some of us I don't need a man to help me build a damn thing!" Jameela snapped.

"What's that supposed to mean?" Naomi said ready to pounce.

"Girl whatever! Do not press me!"

"Or what! You always act like you got some bomb you're going to drop on me, say what the fuck you gotta say *friend!*"

Jameela flicked her off and rolled her eyes, casting her attention on Shantel.

"Ain't had a man claim you for shit since you came out your daddy's nuts but always want to talk heavy shit like you got something on somebody!" Naomi snapped.

"Oh God, Naomi that wasn't nice." Shantel said.

"I'm tired of being fucking nice, fuck her! I told you before you only had one time to play in my face, one!" Naomi yelled.

Jameela was nodding her head but not saying anything. What Naomi said stung and she was fuming inside.

"You're always throwing out the fact that you are so successful and don't need a man for shit like any of us have ever been out here sucking dick to get our bills paid! You know, behind a lot of hyper independent women there's trauma that you clearly have!" Naomi said.

"Oh so you weren't fucking your landlord to pay you rent?" Jameela spat, followed by laughter of her own.

"And Shantel, I despise when you try to psychoanalyze us like your shit is so perfect, I swear to God."

"Clearly you feel that way because I didn't say a word! But you shared how you felt with that low life that isn't worth knowing your real name let alone personal things about your sisters. Hiding behind all this bravado and arrogance only fuels my point Meela, you can fool a fool, but you cannot fool us."

"How long have you been holding this in, huh?"

"Whatever. I hope that the pillow talks and the fifteen minutes of feeling like *that bitch*, over your sisters was worth it. I'm disappointed in you, Jameela! How could you speak on us in that way and not even be sorry, you're just standing here with all this attitude like this is right!"

"So, I'm desperate, sleeping with men and acting like I don't know they're married? You know my story, Jameela. You know what I am product of and how I feel about dealing with married men. You saw the hurt I experienced. You saw the depression that I fell into when I found out that the only man that I've ever loved was married. How could you slander me in that way?"

Jameela put her hands out, "all of my things are in your purse, you can dump it in the trash, just give me my car keys and my wallet." She snapped.

Naomi did say anything. She just opened her purse dumping everything aggressively on the floor.

"You need to get your shit together."

"Who the hell are you to tell me to get it together like you got your shit together? You're running around here fucking everything, just as unstable as they come and you're telling me to get it together? You need to find your father so you can close that gap in your life *and between your legs* and stay the fuck away from mine because Pops can't heal you or help you, he's my father not yours! It's time to stop ingratiating yourself with my damn family, heal your shit already!"

Shantel looked at Naomi who stood there stunned.

"You go any lower and you're going to be in hell." Shantel said to Jameela.

"Oh, like it wasn't you and I having in depth conversations about how loose she's been. You both need to stop acting like I'm the only one talking shit around here." Jameela said, picking up her keys and wallet out of the pile that Naomi dumped on the floor. There were no words for a moment then Naomi just turned around and began walking up the block holding back her tears.

"That mouth of yours…" Shantel pointed at Jameela then did a light jog to catch up with Naomi.

Jameela watched her sisters walk off; Naomi clearly pissed, moving away from Shantel who appeared to be doing some kind of pleading. She watched them until they disappeared around the corner knowing that their friendship was over. She stood for a while watching her parents' living room lights debating if she should jump in her car and go home or go inside. After much thought, she decided to go home.

And fuck them too. She said jumping in her car and speeding off past Shantel and Naomi who were on the corner arguing.

Chapter 22

CRANES IN THE SKY

All was quiet since that warm fall night a month ago when hearts were broken, feelings had gotten hurt, and a sisterhood dissipated. Though Shantel tried to explain what Jameela meant while trying to make it seem as if she and Jameela were talking about her behind her back, Naomi was not trying to hear it. Shantel insisted on driving her home and once she was unsuccessful securing a Lyft or Uber, she was thankful that Shantel had waited and watched to make sure she got in a car safely when she realized that Naomi was having trouble, she pulled up in front of her.

"Get in girl, come on." Shantel said.

She listened as Shantel gave her context on what Jameela was making assumptions about, but Naomi didn't care at this point. Her mind was focused on Jameela's hurtful words, the reality of her life and the fact that her friends were right, but their delivery was wrong. What Jameela said was hurtful, cruel, and triggering.

"We good my love?" Shantel asked once they pulled up in front of Naomi's building.

Naomi breathed in deeply.

"Yeah" She said gathering her things to exit Shantel's Range Rover.

"I love you Naomi, okay? I got hurt out there too and if you know me you know I would never say disparaging things about you or

Jameela. The way she presented it is not how it was. I don't speak like that Naomi, that's not my thing, you know that."

"I love you too." Naomi said getting out of the vehicle before Shantel started on her Iyanla Vanzant shit. Shantel waited until she could see Naomi's living room lights come on.

"Jesus Christ, I need my husband right now." She said calling Yusef to fill him in on her night as soon as she pulled off.

What Gerrod said hurt her to her core. What Jameela said added the last nail to the coffin. And not for one second did she believe that Shantel was dogging her, she knew that Shantel wasn't that kind of person. She was emotionally exhausted and in need of a warm breeze to blow over her and move things around in her life in a positive way.

Shantel was planning for the holidays in advance and begged Naomi to spend the upcoming holidays with her but she just wasn't up to it. The thought of reaching out to Kareem still rained over her head like nimbus clouds.

"Jameela's words haunted her, *"close that gap in your life so you can close the gap between your legs."*

"That bitch."

Naomi cussed Jameela then scrolled through her phone, sending "hey you" texts to whomever. She would jump on the first to respond she thought but the first few responses came too fast, too thirsty, it wasn't the vibe that she was on. She blocked Damon and avoided him when he came into town, so she wasn't left with many choices. Frustrated she went into the puppy's room and woke up Sam and Ginger from their nap.

"Hi, my sweet babies, come on let's go for a walk, let's go." She said dressing them in their adorable puffer coats, boots, and hats. Happily, Sam and Ginger ran ahead of her, down the flights of stairs and pawed at the door that led to the streets.

"Now you know I'm not letting you run out there without your leash, yawl need to stop." she said, securing them and heading out the front door as they dragged her halfway down the block.

Dressed in a short hunter green Sam puffer coat that rested on top of her hips, leggings and Air Max, her locs wrapped up in a loose bun on top of her head, Naomi crossed the street and was met with car horns honking at her to get her attention, but she didn't look. The driver of a black Audi truck insisted on getting her attention. He rolled his window down slightly, "Excuse me." He called out to Naomi who kept walking but slowed her pace kept walking. The car bent the corner and slowly followed her.

"I just want to talk to you, you have a minute?" The voice said.

Naomi slowed down with her pups.

"How can I help you." She made a full stop.

The driver laughed a bit. "I just saw something that I liked and was hoping to get your name, I'm Sello."

"Bobbi."

"Can I give you my number maybe I can call you some time?"

"Sure." Naomi said with nothing to lose.

"You can move closer to the car; I won't kidnap you. I see you have your two killers with you, so you're safe." He said pulling his phone out. Naomi recited her number and Marcelle called her immediately.

"My phone is buzzing in my pocket, it's my real number I assure you."

"I'll call you tonight?"

"Cool." Naomi said and about faced to go home instead of walking a few more blocks with the dogs. Once upstairs, she made a cup of tea and put on her pajamas curling up on the couch to watch one of her favorite Christmas movies, "Almost Christmas."

"Mo'nique is a damn fool in this movie."

She started laughing at herself as if she hadn't seen the movie a dozen times or more. Cozying up to the idea of having a nice evening at home, she lit her electric fireplace and text "the lady" for an appointment. It was time to start therapy and face the music. The buzz of her phone interrupted her texting.

"Hello."

"Hey, it's Marcelle, you still outside?"

"No."

"Oh, I don't live too far from where I saw you walking."

"Oh okay, I love that for you."

Marcelle laughed. "You are feisty, I like that. Anyway I'm on S. Portland, been living over here for about five years now, what about you."

"I've lived in this neighborhood for quite a while now."

"How old are you, if you don't mind me asking."

"I *do mind* actually."

"Okay, I get it. That was rude of me. You're never supposed to ask a woman her age. I'm just trying to make conversation, that's all. I have a son, he's 7. He offered.

"So, you just ride around picking up women for conversation?"

"I was on my way home from dropping my son off and saw you walking. I'm a single man, I saw a fine woman and I hollered, is that a crime?"

"No, I guess not." Naomi said getting comfortable on the couch.

"You have a man or somebody keeping you warm this upcoming holiday season?"

"No."

"That's unfortunate."

"Hey, listen, Marcelle, I'm not really one for the small talk so, what do you want?"

"What do you mean, I'm just making conversation sweetheart."

"So, if I asked you for your address and said I was coming over, would you turn me away or would you settle for some conversation...*sweetheart* because you're throwing out the fact that you live in the neighborhood and all that, so what's up." Naomi pressed.

"I'd say, if you feel comfortable then come on over, I'm not doing anything and if you drink, I have a fully stocked bar, if you want to watch TV, I have three 75 inches. If you're hungry you're in luck because I'm about to cook a mean steak, I haven't eaten all day."

Naomi didn't say anything. All she could think of was she wished she knew him better, because she would go over to his house and eat his steak, watch TV and have a few drinks. But she had to *close the gaps*. She couldn't go on like this.

"Bobbi, you there?" he snapped her out of her trance.

"Yeah, I'm here."

"Do you drive?"

"No."

"I can send an Uber for you or swing around and come get you, you're not far."

"You don't know me, and you want me to come over. I just met you fifteen minutes ago."

"I don't want to be alone tonight, and something tells me that you don't want to be either. You want to take a cab, or should I come get you?"

"Who said I was alone or had a problem with being alone?"

"You're right. It's cool, I'm pushing it. What am I thinking? So, what do you like to do Bobbi, what do you do for a living?"

After hesitating for a few seconds Naomi responded, "I would rather tell you in person. Text me your address."

Naomi rang the bell, and within seconds the door buzzed. She heard a voice tell her to come up a flight. She followed the smell of food cooking and walked through the cracked door and entered a beautifully decorated living room. Black leather sofas, mirrors everywhere, two large floor plants and a beautiful white marble dining room table. To the far left was a set of spiral stairs that led to a lower floor.

"Hello?" Naomi called out.

Marcelle appeared from behind frosted doors where the kitchen was.

"Hey, have a seat I'll be out in a minute, you want something to drink?"

"Do you have Bourbon?"

"I do, give me second." He said disappearing behind the door. She heard pots and spoons clicking, fire ticking and ice dropping into glasses, soon Marcelle appeared with two sifters of brown liquor, he handed her one with the ice in it.

"Thank you."

"My pleasure. I must admit, it was your legs that got my attention and your outfit, I'm a sucker for a fly girl."

"Woman." Naomi joked.

"Yes, definitely a woman but you're really attractive, I love your hair."

"Thank you." Naomi sipped, realizing how young he looked, it made her sort of uncomfortable.

"Do you feel safe?" he said, noticing the look on her face.

"My friends, my father and my two brothers have your address so that's as safe as I'm going to get." She lied.

"You serious?" he asked, looking a bit uncomfortable.

"Problem?"

"No, better safe than sorry." He said.

Naomi sipped her drink with her eyes on him. He had really dark eyes, you could barely see the whites of his eyes. Naomi started looking around the apartment.

"So, you live here alone?"

"Yeah. Why you want to be my roommate?" He tried to joke but there was something about him that was making Naomi uneasy. It wasn't the same feeling she had with other men that she'd swing by for a one-night stand or for drinks and food. This seemed different.

"What's downstairs?" she motioned with her head.

"The bedroom, do you want to see it?"

"No, I'm cool."

"The bedroom being downstairs was definitely the selling point for me, that's my little dungeon down there." he said, a glare coming across his eyes.

"Oh, so you own this spot?"

"I own the building." He spoke. "Give me a second, let me check my steak." He ran off. Naomi pulled out her phone and started googling the address to see what information she could find but he returned very quickly.

"I hope you don't think that I typically do this because I don't." he said.

"What you do and who you invite to your home is your business, you're a grown man."

"You're right, you are absolutely right, and you are a grown woman, so this isn't your first rodeo."

"What do you mean by that?"

"Well at a certain age there's no game to be played. If you want something you go after it, that's all. So what do you do for a living Bobbi. You said you'd rather tell me in person."

"Do you really care?"

"No, but it makes for a good icebreaker." He chuckled. "You seem so uptight, let me get you another drink, finish that one," he said, taking her glass from her and heading back into the kitchen.

"For the record, I just wanted some female company." He said upon his return, handing her the drink, this time with no ice and more liquor.

Naomi placed the drink on the table next to her, "And you don't have anyone else to call so you call a stranger? You want me to believe that?"

"What's wrong with you woman, relax." He said coming close to her and rubbing her shoulders. Naomi's entire body stiffened up at his touch. He put his hands up in surrender and sat back down.

"Hey, listen, you seem really nervous. I promise you are safe but if you feel uneasy, I'm okay with you going home and we can talk on the phone from your place, it's your call."

"I'm okay." Naomi whispered. "But if you could please, just give me a little space."

"Oh, no doubt!" he said taking a seat across from her.

Marcelle guzzled his drink. He took his sweater off and stood before her dressed in a white t shirt that hugged his body, his manhood slightly raised in his sweats. Naomi's nervousness presented again.

"You know what, maybe I should go home, and we can talk on the phone. Let's have brunch or something. You know it's plenty of places to eat down here." She said.

"I understand, I'm a stranger and this is weird. At least finish your drink before you go, and I'll walk you downstairs and wait for an Uber with you." he said and sat down across from her.

She watched him as he casually picked up the remote and began flipping through the channels trying to appear unphased by Naomi who continued sipping her drink with her eyes on him until it hit her out of nowhere. She put the glass down slowly and stood up but felt a little different.

"The food smells great but maybe next time." She said. Marcelle was right up on her.

"Why'd you come." He asked her while toying with one of her locks.

"I don't know, so I need to go." she said, trying to put on her jacket but she felt weak.

"Stay, I promise to make it worth your while."

Naomi was saying no but the words weren't coming out.

"You're not going nowhere." Marcelle said.

Those black eyes that she knew meant trouble stared through her. She felt weak, Marcelle gave her throat a light squeeze then pushed her on the couch and snatched her coat from her, tossing it on the couch. She could feel him pulling at her leggings and then she faded to black, but her eyes were open, and she was paralyzed, she couldn't scream or move as he sodomized and raped her. She could feel him behind her, in her, being rough with her but there wasn't anything that she could do. She just lay there, in a daze while this man violated her.

When he was done, he walked to the back of the house where the kitchen was then came back. She just knew that he was going to pull out a big kitchen knife and cut her into pieces but instead he sat on the couch opposite her and began to quickly put his sneakers on and his sweater over his head. She was trying to move, scream, do something but to no avail. When Naomi finally regained movement in her limbs and woke up with her leggings around her ankles she rolled over and gently pulled her pants up. She had no idea that morning had come. She could hear someone coming back into the house, so she stood up and grabbed her coat scared for her life. A woman entered.

"Who the hell are you?" the woman asked clearly stunned to see Naomi standing in the middle of the living room.

Naomi ran past the woman and down the steps faster than she had ever run before, bursting through the vestibule, ripping open the front door and running 15 blocks to her house, nonstop in the cold weather dropping her coat along the way. She ran straight upstairs and put all the locks on her door jumped in the shower where she scrubbed her body raw. Once out of the shower, she ran into her room and got in the bed, soaking wet, covering herself with her comforter where she let out a blood curdling scream.

Chapter 23

NO HAPPY HOLIDAYS

"Idon't know why this woman insists on having dinner at her house and not ours" Cheryl folded her arms and threw a fit the entire drive from Connecticut.

"Harlem, it's where you were born and raised. You done got rich and switched." Kenny joked.

"Whatever, Kenny. I just like my own house." Cheryl said staring out of the car window taking in the gentrification.

"You're always entertaining at your house, give Shantel the opportunity to entertain for once. She's a great cook so at least we know we'll have a good dinner."

"Hmph."

Kenny kept glancing over at Cheryl as he pushed his Maserati through traffic. The streets of Harlem triggered and humbled Cheryl. She barely visited her daughter and would mostly have Shantel and Yusef visit their homes. Harlem had too many skeletons and memories that she wanted so desperately to forget. Her body tensed up as they drove down Frederick Douglas Blvd. Her husband reached over and grabbed her hand, sensing the shift in her energy.

"You're still so beautiful, fine after all these years. One of the best decisions I ever made was marrying you." He said picking up her diamond encrusted hand and kissing it. He held her hand the entire ride up until they pulled up on Shantel's block.

"Lucky us, parking right here." Kenny said pulling into the parking spot. "Sweetheart, grab the gifts out of the backseat for me please." He asked Cheryl who sat in her seat and didn't budge.

This woman.... Kenny walked to the passenger side of the car and opened her car door, then reached in the back, and grabbed the gifts that he bought for Shantel and Yusef. Cheryl didn't carry bags unless it was one of her designer purses, she didn't open any door for herself. She waited for Kenny to catch up to her to grab her hand and escort her up the stairs like the diva she was in her five-inch heels and full-length Sable.

"Mommy." Shantel warmly greeted her mother and helped her inside of the house.

"You look wonderful ma, yes to this coat!"

"Thank you sweetheart."

"Hey Kenny." Shantel said hugging her stepfather.

"Hi Princess, how are you. The place looks wonderful, absolutely wonderful." He said kissing her cheek and handing her the gifts.

"We probably won't be back down here for Thanksgiving or Christmas so here you are, I hope you love them, but don't open until Christmas, where's Yusef?"

"Upstairs getting dressed he should be down soon, come on in make yourself out at home!" Shantel smiled happily as she led her parents into the large living room.

Cheryl grabbed a seat on the island while she waited for Kenny to pour her a glass of champagne.

"Kenny, you don't have to work for mommy today, let me grab the drinks for you guys, you are guests in my home. Ma, sit on the sofa get comfortable." Shantel insisted.

She then walked over with a flute of Rose' for her mother and gin and tonic for Kenny.

"So what have you been up to? I haven't had a decent conversation with you in about a month." Cheryl stated.

"This place looks stunning. It takes my breath away whenever I come over here." Kenny said truly impressed by the décor and quality of furniture and art pieces.

"Ma, work has been working me." Shantel lied. "And thanks Kenny, I did put a lot of effort into this place. I hired an interior designer at some point so let me not take all the credit."

"Give yourself all the credit. You had to give the designer an idea to bring to fruition, right? This is your vision, own it!" Cheryl said.

"Sure." Shantel said.

Cheryl always encouraged her daughter to never downplay anything about herself or to play small no matter what it was.

"It is quite lovely in here." She said, looking around.

"So, what's on the menu sugar." Kenny inquired.

"Roasted chicken, cream spinach, cornbread stuffing, oxtails, candied yams, lambchops, scalloped potatoes and a very colorful salad. Leafy dark greens with every meal are a must!"

"It sounds delicious baby." Yusef said as he came down the stairs, unaware that Shantel prepared so many dishes.

"Where did you learn to cook so well because your mother here, tuh."

"Kenny!" Cheryl playfully hit his lap.

"Well, it's true baby the only thing you know how to make is reservations, thank God we have a few dollars so we can hire a chef, or I'd starve." He joked.

"Youza a damn lie!" Cheryl laughed.

"I must have learned how to cook from my dad or something, ma did my father know how to cook?"

"It's been so long but I think he knew how to cook. Hey, put on some background music." Cheryl suggested quickly changing the subject.

"You know what I want to hear." Kenny said.

"No Temptations Christmas Album!" Cheryl complained and stood up and huffed.

"Kenny, I'm sorry no Temptations Christmas, it's not even Thanksgiving yet! We're just going to rock out to whatever comes on the Jaheim station."

"Who?" he asked.

"Find my Way Back" by Jaheim started playing.

"I'm not mad at that!" Cheryl said.

"Oh *this brother*, yeah I like him!" Kenny said and stood up to dance with Cheryl. Shantel watched her parents dance, and it made her angry. Kenny wasn't supposed to be here, it was supposed to be Bilal.

Yusef leaned in and kissed Shantel's neck breaking her thoughts.

"You look beautiful babe." He said spinning her around, her pretty coral colored dress twirled in the air.

"Thank you husband. I don't know what I'd do without you."

"Well lucky for you, you will never find out, at least no time soon." He kissed her neck.

"Dinner is ready!" Shantel sang as she began setting the table.

"Baby, do you need help with anything?" Yusef offered from across the room while holding court with Cheryl. Kenny was busy looking at all the art and pictures on the walls, going down memory lane.

"I'm fine baby." She winked at her husband. He mouthed, "you alright?" to which Shantel nodded yes.

"Baby, are you expecting guests? Why do you have extra plates out?" Cheryl asked.

"Possibly." Shantel said while placing a large salad bowl in the middle of the table as she always served her dinner in courses.

"Even your salad is delicious, what's all in this?" Kenny asked.

"Spinach, shaved apples, cucumbers, cranberries, carrots, egg, arugula, and some other stuff." Shantel laughed. "Oh, and Raspberry vinaigrette!"

"This dressing, oh my goodness, it's delightful!" Cheryl complimented.

"Delicious as usual baby." Yusef said.

"What's the next course sweetheart?" Cheryl asked.

"The lollipop lamb sauteed in a garlic butter."

"Cheryl, have you ever had your daughter's scalloped potatoes, to die for!" Yusef said.

"Everything this woman cooks is spectacular. Baby why don't you put all the food out so you can eat, no need for the special presentation tonight, come eat! Let's get some drinks flowing!" Cheryl said, tapping the chair excitedly for her daughter to sit next to her, but Shantel opted to sit across from her mother.

"Look at that gravy." Kenny said loosening his pants as Shantel carved the large roaster.

"Small portions for me dear." Cheryl said placing the linen napkin across her lap as Shantel plated the food.

"So, do you two have plans for the holidays?" Yusef asked Kenny and Cheryl.

"Paris for the New Year, a colleague of mine is having a gala of some sort." Kenny responded in between bites.

"Oh, nice!" Shantel said.

"I was wondering if you both wanted to spend Thanksgiving and Christmas with us?"

"We have plans for the holidays but thank you for the invite." Shantel answered.

"Well okay then. So, how's Jameela and Naomi?"

"They're fine, home with their families." Shantel lied.

None of them have spoken since the blow up at Jameela's house a month ago. Other than the occasional dry response from Naomi when she reached out first that was it. She was still hurt by Jameela and wasn't willing to reach out first. Jameela needed to learn a hard lesson in humility and the dangers of pillow talking.

"Who's at the door then?" Cheryl asked with a mouth full of scallops.

Shantel got up from around the table and headed to the door. Yusef stood up to greet the guest, causing Cheryl and Kenny to turn around to see who was joining them for dinner. Their smiles quickly disappeared. Cheryl dropped her fork. Kenny sat with his mouth agape then stood up and adjusted his collar. Cheryl followed suit and straightened out her dress. Yusef came from around the table to stand by his wife's side. He shook Bilal's hand.

"Good to see you man." Yusef said.

Bilal nodded and said hello to Cheryl and Kenny. Shantel and her mother were having an intense stare down. Kenny continued to adjust his collar. Bilal stepped further into the living room.

"Let me get your coat daddy." Shantel said, relieving her father of his wool Ralph Lauren peacoat and skull cap. He was dressed neatly, like an older J. Crew model or something. His salt and pepper beard were neatly trimmed, his nails manicured. He had on a good shoe and pants with a coral-colored sweater and button-down shirt underneath unintentionally coordinating with Shantel. His simple gold wedding band gleamed.

"Come have a seat." Shantel said happily, leading her father to the table by hand. She made sure that he sat right next to her and across from her parents. Cheryl and Kenny sat down, still speechless. Cheryl couldn't keep her eyes off Bilal, her one and only true love.

"So, ma. Do you care to explain how my father has arisen from the dead?"

Chapter 24

LILAC WINE

*N*aomi called her boss and lied that she had Covid. She was advised to work from home for two weeks and to not return until she could provide a negative test. Naomi spent most of her days demolishing bottles of wine, throwing up, nursing hangovers, and doing it all over again.

Today, she didn't have anything to drink in her house, so she scoured her kitchen draw for the phone number to the neighborhood liquor store for a delivery. The day after she was assaulted, Naomi woke up feeling extremely sore. She didn't have anyone to call so she began drowning her sorrows in the bottle. She so desperately wanted to call her friends, but Jameela would probably make her feel worse and victim shame her. She felt a strong desire to call Pops, the closest thing to a father she ever had, but Jameela also stripped her of that with her hurtful words. She wished she had reached out to her father months ago when her mother gave her the number, she probably would have had him to lean on. She needed male support, but couldn't talk to Yusef, nobody. So, she found comfort at the bottom of the bottle.

She called Marcelle's number, but it was no longer in service. She held the phone in her hand, staring at his number and the hot tears began rolling down her face. *Who was this man? Who's home was it? What the hell happened?* She began pacing the floor as Sam and Ginger pawed at her, it was their walk time, but she was afraid to leave her house. She didn't know if he was circling the neighborhood trying to run into her again. She didn't want him or any man to see her ever again. As she brainstormed and paced back and forth, someone rang the buzzer.

"Yes." Naomi said leaning on the buzzer to let the delivery guy in. She kindly relieved him of the case of wine and gave him a cash tip.

"You having a party?" he smiled and asked politely in his heavy Mexican accent.

Standing at the door disheveled, alcohol seeping through her pores, dressed in nothing but a T-shirt, Naomi smiled and said yes then closed the door. She placed the box on her kitchen counter and was more than pleased to see that they also gave her 6 complimentary nips of tequila.

"Oh, it's up and it's stuck!" she sang to herself, twisting the cap off with her mouth and guzzling her first shot. She then opened her first bottle of wine and put it to her head, guzzling half of it down without taking a break.

"*Aaaah.*" She said sticking her tongue out satisfied, swiping her locs from her face. She paced her apartment, bottle in hand in a manic state unable to sit still, trying to replay what happened. Marcelle clearly drugged and raped her. She hadn't made it to the hospital yet and had no intention of doing so. Her only plan was to get tested for diseases every three months for the rest of the year to make sure he hadn't given her anything. She didn't know a thing about Marcelle and though she knew where he took her, she had no doubt that it wasn't where he lived, and she didn't want to go through the hassle of trying to get the occupant of that apartment to give up his whereabouts. He was in the wind, probably raping someone else by now. His real name probably wasn't even Marcelle.

"*Motherfucker.*" She damn near hissed in the mirror then headed into the bathroom and began rummaging through the drawers until she found a pair of scissors. In between guzzling her wine she began to cut out her faux locs, having cut off a lot of her own hair in the process. Halfway through cutting her hair her arms grew tired. She paused and then guzzled the rest of the bottle, finishing it and tossing the empty bottle in the recycling bin. She immediately grabbed a nip of tequila and drank it, then opened another bottle of wine.

This time she poured some in a wine glass. It wasn't long before that bottle was empty, and she opened another.

Within an hour, Naomi was intoxicated and began calling all the men in her phone, cursing them out and hanging up. Most of them called back, asking her was she okay, what was going on, did she need anything to where she would spazz out, accusing them of raping her, using her, being pieces of shit. In a drunken rage she text Kareem Lawson, blaming him for everything that went wrong in her life, blaming him for her being a whore, a under achiever, a drunk then she called her mother who answered on the first ring.

"Naomi, hi!" Cherisse answered gleefully because her daughter never in the history of their relationship called her first.

"Hi to you too, how do you sleep at night huh?" Naomi slurred.

"Pardon me baby? What do you mean?"

"You let these men do whatever they want to do with me. You couldn't pimp me out, so you left."

"Naomi, what?"

"Don't act shocked, you send these men to rape me to teach me a lesson, I know you're behind this!"

"Baby, are you okay?"

"Are you?" Naomi yelled and let out a maniacal laugh. "You know something, I'll make a really good prostitute. I might as well get paid for this shit instead of fucking for love. Because that's what I'm doing, fucking these men so good ma, I fuck 'em good because I want them to love me, I want attention. I...*your daughter*, even had two men at once. I let two men have their way with me at once and I fucking loved it! But they don't love me ma, these men don't love me, so why not just be a prostitute and get paid for it right? You think I'm too old now to sell pussy on Only Fans? My body is tight I can get paid."

Cherisse listened on the other end. She could tell now that her daughter was drunk out of her mind and completely unhinged.

"Where are you Naomi, are you alone? "she asked cautiously.

"Am I alone? Is that a trick question? I been alone, remember you left me alone when I was seven, are you dumb? I been alone, all my life!" Naomi laughed.

"Are you home?" Cherisse asked.

Naomi didn't answer, she had a bottle in her mouth guzzling. Cherisse could hear the dogs barking so she knew that Naomi was in her apartment.

"Baby, listen to me. I'm not sure what's going on over there, but please, Mimi, please be careful, is there someone that I need to call?"

"Someone to call, to do what Ma, you gonna send another rapist?" She slurred.

"Someone to just check on you sweetie."

But she didn't have anyone's number and her sister Zola was on vacation out of the country. She also didn't even have Naomi's address. That's how estranged they were.

"Incoming! I gotta go ma, bye!" Naomi said clicking over to hear a man's voice asking who this number belongs to.

"Someone text me from this number?"

"Um who are you looking for? I text a lot of men from this number, which one is this? Oooh is this Benjamin with the thick dick? Come over Benjamin and bring a friend, I got something for yawl, I'm not double penetration now."

"I'm sorry, I think there has been a mistake." The man said and hung up.

Moments later, after getting a call from Cherisse, Kareem called Naomi back.

"Naomi?"

Naomi didn't respond, she just held the line.

"Naomi, listen to me. Why don't you send me your address and I'll come by and check on you."

"Nobody is coming in this house, nobody!"

"I just want to put eyes on you Naomi, I want to make sure that you're okay."

Naomi was quiet, again with the bottle in her mouth, taking large gulps.

"Naomi, can you please tell me where you are?"

"You want to have sex?" she slurred.

"Naomi, this is your father."

"Dad?" Naomi sat up erect. "Dad is this you?"

"Yes."

"Daddy is this you?"

"Yes, this is your father."

Naomi tried to stand up, but she stumbled and dropped her phone.

"Naomi!" Kareem yelled into the phone.

Naomi bent down to pick up her phone and fell headfirst. She lay there for a while, unable to get up, her head throbbing. Kareem was yelling into the phone unsure of what was happening on the other end.

"Naomi! Are you okay?" he shouted.

All Naomi could do was groan, her head was pounding.

"*Daddy, come get me.*" She whispered but Kareem couldn't hear her.

"Naomi, say something and let me know you're okay."

"I'm okay," she said in a drunken whisper.

"Naomi, listen to me, what's your address, are you in Brooklyn?"

Naomi was saying yes but the words weren't coming out. She could hear her father asking her a million questions on the other end and her other phone line beeping in.

Cherisse called Zola while she was on vacation and explained to her what was going on. Zola immediately offered up Ms. Monica's number.

"Hello, this is Naomi's mother."

"Yes, hi how are you?" Ms. Monica asked surprised at the call.

"I'm okay but I'm a bit concerned about my daughter. She called me just now and she appears to be very drunk, and I think she's going to hurt herself. Would you mind giving me your daughter's number or perhaps you can call your daughter and have her go check on Naomi please?"

"Oh absolutely, did you speak to her just now?"

"Yes, just now. It sounds bad so please if you could have your daughter or someone check on her for me."

"I'll call Jameela... and Shantel right now!"

"Please thank you and this is my cell please call me back."

"Done." Ms. Monica said frantically calling her daughter who was sleeping and wasn't trying to answer the phone, but Ms. Monica would not stop calling. Her relationship with her parents wasn't the same since that fight in their house so she didn't know why her mother was so eager to talk to her. She answered the phone with an attitude.

"Ma, where's the fire."

"Naomi's mother called me, she said that something is wrong with Naomi, have you talked to her today?"

Jameela sat up. "Her mother?"

"Yes, when was the last time you spoke to her?"

"We're not talking. I haven't talked to her or Shantel since the last time they were at your house."

"What, why?"

"Nobody is speaking to nobody right now. You and I haven't talked. Daddy hasn't called me either!"

"Are you crazy? Did you forget what happened the last time we saw you? Look, go check on your friend!"

"Naomi is probably just drunk, I'm sure she's fine."

"And this is normal behavior and you're okay with that? I'm going to call Shantel. Are you going to check on her or not?"

"Ma, right now I'm in bed, I'm not feeling too well, I'll shoot her a text."

"Okay Meela." Ms. Monica hung up frustrated with her daughter's attitude and called Shantel who wasn't answering her calls. She began pacing then called her husband.

"Preston where are you?"

"Not far, I'll be there in a few, you need something from the store?"

"No, we need to ride to Brooklyn, pull up front and I'll come out."

"Brooklyn for what?"

"Something is wrong with Naomi. Just honk when you're outside."

"Okay." He said perplexed and hung up the phone.

Jameela lay in bed wondering what was going on. By the time she called her mother back, her and Pops were 10 minutes away from Naomi's house.

"You really think it's something serious?" Jameela inquired.

"Well, there's only one way to find out." Ms. Monica said, still annoyed at Jameela but too worried about Naomi to focus on her daughter's nasty attitude.

"Okay, please call me."

"Whatever it is you all got going on you need to fix it." Pops said through the speaker phone.

"Just call me please." Jameela instructed.

Ms. Monica disconnected the call abruptly without acknowledging Jameela's request.

Chapter 25

DEAR MAMA

The tension in Shantel's home was uneasy as everyone kept their eyes on her, to avoid the guilt in each other's eyes.

"What is all of this?" Cheryl asked her daughter.

"You tell me!"

Cheryl stroked her hair and flipped it behind her shoulders.

"If my dad is dead, then who is this?" Shantel asked, sarcastically. Her legs were trembling under the table. Yusef rested his hand on her leg to comfort her. Her father was holding her hand.

Kenny cleared his throat, and Shantel looked at him.

"Maybe you can tell me how this dead man is sitting at our table right now."

Bilal decided to speak up.

"A lot happened back then, and I let her know everything." He said.

Cheryl was still in a state of shock. She didn't know what to say or where to begin so Shantel did it for her.

"I just want us all to go back in time, when I was a little girl, and I asked you about my father and you told me that he was dead." Shantel said, her voice cracking.

"You were so mad when he came up to us that day with the picture and revealed to me that he was my father. Then you tried to force me to call Kenny dad and I could never—not after knowing who my real father was."

"I was just trying to protect you, Shantel. You were a baby when we separated, and I couldn't deal with your father's addiction while being a single mother and going to school; it was so hard for me." Cheryl whispered. "Drugs were running rampant through our neighborhoods; I was not going to let my child become a product of her environment."

"Rightfully so. I can't fault you for that. But don't you think telling me my father was dead for a second time was a bit extreme?" Shantel asked eerily calm.

"I... It..." Cheryl tried unsuccessfully to explain it wasn't as simple as Shantel was making it seem.

"You and Daddy used to get high together until you got pregnant with me, then you were able to kick the habit. I saved your fucking life, and this is how you thank me?" Shantel banged the table.

Kenny turned in his chair slowly and looked at Cheryl, the revelation of her using drugs was news to him.

"He wasn't bothering nobody, especially you and your *new man*. He didn't come around trying to beg for anything. He just wanted to see me as much as I wanted to see him. He was harmless!"

"Shantel, I told you that your mother did what she had to do to protect you," Bilal said softly.

"Nah, no! Why did me acknowledging that this man was my father bother you so much? I need answers!" Shantel shouted. "Say something instead of sitting there looking like plucked bird!" she instructed her mother.

Cheryl rolled her eyes and breathed in heavily trying her best to not go "Harlem" on Shantel.

"I was doing everything in my power to protect you. I don't really know what else to say to you, I don't." she mumbled, remembering the day Kenny came home from work and told her that he had a talk with Bilal. She never knew all of what he said to make Bilal go away, but she was about to find out.

"Kenny, you took your hard-earned money, visited my father weekly and gave him money for drugs in exchange for staying away from me, why?"

Now it was Cheryl who turned in her chair and looked at Kenny like he was crazy.

"Because I loved you, Shantel. I loved you so much, and I didn't want you to get hurt."

"Hurt by who?" Shantel said, looking around in disbelief.

"The situation, everything that was going on. He was on the streets...he was on drugs...anything could have happened to you standing on those street corners talking to him. We just did what we thought was best because we loved you. We didn't want you to get so attached to him and then he leaves or even worse, die."

"The irony in that entire statement. Kenny, if you loved me as much as you say you did, then you would have taken that money and put my father in rehab so that he could get better and so that I can be happy. Because, when you truly love someone, you want to see them happy and you will do whatever it takes," Shantel's voice cracked.

With tears streaming heavily down her face she looked at her mother, "Ma, how could you let this happen? How could you be a co-conspirator to this? Or were you the mastermind? Whose idea was it to try to get my father to overdose?" Shantel said with wild eyes, looking at Kenny and Cheryl.

Chery looked over at Kenny, who once again began fussing with his collar.

"Your mother went to your little friend's house up the block one day when you told her that's where you would be. She wanted to bring you the snacks you left behind, but when she got there, the girl's mother said you weren't there yet. So, she panicked and began walking the neighborhood, frantically looking for you, and saw you two blocks over, sitting on a crate, talking to your father. She would follow you most days and see you talking to him and, well, I guess it just upset her," Kenny offered with a sigh.

"She approached me one day and told me to stay away from you, and I told her I wouldn't. You're my daughter, and I looked forward to seeing your pretty little face every single day. It gave me hope. But your mother cussed me out badly and warned me that something worse would happen if I didn't push you away." Bilal said.

"I was just trying to scare you. I am not the bad guy! You chose to put that glass dick in your mouth; I had to protect my child! She would have nothing if I didn't do what I did!"

"Baby, you were sucking on that glass dick right along with me, *respectfully*," Bilal clapped back.

"So, what the hell happened then, huh Kenny? It was your idea?" Shantel asked.

Everyone started yelling over one another and things turned chaotic. Yusef stood up, picking up one end of the table and shook it to get everyone's attention.

"We are not going to get anywhere with everyone yelling. Be respectful to one another in this moment, please! My wife needs and deserves answers, so please can we all just say our piece for the sake of healing and clarity?"

Cheryl began to speak, her bourgeois accent turned off and Uptown Cheryl from Harlem was now in the building.

"Kenny told me that he wasn't going to have his name attached to no bullshit and that Bilal had to go if he was going to adopt you." Her eyes teared up. "He said that we couldn't get married and move forward as long as you were calling Bilal your dad."

"And so, you gave him the okay to go through with his plan to give my father money in hopes of him blowing it on drugs, overdosing and dying? Kenny..."

Cheryl was fixated on Bilal, staring at her first love—her only love—fascinated by how healthy and good he looked. She could have never imagined him ageing so fine and fit. She hadn't even loved Kenny the way that she loved Bilal. If Bilal never got hooked on drugs, he would be her husband, not Kenny. Shantel watched her mother gawking at her father. She then glanced at Kenny, who was staring at Bilal with so much hatred. It all began to make sense at that moment.

"I completely understand now. Kenny, you were jealous of my father."

"What an insane thing to say."

"No, you knew how much my mother loved my father. And you didn't want any chance of him rehabbing, getting on his feet again, because you knew that you would lose my mother. Isn't that right ma? Isn't that the truth?"

"No, you're wrong about that Shantel."

"Ma, I am sitting here right now looking you dead in your face and you can't keep your eyes off of him!"

"No, don't do that Shantel." Bilal said.

"Kenny, you tried to kill my father over a woman?"

"I'm not dealing with this shit here." He stood up. "I'm glad that you got on your feet brother, it really makes me happy to see that you're doing well and that you're back in my baby girl's life."

"Don't you ever call me your baby girl again! You know Kenny did it ever dawn on you that through adoption and all I have never called you dad, never acknowledged you as my father, always putting emphasis on the *step*, in stepfather, or calling you my mother's husband. I didn't even let you walk me down the aisle because something in my spirit just didn't connect with you. I didn't let you drop me off at college, nothing. I cared about you, but we never connected, you noticed that right? There was just something about you that wouldn't allow my divine spirit to connect with you in that way and it wasn't about knowing you weren't my father, it was something more, but now I see what it is, you are wicked."

"You're going to let this girl talk to me like that?" he asked Cheryl who rubbed his arm to calm him down.

"Everyone just please, let's keep things calm," Cheryl said switching her bourgeois accent back on. "Honey please, she's just upset, this is a lot for all of us."

"I took you and your mother out the ghetto if it wasn't for me, she would probably be in an alley way sucking strange dick to get your father a fix, how dare you!" he yelled.

"Oh, there it is.... there is the real Kenny, there he is," Shantel said her eyes welled up with tears.

"Kenneth!" Cheryl exclaimed.

"I worked too damn hard and supported this woman too damn long and hard for her to come at me like this because her junkie father came back from the dead. He chose a fucking pipe over you and your mother! Yet you both can't seem to just let him go!"

"Wow." Yusef said walking over to his wife as Kenny went on a rant.

"You think I don't know that you held on to me because you wanted to get out of Harlem? You think I don't know that you didn't love me for the first few years we were together? You think I'm dumb? But I loved you anyway, and I gave you time and I loved Shantel, you both deserved the world and I tried to give you that. But not in a million years would I have ever thought that I would be scammed by a fucking crack whore and her crack baby." He said, removing himself from the table.

"Where's my coat?" he barked.

"Kenny, don't you dare talk to me and my child like that!" Cheryl said.

"Or what, what are you going to do Cheryl, where are you going to go. I got two words for you, *prenuptial agreement*, so spare me, you got your shit together but you can't afford the lifestyle you love without me."

Yusef was on his way over to check Kenny who braced himself when he saw Yusef coming his way, but Shantel intervened.

"I know who I am and thank God I know who you are too. Your little feelings are hurt so now you want to hurl insults?" Shantel followed behind him.

"Shantel, you just said it, you never cared about me, your mother didn't either. She just needed someone to take care of you both. Her heart has always been with your father. Have you heard her deny it yet?" he said, causing everyone to look at Cheryl.

"That's not true Kenny, the truth needs no explanation. I love you so much darling, please." She said hugging him tight. He pushed her off him.

"Grab your coat and let's go. Save the dramatics. Shantel, get our coats now!"

"Please don't raise your voice at my wife not one more time. This is difficult for everyone to process. But please keep your voice down in my house and don't talk crazy to my wife." Yusef warned. "The house that I bought?" Kenny scoffed.

"This is *my* house. My name is on the deed, this is mine, all of it!"

"I wish you had all that sass and attitude when your little ass was plucking roaches out the cereal box."

Cheryl almost tripped over her own feet trying to get at Kenny.

"My child ain't never been poor! You got me fucked up Kenny, hold on now!" Cheryl intervened. "I was doing well for myself despite so don't come over here like you saved me! You weren't rich when I met you and you weren't the only dog pawing at my door. I chose you and don't you ever forget it! There wasn't a man in Harlem from big time dope dealers to white collar executives that didn't want to be with me, including you so let me remind you of who you are married to!"

"I'd watch it if I were you." He said very sinisterly as Yusef handed them their coats.

"You all have a good evening." Kenny said walking out the door.

Normally he'd hold Cheryl's hand to escort her, but he was at the bottom of the steps about to jump in his car while Cheryl was still trying to get into her coat. Bilal came from around the table and the three of them stood in front of Cheryl.

"You did what you had to do, and I forgave you a long time ago, I had to. Thank you for raising our daughter so beautifully, she's perfect." he said, draping his arms around Shantel who was physically shaking.

"I'm so sorry, I'm so very sorry, I didn't know what Kenny did." Cheryl said as the tears came down hard and fast. Bilal reached out and grabbed her hand. The warmth of his hand brought the tears down even harder for Cheryl. She had longed for his touch for years after they parted ways and always wondered if he died, was in jail or how he was doing. Bilal had been her friend since they were kids, turned high school and college sweethearts. They had their entire life planned out and just like that, drugs came into the city, they both got caught up and Bilal got stuck and had to get left behind.

"Let's go!" Kenny said loudly while leaning on the horn.

Cheryl snapped out of her trance at the sound of the horn going crazy outside, "Shantel, baby we will talk." She said in rushed tones. But Shantel just turned her back as Bilal escorted her inside.

"I'll walk you down." Yusef said holding Cheryl's hand escorting her down the long brownstone steps to the car door.

"Please tell my daughter I love her, and I am sorry." She looked up at him.

"Will do." Was all Yusef said before turning his back and jogging up the stairs to get out of the cold. Cheryl kept her eye on the door as it slammed shut. She cried the entire ride home to Connecticut, aggravating Kenny who turned on his Temptations Christmas play list to drown out the sounds of her tears.

Chapter 26
FADED PICTURES

*N*aomi managed to get off the floor and onto the couch. She grabbed the half bottle of wine that was on the end table and sipped slowly with her eyes closed as Sam and Ginger pawed at her shin.

"It's hot in here." She slurred and walked to her window, struggling to open it because she was too drunk and too weak. She slapped the window and screamed, "I'm hot!" pulling her shirt over her head, revealing her naked body. She looked at her body in the mirror, turning from side to side checking herself out. The thought of being raped crept back into her head as she stared at her beautiful body now looking at it as if it were dirty. She grabbed the full-length mirror and sent it crashing to the ground. In a rage she began slapping things off counters and mantels.

"Where's my drink?" she asked, heading back into the living room, finding her wine bottle on the end table. She guzzled some more and looked at the bottle.

This shit ain't done yet? She said and put it to her head and chugged until there was nothing left.

Where's my phone. She said stumbling looking around. The call with her father had long dropped but her phone began vibrating again but she couldn't remember where she left it. She spun around and made herself dizzy, flinging the empty wine bottle on the love seat next to her. Her phone began ringing again. In a hurry to chase the sound before it stopped vibrating again, she attempted to run, bumping into the wall sending herself crashing to the floor, her head banging against the concrete knocking her out cold.

Upon hearing the dogs barking and going mad, that alarmed Ms. Monica that something had to be terribly wrong in the house and she was fearing the worst, so she called Naomi's mother back with an update from the hallway of Naomi's apartment building while Pops was dialing 911.

"What's her address, I'll call her father, he lives in Brooklyn." Cherisse panicked.

Jameela was now on the line. "Ma, what is going on?"

"We don't know, is there a spare key or a super around here somewhere that can get us into this apartment?"

"Is that her dogs barking like that?" Jameela asked now in a panic.

"Yes, Meela yes is there a key or a super!"

"She keeps a spare key on top of the door on the ledge!"

Pops reached up and grabbed the key letting himself and his wife in to find Naomi on the floor.

"Naomi!" Ms. Monica screamed as Pops ran to her side.

"Ma, ma what is it?"

"We don't know, she's on the floor not moving, I'll call you back!"

"I'm on my way!" Jameela jumped out of her bed.

"No, don't do anything until I call you, we don't know what's going on right now, your father is dealing with it and the ambulance is on the way, just sit tight."

"Ma what do you mean she's on the floor? Is there blood?" But Ms. Monica hung up. She looked around noticing the massive amounts of liquor bottles that were around the apartment. The dogs were barking crazy and pawing at Naomi, so Ms. Monica picked them both up and walked around the apartment. She peeked into Naomi's room, two wine bottles on her nightstand, glass shattered everywhere, *was she attacked?* The entire apartment reeked of liquor as did Naomi's body. She gasped when she noticed chunks of Naomi's hair was cut out.

"She's breathing." Pops crouched over her checking her pulse. "Get a blanket or something." Pops instructed Ms. Monica who was trying to keep herself calm.

Ms. Monica found a duffle bag and began throwing items in it for Naomi. The EMS workers came hurriedly up the stairs as Pops held the door open for them.

"Do we know what happened here?"

"No. Her mother lives far and asked us to do a wellness check on her because she wasn't sounding right." Ms. Monica offered as Kareem came bursting through the door. Everyone turned and looked at him.

"I was on the phone with her, but I don't know what happened, it sounded like she fell or something. I'm her father." He offered.

"Can you tell us what you heard sir."

"She was yelling and crying. I was asking her to tell me what was wrong then it sounded like she fell or something. I don't know."

The medics continued working on Naomi, while Pops and Ms. Monica introduced themselves.

"I don't know what was happening, but this was the messages that she sent me."

He showed them the disturbing messages and they all stood trying to figure out what was going on. Kareem didn't have much to say as they put the oxygen mask on his daughter and lifted her onto the gurney.

"Please put some clothes on her please." He spoke. Ms. Monica swiftly pulled sweatpants out of the bag and Kareem assisted one of the workers in putting pants on her.

"Is she going to be okay?" Ms. Monica asked.

"Let's hope so," the EMS worker said as they pushed the gurney out the door.

"Where are you taking her?" Pops asked.

"Long Island College."

Everyone ran downstairs and jumped into their respective vehicles and followed the ambulance to the hospital.

"Did you see those messages? What do you think that was about?" Ms. Monica asked Pops as they pulled off.

"I don't know, but something happened to that woman that sent her over the edge, and I just hope that whatever it is, she can recover from."

"Do you think it's a good idea for her father to be there?"

"This is extremely sensitive. I don't know what to do, if I should protect her or if she even needs protection from him right now. She sounds like she snapped or something."

Chapter 27

COUNT ON ME

The time spent alone since Shantel confronted her mother and Kenny about conspiring to kill her father were long, depressing, dim. Not being able to call her sisters to vent to them about all the changes and emotions she was going through was stressful, she couldn't give Yusef a break, but he was the only one around.

She stared out the window of her office overlooking Rockefeller Center, watching everyone just milling about, holding hands and taking pictures. Someone was performing in front of NBC, she could hear screaming and cheering in the distance. Folks were outside happy, laughing and enjoying the upcoming holidays and here she was with all this drama and trauma.

"Lord knows I need a vacation; I need some time off," she said to herself when one of her staff knocked on her door.

"Mrs. James?"

"Please call me Shantel, I told you that. What is it?"

"Someone is on the phone at the front desk for you, they say it's an emergency."

"Why would someone be calling the front desk for me?" She said picking up her cell phone to see if she had any missed calls, and she did, all from Jameela. She hurried to the front desk and picked up the phone.

"This is Shantel."

Shantel listened on the other end as Jameela frantically told her how her parents had to go to Naomi's house, and they found her on the floor unresponsive. Nobody knew what was going on at the moment.

Shantel hung up, rushing into her office for her laptop and purse as one her colleagues rushed into talk business but she shut her down, "Lydia, we have to discuss this tomorrow, I am so sorry, but I have a family emergency." She said wrapping herself in her floor length cashmere coat.

"Oh, I hope everything is okay."

"I'll email." She said hurrying out the door, changing her mind from catching a cab to taking the train. She couldn't risk getting stuck in traffic.

"*Naomi, what the hell girl?*" she said, her leg shaking all the way to Brooklyn. Shantel all but ran to the hospital, calling Jameela when she got to the lobby.

"I'm not there yet, wait for me in the lobby I'll be there in about fifteen minutes." Jameela advised but Shantel couldn't wait. She called Ms. Monica's phone.

"Hi, Ms. Monica, it's Shantel, what floor are you guys on?"

Shantel was rushing through the halls until she spotted Pops at the far end standing with his wife and another gentleman.

"What's going on?" she said hugging both Pops and Monica.

"We don't know anything yet. She sent strange messages to her father that we're trying to decipher."

"Her what?"

Pops motioned with his head to the man standing alone at the other end of the corridor on the phone in deep conversation with someone.

"He was the last person to speak with her then he heard her fall or something. He called her mother, her mother called me so on and so forth, where's Jameela." She said exhausted looking at her watch.

"She should be here any second now, I couldn't wait for her in the lobby, but I told her where to find us, oh Naomi baby, what is going on?" Shantel said looking toward the room where Naomi was.

"She had so much alcohol in her apartment, empty bottles everywhere she reeked of alcohol, coming out of her pores and everything. She's drinking like she's in pain." Pops said.

"What happened between the three of you, I'm understanding that you all had some kind of altercation, what happened?" Ms. Monica inquired.

"Ms. Monica, I don't want to get into that, respectfully. There were a lot of terrible things that was said."

"Let me guess, my daughter is the cause of all of this."

Everyone watched Jameela as she sped down the corridor in a long black mink vest with the head wrap to match. She hugged everyone briefly and asked to be updated. Her nose was red and swollen, as if she was crying or it could have been the cold weather or both. Shantel made a motion with her mouth, like how Jamaican women do, pointing toward Kareem.

"Her father?" she asked with her lip curled up in disgust.

"Mmm hmm."

"Where the hell they find him at?" Jameela said looking him up and down, growing more and more disgusted as she looked at him. "So, what's up, nobody knows anything? Where's the doctor?"

"Relax we're all waiting to hear something" Pops said irritated. The women sat down on a row of chairs nearby, rocking back and forth, looking in their phones and being awkward as Ms. Monica sat in between them.

"You see how important it is to forgive? Whatever you all were fighting about doesn't even matter because one of your best friends is in a hospital bed right now and we don't know what the outcome is going to be. I don't need to know what was done or said to know that it had to be pretty terrible for the three of you to not have talked in this long!" She said sucking her teeth.

"This is my fault." Jameela said.

Shantel didn't stop Jameela's pity party. She needed to feel what she was feeling to bring forth change. Her mouth was nasty when she was ready, and she had to learn that sometimes you won't have the opportunity to apologize and make it right. The doctor came out looking around for everyone, the women ran close to Pops as Kareem stepped up to hear what was going on.

"You're her father, correct?" he said to Pops. Pops hesitated to say anything.

"Yes? No? Who are her parents?" the doctor asked impatiently.

"Us." Pops said, putting his arm around Ms. Monica.

"We're her sisters." Shantel said. The doctor looked at Kareem.

"Family." he said barely audible.

"Naomi has alcohol poisoning and suffered a stroke. She had a blood alcohol level of .35, she has some trauma in her brain. She is also in an induced coma right now."

"Oh my God." Jameela said hugging herself.

"A coma? What the hell does that mean, she's going to wake up right?" Shantel asked.

"Is she going to be okay?" Jameela asked softly.

"We're just hoping to stabilize her in every way. That's the only way that we will know how much damage there is. We won't know much until she's stabilized. The swelling in her brain has to go down. That's all I have for now."

Jameela put her hands over her face and began to bawl. Shantel pulled her in and consoled her friend.

"She's going to be okay Jameela, come on now."

"It's my fault, I shouldn't have said what I said to her, it's my fault." She cried.

"We gotta just pray for our girl." She said as Kareem walked up.

"Hello, I am Naomi's father." He extended his hand. Shantel and Jameela both looked him up and down unwelcomingly.

Pops walked up and joined the circle, "everything cool?"

"Yeah." Jameela said hugging her father. He embraced her and rubbed her back, kissing her on top of her head. She was inconsolable. Pops walked his daughter to a chair, and they sat down together, he pulled her head into his chest and continued rocking her leaving

Shantel and Kareem standing together awkwardly. Shantel looked over to Pops who motioned for her to come over. The big man consoled the two adult women like they were little girls. They held on to him and cried until they were out of tears. Kareem, feeling as if he had no place there, started to head out. Pops excused himself from the women and caught up to Kareem.

"You're not going to go inside and see your daughter?"

"She doesn't even know I'm here."

"But *you know* you're here." Pops said, staring him in the eyes. "Listen, Naomi has been in my life since she was about 7 years old. I know enough to know and say this with all confidence, that that young woman has a hole in her heart the size of my fist if not bigger because of the things she experienced as a child. And now she's in a coma. Don't walk out of here or I'll be forced to make sure you don't walk back in." Pops warned.

"You don't know my life. You don't know the guilt I carry as a man, a father for treating my one and only daughter that way." Kareem snapped.

"That's a conversation for your therapist not me. You can at least go in the room and look at her, talk to her, do it for you." Pops said giving Kareem a hearty slap on the shoulder. "We're not judging you, *not yet.*" He said and walked off.

Kareem walked the green mile passed the women, toward the room where his daughter lay with tubes in her. He wiped his tears before stepping into the room as the rest looked on.

"She sent her father the most bizarre messages, something about being raped over and over by men. Her mother said the same thing, that she accused her of pimping her out to men." Ms. Monica informed the girls.

"What?" Shantel said, looking at Jameela.

"I don't know, something happened, and it isn't good." Ms. Monica said softly, rubbing both women's legs.

"Rape? What in the world!" Shantel said, looking at Jameela.

Kareem sat down in a chair next to his daughter's hospital bed but couldn't look at her.

"I saw you that day, a long time ago when you came by the barbershop. It didn't dawn on me that it was you until you ran off and by the time, I came out of the shop you were gone. I couldn't get you off my mind since that day. I just didn't know what to do. I'll save some for when you wake up because *you will* wake up Naomi and *you will* get better and life is going to be different because I'm here now, I'm here and I promise…" he said, his voice cracking. He stood up and decided not to look her way then headed out the door without looking back.

Everyone watched Kareem until he disappeared around the corner.

"I don't know how I feel about him showing up after all of this time." Ms. Monica admitted.

"Her mother ain't about shit either." Jameela said.

"Jameela, don't put your mouth on people alright. It's okay to have an opinion but sometimes you gotta know where to draw the line!" Ms. Monica snapped. "Why don't the two of you go in and see your friend, how about that."

Shantel got up first and led the way.

"I don't want to go in there right now." Shantel said.

"Me either." Jameela started crying again. The guilt of the things that she said was weighing heavy on her.

"We can't lose her." Shantel said out loud.

Jameela nodded in agreement as a flurry of tears came down her face.

Chapter 28

WHEN A WOMAN'S FED UP

Tiffany knew that deep in her heart, this marriage had run its course when Gerrod stopped trying to impress her by doing the little things such as taking her out on dates, coming up with ideas for vacations and quality time. He would use her being busy as an excuse as to why they could never spend quality time or say things like, *I can no longer afford to take you to the places that you like to go. You're too good for Capital Grille! I have to take you to Eleven Madison Park and Jean-Gorges!* He found ways to attempt to make her feel guilty about her success and she was tired of it. Once she involved her mother and sister, providing them with all the details, there was no turning back. They constantly urged her to get a divorce as they had never been fond of Gerrod and after learning of him giving away her things and proposing to another woman, there was no turning back for her family.

A month passed and Gerrod was still begging for forgiveness while sleeping in the guest room. A part of him felt as if he had a chance since Tiffany hadn't filed for divorce....*yet.*

"Gerrod I'm all out of talks." she said hurrying down the stairs toward the kitchen as he trailed behind her.

"I fucked up Tiff, I fucked up." Gerrod said banging himself on the forehead.

Tiffany began talking out loud to herself while prepping her tea. "I have never been so embarrassed in my entire life."

"It was all a game baby, I didn't want to marry that woman! You know that's some bullshit, I'm already married!" Tiffany turned around upon feeling him nearing her.

"You think that makes it any better? Do you have any idea what you have done to that woman? You have broken her, you have disappointed, broken and disrespected me. I'm embarrassed, aren't you?"

"Tiff, listen I'm not trying to blame you at all but with you out of town all the time, I needed some affection and attention as well. And who knows who you're out there fucking when you're gone weeks at a time then when you come home you have no desire to fuck your husband."

Tiffany's eyes widened with shock. "Oh wow, now that's a good one Gerrod but you're not dealing with no average bitch boy. I got billionaires after me, multimillionaires! But I have morals and I respect my vows! This is solely on you 100%."

"You keep forgetting that when I met you, you didn't have any of this."

"You're my biggest hater Gerrod and I will not let you be my downfall." Tiffany said.

"I want a divorce and you will give me one." She sipped her tea.

"You don't mean that. I swear this is the last time!" he said reaching for her hand.

"You can't sex me into forgiveness, you can't be a good boy for a few months by staying home or coming straight home to show me that you're not outside. You're not even on my level financially to make it up to me with a gift." She scoffed.

"So this is what we're doing now?" he asked.

"We have that infidelity clause in our prenup too, thank God I made you sign one way before we… I mean I got rich. Your ass is fucking through!"

"You wanted this marriage to be over because you're probably out there fucking some old white motherfucka!"

Tiffany laughed. "I pity you, Gerrod. I'm not allowing you to deflect, sorry." She sang. "It never sat right with me that I had to put the majority of the money up for my own damn ring so that you wouldn't be embarrassed."

"Everything is about money to you."

"Had you done what we planned you would have been able to afford the ring that I wanted and deserved. I'm so tired of pretending, aren't you?" Gerrod stood silently, rubbing the top of his head out of frustration wondering what on earth he could do to change Tiffany's mind. He hadn't left the house other than to go to work in a month. And Tiffany hadn't traveled either.

"I need you to start looking for a place to live. I'm done letting your mediocre ass cheat on me and before you give me something that I can't get rid of I need to cut my losses and move on!" she yelled.

"We can work through this." Gerrod said but it came out weak as he wasn't so sure.

He thought Tiffany would have divorced him years ago, but he knew she loved him deeply and wanted the marriage to work. She fought for them time and time again and he thought this time wouldn't be any different. He hopped in the shower, allowing himself to release his emotions while Tiffany lay in bed, angry and feeling vengeful.

The next morning he was awakened to the sounds of his wife moving around the room while reappearing from her walk-in closet dressed in yoga pants, a white body-hugging V-neck t-shirt, smelling like Givenchy perfume, one of her favorite fragrances. Gerrod concluded that she was going to blow off steam in the gym. She continued moving around grabbing one thing or another, lastly snatching up a pair of car keys. She looked up at Gerrod who was at the top of the steps watching her.

"Do not be here when I get back. I want you out of this house. Find somewhere to go and don't come back...unless I ask you to." She said walking out.

Once Tiffany left the home, Gerrod gathered some clothes and decided that he'd stay in Four Seasons until Tiffany calmed down long enough for them to have a conversation on how to save their marriage. He was more than capable of becoming a better man for his wife and wasn't going to lose her.

Gerrod entered the Four Seasons, drawing attention as always from mainly white women as most of them believed him to be some kind of famous athlete. He arrogantly approached the front desk and asked if the Hudson Suite was available.

"I'll take the Soho Suite if the Hudson isn't available." He said while reaching for his wallet in his back pocket. Gerrod realized that the concierge was having some kind of difficulty, so he offered up a name, "I'm Gerrod Michaels, my wife is Tiffany Michael's."

"Yes, sure Mr. Michaels, I do understand. We have the Hudson available for you for the week, checking in today and checking out Friday a total of 6 nights, 5 days, the total is $16,390.00 that will include a daily breakfast and transportation to and from the hotel if needed. You may extend your stay after Friday if you choose. What card will we be using today Mr. Michael's?" the concierge asked as a line formed behind Gerrod. He proudly handed over his black card and leaned against the counter while the concierge whose name tag read Audrey pushed buttons.

"I'm sorry, Mr. Michaels, but this card isn't going through, is there another card that you would like to use?"

"Can you try again?" he asked politely. Audrey obliged then shook her head "I'm sorry. Is there another card you would like to use?"

"Sure." He said, handing her his platinum card which also declined. Furious, Gerrod began calling Tiffany to get things sorted but his calls were going straight to voice mail. The guests behind him began to grow impatient so he excused himself off the line and began scrolling through all his credit card and banking apps and learned of his fate. He had no access to any of Tiffany's credit cards or bank accounts.

"Fuck!" he yelled loud enough for people in the lobby to look at him. He grabbed his bags and stormed out of the hotel and walked about two blocks before he stopped to take a deep breath.

"Come on Tiffany don't do this." He said calling her again and again, but he could not get through. He made his way to the Dream Hotel and handed over his card to pay $3500 for the week to get him the best room that they had to offer. As Gerrod lay in bed, feeling as if he was sleeping someplace beneath him, he realized how bad he had fucked up, not because of what Tiffany provided but what he vowed to be a part of. He failed as a husband and most importantly a friend to Tiffany who had went above and beyond as a woman and a wife. He was going to find out the hard way that when a woman's fed up… there ain't nothing you can do about it.

After a much-needed spa treatment, hair wash and facial, Tiffany treated herself to lunch and then headed to Jameela's house. Jameela was surprised to hear from Tiffany after a month, asking could she come by to retrieve her possessions. Jameela wanted to leave the bag at the front desk but didn't want to risk something happening to it. But she wasn't too fond of seeing Tiffany or Gerrod.

Anxiety was getting the best of her, but she wasn't about to be unhinged when they arrived. She guzzled a flute of champagne and answered the intercom.

"This is Jameela White." She answered.

"Tiffany Michaels." The woman said just as assertive on the other end.

The women held the line, Tiffany wondering if Jameela would invite her up to get her things or if she would announce that she was coming down. Jameela was feeling heavy with sorry while her best friend lay in the hospital and couldn't take on any more drama.

"I'm alone." Tiffany offered.

"Press PH on the elevator, I'm 4102." Jameela said blandly.

"Noted." Tiffany said and hung up.

Tiffany stood on the other side of the door waiting for Jameela to open the door. She couldn't believe that this was her reality, visiting her husband's mistress to get back her things. Jameela opened the door to find Tiffany standing there in large shades covering most of her face, her long freshly styled and layered ash blonde and brown hair cascading down her left shoulder swept to one side. She was dressed plainly but still gave a "rich bitch" allure that Jameela couldn't even be mad at. Without a word, Jameela handed her the large shopping bag through the door.

"I appreciate it." Tiffany said.

Tiffany realized that Jameela didn't have to give the bag back. She could have ditched Gerrod, changed her number and went missing and in all actuality, there was nothing that she would have been able to do about it except file a claim like she already did to receive another bag. So the fact that she was gracious enough to return it spoke volumes. The women lingered, Jameela not closing her door and Tiffany not walking off.

"Is there anything else I can do for you." Jameela stated more than asked. She wasn't about to sit around and have this woman hurl insults at her like she did before.

"I want to apologize for the things that I've said. I was just pissed."

"I understand." Jameela said through the cracked door.

"You clearly aren't like the others." She scoffed. "By that I mean, you got your shit together. I hope he didn't do too much damage to your pockets."

"Oh, no damage at all. I may have been a fool, but I don't spend on men." Jameela said as seriously as cancer.

"I hear that." Tiffany faintly smiled.

"I'm sorry that this happened to you, truly. Something similar happened to my best friend and it was just egregious to say the least. And I'm not sure if it helps but I meant it when I said I never been in your home or anything like that."

Tiffany shook her head. She attempted to hide her tears, but they were coming down softly behind her shades.

"I'm sorry, thank you for the bag."

"Don't mention it. I wish you healing sista. I truly do." Jameela said.

"Same to you." Tiffany said.

The two women still lingered on as if there was more to say. Tiffany was trying to take Jameela in, after all this was the woman that her husband proposed to and spent her money trying to impress. She needed to know what it was that Jameela had that she didn't, clearly there was something. Perhaps her husband was just as unhappy with her as she was with him.

"I'm not sure if I'm doing the right thing, but... would you like to come in." Jameela asked cautiously. Tiffany didn't respond, she just stepped toward the door and Jameela opened it wide enough for her to pass through.

"The Delano." Tiffany said inhaling the fragrance as she entered the apartment and began looking around.

"My favorite Aroma 360 fragrance." Jameela said.

Mine as well. Tiffany thought but wasn't about to get all Lavern and Shirly with her husband's side piece.

"Can I offer you some champagne, spirits, water."

"I'll take a glass of champagne please."

"Dom, Veuve, OJ, no OJ."

"Dom, light OJ." Tiffany said grabbing a seat at the island while Jameela popped open champagne and moved around the large kitchen.

"This place is beautiful." She admired it.

"Thank you." She said setting the glass down in front of Tiffany then grabbing a seat across from her.

"So, I just want to speak with you about everything." Tiffany started.

"Of course." Jameela complied.

"You meet my husband..."

"At a woman's empowerment event and he was with his sister Robin."

"That messy bitch. He used to date her many years ago, then she realized she likes women."

"Oh, so that's not his sister!"

"I hope not!" Tiffany laughed.

"Well, we met, and it was a whirlwind we spent almost every day together for about three weeks."

"That had to be when I was in Toronto. He came out to meet me around that time."

"Yes, I guess that was when he told me that he had to go out of town on business for a week."

The women shook their head.

"We would spend weeks together then he would leave for a week *on business* things like that. I see now he was going home to spend time with you once you were back from business."

"Gerrod has *no business* and he's fine just where he is. I tried to push him to be greater, do better, get out and see the world but he was just so content riding my coattails. It wouldn't be so frustrating if this was who he presented himself to be from day one."

"He talked a good one." Jameela said very low.

"Did he have anything to do with this place?" Tiffany looked around at the ginormous luxury apartment.

"No, well...not in the sense that I think you are asking. My credit, my business, my income, my name, this is all me. I own a 24-hour day-care center, one in Queens and I'm about to open one in lower Manhattan near Maiden Lane, hopefully if all goes well, then another one in Dumbo, just waiting for approvals, paperwork, you know."

"That's amazing, congratulations. I wish you so much more success." Tiffany said truthfully. She picked up her glass to toast with Jameela.

"Thank you."

"No, thank you for being an inspiration to your people, our people. My father was a successful black man and he instilled that in my sister and I very early on to not settle, to go out there and chase our dreams and do more than enough. He would always tell us that there was enough money for all of us and to make sure we got our piece of the damn pie, don't settle for crumbs. He was a successful financier for a while then went into business for himself. He married my mother while he was working his way up, she loves to let us know that she was not with him for the money and that she was with him when he didn't have shit." Tiffany chuckled a bit.

"Sounds like my mother."

"No kidding." Tiffany said. "My dad passed away about 6 years ago, liver cancer. That's why I don't drink much at all. They say it wasn't caused by alcohol, but I don't do anything that will contribute to an early death. The occasional wine and champagne are fine, and I do mean very seldom, at least for me. Some occasions call for it, celebrations, birthdays, *this*...." she said and guzzled the last of her champagne.

"Would you like another."

Tiffany answered by extending her glass.

"So my sister, *the white* one as everyone calls her did what white girls do, latched on to an up-and-coming athlete and the rest is history."

"So this is the sister in Dallas aka your husband's ex-wife."

"Exactly. Sometimes I envy her. She got away easily, no hard work, no rejection, no college, no grinding. Just be pretty, have long hair, look exotic and have a baby by an athlete oh and turn the other cheek when he cheats because you can't lose the lifestyle. I did all that turning of the cheek and was the provider of the lifestyle. Life's a bitch sometimes. I should have left his ass a long time ago that's word to Mary J. Blige." She laughed.

Jameela did too, she wasn't expecting that to come out of Tiffany's mouth. She seemed so far removed and uppity but the more she spoke, the more Jameela realized they had so much in common.

"You know, I blame my mother. May he rest in peace, my father was my world but he use to put my mother through some shit!"

"Oh, you sound like me right now!" Jameela chimed in.

Tiffany laughed but she had tears in her eyes and Jameela realized that this woman was venting and needed someone to talk to, so she pulled back on her own stories and let Tiffany get whatever off her chest.

"Yeah, my dad was a piece of work, he's behaving now." Jameela said.

"The big guy was your dad right? Your family looks nice. Reminds me so much of how my family is, optics at least. I apologize for disrespecting your home. I truly didn't know what I was walking into. Please extend my apologies to your lovely family."

"I understand and I appreciate your apology."

"So, how did Gerrod arrive at the point of proposal, who's idea was it."

"My parents have been married all my life, my best friend is married, but I have never been in a serious relationship. Gerrod was the first man that I actually put my guards down for unfortunately. I work hard, I have financial aspirations, I knew that the man I settled down with would not be basic, on the come up, or anything like that. I am too old for potential."

"Preach!" Tiffany said, raising her glass.

"So when I met Gerrod, and he convinced me that he use to play for the NFL and now was an entrepreneur and all this big money talk I was intrigued."

"I understand totally." Tiffany sipped.

"How could I not believe it with the cars he drove, the watches, the threads. So as time went on, I did find it interesting that he didn't want to meet any of my folks. He fed me many excuses and I chose to believe them because I wanted what I wanted. I own a home on Long Island, but he said it was too far from everything, so I rented my house out and found this space. He said he would take on the overhead once the divorce was finalized. My friends were getting in my ass so terrible behind this and I just would not listen."

"Oh the two women that were there."

"Yeah." Jameela shook her head somberly thinking about Naomi.

"I'm so sorry about the terrible things that Gerrod said. You know it made me look at him in a different light. I don't delight in any man talking to women that way. I was dumbstruck. I hope your friends are okay."

"You have no idea how okay they are not."

"He's a dirty son of a bitch for this. I didn't want my marriage to fail in front of my sister and mother. They are the proud founders of the first wives club and they get on my damn nerves with all of this talk about what a wife should do, and what a woman should do, a wife this, a man that, like there is so much more to life than being some foolish man's wife!"

"Amen."

"Has he contacted you."

"No, and I pray it remains that way."

"Would you let me now if he does?" Tiffany asked, easing up from her seat.

"Absolutely."

"Well, thank you so much for this talk and for your time. I'm not sure if you remember the business that I'm in but I can move things along for you regarding your business locations."

Jameela didn't know what to say and wasn't about to get too excited, so she just smiled, unsure of how to respond.

"I'm all for black women empowering one another."

"Thank you, Tiffany." She said walking her to the door.

"Text me the paperwork etc. and let me call in some favors."

"I appreciate that so much. With everything going on right now, I could use some good news. Oh before you forget the reason why you came, here." Jameela said, handing her the purse.

"I've been a loyal customer for years. I absolutely love Chanel. I look around and I see that you're a woman about her business, and I honor women like you, I truly do. Chanel is replacing my bags once the investigation is complete. So keep it for your pain and suffering, my new one should be arriving soon."

Jameela was elated, "I don't know what to say Tiffany this is beyond kind."

"If we met under different circumstances, we would be friends, I could tell." Tiffany winked.

Jameela was compelled to hug Tiffany but all she could say was thank you.

"You will let me know if that man reaches out to you and tries to get you back or do anything right? I need all the proof and resources possible to make this divorce smooth for me because that motherfucka ain't getting a dime from me."

"Allow me to gather any and all info that I have, text me your email address." Jameela said.

She watched Tiffany walk down the hall then twinkled her fingers goodbye as she disappeared onto the elevator. *I fucking like her!* Jameela said as she picked up the large Chanel shopping bag and twirled it around happily. Her happiness faded quickly upon thoughts of Naomi that seeped into her mind.

MOMMY DEAREST

Once Ms. Monica no longer felt obligated to keep Cherisse up to date on what was going on with her only child, Cherisse made it to New York, checking into the Tillary Hotel in Brooklyn. With a bouquet of flowers and a small teddy bear, Cherisse slowly walked down the hall looking into each room until she came across the room where her daughter was. The machines around her whirled and beeped softly, Naomi's chest moved slightly, her face covered in masks and tubes. A nurse approached her and asked who she was.

"Her mother," she said offended.

"I'll grab her doctor," the nurse said hurrying off.

About twenty minutes later, Dr. Nin came in and introduced himself.

"In conjunction with the alcohol poisoning and stroke right now we are monitoring her brain activity. She still has some swelling. Though slowly, the swelling has gone down, but she isn't out of the woods yet."

"So is she going to be in a coma for a few more months, weeks?"

"Again, I can't say right now. We need the swelling to not only dissipate but we must ensure that it doesn't come back. We need all her vitals to be stable and consistent. So for now she's on ice so to speak. But we're doing everything possible to preserve her, I promise you."

"Have you ever experienced this with other patients and what's the turn around? Be honest with me."

"Well, we've seen worse conditions that had a 100% recovery over time, and we've seen conditions nowhere near as bad however, due to preexisting health conditions and things like that, recovery was minimal. It's really on a case-by-case basis and I don't want to give false hope or false fear. All I can tell you is that the swelling is going down, the internal bleeding has stopped, and we just need to monitor her closely. We won't know how much damage is done until then."

"It's been a week now. When she recovers, what can we expect?"

"It's hard to tell at the moment I wish I could give you more."

"I understand and thank you for all you've been doing for her."

"Absolutely, it is my pleasure." He said and hurried off.

Cherisse sat next to Naomi and gently rubbed her hand.

"God, please give us another chance to get it right, please." She begged.

Having never met Cherisse other than briefly when she came to visit Naomi when she was about nine years old, Jameela made it her business to head to her parents' house once they informed her that she was in town and wanted to meet the people that served as "*second parents*" to her daughter as if she had first parents to compare it to.

"This woman took days to come see her child and if I hadn't stopped feeding her information she wouldn't have come. I think she would have been content with getting feedback from me rather than come see for herself."

"I don't know what she expects to get from us." Jameela said while loading the dishwasher for her mother.

"Well you know me, I'm always pleasant but she bet not say nothing too foolish." Ms. Monica scoffed as Pops entered the kitchen.

"What time is this woman coming, I got shit to do." He said looking at his watch.

"Like what?" Ms. Monica inquired.

"Like take a fucking nap I'm tired." He said causing everyone to laugh.

"Seriously, I definitely rather be shampooing my pet roach ralph than to meet this poor excuse of a mother." Jameela said.

"I just don't understand. But I guess she's coming here to explain to us what was on her mind when she left her baby with her sister."

"Now Zola is alright with me." Pops said.

"Of course she is. You gotta be a stand-up kind of person to take on someone else's child when you don't have any of your own. Much respect to Zola always." Ms. Monica said.

"I second that." Jameela said.

"That must be them now." Pops said, heading to the door to find Cherisse, Zola and Kareem to his dismay at the door.

"Come in." Pops stepped aside as Ms. Monica warmly greeted Zola and exchanged pleasantries with Kareem and Cherisse. Jameela was in the living room drinking a cup of tea as she had been feeling a bit under the weather.

"You must be Cherisse." Ms. Monica said.

"Yes, and you're Monica?"

"That would be me, this is my husband Preston, and my daughter Jameela."

"The infamous best friend how are you dear. I haven't seen you since you were knee high to a grasshopper!" Cherisse said, approaching Jameela with her hand extended.

"I'm well. Thank you for asking." Jameela responded curtly.

"Can I offer you all any beverages, wine, beer, water, tea, coffee, anything?"

"I'll take water with lemon?" Kareem asked cautiously.

"Oh come on you can do better than that, I got bourbon, scotch..." Pops said always forcing spirits on someone.

"Gin?"

"Baby get the man some Gin, neat right?"

"Yes sir." Kareem said.

"For you ladies?" Pops pushed.

"I'll take a Tequila with fresh lime, soda water with a bit of agave if you have?" Zola said.

"That's where Naomi gets that drink from, she loves that!" Jameela said.

"Is that right?" Zola said.

"Yup, right mommy?"

"That is correct!"

"Well then I'll have the same." Cherisse said.

Ms. Monica went into the kitchen to shake up drinks. She returned quickly with all the drinks on a tray and set them down in the middle of everyone for them to grab their glasses.

"A toast, first and foremost to Naomi. May God keep her covered and recover her 100%" Pops said. A chorus of amen's followed as everyone sipped.

"So what brings you all here aside from the obvious." Pops jumped right into it.

"I just thought that a meet and greet was long overdue. You all know my daughter better than I do. And I know what your perception of me might be and I would like to just clear up some things." Cherisse said.

"So you're here to clear your name." Jameela stated blandly from the back of the room as she decided to sit at the dining room table and observe everyone.

"Precisely yes."

"Well, we don't have any judgement of you either way but if you feel it necessary to speak up for yourself then by all means, go ahead." Pops said.

"Let me just say this first before Cherisse says anything. I take full responsibility for everything that has happened. It was a domino effect once I dropped my responsibility. She did what she had to do, and I am in no position to fault her for leaving Naomi behind when my track record isn't great at all."

Jameela sucked her teeth so long and hard any Jamaican woman would be proud.

"What is it, Jameela." Ms. Monica said.

"Jameela, why don't you go lay down you said you weren't feeling well." Pops offered, knowing that his daughter's mouth was lethal, and he didn't' want her to say anything foul to these people even though they deserved it.

"I'm fine right here. I just think that it's crazy how you both are leading with the perception of you as opposed to Naomi. We don't care about what you did or why, what we care about is Naomi getting better and what the two of you have to offer her because all the events in her life lead up to this moment, the drinking, the promiscuity, and everything else that she had to internalize. Her mental and emotional state has been in shambles most of her life and the two of you show up here while she's in a coma to clear up what people think about you?"

"I understand your frustrations Jameela, I do. I know that you firsthand can appreciate what Naomi has gone through, but you don't know everything. I did not leave Naomi. I've long since wanted to move out of New York to raise my daughter. And I know that she experienced a lot. She was so happy with her aunt because she had a friend now, which was you, Jameela. And it wasn't lost on me that she yearned for a father figure in her life, which was what really made her want to stay with Zola, so that she could be around this family. I did bring Naomi down south with me during winter break once and she hated it. She just wanted to come back home and be with Zola, the dog, the Whites. I honestly had so much on my plate, finishing school, saving money for a house, trying to get everything in order so that I could provide a loving environment for Naomi, but she didn't want to come and so Zola and I had a talk and she agreed to keep her as long as she remained respectful and got an education."

"I don't recall her going down south in the winter." Jameela said.

"Well, she did come once. I would call every single day and come visit when time allowed but life started to happen and if I'm guilty of anything then it's not making time, but I was trying to heal from my own traumas and get on my feet. I asked Naomi when she was entering Junior high if she wanted to come live with me and she said no. I asked again when she went into high school and she said no. When she graduated high school, I expected her to go away to college, hopefully in the south so that we could be closer."

"But you were highly disappointed when she didn't continue her education and that's when you started to berate her and talk down to her. I remember that clearly." Jameela said not allowing Cherisse to tell a sob story.

"I don't recall berating her. I was disappointed because she has been surrounded by education her entire life, everyone around her has higher education."

"I was there, right next to her when you called her and said some awful things to her when you learned that she was not going away to college. Initially she was just taking a year off but after that phone call with you she just threw away any thoughts of going to college. Do you remember that phone call?" Jameela challenged.

"I just wanted her to secure her future, does that make me a bad mother?"

"No, I can't say that. But what makes you a bad mother is disowning her when her lifestyle didn't align with your vision of what you wanted your daughter to be. To you, she wasn't anything to show off, so you just forgot about her during a time in her life when she needed you most. She was becoming a woman and didn't have you to nurture her. And when you asked her to come stay with you before junior high school was that before or after ignoring her calls. Or when you asked her to come stay with you to attend high school, was that before or after you called her worthless for not making valedictorian or salutatorian? And after high school when she actually mentioned coming to stay with you after I had gone off to college already, you told her she'd be changing toilet paper for offices in large corporations instead of running one because she chose not to go to college and that the only thing waiting for her down south was a job at Waffle House or the strip club since she chose not to go to college."

Not knowing all of this, Kareem glanced over at Cherisse briefly then sipped his drink.

"Yeah, I was around for all of those phone calls." Jameela folded her arms.

"I just wanted her to be better than average. I won't apologize for that. My delivery may have been wrong and hurtful, but I wasn't wrong for how I felt."

"You were dead wrong for how you felt because raising her was *your* responsibility and you failed, period. You didn't want to raise her once you realized that this man wasn't leaving his wife. You gave up and let Zola have her. And you did the bare minimum just to keep the smut off your rep when in fact all you did was make things worse. You did things for her just to say you did something."

Monica gave Jameela a warning look to watch her mouth.

Calmly Cherisse asked Jameela, "What would have made me a better mother then in your opinion."

Jameela put her tea down and met Cherisse's sarcasm. "According to what your child said, you were supposed to fight for her, drag her down south whether she liked it or not and raised her regardless of what she wanted to do. You could have sent her to visit in the summers and recesses. You dropped the ball, her words not mine." Jameela said.

"I have been made aware that there were quite a few things that my niece experienced but she hid from me because she didn't want her mother to know," Zola said.

"Zola let me just say this, Naomi thanks God for you and she by no means meant to hurt or disrespect you by hiding anything. She just didn't want Cherisse to know anything about her at all." Jameela said.

Ms. Monica then cleared her throat to speak, "and let me just also add that I by no means meant to overstep but Naomi practically grew up in this house. She went on family vacations with us, she spent holidays with us when Zola would go on trips and things. Zola has spent holiday seasons with us as well and so I guess I'd like to know why you never made the time to come home to see your daughter?" Ms. Monica asked.

"Again, I just took for granted that she was safe with my sister and seemingly happy. I really don't have anything further to add except that I did not just abandon my daughter."

"Oh but you did, the both of you did. Kareem, did you ever say anything to your wife about pressing a little girl about you sleeping with her mother and your son physically assaulting her? Can you even fathom what that would do to the psyche of a little girl? Her mother being villainized by her father's wife and her brother all while her father didn't do anything to protect her or stop the madness? What about you Cherisse, what did you do when you heard about this?"

"I wasn't made aware of that incident until sometime after the fact." Kareem said.

"Bullshit," she told her mother as soon as she got home so I am inclined to think that any mother would call up the father and share what happened. So you're telling me something as diabolical as that happened to a little girl on her way home from school and nobody jumped into immediate action to correct and protect her?" Jameela said getting angrier. Pops just sat back, taking it all in letting the woman sort it out as he had nothing to add at the moment. Kareem and Cherisse, realizing how ridiculous they looked and not understanding how much Naomi hurt and shared with her best friend decided to stop coming up with excuses.

"She is almost forty years old and her entire life all she ever wanted was her daddy. Do you know that she would go to Brooklyn and watch you from afar just to get a look at you?" Jameela said tearing up as she imagined the pain her friend was in. Zola's eyes opened wide as she had no idea this was happening.

"I did in fact see her one time but by the time I came out of the store she was gone."

"And you didn't follow up with her mother to ask where she was staying so that you could build a relationship? You saw her and that was it?" Jameela yelled. "My girl is in a coma. We don't know if she will ever come out of this and if she does will she ever be coherent enough to live a decent life and get the love that she deserves. And I blame it on the both of you, 100 percent. You both just sat back and let her life go whichever way. Let me ask you, how is your son, how's life for him, are you still with his mother?"

"Yes, I am still married. My son is a Morehouse graduate and is doing well for himself."

"Educated, married, children, the whole nine."

Kareem didn't answer.

"That's what I thought. And we know that you went on, met you a woman, got married and raised a lovely stepson, also college educated, good kid, right? Just living life, family vacations and what not, any of your children drink?" She looked from Cherisse to Kareem.

"Not that I know of, maybe occasionally out with friends." Kareem asked.

"I've watched my friend drown her pain in the bottle for so many years. She would fight so hard to live a healthy life. And all she needed was parents that didn't give up, that didn't take the easy way out. Now it might be too late to say sorry how do you feel about that?" Jameela asked, her voice shaking as her own guilt made her sick.

"I was young and scared and made a mistake by stepping out on my marriage and having a child. Naomi didn't deserve to be treated this way and there isn't anything that I can do about the past, but I am willing to die making this up to her, that's all that I got."

"How did you think it made her feel when you told her not to call you dad." Jameela snarled.

"Woah." Pops said.

"I didn't think my presence even mattered to her after all of this time you know?"

"Does your presence matter to your son?" Pops finally said something.

"Yeah, it does."

"So why wouldn't it matter to your daughter."

"Because I wasn't in her life so I figured you can't miss what you never had."

"Did you grow up with your father?"

"I did not."

"And did you ever miss him or wonder why he didn't come around or stay in your life?"

"I did but once I reached a certain age, I just let it go. It made no sense to dwell on something that wasn't going to happen. He wasn't going to be in my life, his choice."

"We're obviously cut from two different cloths because I can't imagine fathering a child in or outside of my marriage and walking away. I knew that pain through my sisters. I've seen them go off and be successful but pick the wrong men, have low self-esteem, go through so much bullshit and I vowed as a man, that if I could help it, to never abandon any woman that I claim to love be it my children, my wife, my sisters, it didn't matter."

Jameela once again felt foolish for being even slightly jealous of Naomi and Preston's bond now that her father painted a picture as to why he sometimes favored Naomi over her.

"So what's the end game, why are we all here and how do we move forward?" Ms. Monica asked as Cherisse and Kareem's energy had become draining. They had nothing to offer, they didn't ask about Naomi or inquire about her life, her past or anything. They were simply here to save face and make excuses for being shitty parents.

"I want us to just continue to support Naomi and stand together to be there for her. I don't want to be pushed out or shamed because of our history. Her father and I have a right, the only rights if you will, should anything happen to her, or any decisions need to be made."

"You mean like a DNR or something?" Ms. Monica inquired.

"Considering all things." Cherisse said.

"We won't get in your way, just don't get in ours." Jameela stood up from the table in the back.

"I understand that you are concerned and have a deep love for Mimi and despite my shortcomings I am her mother, and you can't compete with a parent's love."

"Now hold on, this isn't a competition," Ms. Monica said.

"Ma, don't worry because one can't compete where they don't compare. I'm done with all of this. It was *not* a pleasure to meet either of you. Mommy, daddy I'm going to lay down, I'm not feeling too well." She said kissing them both. "Zola, always a pleasure."

"Likewise." Zola smiled at Jameela as she walked away.

"I'll see you out," Pops said escorting them to the door.

"We are her parents, regardless. I just want to make sure we have a clear understanding." Cherisse said.

"Noted." Was all Ms. Monica said as she hugged Zola who softly said good night. Ms. Monica shut the door strongly behind them.

"Can you believe the nerve of that woman?" she asked her husband with wide eyes.

"I can and I don't care what they're talking about, they're not coming over here with this self-righteous we are her parents bullshit, it ain't happening. Now I'm willing to step aside and let them do what they should have been done but you're not about to erase us like we weren't the ones holding her down."

"Nor would Naomi want that, so we have nothing to be worried about."

Jameela appeared at the top of the steps, "let's go visit her tomorrow, give her some loving energy."

"That sounds like a plan. Are you and Shantel all right, will you invite her to come along?"

"I will, Naomi needs all of us now more than ever and I really do not like the vibe that her fake ass parents are coming in on, I swear. It just seems like they are up to something."

Pops didn't say anything to that, but his silence was confirmation enough.

Chapter 29

THE BIG PAYBACK

*T*iffany returned home and did a thorough walk through of her large home confirming that Gerrod was not there. She didn't know where he was resting his head, and she didn't care at this point. She opened her laptop and curled up on her couch with a mug of ginger tea and searched Jameela White's credentials then made a few calls.

"Hey, Cliff how have you been?... I am great, wonderful...oh he's fine, business is fine, everything is great. I do have a favor to ask of you please, you said to call you should I need anything, you owe me one or two favors...Thanks, there's a lot in Dumbo, how much is that going for, who's up for that?"

Tiffany began jotting numbers down in her notepad on her cell phone as Cliff spoke.

"That's a good number, do you think you can get me to the front of the line on that deal? I have a new business venture I'm embarking on, I think that lot might be perfect for it."

"Oh really, what do you have in mind now? Something outside of the normal scope?" Cliff asked.

"I have a few ideas, I'll share with you soon, just stop any sales on it."

"You know that's nothing but a flip of the switch, is that all?"

"No, one more favor. Can you check and see if anyone is close to or interested in buying a lot near Wall Street, around Maiden Lane area?"

"Looks like it's going to be city funded." He said as he typed.

"And the city can pull out or is it too far in the process?"

"It all depends on who wants to know Tiffany, what are you up to?"

"I think that area would be perfect for a salon. Areas like that, upper east side, they don't have many salons that cater to the tons of black women that work in that area. We need a place to go on our lunch breaks or right after work."

"So what do you need me to do?"

"Pull the plug on that deal and the other one in Dumbo. I'm willing to pay whatever."

"Money talks, you got it!"

"Oh and get me the information on the landlord for this address in Queens will you." She said giving him the address to Jameela's day care.

"What's this place?" he asked.

"I think it has a day care in there, see if it has a vacant floor. I'm thinking about possibly renting office space or buying the building from the landlord."

"Okay, sounds good."

"Thanks Cliff, how long before I know something concrete?"

"It's the weekend so allow me to get back to you end of next week."

"You are the best, Cliff!"

"Tell that to my wife!" he chuckled.

"I'll be sure to put in a good word, just buy her something expensive on top of that and she's silly putty in your hands!"

"If it were only that easy, boss lady. Well I gotta run, I'll revert next week, you enjoy your weekend."

"Oh I will, same to you." Tiffany said hanging up.

"*I'm going to run your ass right out of business.*" She laughed sinisterly and picked up the phone to call her sister.

Chapter 30

SHOOP, SHOOP, SHOOP

It was all about Naomi at this point and the rift between the women and her illegitimate parents didn't matter. As long as everyone came around with good vibes, love and healing energy for Naomi, there wouldn't be an issue. Shantel and Yusef were the first to arrive at the hospital, carrying fresh flowers, cards, and stuffed animals. With everyone having busy schedules and not being able to come to the hospital every day, they did ensure that she was being properly taken care of by flooding the hospital with phone calls.

Everyone seemed to have the same idea to visit Naomi today.

"It's crowded in here, and we don't need the doctors to get riled up. The two of you want to spend some time with her first since you're her parents and then we rotate?" Ms. Monica asked Cherisse and Kareem who searched for the sarcasm in her comment, but Ms. Monica stood ever so elegantly and politely that they were unsure.

"Maybe you all should take turns, and we'll go in last, this way we don't hold up the line by spending so much time with her, *as her parents*." Cherisse stated.

"Sure," Ms. Monica said, turning away from her and giving her no energy. Shantel and Jameela, who were in a heated discussion in the corner about Tiffany's visit paused the conversation once Ms. Monica got closer.

"That woman is a trip, coming over to our house yesterday trying to get some sympathy and making all kinds of excuses for leaving Naomi." Ms. Monica huffed.

"Girl, I got them the hell up out of my parents' house with that foolishness in under 20 minutes, I couldn't take it." Jameela said holding her stomach.

"Baby are you okay, you've been cramping since yesterday."

"I'm really stressed, and I've been eating all the wrong things. I could probably use a detox. I haven't been working out or anything I'm just drained." She winced again in pain.

"You might as well get checked out while we're here." Shantel said, walking Jameela to a nearby seat. Jameela continued keeling over and holding her stomach.

"I'm grabbing a nurse."

"I think it's gas." Jameela said holding her stomach attempting to follow Shantel to the nurse's station as Kareem and Cherisse looked on. Pops came out upon seeing Jameela limping.

"What's going on." he asked while rubbing her back.

"She needs to get these stomach pains sorted." Ms. Monica said.

"Oh, okay well you know what happens when you approach 40. That check engine light comes on, you sneeze and paralyze yourself." He joked.

"You got that right!" Jameela laughed.

After some paperwork, Shantel and Jameela sat side by side waiting for her to be called while Ms. Monica continued looking down the hall at Naomi's parents.

"That girl deserved better." She disapprovingly shook her head.

"I have no desire to meet that woman." Shantel said.

"Ms. White?" The nurse approached the women.

"Yes that's me."

"How are you, I'm Joanna, I assist Dr. Giles. He would like for you to give a urine sample before observation if that's okay."

"That's fine." Jameela said, taking the cup from Joanna and heading to the bathroom. She returned a few minutes later and sat down, waiting to be called.

"I really do think that it's gas. I haven't been cooking so I've been eating bullshit, running around, then Naomi, I'm just super stressed out right now."

Dr. Giles entered the examination room interrupting the conversation.

"So Jameela how can I help you." Dr. Giles, a tall lanky Caucasian man asked as he pulled up a seat.

"I've been having stomach pains for a few weeks now. I'm here visiting my sister, so I thought it made sense to get checked out. I really do think that it is stress related." She said as she ran down the list of stressors she had been dealing with lately.

"What was the date of your last menstrual cycle?"

"Last month on the 4th and it only last two days and it was very light."

"Okay, do me a favor and lay down please, I'm going to just check your abdominal area." He said and began pressing on her stomach. "Okay, you can sit up now." He said as the nurse came in and handed him a chart. He gave the chart a good once over then placed it on the table next to him.

"So, stress, poor diet, not getting enough rest, gas, fatigue, so many factors can contribute to your stomach issues. But I can assure you that none of these are the reason why you're experiencing such discomfort."

"So what is it then?" Jameela asked impatiently.

"Well, you are in fact pregnant."

Mrs. Monica immediately grabbed her necklace and began fidgeting with it. Shantel firmly pressed her hand on Mrs. Monica's knee, bracing herself.

"Come again?" Jameela asked, her eyes widened.

"Yes, pregnant about five or six weeks."

"Pregnant? Oh no this can't be right, are you sure?" Jameela looked up at Dr. Giles.

"Yes, I'm sure." He said seeing this disappointment on so many women's faces over the years.

Ms. Monica asked to be excused.

"Where are you going? Don't tell Dad!" Jameela said with a look of fear on her face.

"No, no, no of course." Ms. Monica touched her daughter's hand gently before exiting. She felt as if she was about to pass out.

"I'll step out and give you a moment." he said and scurried out.

"I cannot be pregnant, oh my God!" she covered her face.

"*A whole ass baby.*" Shantel said to herself.

Dr. Giles reentered the office, "I'd like to see you in next week, you can make an appointment at the front desk. Congratulations, Jameela." he said and shook her hand. He nodded at Shantel and walked out.

"I need a moment alone, please." She snapped at Shantel who stood up.

"Not a problem, I'm going to head back to see Naomi."

She encountered Jameela's parents at the end of the hall and informed them that Jameela was fine and getting dressed.

"I'm going to sit with Naomi for a moment." She smiled softly at Jameela's parents leaving them in the hall. She pulled up a chair next to Naomi and softly covered her hands with her own.

With her voice low and soft she began conversing with her best friend.

"Sister, so much is going on. You don't know how bad I wish the three of us could go to Blvd Bistro, Brooklyn Chop House, Bobby Vans right now." She sniffled.

"As soon as you wake up, *and you will wake up*... I'm taking you to get that big, beautiful mane washed, then we're going to get mani and pedi's and you're going to stay with me and I'm going to take care of you. I promise I am. I'm going to put you up on the first floor of my Brownstone. Sam and Ginger are already with me, don't be silly." She smiled softly. "Mimi, wake up girl." Her voice cracked.

"Hey." She heard a man's somber voice behind her. She turned to find Cory standing in the doorway.

Chapter 31

GOTTA FIND MY WAY BACK

*S*hantel stood up slowly at the sight of Cory, wondering how on earth he knew to come to the hospital. Cory looked past Shantel and set his sights on the love of his life, who seemingly seemed to be losing hers.

"What happened." He stated rather than ask as he stepped up closer to her bedside, looking over her entire body. Shantel took a deep breath and began rubbing her temples. First Naomi's wayward parents had the nerve to show up trying to pull rank and now Cory was here as if he didn't play a role in her downward mental spiral.

"What are you doing here?" Shantel inquired in an annoyed tone.

"I don't want no smoke, what happened?" Cory asked softly.

"We won't know until she wakes up and tells us."

Shantel grew sadder the more she recounted in her mind the events that led up to Naomi being in her current state and she wasn't willing to share that with Cory. They were barely in touch because of Jameela's vitriol toward her and with her own family history coming back to bite her, Shantel didn't have much time to keep trying to spend time with Naomi. So she kept her in prayer, set a reminder to reach out to her friend every Sunday around the time she normally would, and if she didn't answer, which she rarely did, she would send her a loving text message, letting her know that she loved her so much and missed her. As for Jameela, she didn't extend that same grace. She was done being the bigger person in the group. But even knowing what she knew, she didn't know the depth of Naomi's sorrows, moreover, she couldn't even fathom that Naomi had been drugged and sexually violated.

Cory and Shantel said nothing for a while, the silence was heavy until Shantel inquired again about how Cory knew what was going on.

"I have a cousin that moved up here from Georgia, he moved a block up from Naomi's, crazy right. When he gave me his address, I was like no fucking way, but I took it as a sign because she was on my mind so heavy to be honest. For the past couple of months I couldn't stop thinking about her. So since I was in the neighborhood, I figured I'd ring her bell, see if she was home or if she even still lived there and one of her neighbors told me she saw the ambulance take her last week."

"So how did you know what hospital she was in?" Shantel folded her arms.

"The neighbor overheard where they were taking her." He said, his eyes on his beloved.

"And what made you think that she would still be here?" Shantel grilled, trying to get his attention, not happy at all about his presence.

"I called the hospital."

"They're not supposed to give out that kind of information."

Shantel folded her arms not letting up on him.

"Yeah, that's what they told me, so I assumed that meant she was still here, so I took a chance and came, and they told me her room number."

"You know what, your name is not even on the list, and they're not supposed to give out that kind of information, so they still violated!" Shantel stood firm.

"Is there a problem with me being here?" Cory asked realizing that Shantel was becoming confrontational. He remembered her as "the soft, nice friend." He would expect more of this push back from Jameela who was always up in his face about ain't shit men and questions about why men cheat.

"It's been a long time and I hate to even bring it up under these circumstances, but you have no idea the mess you left behind and what it took for that girl to recover."

"I never meant for none of this to happen."

"Cory, come on brother make it make sense." Shantel said getting pissed all over again.

"I saw her through the pregnancy, and she had my son then we got a divorce. We couldn't repair what was already broken *before* Naomi and then when she found out about Naomi, she couldn't move forward knowing that I truly loved someone else."

"Well good for her." Shantel said unimpressed. "But do you have any idea what it feels like to love someone and there's nothing that you can do to turn that love off, so you turn on yourself, because you feel like a fool? So you beat yourself up in so many ways as if that's going to change something. It's like dying with your eyes open, drowning while watching the one that's supposed to save you standing over you holding on to *your* life jacket and not giving it to you. I've watched that girl go through it. You were supposed to be her safe space Cory. I may be overstepping when I say this, but she's been afraid to get close to any man, so she switches them like draws."

Cory began rubbing his dark waves out of frustration. He knew that he hurt Naomi and couldn't deal with hearing the aftermath of his carelessness. The guilt in him began to rise again, something that he thought he healed from. But Shantel was there to remind him of what a fuck up he was.

"I can't change the past, I'm here now. Just tell me what I could do to help."

"Look at her Cory, what can you possibly do?"

"I know ya'll hate me, that's cool but I'm here for anything Naomi needs." He said hoping deep down that Naomi recovered from whatever this was so that he could extend himself to her in any way she could possibly need.

Shantel looked over at her friend and the memories of them growing up together flashed before her eyes as she thought to herself what life would be like without her best friend. Cory, noticing the shift in Shantel's energy and how sad she got, reached for her hand, and pulled her close, embracing her.

"She's going to be okay. Her story isn't going to end like this, she has too many people that love her." Cory offered as Yusef appeared from getting food downstairs. He took a step back upon seeing a strange man hugging his wife and was shocked upon seeing who the man was as he approached.

"What's up man!" Cory said, extending his hand for a shake.

"How you been?" Yusef asked Cory while handing Shantel a bottle of water.

"You know..." Cory shrugged.

No one said anything as the three of them stood awkwardly in the hospital room trying to avoid looking at the bed with their loved one laying in it.

"Let's give him his space to spend some time with her, come on baby." Yusef said grabbing Shantel's hand, leading her out of the room. Cory grabbed the seat next to Naomi's bed, but he didn't look at her, instead dropped his hands between his legs with his head hung down low, thinking of her beautiful smile, her laugh, her jokes, and good energy. He replayed the day they met in Miami and how radiant she was, her locs so beautiful, long, healthy. She had the most infectious smile and she always smelled so good. He fought hard to only think good thoughts but the memory of how they parted, what he had done, and how hurt she was, the tears she cried when they made love for the last time crept into his psyche. Little did she know, he cried too.

"*Damn Mimi.*" He choked up.

Unable to sit in the room for more than a minute, he abruptly stood up and exited the room, wiping his tears quickly before anyone could see but Shantel and Yusef were both watching. He hurried down the hall with Shantel jogging behind him. She caught up with him as he pressed for the elevator.

"Leaving so soon."

"Yeah, I gotta go do a thing." He said not making eye contact with Shantel who began to feel pity for him.

"Take my number." she offered.

"What happened to my baby." He asked no one in particular as Shantel put her number in his phone.

"Call me, she needs all the love and support and regardless of what I know you have that for her. You can call me for updates. I know you live far and probably can't make it out here often."

"I'm definitely around and will make it my business to see about her, thank you Shantel." he said, stuffing his phone in his back pocket as Jameela came flying around the corner angry at the news she had just heard.

"Cory?" She looked from him to Shantel bewildered.

"How you been Meela." he asked somberly.

"Great! You know, bestie in a coma, but life is good, what about yourself, you look well. How's the family, the wife and kids, the kid gotta be about five or six now, right? What did you end up having?" she snarled.

"I'll be in touch." He said to Shantel, not willing to go there with Jameela. The elevator doors opened and closed with Jameela mean mugging him. She turned her attention to Shantel.

"What the fuck is he doing here?"

"The same thing everyone else is Meela." Shantel said annoyed at Jameela's energy.

"What, you called him or something? How did he know she was here? We don't need no bad energy around our girl!"

All Shantel could think was that the only bad energy around was Jameela. She still wanted nothing to do with her but for the sake of Naomi, she gave her the time of day.

"Listen, none of that matters. Naomi needs all the love and support right now."

"And you think that *he's* going to love and support her? You didn't tag his ass for what he did to our girl? You all chummy chummy with him? He's the fucking enemy! He's part of the reason that she's in this situation!"

Shantel began rubbing her temples. "Meela, our girl is in a coma, none of this other shit matters."

"You are so damn soft sometimes I swear, *anyway*. Are you guys leaving, what's the plan?" Jameela asked looking up at Yusef.

It took everything in Shantel to not go off on Jameela, but she just wanted to go home and get away from her for now. Her energy was overbearing.

"I need to take my wife home so she can get some rest." Yusef said answering for Shantel who had nothing to say.

"Okay, then me too. Let me run and say bye to my parents, don't leave me, we can walk to our cars together!" she said scurrying off.

As soon as Jameela left, Shantel pressed for the elevator to come and got on it. She had no intentions on waiting for Jameela. She didn't need her to visit or for any updates on Naomi. She didn't want to be bothered with her at all. Yusef didn't question Shantel's choice to not wait for Jameela.

"She must have really said some terrible things for you to still not want to tell me or be bothered with her." Yusef said as he opened the door for her to exit the hospital. Shantel took a beat before responding to her husband. She softly reached for his hand immediately feeling a sense of security as they headed to his truck.

"Pillow talking is what got us in this mess, so I rather not go there with you. But the bottom line is, she's clearly not good for the nervous system. I'm not sure when I'll be okay to talk to her and when Naomi wakes up, because my best friend will wake up, I'm going to do my best to keep her away from Jameela until she changes her ways." Shantel said, her voice cracking.

Yusef didn't respond but instead opened the door for his wife, guiding her as she hopped into the large vehicle.

www.ingramcontent.com/pod-product-compliance
Lightning Source LLC
Chambersburg PA
CBHW071533260626
47170CB00002B/611